The
GIFT

The GIFT

PRAIRIE STATE FRIENDS *Book Two*

WANDA E. BRUNSTETTER

SHILOH RUN PRESS

An Imprint of Barbour Publishing, Inc.

ISBN 978-1-61626-082-8

eBook Editions:
Adobe Digital Edition (.epub) 978-1-63409-561-7
Kindle and MobiPocket Edition (.prc) 978-1-63409-562-4

All scripture quotations are taken from the King James Version of the Bible.

This book is a work of fiction. Names, characters, places, and incidents are either products of the author's imagination or used fictitiously. Any similarity to actual people, organizations, and/or events is purely coincidental.

Cover image: Faceout Studio, www.faceoutstudio.com

Published by Shiloh Run Press, an imprint of Barbour Publishing, Inc., P.O. Box 719, Uhrichsville, Ohio 44683, www.shilohrunpress.com

Our mission is to publish and distribute inspirational products offering exceptional value and biblical encouragement to the masses.

Member of the
Evangelical Christian
Publishers Association

Printed in the United States of America.

DEDICATION

To my dear friend Irene Miller, who has
helped many people with her special gift.

In quietness and in confidence shall be your strength.
ISAIAH 30:15

CHAPTER 1

Arthur, Illinois

As clouds, black and boiling, filled the darkening sky, Leah Mast pedaled her bicycle harder, knowing that if she didn't get home soon, she'd be caught in a downpour. The muscles in her calves felt as if they could give out at any moment, but she ignored the pain, concentrating on just getting home. Leah had noticed the sky darkening before she left the house. So much for thinking she could outsmart the weather.

"Guess this is what I get for taking my bike instead of the horse and buggy," she muttered, moving to the shoulder of the road as a car sped past. *Too bad I can't pedal as fast as that car.*

Right after eating breakfast and helping her mother with the dishes, Leah had bicycled to Family Health Foods, a mile south of Arthur, to buy some massage lotion. She'd scheduled a few people for foot treatments this afternoon and needed to restock her supply.

With determination, Leah continued her trek toward home. Attempting to keep her mind off the leg cramps that threatened with each downward push, she thought about the special relationship she'd had with her maternal grandmother, who had taught her reflexology. During her lifetime, Grandma Yoder had helped a good many people with her gift of healing.

Leah had the gift, too. At least that's what Grandma had always told her. Many Amish people in Leah's community, as well as some Englishers, came to her for foot treatments. Of course she couldn't charge a set fee for her services, since she didn't have a license to practice reflexology. But the people who came to Leah always gave her a donation. She treated back and shoulder pain, sinus congestion, sore throats, headaches, and insomnia. She also used reflexology to help folks relax, balance their body, and increase blood circulation. When people came to her with more serious illnesses, she always suggested that they see a doctor, because some things she simply could not help.

A clap of thunder sounded, bringing Leah's thoughts to a halt. Big drops of rain pelted her body and stung her face. This was a cloudburst, not an ordinary gentle rainfall. If it kept up, she'd be drenched by the time she made it home—that is, if she could see well enough to get there. The rain came down sideways, and Leah could hardly keep her eyes open. She hoped this was just a freak storm that would move out as quickly as possible. Well, there was nothing she could do about the weather except keep pedaling as fast as she could.

The *clip-clop* of a horse's hooves caused Leah to look over her shoulder. She guided her bike farther off the road and was surprised when the horse and buggy stopped behind her. The driver's side door opened, and Adam Beachy called, "Do you need a ride?"

Astonished by his invitation, Leah quit pedaling. "What about my bike?" she asked as the rain dribbled over her face.

"Not a problem." Adam stuck his blond head out and pointed to the rear of his buggy. It was then that Leah realized he was driving his market buggy. Partially enclosed, it had an open wooden bed that extended from the back. If it was empty, there would be plenty of room for her bicycle in the bed.

Leah climbed off and was about to push the bike around back, when Adam shouted, "If you'll get in my buggy and hold the reins, I'll put your bicycle in and snug it in place."

Shivering from the drenching rain, Leah climbed into Adam's buggy and grabbed the reins, while Adam stepped out and picked up her bicycle.

Leah felt soaked clear through to her skin, and her muscles continued to cramp. It would be a miracle if she ever warmed up. Even though it was the middle of June, a storm like this could chill a person to the bone.

"*Danki*," Leah said when Adam climbed back into the buggy. Her breathing was getting back to normal, but her wet clothing clinging to her drenched skin made her feel icy cold.

Leah handed the reins back to Adam, and using the sleeve of her dress, she wiped rainwater from her face. "I appreciate you stopping, because I need to get home and change out of these wet clothes before Sara Miller comes for a reflexology treatment this afternoon."

With water dripping off his chin, Adam's brown eyes squinted as he wrinkled his nose like some foul odor had permeated the buggy. "So you're still foot doctoring, huh?" He reached behind his seat and handed Leah a small blanket.

She gave a quick nod, wrapping the cover around her shoulders. Even though the blanket pressed her soggy dress against her skin, Leah was grateful for its warmth.

"Humph! I can't believe there are still people who believe in all that hocus-pocus."

Gritting her teeth, Leah pulled the blanket tighter. "Reflexology is not hocus-pocus; it's a form of bodywork that focuses on the feet, and—"

"And nobody's ever been cured of anything by having their feet massaged." Adam snapped the reins and directed his horse onto the road. "You oughtta quit taking people's money for something that's fake and get a real job, Leah."

Fuming, Leah nearly had to bite her tongue to keep from shouting at him. In all her twenty-five years, she'd never met such an opinionated, rude man! Adam had only said a few words to her whenever she'd visited his hardware store, and he had never made eye contact until now. Leah had also observed how, after their biweekly church services, Adam often hurried off, sometimes not even staying for the meal that followed. She'd always thought it was strange that he didn't linger to visit with the men after church, like most others did. Apparently he wasn't much for socializing. *No wonder he isn't married*, she thought. *No woman looking for a husband would put up with being talked to like that. And what does he know about reflexology, anyway?*

Unable to hold her tongue, Leah snapped her head in Adam's direction. "For your information, Mr. Beachy, there are reflex areas on people's feet that correspond to specific organs, glands, and other parts of the body. Those who practice reflexology believe that applying pressure to these reflex areas can promote health in the corresponding organs through energetic pathways."

"Puh! Is that so? Just what illnesses have you helped cure, Leah?"

"Many, in fact." Leah held up one finger. "Some people who come to me get relief from headaches and stress."

Adam flapped his hand in her direction, which only fueled her irritation. "Any kind of massage can make a person relax and feel less tension. Besides, I wouldn't call stress an illness."

"Maybe not in itself, but stress can lead to many different ailments, including headaches." Leah held up a second finger. "Some folks who get reflexology treatments have found relief from back pain." Before Adam could respond, a third finger came up. "And some with digestive disorders or insomnia have felt better after I've worked on their feet. I believe my ability to help them is a gift."

Adam shook his head. "I'm not interested in hearing a bunch of mumbo jumbo. If people are willing to pay whatever fee you're charging and believe they'll get well, that's up to them, but I'm not a believer in that sort of thing."

His tone cut like glass. Leah crossed her arms and glared at him. "The people who come to me for treatments believe in what I'm doing, and I don't have a set fee. I work on anyone's feet for a donation, which means whatever they can afford."

Adam glowered at her. At least Leah thought it was a glower. To give him the benefit of the doubt, she supposed he could have a case of indigestion. "Well," he said with a huff, "you'll never catch me taking off my shoes and socks so someone like you can press on my feet."

Someone like me? Leah's face burned. *Oh, you don't have to worry about that, Adam Beachy. Even if you gave me a hundred-dollar donation, I would never touch your smelly feet!*

"You have a right to your opinion," she muttered.

"That's right, I sure do."

"And I have a right to mine." Refusing to look at Adam, Leah focused on the road ahead. Her folks' house wasn't too far from here, so she should be able to make it that far without saying anything more. She would have liked to give Adam some specific details on reflexology, but what would be the point? He had obviously made up his mind, so she probably wouldn't get very far defending her skill.

I wish now I'd never accepted a ride from him, she fumed. *I'd have been better off riding my bike the rest of the way home, even in the drenching rain.*

"Where have you been that you got caught in this storm?" Adam's deep voice penetrated Leah's angry thoughts.

She looked down at the plastic sack in her hands, unwilling to tell him that she'd bought massage lotion to use on Sara's feet. He'd probably have something negative to say about that, too. "I just needed something at the health food store," she murmured, wiping a drop of water as it trickled down her nose.

Adam clucked to his horse to get him moving a bit faster. He was probably as anxious to drop Leah off at her house as she was to get there.

Leah watched Adam pull back on the reins, guiding his horse through a waterlogged area. The small creek, which normally flowed through a pipe under the road, now splashed across the asphalt pavement. As the horse walked slowly through the fast-flooding creek, she noticed the cause of the rising water. The pipe was clogged with debris that had washed down from farther up. Small branches and clumps of dead leaves had caused the creek to detour from its natural flow. The water was still shallow, but if the rain kept coming down like it was, the road might become impassable. Thankfully, they'd made it this far and would hopefully make it home before the storm got any worse.

They rode in silence the rest of the way, and Leah felt relief when Adam directed his horse and buggy up her folks' driveway. Except for that one small area of flooding, the drive had been without incident.

"I'll get your bicycle." Adam guided his horse up to the hitching rack. Before Leah could respond, he jumped out of the buggy, secured the animal, and went around back.

Leah climbed out, too. "Danki for the ride," she said when Adam pushed her bike around the side of the buggy. She noticed how the rain poured from the top of his hat.

"Sure, no problem." Adam speedily untied his horse, stepped back into the buggy, and as he backed the horse away from the wooden rail, he gave a quick wave.

Leah waved in response then, dodging puddles, made a dash for the house. If Adam hadn't acted so negatively toward her reflexology, in appreciation of him bringing her home, she might have invited him in for a cup of hot tea and the chance to dry off a little while waiting for the storm to subside. But after that conversation, Leah hoped she would never again be put in a position where she'd have to be alone with Adam Beachy. He might be the most attractive single Amish man in Arthur, but as far as she was concerned, he had the personality of a donkey!

CHAPTER 2

*L*eah Mast may be pretty, but she's sure opinionated," Adam muttered as he headed for home. "No wonder she's not married."

Adam had never met a woman as independently determined as Leah. Of course, he hadn't known that many women personally, since he kept to himself as much as possible when it came to socializing. At a young age, Adam had reached the conclusion that he would never marry. It wasn't that he had no interest in the opposite sex—he just didn't trust them.

Bringing his thoughts to a halt, lest he start feeling sorry for himself, Adam concentrated on the road ahead. It was still raining hard, making it difficult to see. If he didn't pay close attention, he could end up off the road. So far, his horse, Flash, was behaving himself and didn't seem to mind the driving rain. Unfortunately, Adam couldn't say the same about his own demeanor. Thanks to his generosity in giving Leah a ride home and then getting out in this horrible weather to transport her bike, he was wet and cold. Drips of rainwater still hung on the brim of his hat, and his shirt and trousers felt like a second skin. He couldn't wait to get home and out of the soaking wet clothes. First and most importantly, though, Adam knew he had to keep his mind on the road, or he might not make it home at all.

Maybe I should have kept going when I saw Leah riding her bike. She was already soaking wet by the time I came upon her. If I hadn't picked her up, we'd never have had that conversation about foot doctoring.

The more Adam thought about it, the more upset he became. Leah reminded him of someone he'd rather forget—not in looks, but in that sure-of-herself attitude. Well, the pretty woman with blue-green eyes and golden brown hair could practice reflexology all she wanted, but it wouldn't change the fact that it was a waste of time. If certain people thought otherwise and wanted to give her a donation, that was their business, but Adam would never let Leah touch his feet!

"*Ach*, my, you're sopping wet!" Mom exclaimed when Leah found her in the utility room, washing clothes.

"I got caught in the downpour," Leah replied.

"I wish you would have taken the buggy instead of your bike. I'm guessing by now you probably wish that, too."

Leah nodded. "Where's Sparky?"

"Last time I looked he was lying just inside the barn."

"Guess he doesn't want to get wet, either." Leah chuckled, wiping another drop of rainwater rolling down the middle of her forehead. "*Schmaert* dog."

"Until I closed the window, the rain was actually blowing into this room, even with the large overhang on the porch to protect it." Mom handed Leah a clean towel. "You'd better dry off some before you head to your room to change, or you'll be leaving a trail of water."

"Danki, Mom." Leah removed her saturated head covering and hung it on a wall peg; then she blotted her hair with the towel. "I'd probably look even worse if Adam Beachy hadn't come along and offered me a ride home."

A wide smile stretched across Mom's face, and her thinning eyelashes fluttered above her dark brown eyes. "That was sure nice of him. Did it give you a chance to get better acquainted?"

A jolt of heat traveled from Leah's neck to her face, despite the chill she felt on the rest of her body. "Oh, we got better acquainted, all right. I found out that Adam doesn't believe in reflexology, and he really didn't have much of anything nice to say."

Mom's lips compressed. "I'm sorry to hear that. I was hoping. . ."

"What were you hoping. . .that Adam might be interested in courting me?"

Mom pulled a towel free from the wringer washer and placed it in the wicker basket at her feet. "Now that you brought up the subject, it would be nice if you had a suitor, don't you think?"

Leah shook her head. "I don't need a man in my life right now. What I do need is to get out of these wet clothes so I'm ready when Sara Miller shows up for her reflexology appointment."

Mom glanced at the battery-operated clock on the wall to her left. "Oh that's right. You did mention before you left that you had a few appointments this afternoon."

Leah nodded and turned toward the stairs but paused when she smelled a delicious aroma coming from the kitchen. "Do you have something on the stove, Mom?"

"*Jah.* It may be the middle of summer, but on a rainy day such as this, I thought a pot of vegetable soup would taste good for our supper tonight. I also made a loaf of homemade bread." Mom gestured to the adjoining room. "Would you mind checking on the soup before you go upstairs?"

"Sure, Mom, no problem. Oh, and if Sara gets here before I've changed, please tell her to go on down to the basement, and that I'll meet her there."

"Okay, I'll let her know."

Leah blotted her arms and legs with the towel then went to the kitchen to check on the soup. Taking a sip of the broth, she smacked her lips. "Yum. I can't wait till suppertime." Turning the burner down so the soup could simmer, she left the room.

As Leah made her way up the stairs, she thought about her mother's comment about a suitor. Although Leah acted like she didn't care, she longed to be a wife and mother. But so far, the right man had not come along. No one, that is, who had swept Leah off her feet. It was probably wishful thinking, but she wanted to fall in love with a man who made her heart beat like a thundering herd of horses. Leah's friends Elaine Schrock and Priscilla Hershberger both had boyfriends. Priscilla was being courted by Elam Gingerich, and Elaine had recently started seeing Ben Otto, who was fairly new to the area. She figured they'd both be married with children long before she had a suitor.

Leah entered her room, removed her wet clothes, and changed into a clean, dry dress. *Here I am, twenty-five years old already, and I don't even have a boyfriend, much less the prospect of marriage. Maybe it's not meant for me to get married.* Leah wasn't going to marry just anyone merely because time was running out before she'd be considered an old maid. *I must leave things in God's hands and remember Isaiah 30:15, the verse I read last night: "In quietness and in confidence shall be your strength."* Leah sighed. *I am certainly not quiet by nature. Adam sure got under my skin today, and I probably said more than I should have in defense of myself. Well, he said more than he should have, too.*

When Leah entered the basement a short time later, Sara was sitting in the recliner with her shoes and stockings off. Her normally slender legs and feet looked a bit swollen, and several strands of her medium brown hair peeked out from under her head covering. Sara's shoulders were slumped, and Leah noticed dark circles beneath her friend's brown eyes.

"Sorry for making you wait," Leah apologized. "I rode my bike to the health food store earlier and got caught in that downpour, so I had to change out of my wet clothes."

"It's not a problem; I haven't been here that long." Sara motioned to a plastic container on the small table to her right. "I brought you some chocolate-chip cookies that I baked this morning."

"Danki. That was nice of you. Except for bread, neither Mom nor I have done much baking lately. We've been too busy picking strawberries from our garden and making them into jelly." Leah smiled. "Last night, I was going to make a strawberry cheeseball but decided to make a chocolate-chip one instead."

Sara smacked her lips. "I'll bet that was good."

Leah nodded and took a seat on the stool in front of the recliner to begin working on Sara's feet. "I enjoy making cheeseballs, and it's always fun to try out new combinations." She picked up the bottle of lotion, poured some into her hands, and rubbed it gently into Sara's feet. "How have you been feeling lately? Are you having any unusual symptoms with your pregnancy?"

"No, not really. In fact, my symptoms have actually diminished, which the doctor said often happens to pregnant women who have MS."

"That's good to hear. So you're not having any problems at all?"

"Not with my MS, but my lower back has begun to hurt, and it's hard to sleep." Sara frowned. "I'm only four-and-a-half-months pregnant, so I wasn't expecting back pain this early. I didn't experience it at all when I was carrying Mark, but I know that many women have trouble with their back—especially toward the end of their third trimester."

Leah began to work on the heel of Sara's right foot. After a while, she moved to the other foot. "Is that tender?" she asked when Sara winced.

Sara nodded. "Jah, a little."

Leah worked on Sara's left foot for several minutes, then she asked her to stand and walk around for a bit.

"My back feels much better. Danki, Leah." The dimples in Sara's cheeks deepened when she smiled.

"You're welcome. Let me know if it flares up again or if you need another foot treatment just to help you relax."

"I will." Sara put on her shoes and stockings.

"Now let me rub your neck a bit before you go." Leah usually did that for most of her patients. It helped them relax and finished the treatment on a positive note.

As Leah massaged Sara's neck, they talked about the weather.

"How were the roads when you came here?" Leah asked. "Were any sections flooded?"

"At one place," Sara said as Leah worked the knots out of her neck, "but my horse cooperated well and walked right through it without a problem."

"That's good. Some horses get spooky over things like water in the road."

"You're right about that." Sara slipped some money into the jar Leah had set on the small table near the chair. "Guess I'd better go. Jonah took some time away from his buggy shop to watch Mark so I could come here, and I'm sure he's anxious to get back to work."

Leah hugged Sara, and as the young woman headed up the stairs, Leah thought about her friend Elaine, who had once been courted by Jonah. Listening to Elaine talk about Ben, Leah wondered if she cared for him as much as she had Jonah.

Since she had a few minutes until Margaret Kauffman, their bishop's wife, arrived for her treatment, Leah washed her hands and tasted one of the cookies Sara had brought. It was soft and chewy, and she relished the taste of chocolate along with the little bits of nuts inside. Tempted to eat a second cookie, she put the lid back on the container and took a seat in the recliner to wait for Margaret. Maybe later this evening, she'd have another cookie with a cup of hot tea.

Drawing in a deep breath, Leah closed her eyes. If she wasn't careful, it would be easy to succumb to sleep. A vision of Adam Beachy flashed into Leah's mind, and her eyes snapped open. *Now why was I thinking about him again?*

Leah stood and opened the lid on the plastic container. She was on the verge of taking another cookie, despite her resolve, when she heard footsteps coming down the stairs. Closing the lid, she turned and smiled at Margaret. "Did your husband bring you here today, or did you come alone?"

"I brought my own horse and buggy." Margaret placed her black umbrella on the floor near the chair. "It's stopped raining, but it sure came down hard for a while there." She removed her cape and black outer bonnet, revealing her white head covering, perched on top of her salt-and-pepper hair.

"I know. I got caught in the downpour when I was riding my bike earlier." Leah motioned to the recliner. "If you're ready, why don't you take a seat? Oh, and if you're hungry, there's some chocolate-chip *kichlin* there on the table. Sara Miller made them."

Margaret's pale blue eyes twinkled when she smiled and took two cookies. "Anything with chocolate in it appeals to me." She took a seat in the recliner and ate both cookies before removing her shoes and socks. Suddenly, a strange look came over her face and she started wheezing, as though she was having trouble catching her breath. "I—I think I'm having a reaction to what I just ate. I feel a strange tightness in my throat and chest—it's like I can't breathe."

Leah's shoulders tightened as perspiration beaded on her forehead. She'd heard about allergic reactions to certain foods, but she'd never dealt with one before. "Have you ever had an attack like this?"

Margaret shook her head.

Knowing she needed to get help for their bishop's wife, she told Margaret to lie back in the chair and try to stay calm. Then Leah rushed upstairs, quickly told Mom what had happened and asked her to go downstairs and keep an eye on Margaret, while she ran outside. Her heart hammering, she raced for the phone shack to call 911.

CHAPTER 3

I heard that Margaret Kauffman had an allergic reaction while you were working on her feet yesterday," Leah's friend Priscilla said as they ate supper together at Yoder's Kitchen the following day.

Leah nodded and reached for her glass of lemonade. "I never even got started on her feet, because it came on after she'd eaten a couple of the cookies Sara Miller had brought earlier. When Margaret said she was having trouble breathing, I knew I needed to get help for her right away."

"Did you know it was a reaction to what she ate, or did you think it might be something else?" Priscilla's coffee-colored eyes revealed the depth of her concern.

"I wasn't sure what to think at first, but then Margaret said she thought she was having an allergic reaction. So I asked my *mamm* to stay with her, while I rushed out to the phone shack and called 911." Leah paused to take a drink. "When the paramedics got there, they knew what to do, and at the hospital, they ran tests that revealed Margaret's allergic to walnuts, which were in the chocolate-chip cookies."

"It's good she found that out so she can be careful not to eat anything else with nuts," Priscilla said before taking a bite of salad. "If she's allergic to walnuts, she might have that same reaction to other kinds of nuts as well."

"The doctor wrote Margaret a prescription for an EpiPen, which she will keep with her in case an incident like that ever happens again," Leah explained.

"That must have been frightening, not only for Margaret, but for you as well."

"Jah, it was." Leah sipped more lemonade. "You know, it's too bad

Elaine couldn't join us this evening. It's been awhile since the three of us had a good visit."

"I was hoping she could come, too, but she has a dinner scheduled this evening for a large tour group."

"That's right; I do remember her saying that." Leah paused to eat some of her salad. "Oh, I forgot to mention that Mom sent a container of vegetable soup for you and your parents. It's in a cooler out in my buggy. I'll get it for you after we eat. It might be something you can enjoy for lunch tomorrow."

Priscilla smiled. "Please tell your mamm I said danki."

"I will. She made enough soup to feed a small barn-raising crew, so she was more than happy to share."

"We enjoy anything your mamm makes because she is such a good cook."

"You're right about that. I do all right in the kitchen, but my cooking skills aren't nearly as good as hers." Glancing to her left, Leah cringed when she noticed Adam enter the restaurant. Trying to suppress a cough, she almost choked on the little tomato she was chewing. She was relieved when the hostess handed Adam a takeout box, which meant he wasn't planning to stay.

Before Leah had a chance to look away, Adam glanced in her direction and gave a brief nod. She smiled in return then quickly focused on her salad.

Priscilla bumped Leah's foot under the table. "Your face is red. Are you okay?"

"I'm fine," Leah muttered. She glanced back at Adam and was relieved when she saw him go out the door.

Priscilla tipped her head, looking curiously at Leah. "Are you interested in Adam Beachy? Is that why your cheeks are so pink?"

Leah touched her hot cheeks. "No, of course not!"

"Is he interested in you?"

"The only person Adam's interested in is himself and his biased opinions."

"What makes you say that?"

Leah proceeded to tell Priscilla about the ride Adam had given her and his attitude toward reflexology. "He thinks it's hocus-pocus."

Priscilla's eyes narrowed. "That's *lecherich*."

"You're right, it is ridiculous."

"How would Adam know anything about reflexology?"

Leah shrugged. "All I know is that man is unsociable and too sharp with his words. Makes me wonder how he can run a business and keep customers coming back to his store. Guess it's a good thing he has Ben Otto and Henry Raber working there, because they're both friendly and quite pleasant."

"You're right," Priscilla agreed. "The last time I went there to get some nails for my *daed*, Adam was behind the counter, and he barely said two words to me. What do you think his problem is, anyway?"

Leah shrugged again. "I have no idea. The only thing I do know is that I'll never accept another ride from him, no matter how hard it's raining. I'd rather be waterlogged than listen to him say negative things about the very thing I feel called to do."

"I can't blame you for that. Personally, I see your foot doctoring as a gift from God." Priscilla smiled. "Not everyone has the ability to help people the way you do, Leah. Maybe someday Adam will have a sinus headache or some other type of problem and come to you for help."

Leah shook her head. "I doubt that. I'm sure he'd be the last person in our community who'd ask me for help. For that matter, I have no desire to work on Adam's feet."

When Adam entered his house that evening, a deep sense of loneliness encompassed him. He should be used to coming home every evening to an empty house, but he'd never quite adjusted to it. He missed his dad and the conversations they used to have, and he missed his sister, Mary, whom he'd been close to during their childhood. But Mary lived in Nappanee, Indiana, with her husband and three girls. Two years ago, Adam's dad had passed away after a freak accident when he'd been helping a neighbor in his field. After six months of grieving his loss, Adam had left Indiana and moved to Arthur, Illinois, seeking a new start with the hardware store he'd purchased. He didn't have any relatives in the area, but that was okay. Adam was used to moving and starting over. Dad had uprooted them several times after Adam's mother walked out on them when they lived in Pennsylvania. Adam didn't know why they'd moved, but he'd later found out that Dad didn't want Adam and Mary's mother to have anything to do with them if she ever came back. He'd said she was a wicked woman and didn't deserve to spend any time with her children. Well, that was fine with Adam, because he wanted nothing to do with her. When she'd left the Amish faith and divorced his dad, Adam had been five years old and Mary had been eight. How any woman could walk out on a man as great as Dad and leave her children behind was a mystery to Adam, and he'd never come to grips with it. He had struggled the last twenty-five years to keep from hating her for what she'd done. It was wrong to dislike anyone that much, but Adam's anger festered like a splinter that wouldn't come out. It had kept him from getting close to anyone except for Mary and her family. Adam loved his sister and would do anything for her. He cared about her husband, Amos, and their daughters, Carrie, Linda, and Amy, too, although he didn't see them as often as he would like.

Adam hung his straw hat on a wall peg in the kitchen and, after pouring himself a glass of milk, took a seat at the table. He'd put in a long day, and it felt good to be off his feet.

As he sipped some milk, his gaze came to rest on the coloring book lying on top of the desk across the room. He'd purchased it so his nieces would have something to do when they came here for Christmas last year, but the girls had forgotten to take it home with them. Several months before the holiday, Adam had asked Jonah Miller, the local buggy maker, to build him a buggy that would accommodate six people so all his guests could ride together. Having his sister and her family with him to celebrate the Christmas season had been nice, but he hadn't gotten much use out of the larger buggy since they went back to Indiana. He hated to admit it, since he'd paid Jonah Miller a good price for making the buggy, but it seemed like a waste to have the larger rig sitting out in the buggy shed. At least he would have it for the next time Mary and her family came to visit.

Sure wish Dad could have celebrated Christmas with us, Adam thought with regret. *If his life hadn't been snuffed out that way, we'd be together right now.*

"We never know what's coming in life," Adam mumbled, setting his empty glass on the table. "Never know what the future holds."

CHAPTER 4

*E*laine Schrock had never been one to give in to self-pity, and tonight was no exception. She'd just told her helper, Karen Yoder, good-bye and had put the last of the dishes away from the tourists' dinner she'd hosted. Every time Elaine hosted another dinner, she pictured Grandma working beside her, wearing a cheerful-looking smile. Oh, how she missed their conversations and the humorous stories Grandma often shared from her childhood, but the memories of Grandma were also what motivated Elaine to continue providing these dinners. Knowing how much her grandmother had loved doing them, wasn't she, in a way, helping to keep Grandma's memory alive by continuing this tradition?

When Grandma died, Elaine had considered selling the house and moving away, but this had been her home since she was a girl, and she couldn't bring herself to leave the old house where so many memories lived. Perhaps if Elaine ever got married, she would raise her own children in this place where so much love had abounded when Grandpa and Grandma were alive. The swing in the yard, the big back porch, and even the bedrooms upstairs with their creaky floorboards needed children to fill them.

If only Grandma and Grandpa could have lived long enough to see great-grandchildren, she thought, moving over to her desk on the other side of the room to get the book on gardening she wanted to read. *I know they would have loved my* kinner *as much as they loved me—if I ever have any children, that is.*

Bringing her thoughts back to the dinner she'd just hosted, Elaine chuckled over the group's reaction to one of the guests. An Asian man, Mr. Lee, burped out loud after eating his salad. Then he did the same thing after finishing his mashed potatoes. At that point, the whole dining area grew silent, and the other guests stared at the man. An uncomfortable hush settled over the room. Mr. Lee must have noticed it, for he stood up and explained that in the part of China he came from, it was customary to show appreciation for the food by burping out loud. He even offered to stop doing it if anyone was offended, but the other guests seemed to be satisfied with his explanation. Everyone continued eating, accepting the fact that Mr. Lee was going to burp during the whole meal. Bethany, a young college student, even thanked Mr. Lee, saying she had signed up for the dinner to learn about Amish customs but had learned something about another country's customs, as well. She went on to say that she could use this information for her thesis. Everyone clapped, and the group seemed to relax even more.

Later Elaine served strawberry pies for dessert. After they were done eating, everyone burped. One of the ladies said that it was the best pie she'd ever eaten, and if burping was a way to show her appreciation, then she was glad she had. More clapping and laughter followed.

Elaine joined in, feeling almost weightless in her joy. She wasn't sure how Grandma would have reacted to the burping that went on around the dinner table, but to Elaine, it felt good to see the whole group get along so well.

Pushing those memories aside, she started toward the living room. She thought she heard a horse and buggy coming up the lane. Wondering who would be calling at this time of night, she peered out the window into the darkened yard. Lights on the buggy revealed little, and she couldn't make out whose rig it was. Thinking it might be Ben Otto making a surprise call, Elaine left the kitchen and hurried to the back door. Moments later, Leah stepped onto the porch, holding a flashlight in one hand. "*Wie geht's?*" she asked.

"I'm doing fine," Elaine answered, "but I'm surprised to see you. I didn't expect you'd be coming by tonight."

Leah smiled. "I wanted to see how things went with your dinner. Were there lots of people? Was Karen Yoder a big help to you?"

Elaine opened the door wider. "Come in. I'll tell you about it." She led the way to the kitchen and asked her friend, "Would you like a cup of tea?"

"That'd be nice."

Elaine gestured to a chair. "Take a seat, and I'll join you as soon as I get the water heating."

"Is there anything I can do to help?" Leah offered.

"That's okay. It'll only take me a minute." Elaine filled the teakettle and turned on the propane stove. "Now in answer to your earlier questions, things went quite well tonight. But I couldn't have done it all without Karen's help."

"I'm glad to hear that. When I was having supper with Priscilla tonight, I kept thinking I ought to be here, helping you."

"No need to worry about that. Karen and I managed just fine." Elaine took a seat beside Leah. "I did miss Grandma, though."

Leah reached over and clasped Elaine's hand. "That's understandable. You helped her with the dinners for several years. It's only natural that you'd miss her when you were doing something you knew she enjoyed."

"Hosting dinners for tourists brought Grandma much happiness," Elaine agreed. "I only wish we hadn't been forced to quit doing them because of her dementia."

"You did what you had to do." Leah's sincere smile conveyed heartfelt sympathy. "There was no way you could keep hosting the meals with Edna going downhill so quickly."

Elaine sighed. "I know, but I missed doing the dinners, and Grandma did, too—at least until her memory got so bad that she forgot about the tour groups."

"Now you're carrying on her legacy. I'm sure she would be pleased."

When the teakettle whistled, Elaine fixed their tea and got out the leftover strawberry pie. "Would you like a piece?"

"Sure. That looks good."

Elaine cut them each a piece and returned to her seat. "How are things going with you? Have you given many foot treatments lately?"

Leah nodded. "I saw Sara Miller yesterday, and our bishop's wife came after that. Unfortunately, Margaret had an allergic reaction to the walnuts that were in the cookies Sara had given me. The poor woman ended up at the hospital."

"That's *baremlich*. Is she doing okay?"

"It was terrible, but she's much better. Now she'll have to carry an EpiPen at all times in case something like that should happen again."

Elaine sipped some tea. "I'm sensitive to some chemical odors, but I've never had difficulty breathing."

Leah leaned her elbows on the table. "I hope you never do."

As they ate their pie and finished the tea, Leah told Elaine about her encounter with Adam Beachy. "I'm not sure why, but he's against reflexology."

"Maybe he ought to give it a try." Elaine got up to clear their dishes. "Personally, I find your foot treatments to be very relaxing. Since Adam seems to be so uptight, maybe reflexology would help him unwind."

Leah's forehead wrinkled. "I doubt that he'd ever come to see me. Even if he did, I wouldn't want to work on his feet."

"How come?"

"I just wouldn't, that's all."

"Adam is a handsome man. As far as I know, he's not courting anyone."

"He may be handsome, but his personality leaves a lot to be desired." Leah carried the teakettle back to the stove. "Can we talk about something other than Adam Beachy?"

"We can talk about anything you like, but let's go in the living room where the chairs are more comfortable."

Elaine followed Leah out of the kitchen, and they took seats on the sofa. "How are things going with you and Ben these days?" Leah asked.

Elaine shrugged. "Okay, I guess. He drops by fairly often to see how I'm doing, and we went out for supper a few times last month."

"I don't mean to pry, but are you two getting serious?" Leah questioned.

"I'm not sure how Ben feels, but right now, I see our relationship as more of a close friendship than romance. I'm comfortable when I'm with him, but the feelings I have for Ben aren't the same as what I felt for. . ." Elaine's voice trailed off. "Sorry, I didn't mean to go there."

"As what you felt for Jonah?" Leah prompted. "Is that what you were going to say?"

"Jah. Jonah was my first love, and the feelings I had for him will probably remain in my heart. But he's married to Sara now, and they seem to be happy. I wish them well."

Leah squeezed Elaine's arm tenderly. "You're one of the nicest people I know. Despite what you told Jonah about not loving him, I know you ended your relationship so you'd be free to take care of your grandma. When he married Sara, you were gracious. I'm not sure I could have been that understanding. It seems like he rushed into it, if you ask me."

Elaine leaned heavily against the sofa cushions. "Jonah did what he wanted to do, and I did what I had to do. I loved him enough to let him go so he could find the happiness he deserved with someone else. Now he has Sara and little Mark to fill up his life, and they have a new *boppli* on the way."

Leah rubbed the bridge of her nose, the way she often did when deep in thought. "Have you ever wondered if Jonah married Sara just so he could be Mark's father?"

Elaine leaned slightly forward. "It's not my place to wonder things like that, and it doesn't matter what Jonah's reason was for marrying Sara. They're husband and wife now, and I'm no longer a part of Jonah's life. I'm determined to move on and leave my regrets in the past. Someday, if the Lord wills it, I'll fall in love, get married, and fill this house with enough kinner to take up all the empty places. In the meantime, I'm going to take one day at a time and keep hosting tourist dinners."

Leah smiled. "Everyone should learn to take one day at time, but I do hope that someday we'll both find the man of our dreams."

When Leah arrived home, she found her parents in the living room playing a game of checkers. "Where have you been all this time, Leah?" Mom asked. "It's after ten, and we were starting to worry."

"More to the point, your mamm was worried." Dad chuckled as he jumped one of Mom's checkers.

"We knew you were meeting Priscilla for supper, but I thought you'd be home before this," Mom said.

"I'm sorry. I did meet Priscilla for supper, but I decided to stop by and see Elaine on my way home," Leah explained. "I wanted to see how things went with the dinner she hosted this evening."

"Did things go well?" Mom asked.

"Jah. Elaine seemed quite happy and relaxed."

Mom removed her glasses, blew on them, and wiped the smudges with the edge of her apron. "It was nice of you to stop and see your friend, and it's good to hear that Elaine's evening went well. But Eli and Kathryn Byler were here earlier with their son, Abe, who wasn't feeling well. They wanted you to work on his feet. When I told them you weren't here, they were disappointed."

Leah felt bad, but at the same time, the Bylers hadn't made an appointment, so she'd had no idea they were coming. And she couldn't stay home all the time in case someone might need a reflexology treatment.

"Did you tell Eli and Kathryn to take Abe to the clinic for help?" Leah questioned.

Mom gave a nod. "I did, but they asked if you'd be here in the morning."

Leah sighed, wondering if the Bylers had found help for Abe or if she would see them in the morning. If that turned out to be the case, she hoped a foot treatment would be all that Abe needed. If there was something seriously wrong with the boy that was beyond the scope of her abilities, she would certainly tell them so.

CHAPTER 5

*L*eah smiled as a male hummingbird hovered directly above her head while she filled one of their numerous feeders in the backyard. To describe these little birds as curious was an understatement. The hummer was so close to Leah that she could actually feel the breeze from its fast-moving wings, which buzzed like a bee.

Leah loved watching the beautiful flying jewels. It never ceased to amaze her how quickly the hummingbirds could get from one place to another. She'd even observed them flying backward a few times. Occasionally, after she had the feeders cleaned and refilled before hanging them back on their hooks, Leah would hold a feeder and watch the hummingbirds close up when they flew in to feed. One time she held a feeder with one hand at the top then opened her other hand real wide, holding it directly under the feeding perches. Leah could hardly believe it when one of the little hummers landed on her finger and drank from the flowered portal. Although her arm grew tired, she didn't move a muscle, wanting to make the experience last as long as possible.

This year, they seemed to have a lot more hummers than usual, and every other day she had to refill their five feeders. Leah was glad she'd stocked up on sugar in early spring, because it wouldn't be long before the feeders would need to be filled every day—especially in mid-July, when the birds started migrating to their area from the north. It wasn't unusual for Leah to go through ten pounds of sugar in a week's time while the hummingbirds stayed over for a few weeks before heading to the Gulf of Mexico. From morning until just before dark, the hummers chattered nonstop as they flitted from one feeder to another. Sometimes they dive-bombed one another in a fierce battle to get to the feeders. Other times, the tiny birds took turns at the feeders and everything seemed quite peaceful.

Leah was excited that Alissa Cramer, one of their English neighbors, would be coming over during the active time in August to band the hummingbirds. She couldn't imagine a metal band being small enough to fit on their little legs but big enough to have a number inscribed on it for tracking future behavior. It would be interesting to see the process.

Leah had just filled the last feeder when a horse and buggy pulled in. Sparky raised his head from where he laid on the porch, but he didn't bother to bark.

Leah recognized the Bylers' rig as it pulled up to the hitching rack. Kathryn got out and helped three-year-old Abe down while Eli secured their horse.

"I'm so glad you're here," Kathryn said, carrying her son as she rushed over to Leah. "Our boy has a nasty cold, and with his asthma, I think it's gone into his chest." Dark circles stood out beneath the young woman's pale blue eyes, and Leah figured Abe's mother hadn't gotten much sleep.

"I'm sorry to hear that, and I feel bad that I wasn't home when you stopped by last night." Leah motioned to the house. "Come inside, and I'll see what I can do for Abe."

Leah led the way, stepping around Sparky. Once inside, she suggested that Eli wait upstairs with her dad. Since this was Saturday and Dad wasn't working, the two men could visit while Leah worked on Abe's feet in the basement. The boy's mother would want to be with him, so she didn't ask her to wait upstairs, even though Kathryn could have visited with Mom.

When they entered the basement, Leah asked Kathryn to place Abe in the recliner, and then Leah took a seat on the footstool in front of him while his mother seated herself rigidly on a nearby chair.

"How long has Abe been feeling *grank*?" Leah asked.

"He's been ill almost a week." Kathryn sighed. "We thought he'd be better by now, but when his wheezing seemed worse, we decided it was time to bring him to you."

"Did you take him to the clinic?"

Kathryn shook her head. "It's expensive to go to the doctor, and we were hoping you could help."

"I'll do what I can." Leah picked up the little boy's left foot. "But I'm not a doctor and make no promises."

"I understand. Please, just do what you can."

As Leah began working on the little guy's feet, she discovered that the areas representing his adrenal glands were tender and inflamed. "I have never found a case of asthma where the reflexes to the adrenal glands weren't tender," she told Kathryn. "It may take awhile, but I believe with a little persistence, stimulating the adrenals will help."

Kathryn's face seemed to relax a bit, and she leaned back slightly in her chair. Meanwhile, Leah kept applying pressure to the two spots on Abe's small feet that needed the most attention.

After she'd been working on him nearly half an hour, his color improved and he seemed to be breathing better. "I'd like to see Abe again in a few days," Leah said. "But do keep an eye on him, and if he gets any worse, please don't hesitate to take him to the doctor. I'm sure your church district will help financially."

"Danki, Leah. I appreciate what you've done." Tears welled in Kathryn's eyes as she placed a few dollars in the jar on Leah's table.

Leah touched the woman's hand. "You're welcome."

When the Bylers left, Leah went to the kitchen to see if her mother needed help with anything.

"If you have time, would you mind running an errand for me?" Mom asked.

"Sure. I don't have anyone scheduled for a foot treatment until this afternoon. Where did you want me to go?"

"I need a few things from Rockome Garden Foods." Mom handed Leah a list. "I'd go myself, but I'm in the middle of making bread and don't want to leave it."

Leah thought about offering to finish the bread but decided it would be more enjoyable to take a buggy ride. Besides, she usually found a few things to buy at the store, and it would be fun to browse. "No problem, Mom. I'll go there right now."

Arcola

As Adam headed down the road in the direction of Rockome Garden Foods, he made sure to keep a tight rein on his horse, because for some reason the normally docile animal wanted to run at full speed. Maybe it was the smell and feel of summer that caused Flash to be so frisky. Sunny days like today certainly put a spring in Adam's step, so why wouldn't they have the same effect on his horse? The way Flash was acting, his name truly fit.

Since both of Adam's employees were working at the hardware store, he had decided it would be a good time to do some grocery shopping. His cupboards were getting bare, and there wasn't much in the refrigerator. If he didn't restock, he would either have to eat supper at one of the local restaurants this evening or get by on crackers and cheese. Of course, Adam could have gone to one of the other stores closer to his home, but he liked going to Rockome because they had a good selection of canned goods, butter, cheese, pastas, and bulk foods—not to mention all the baked goods and homemade candy. Adam's mouth watered just thinking about the cookies and sweet breads he planned to buy.

"If you had a wife, she'd cook and bake for you." Adam shook his head, thinking about what his sister had said the last time they'd talked on the phone. Mary was determined to see Adam married, and he was just as determined to remain single.

Who needs a wife? Adam thought. *I'm perfectly capable of washing my own clothes, cooking, and cleaning.* If he were completely honest with himself, he'd have to admit that he wasn't the best cook or the tidiest housekeeper. He got by, though, and he was fine with that. Of course, no wife meant having no children or future grandchildren. It also meant he'd be a lonely bachelor for the rest of his life, without the warmth, companionship, or love of a woman. But even if he found someone and fell in love, how could Adam trust her not to break his heart the way his mother had broken his dad's? Adam never wanted his children to go through life feeling like they were unwanted. No child deserved that.

No, Adam told himself, *even if I have to spend the rest of my life in solitude, I'll be better off alone.*

When Rockome Garden Foods came into view, Adam directed Flash into the parking lot and up to the hitching rack. After he'd made sure the horse was secure, he headed into the store.

It took awhile to get everything on his list, and as he was heading to the checkout counter, he remembered he still needed some honey.

Hurriedly, he headed back to the aisle where several varieties of honey were located and picked one off the shelf. It slipped out of his hand and smashed on the floor. "Oh no!" he groaned. "This is not what I need today."

Using the toe of his boot, Adam pushed the broken glass aside and rushed to the front counter, where he told the clerk what had happened. "Do you have something I can put the broken glass in?" he asked.

"Don't worry about that," she said, smiling. "I'll get one of the other clerks to take care of it."

Just then, Adam spotted Leah entering the store.

Leah was looking over her mother's list when she glanced up and saw Adam standing near the checkout counter. *Oh, great. I hope he doesn't say anything to me.*

Hurrying, she zipped down the pasta aisle, grabbing a bag of noodles, the first item on Mom's list. She turned and was about to head down the canned-goods aisle when she stepped in something goocy. Her feet slipped out from under her, and down she went.

"Ach, my!" Leah gasped, seeing that she had sticky honey on her hands, knees, and the lower part of her dress. Then she noticed the broken glass pushed off to one side, nearly hidden under the bottom shelf. Someone must have either knocked the jar off the shelf or picked the honey up and dropped it.

As Leah attempted to get back on her feet, she heard Adam's voice. "Are you all right?"

She looked up and grimaced when she saw him staring down at her. "I–I'm not hurt. I just slipped in some honey."

"That's my fault," he mumbled, extending his hand to Leah. "I dropped a jar a few minutes ago. The clerk said she would ask someone to clean it up, but I guess you got here first."

Despite her best efforts, Leah couldn't seem to stand on her own, so she reached up and clasped Adam's hand. It was surprisingly warm, and as he helped her stand, she noticed his look of concern.

"Are you sure you're not hurt?" Adam's tone seemed sincere.

"I'm fine. Just a sticky mess." Leah let go of Adam's hand and noticed that she'd transferred some of the honey onto his hand, too.

"I'm really sorry." He took off his hat and ran his fingers through his hair. "Oh, now look what I've done."

Leah held her breath, gazing at the sticky goo that had shifted from Adam's fingers to his hair, making it clump in several places. He stood several seconds with a peculiar expression; then he burst out laughing. It was the first time Leah had heard him laugh, and she couldn't keep from giggling herself.

"We're a mess, aren't we?" Leah grew serious, trying to contain her laughter. "Anyway, it's not your fault. If someone said they'd clean it up, they should have followed through."

"I'm sure they were planning to," Adam said. "This just happened right before you got here."

"Well, I'm glad it was me who fell and not some elderly person. Besides, I didn't get cut by the broken glass, and that's a good thing." Leah looked down at her hands and groaned. She really was a sticky mess, and wondered how she would ever get all that honey off her shoes, not to mention her dress. "I'd better head to the restroom and get cleaned up," she said.

"Jah, me, too."

"Danki for your help, Adam."

When Adam nodded, Leah noticed that he was smiling, as though trying to hold back more laughter. Was that smirking because he thought she looked funny, or was it just a friendly smile? Maybe Adam had an agreeable side that she hadn't seen before. Well, there was no time to figure it out now. After she got cleaned up, she needed to get her shopping done quickly, because she had two more people coming for foot treatments this afternoon. Her shoes sticking to the floor with each step she took, Leah tiptoed her way to the restroom. She hoped someone would get the mess cleaned up soon, because she was making sticky spots all the way to the bathroom. *I hope Adam doesn't have any trouble washing that honey out of his hair*, she thought, suppressing another giggle.

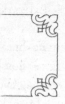

CHAPTER 6

Arthur

*A*dam glanced out the window of his store and grimaced. Several soda pop cans were strewn about the parking lot, as if someone had just pitched them out the window of their vehicle. Most likely some thoughtless Englisher's action, but then it could have been done by one of the local Amish youth. The litter made his business look scruffy, so he needed to dispose of it right away.

"I'm going outside to pick up some aluminum cans," he told Ben Otto, his newest employee.

Ben looked up from behind the counter where he'd been waiting on an elderly Amish woman. "Want me to get 'em?"

"No, that's okay; I'll take care of it." It was getting hot and stuffy inside the store, even with the overhead ceiling fans that were run by a diesel air compressor, so this was a good excuse for Adam to get some fresh air.

"I'll keep an eye on things in here." Ben ran his fingers through his wavy brown hair. "I enjoy working in your store, Adam, and I appreciate you giving me this job."

"And I appreciate everything you do." Adam was glad he'd hired Ben. The twenty-three-year-old Amish man had a good work ethic. Adam had quickly discovered that he could depend on Ben, who aimed to please.

When Adam stepped outside, the heat and humidity almost took his breath away. Not even a hint of a breeze was blowing. So much for the fresh air he was hoping to find. No wonder it had gotten so hot and stuffy inside the store. It was the middle of July, so warm temperatures could be expected. But this extraordinary heat surprised him.

Gathering up the empty cans, Adam tossed them into the recycle bin. Then he headed around to the back of the store to make sure his and Ben's horses had plenty of water. He'd built a lean-to for the animals so they had enough shade inside the small corral. Adam's other employee, Henry Raber, usually rode his bike to work, but today Henry hadn't come in because he'd pulled a muscle in his shoulder yesterday while picking up a heavy sack of cement at the close of work. Adam had suggested that Henry take today off and see one of their local chiropractors. Hopefully he'd done that and would find relief. Adam figured they could get by without Henry for a few days, but so far this summer, business had been brisk. He couldn't afford to be shorthanded for any length of time.

Try not to worry about it, he told himself. *As Dad used to say, "Just take one day at a time." What was that verse Dad always quoted? Oh, yeah, Matthew 6:34: "Take therefore no thought for the morrow: for the morrow shall take thought for the things of itself."*

Adam glanced around the parking lot once more to be sure he hadn't missed any cans or other litter. A few weeks ago, he'd discovered that someone had emptied their car's ashtray in the planter box by the entrance door of the store. The planter had colorful petunias growing in it, so surely the person knew it wasn't a container for waste. He wondered what would make someone get out of their car, walk up to the entrance door where the planter sat, and empty their cigarette butts. Adam didn't know if he was being overly critical because of the way things were these days, but he sure wished folks would be more considerate.

Satisfied that the parking lot looked clean and inviting, he returned to the store. He found Ben waiting on their bishop, Levi Kauffman. Since Ben seemed to have everything under control, Adam started toward the other side of the store to see if he was getting low on any gardening tools. First though, he needed to make sure the dolly was readily available, because anytime now, the delivery truck should be pulling in with his most recent order. Various-sized bags of thistle and sunflower seed were due in today, which was good, since there wasn't much left of either in the store right now.

Adam went to the storage room, which was in the rear of the building and led to the back door where deliveries were usually dropped off. He always liked to help the driver unload supplies, so he pushed the dolly over and left it sitting close to the back door. That would be one less thing to look for when the truck arrived.

As Leah headed to the health food store to buy some vitamins, she found herself panting for breath. The road was perfectly flat, so pedaling the bike wasn't causing a problem. What had zapped her strength was the unrelenting heat. Summer was nice, but when it was humid and hot like this, Leah longed for the cooler days of fall, but they hadn't even reached the dog days of August yet. What she wouldn't give for a gentle breeze right now. Up ahead, she was glad to see a huge maple tree that provided some shade along the road.

Leah stopped to catch her breath, and took a drink from the Thermos of iced tea she carried in her basket. The next time she made the trip to town this summer she would take the horse and buggy. At least then the horse, who was trained to pull and could withstand the heat, would be doing all the work and not her.

She watched as a delivery truck approached. It wasn't unusual to see trucks on this road making deliveries into Arthur or to businesses just outside of town. As the truck whizzed by, it created a breeze that felt really good for the few seconds it lasted, even though it smelled of exhaust. All too soon the air grew still again.

Leah looked up into the tree. The thick cover of maple leaves hung motionless. She wiped her forehead with the back of her hand, standing there just a bit longer. She took the cap off the Thermos and guzzled more of the iced tea, grabbing a small ice cube with her teeth to let it melt in her mouth. When she peeked into the Thermos and saw only a few ice cubes left in the remaining tea, she snapped the lid back on, knowing if she stayed any longer, the humidity would get worse and her tea would no longer be cold. Taking one more look around, she watched a butterfly slowly flitter past and land on some chicory weed that was growing in clusters along the road. Even the butterfly's wings looked bogged down from the clammy, moisture-laden air as it sat on the blue, daisylike flower.

Leah moved on, trying to keep her focus on the scenery instead of how miserable she felt. Sweat ran down her back as the sun beat relentlessly on her body. The creek, running from one side of the road and through a pipe to the other side, looked inviting as Leah pedaled over it and continued onward.

She knew how good the cool water would feel, but there was no time for such a childlike venture. She giggled, thinking how silly it would look if she showed up at the health food store soaking wet.

As Leah proceeded, her bicycle pedals kept slipping. Something must be wrong. When they quit working altogether, she had to stop and get off.

Looking down at her bike, Leah groaned. The chain was loose, and she had nothing to tighten it with. "At this rate, I'll never get to the health food store," she mumbled, making sure her bike was on the shoulder of the road as she began to push. Even when she did get there, she'd either have to walk the bike home or find some way to fix the chain.

While Adam waited for his delivery to arrive, he went back to the main part of the store and headed to the first aisle, where the garden tools were kept. There he caught sight of a freckle-faced English boy who appeared to be in his early teens. The kid had his hands in the pocket of his jeans, and a worn-looking baseball cap covered most of his red hair, which was pulled back into a ponytail. He stood staring at the shelf full of gardening gloves and hand shovels and didn't seem to notice Adam standing nearby. Adam thought it was strange that the boy was wearing a denim jacket, buttoned up to his neck. On a day as warm as this, he didn't think anyone would feel the need for a jacket.

Just as Adam was going to ask the boy if he needed any help, the kid grabbed two pairs of gloves off the shelf, along with two of the small shovels, and stuffed them inside his jacket. Then he turned, caught sight of Adam, and froze.

Adam didn't say anything at first, hoping the boy would take the items to the checkout counter to pay. Of course, that wasn't likely. Most people who planned to buy something didn't stuff the articles inside their jacket.

Time seemed to stand still as they stared at each other. Adam didn't back down, and the kid nervously broke eye contact, glancing toward the front doors. Adam didn't have time to blink before the boy ran past him, headed for the exit.

"Stop where you are!" Adam shouted, convinced the boy was shoplifting. He raced after him. "You'd better give me those items you took!"

Glancing to her right, Leah saw Adam's hardware store come into view. Thinking she might find some type of tool there to fix her chain, Leah pushed the bike into the parking lot and set the kickstand. She noticed the delivery truck that had passed her earlier was parked along the side of the store. The driver, talking on a cell phone, stood by the rear of the truck.

Leah went up the front steps and reached for the door handle. The door flew open, and—*wham!*—a teenaged boy crashed into her, knocking her down. As she tried to clamber to her feet, Adam barreled out the open door, shouting for the boy to stop. In his haste, Adam plowed into Leah, and they both landed on the porch in a heap.

CHAPTER 7

*A*re you okay?" Adam and Leah asked at the same time.

Leah looked at Adam and bobbed her head. "When I reached for the door to your store, I never expected to get plowed down by that boy. He didn't even look back or apologize." She looked at her hands and noticed that they were a bit scraped. Nervously brushing them together, she added, "The least he could have done was to ask if I was all right."

"I'm sorry about that." Adam stood and reached for her hand. "And I never expected to catch someone shoplifting in my store." He grimaced. "I didn't actually catch the fellow, now did I? Thanks to me tripping over you and falling, that young thief got away."

Leah scrunched up her face, realizing the hand Adam held in his stung more than she'd first thought it did.

"Let me look at those hands," Adam said, his voice filled with concern. Before she could react, he took her other hand and examined it as well. "I have some witch hazel in the store. We'd better get your hands cleaned off."

Leah quickly pulled back from Adam's grip. Confusion mixed with a bit of irritation bubbled in her soul as she gazed up at him. Wiping her hands on her dress, she asked, "Are you suggesting that it's my fault you didn't capture the boy?"

He shook his head. "You were just in the wrong place at the wrong time."

"So if I hadn't come to the hardware store, you'd have your merchandise back by now?"

Adam shrugged. "Can't say for sure, but there's a pretty good chance I would have caught the kid."

"Maybe you should go after him now. Did you see what direction he took?"

"No. Did you?"

Leah's hands went straight to her hips. "Of course not. How could I see anything with you lying in a heap beside me, blocking my view?" She bit back a chuckle, thinking how silly Adam had looked when he fell down. His thick blond hair was in a disarray, and she resisted the urge to reach up and comb it with her fingers.

Adam stared at Leah. Then, in a surprise gesture, he reached out and touched her head covering.

She pulled back slightly. "Wh–what are you doing?"

"Your *kapp* is crooked. Looks like it's about to come off." Adam's voice seemed deeper than usual, and Leah swallowed hard as she stood, letting him readjust her covering.

"Are you going to call the authorities about the shoplifter?" Leah questioned, hoping the change of topic would get her mind off his dreamy brown eyes.

"I'm not sure what I'm going to do." Adam grunted, rubbing his chin. "If I call the sheriff, I should do it soon, but if I wait, maybe I'll see the boy in Arthur or somewhere else in our area and approach him myself."

"That could be dangerous, don't you think?"

"He's just a kid, Leah. Maybe there's a reason he stole from my store."

"I can't understand why anyone would steal. Even if a person is poor, they should ask for help. Our community is always willing to help out when Amish or English have a need." Leah reached up and felt her head covering, noting that it seemed to be in place. "Danki for fixing my kapp." Feeling a bit tongue-tied, she could feel her cheeks warm. Why was Adam staring at her like that again? Was something else off-kilter? Should she ask?

After what seemed like forever, Adam blinked and looked away. "So, uh. . .what brings you to my store today?" he asked, looking down and brushing at the dust on his trousers.

"The chain on my bike came loose. I was hoping you might have something here that would help me fix it."

Adam chuckled. "I'm not a bike shop, Leah."

The heat she felt on her face intensified. "I know that, but I thought maybe—"

"Come to think of it, I do have a tool in the back of my buggy that's exactly what you need."

"Would you mind if I borrow it?" she asked.

His eyes narrowed. "You really think you can fix the chain?"

Leah's defenses rose. "Despite what you might think, Adam, I'm not *dumm.*"

"I never said you were dumb. Just didn't know if you'd ever tightened a bicycle chain."

She relaxed a little. "I've never done it before, but I think I can figure it out."

"Okay." Adam shrugged. "If you'll wait right here, I'll get it."

That young woman is sure hard to figure out, Adam thought as he made his way around the back of the store to his buggy. *One minute she's sweet as date pudding, and the next minute she acts like she has a bee under her kapp. Sure wish she hadn't come along when she did; I'd have my shoplifter by now. Who knows where he ran off to, or why he took those things from my store.*

Adam picked up his pace, noticing that the delivery truck was already there. Luckily, the driver was talking on his cell phone, so that would give Adam a few extra minutes before he'd need to help the guy unload his order. *Sure wish Leah wasn't so pretty. Makes it hard for me to look at her and not long for a wife. I wonder how well she cooks.*

He slapped the side of his head. *Now where did that foolish notion come from? I'm just not thinking straight today. Must be all the excitement.*

When Adam reached the buggy, he opened his toolbox and took out what he needed. Then he went back to where he'd left Leah but discovered she wasn't there. He glanced at her bike, parked in one of the bicycle racks. No sign of Leah over there, either.

Adam crouched down to examine the chain and realized that it needed to be shortened. Thinking Leah may have gone into the store, he went inside, where he discovered Leah near the checkout counter, talking to Ben.

"Here you go, Leah." Adam handed her the tool.

She stared at the object. "What's that?"

"It's called a 'chain tool,' and it's used to push the pin out of the chain so you can take out links to make it the right length. I took a look at your bike before I came inside, and it appears that the chain has stretched. That's why it's loose."

Leah stared at the small metal tool with a curious expression. "Are you sure this will work on my chain?"

"Course it will. If you know what you're doing, that is. Since there aren't any common tools you would find in my store that can do a decent job of removing and reinserting chain pins, you really do need this tool."

"Oh, okay." Leah hesitated, glancing at the chain tool then back at Adam. "Umm. . . I'm really not sure how to use this."

"Figured as much. Want me to do it for you?" he asked.

"I appreciate the offer, but you have a store to run, and I noticed a delivery truck out back when I entered the parking lot, so you'll probably be busy with that."

"It's not a problem." Adam looked at Ben. "Since there are no customers in the store at the moment, would you open the back door and help the driver bring in those bags of seed? The dolly is inside the door, and you can just stack them anywhere in the back room. I'll get to them as soon as I help Leah."

Ben nodded. "Sure, no problem."

Adam followed Leah out the door. While he knelt next to her bike, Leah stood off to one side, watching. "I've done this a good many times," he said, looking up at her. "My daed owned a bike shop when I was a boy, so I've had lots of practice fixing chains and a whole lot of other things related to bikes. Fact is, I've repaired my own bike chain several times."

Her eyebrows lifted. "Really? I didn't know you owned a bike. I've never seen you riding one."

"Jah, well, there are a lot of things about me you don't know."

CHAPTER 8

"*Ich hab's im rick*," Priscilla complained to her mother as they pulled weeds from their garden. Mom straightened, rubbing an area on her lower back. "I can understand why you have a backache. My back's about to give out, too." She gestured to the wicker chairs sitting under the gazebo Dad had built a few years ago. "Let's take a break. I'll go get us some lemonade, and we can sit out there in the shade and rest awhile before we finish up for the day."

Priscilla smiled. "That sounds good to me, only why don't you sit and let me get the lemonade?"

"That's okay," Mom said. "I need to go inside anyhow. While we've been weeding, I thought of a few things I want to put on the grocery list. If I don't do it now, I'll probably get busy doing something else and forget." She frowned. "I've been kind of forgetful lately."

"That's fine, Mom, but if you need me for anything, just give a holler."

Watching her mother go toward the house, holding her lower back as she walked, Priscilla sauntered around the yard for a bit, hoping to get the kinks out of her own back. All that bending, stooping, and pulling of weeds had really done a number on her this morning. She glanced at the small store connected to their home, where she and Mom sold homemade jelly and several kinds of home-canned fruits. It was closed today. Otherwise, she would have been working there instead of in the garden. Priscilla helped her mother process all of their fruits, vegetables, and berries, which she found somewhat rewarding, but weeding was not one of her favorite things to do. Mom's either, for that matter, but it needed to be done.

Priscilla looked up at the house, thinking about how Mom had said she'd been forgetful lately. She hoped it was just a case of having too much to do, and that Mom wouldn't end up with dementia someday, like what Elaine's grandma had gone through. It had saddened Priscilla to watch her good friend deal with the heartache of losing her grandma to such a horrible disease. Priscilla, as well as Leah, had offered Elaine their support. Priscilla knew if she were ever faced with an adversity that her two best friends would be there for her, too.

Rubbing at the knot in her lower back, Priscilla glanced toward the road and was surprised to see Leah pedaling up the driveway.

"I was just thinking about you," Priscilla said when Leah rode up.

Leah grinned. "I hope they were good thoughts."

"Of course. I was thinking how fortunate I am to have good friends like you and Elaine, and how we've always been there for one another."

"That's true, and I feel blessed because of it." Leah climbed off her bike and set the kickstand. "I'm on my way home from the health food store and decided to stop here and ask for a cold drink of water." She fanned her face with one hand while holding up her Thermos with the other. "All the ice cubes melted, and what little tea I have left is now warm. When I left home, I didn't realize it was going to be such a hot day. After all I've been through, I'm drenched with perspiration."

Priscilla felt concern. "What do you mean, all you've 'been through'? Did something happen on the way to or from the health food store?"

"It was on the way. My bicycle chain became loose, so I stopped by Adam Beachy's hardware store to see if I could find something to fix it, and then. . ." Leah paused and blotted her damp forehead with her dress sleeve. "Whew, the air is so humid today. My clothes are actually sticking to me."

Priscilla motioned to the wicker chairs under the shade of the gazebo. "Take a seat. I'll run in the house and get you something cold to drink. You look miserable, and I'm worried that you may have been in the sun too long."

"Danki," Leah said. "I really do need to rest awhile. When you come back, I'll tell you what happened after I got to Adam's store."

" 'Here you go; I brought lemonade, and it's nice and cold," Priscilla said when she returned from the house carrying two glasses.

"Danki." Leah took a big drink then held the cool glass against her hot cheek. "This is so refreshing. It's just what I needed right now."

"I know what you mean." Priscilla took the seat beside Leah and drank from her own glass. "Mom and I have spent most of our morning weeding, and it didn't take long till we were both hot and sweaty; not to mention that our backs are hurting."

"I'm sorry to hear that. By the way, where is your mamm?"

"She's in the house, adding things to her grocery list."

"I have a couple appointments early this afternoon, but I'm free around four o'clock, if you'd like to come by for a foot treatment and neck massage. You can bring your mamm along, and I'll work on her, too."

"That sounds nice, and if Mom doesn't have anything important she needs to do, we both may take you up on that offer." Priscilla sipped her drink and set her glass on the wicker table between them. "Before you leave, I'll refill your Thermos with cold water and lots of ice cubes. That way you'll have something to drink on your trip home."

"That'd be great. Danki."

"So tell me now; what happened at Adam's store this morning?"

Leah fiddled with the ties on her head covering, remembering how flustered she'd felt when Adam fell beside her on the porch.

"Your cheeks are bright red." Priscilla's voice was edged with concern. "Maybe you need to drink more lemonade."

Leah shook her head. "No, I'm fine. Just thinking about what happened is all."

"Please tell me. I'm anxious to hear."

Leah recounted the events, from when the teenage boy rushed out the door and knocked her to the porch to when Adam had nearly fallen on top of her.

Priscilla giggled. "I'm sure it wasn't funny, but I can just picture you and Adam lying there beside each other."

"You're right, falling wasn't funny, but if you'd seen the look on Adam's face, you would have laughed." Leah suppressed a giggle. "I seem to be falling a lot lately whenever Adam's around."

"What do you mean?"

"I saw him at Rockome Garden Foods the other day and managed to slip in some honey that got on the floor when he dropped a jar of the stuff."

"Oh no! Maybe it's a sign that you're meant to *stick* together." Priscilla snickered.

Leah shook her head. "No way! Adam's not my type, and I'm sure the feeling is mutual."

"I didn't think Elam was my type when he first seemed interested in me, but look at us now—we're courting."

"That's different. You've known Elam since we were kinner, and he was your friend before he asked if he could court you." Leah took another drink. The tangy, cool lemonade felt good on her parched throat. "Adam and I don't even like each other, so there's no chance of him ever courting me."

"Who let this mutt in my store?" Adam asked Ben. A bedraggled-looking black Lab was sniffing around the garden rakes.

Ben shrugged his broad shoulders. "Beats me. I didn't even notice him till now."

Adam inhaled a long breath. "Well, he needs to go out. No dogs are allowed in here, unless they're service animals." He pointed at the Lab. "And that mangy critter definitely doesn't qualify!"

"Want me to get him out?"

"No, I'll take care of it." Adam opened the front door, pointed at the dog, and hollered, "Go on outside where you belong!"

The dog looked up at Adam as if he had no idea what he wanted.

Adam wasn't keen on touching the dirty animal, so he grabbed a broom and shooed the dog out the door, quickly shutting it behind him. Hopefully, by the time the next customer came in, the dog would have gone back to wherever it came from. In the meantime, Adam had a box of paintbrushes to unpack, as well as the bags of birdseed to unwrap and stock on the shelves. He decided to work on the seed bags first. The bags weighed from ten pounds all the way up to fifty pounds, so that would keep him busy for a while.

"I'll be in the back room if you need me," he called to Ben.

"No problem. I'll take care of any customers who come in," Ben responded.

Adam finally got the bags off the pallets and used the dolly to wheel them out to the shelves. First he put the smaller bags on the higher shelves, then the forty-and fifty-pound bags went on the lower shelves. In the same aisle, opposite the seed, were various-sized bird feeders, along with boxes of suet cakes.

After several trips, Adam brought out the last two fifty-pound bags of seeds. His shoulders had started hurting. *I wonder if Leah could help my shoulders.* Pausing, Adam thumped his head. *Now what made me think that?*

Making sure there was room for the last bag, Adam picked it up and felt his fingers poke through the middle of the bag. As if watching it in slow motion, he saw the birdseed pour out, spreading all over the floor.

"Oh, great! What more could go wrong today?" Adam moaned as he inspected the almost-empty bag. Apparently there'd been a tear in the bag, which his fingers had made bigger when he'd lifted it. "Now how did I not see that before?" He looked down at the seed-covered floor, slowly shaking his head.

"Do you need some help here?" Ben offered, joining Adam in the aisle.

Adam looked at him and rolled his eyes.

"I'll go get a container, and we can put the seed in there." Ben left quickly. When he returned, he held a garbage can, two brooms, and two dustpans. As they worked together to clean up the mess, Adam decided to question Ben.

"I don't know if you realized what happened a little bit ago, but we had a shoplifter in the store. That's who I was chasing when I ran out the door and bumped into Leah Mast."

"No, I didn't realize that." Ben's dark eyebrows squished together. "Guess I must have been busy with a customer at the time."

"Did you notice a teen enter the store before that? He had on a denim jacket and a baseball cap. Oh, and he had red hair, which he wore in a ponytail."

"I was up at the front of the store, but I didn't see anyone like that come in." Ben scratched his head with a quizzical look. "Course, I may have been helping a customer and just didn't notice the boy. What are you going to do about this, Adam? Will you call the sheriff?"

"Think I'll wait on that." Adam shoveled another dustpan full of seed and poured it into the can. "He only took some garden gloves and two hand shovels, so I'm really not out that much."

"Okay, whatever you think is best," Ben responded with a shrug.

"Would you mind finishing this up while I take care of the paintbrushes that need to be put out?" Adam asked.

"Sure, no problem."

Adam headed to the back of the store, tore open the box, and had begun sorting the paintbrushes but had to stop. "Guess I overdid it with all those seed bags," he mumbled, rolling his shoulders, hoping to get the kinks out. "Well, this isn't going to get done by itself." Reaching inside the box, he stopped again when he heard a whimper. Standing a few feet away was that same black Lab.

"You again? What are you doing back in here, boy? Are you lost or just looking for trouble?"

The scraggly-looking dog walked timidly over and pawed at Adam's pant leg. It looked as if the mutt had something in his mouth. At Adam's command, the Lab dropped it and backed up when Adam's voice grew stern. "I don't know what you want, but whatever it is, you won't find it here." Adam opened the back door this time and practically pushed the dog outside. "Go home!"

With his tail between his legs, the Lab slunk off, but before Adam saw which direction the dog took, he quickly shut the door. *I wonder how that* hund *got in here again.*

Massaging his shoulder, Adam walked back toward the box of supplies but stopped short when he kicked something with his shoe. Bending down to pick up the article, he realized it was a pair of garden gloves, still packaged together and unopened. It looked to be the same type, or perhaps even one of the pairs the shoplifting kid had snatched earlier today. But that couldn't be—he'd seen the boy run out the door with the gloves. Could he have dropped one of them as he was running away, and had the dog picked it up? Adam would probably never know the answer to that, and right now, it didn't seem that important.

Scratching his head, Adam groaned. If the rest of this day didn't turn out any better than the first part had, tomorrow he might decide to let Ben run the store by himself and stay home in bed.

Of course, Adam told himself, *that's really not an option.*

CHAPTER 9

*H*ow are you doing today?" Leah asked when Margaret entered the basement for another foot treatment.

"I've recovered from my reaction to the walnuts, but since I never got a foot treatment that day, my back is still hurting." Margaret reached around and touched a spot on her lower back. "Seems like the older I get, the more aches and pains I seem to have. Even when I do the simplest chores, some part of my body ends up hurting."

"Well, have a seat in my chair, and I'll see what I can do to ease some of that." Leah motioned to the recliner.

Margaret did as Leah told her. "When I was walking up to your house, I noticed all the hummingbird feeders you have. I paused a few minutes to watch them flitter around. Now that was kind of fun."

"They are fun to watch." Leah took a seat on the stool in front of Margaret. "We have so many hummers this year that I've had to add a few extra feeders to accommodate them all."

"I've only seen a couple at our place," Margaret said as Leah applied lotion to her left foot. "I don't have any feeders out, but they seem to like our honeysuckle bush."

Leah nodded. "Several bushes and flowering plants attract the hummers, but with so many coming into our yard, keeping the feeders filled seems to work best."

"That makes sense," Margaret agreed.

"Isn't it amazing how watching something that simple can help a person relax and forget all their troubles, even if only for a few minutes?"

"Jah. My husband often says it's a shame more people don't take the time to stop and look at a pretty sunset or observe God's creatures that are here for our enjoyment."

Leah smiled. "He's right about that. A lot of times the beauty God's given us goes unnoticed."

"It's good to know you're not one of those people," Margaret said. "The world would be a lot better place if folks just slowed down and uncomplicated life a bit."

"It could certainly be good therapy. I know it is for me."

As Leah began working, she found several sore spots on Margaret's left foot. Moving to the right foot, she uncovered more tender areas, which she pressure-pointed and massaged. "The areas I worked on that were so tender are related to your back," Leah explained, "so I'm hoping I was able to open the pathways and offer you some relief."

When Leah finished, Margaret put her shoes on and stood. Walking around the room for a bit, she smiled and said, "Danki, Leah. My back feels much better than it did when I first got here."

Leah smiled. "I'm glad it helped, but you may want to take it easy for the rest of the day, and if your back begins to hurt again, be sure to ice it for a while."

Margaret placed some money in the jar and gave Leah a hug. "What you do here in this room is a good thing, and I hope you won't ever quit, because you've helped many people."

Leah was pleased to hear that. It was a reminder that she was using the ability God had given her to help others, and that was reward enough. Too bad people like Adam didn't appreciate or believe in reflexology.

Well, to each his own, Leah thought after Margaret said good-bye and went upstairs. *I don't know why I'm thinking about Adam right now, because I certainly don't need his approval.*

Leah glanced at her appointment book and realized that she didn't have anyone else scheduled for the rest of the day. Maybe this would be a good time to sit outside, enjoy the sunshine, and get a little reading done. She'd started a new novel set in the Old West the other day but had only read the first two chapters. Most days she was too busy to read, and by the time she went to bed at night, Leah was so tired she couldn't keep her eyes open.

After putting away her massage lotion and washing up, Leah went upstairs. She found Mom in the kitchen, peeling potatoes at the sink. "It's only four o'clock," Leah said, glancing at the clock on the far wall.

"Are you starting supper already?"

"Just thought I'd get the potatoes peeled and cut; then I'll put them in a kettle with cold water till it's time to start cooking." Mom smiled at Leah. "How'd it go with Margaret? She looked quite relaxed when she came upstairs."

"She said her back felt better after I worked on her feet, so with less pain to deal with, I'm sure that's why she was relaxed." Leah took a pitcher of iced tea from the refrigerator and opened the cupboard where the glasses were kept. "Would you like some iced tea, Mom?"

"Maybe later," Mom replied. "Right now I just want to finish this."

"I was going outside to read awhile," Leah said, "but if you need my help with supper, it can wait."

Mom shook her head. "You go ahead. I can manage. Besides, there aren't many potatoes left to peel."

"Okay then, call me if you need anything." Leah poured herself some tea and put the container back in the refrigerator. Taking her book from the drawer where she'd put it the other day, she went out the back door.

Leah had just seated herself on the porch when a hummingbird zoomed in. At first it hovered above the book she held. Then it flew right over her head and found its way to the nearest feeder hanging from one of the shepherd's hooks near the house.

Glancing down at the book, Leah realized that the hummingbird had probably been attracted to the red in the cover. She grinned, watching the tiny bird at the feeder dip its beak in and out to get the sweet nectar. Leah never tired of watching the hummers and wished they could stay all year. Since that wasn't possible, she would enjoy them for the few months they were in the area. And next month, when Alissa came to band the birds, Leah would make sure she was available not only to watch the procedure but also to offer Alissa assistance if needed.

Pulling her gaze from the hummingbird, Leah set her drink on the table and opened the book. She'd only read a few pages when Priscilla rode up on her bike. Leah figured she was probably here for the foot treatment they had talked about working in.

So much for getting any reading done, Leah thought. But then, she quickly corrected herself. Priscilla had complained of back pain, and if Leah could help, she would gladly set aside her free time to accommodate a friend.

Sparky ran out to greet Priscilla, although he didn't bark.

"Hey, pup. How are you doing?" Priscilla bent down and scratched behind the dog's ears.

"Mom and I did some more weeding after lunch, and now my back hurts even worse than it did before," she said, joining Leah on the porch. "Would you have time to give me a treatment?"

Leah bobbed her head. "Of course; I told you I would."

"Jah, but I don't want to take you away from your book. It looks like you've been enjoying having some time to relax."

"It's fine, really." Leah set the book aside. "Where's your mamm? When you mentioned earlier that she was also sore from weeding, I figured she'd want a treatment, too."

"That's what I thought, but Mom said that she had some other things she wanted to get done today. If she's still hurting tomorrow, I'm sure she'll make an appointment to come see you."

"Okay, let's go down to the basement."

After Leah finished working on Priscilla's feet, she asked her to sit in the straight-backed chair so she could massage her neck and relieve some tension. "Oh my, you have some knots in there, too."

"After all that yard work, I'm not surprised, but I'm feeling better already."

Leah smiled. She didn't always get immediate results with those who came to her for help, but when she did, it gave her a sense of satisfaction. But the ability to help others was her gift, and she reminded herself once more that it came from God.

"When we were outside, I couldn't help noticing all the humming-birds in your yard. They seemed to be flitting around everywhere. Some even went to the bee balm flowers you have near the porch," Priscilla commented.

"They do love that bee balm." Leah laughed. "But I think the main reason we have so many hummers is because of all the feeders we have out. It's a lot of fun to watch them chirping at one another as they zoom in and out all day. You should hear all the commotion they make."

"Makes me wish we had some feeders in our yard," Priscilla said. "Is it too late in the season to hang them out?"

"I don't think so, but the peak of the season for hummers in our area is just a month away, so if you're going to try luring them into your yard, I'd suggest you get some feeders hung out soon. When I was talking to my neighbor the other day, she explained how the hummingbirds start migrating down here around mid-July, and that's why it gets extra busy at the feeders. With our local hummers sticking around, as well as the migrating ones from up north, it's like watching a swarm of bees."

"Think I'm gonna get a feeder or two right away."

As Leah started massaging the other side of Priscilla's neck, Priscilla screamed and jumped onto the seat of her chair.

"What's wrong, Priscilla? Was I massaging your neck too hard?"

"No, it wasn't that." Priscilla pointed. "Look, there's a *maus*! It's nibbling on the laces of my sneaker!"

Leah grabbed a broom and chased after the mouse. It zipped across the room and disappeared behind a stack of boxes.

"You can come down now. The *maus* is gone." Leah extended her hand to Priscilla.

Priscilla looked a bit hesitant but finally stepped down. Quickly grabbing up her shoes, she took a seat in the chair and slipped them on her feet.

"I wonder why that little mouse was so interested in your shoelace." Leah snickered. "It's certainly not covered in peanut butter or cheese."

Priscilla's fingers touched her parted lips. "No, but I spilled some chicken soup during lunch, and a little of it ended up on my shoes. Guess I didn't get it all cleaned off."

Leah looked at Priscilla's shoes and giggled. Priscilla did the same. Soon, Leah was laughing so hard she had to sit down. It felt good to find some humor in such a small thing. With all the horrible things that went on in the world, a little bit of laughter was good medicine.

⌒

When Adam secured his horse to the hitching rack outside his house that afternoon, he was surprised to see the black Lab that had come into his store, prancing up the driveway. "Oh no," he moaned. "Not you again! What'd you do, boy, follow me home?"

Woof! Woof! The dog raced up to Adam and pawed at the leg of his pants.

"I can't believe this. Why me, of all people? I don't even like dogs that well." Adam clapped his hands and pointed toward the road. "Go home, boy! Go back to where you belong!"

After Adam brushed his horse down, he went into the kitchen so he could get his Thermos and lunch pail ready for the next day. Cleaning the Thermos, Adam watched out the window and rolled his eyes. The dog had made himself comfortable lying near the wheel of Adam's buggy.

"That crazy mutt has a mind of his own," Adam muttered. "Maybe if I stay inside awhile longer, he'll leave." Adam took a few celery stalks from the refrigerator and snipped off the ends. After rinsing the pieces, he got the peanut butter and spread it on the celery. He munched on one and wrapped the others to put in his lunch pail for the following day. After placing the rest of the celery back in the fridge, he paused a minute, making sure he had enough bread, lunch meat, and cheese to make a sandwich in the morning to take to work. Satisfied that there was plenty, he shut the refrigerator door. He looked out the window but didn't see the dog.

"Oh, good." Adam grabbed the peanut butter and went to the pantry. After putting the jar away, he took out a pack of crackers and a few cookies to add to his lunch box. Now all he'd have to do in the morning before heading to work was make a sandwich.

"Guess it's safe to go back outside." Grabbing his hat, Adam went out the door but halted when he approached the barn and saw the mutt lying there, looking up at him.

"Are you still here?"

The dog wagged his tail but didn't budge.

Adam wondered if the critter might be lost or abandoned. He'd heard of people driving to an area outside their neighborhood and dropping off their unwanted pet. Even though Adam didn't care much for dogs, he thought it was terrible if someone had deserted the Lab.

Flash nickered when Adam drew near and ran a hand down the horse's neck. "What do you think of that pesky dog?"

Flash snorted and shook his head.

"I feel the same way." Adam chuckled as he unhooked the horse, leading him past the dog and into the barn.

Before leaving for work, Adam had raked out the stall and put fresh bedding inside for his horse. At least that was one chore he wouldn't have to do this evening. Adam led Flash into the stall and started brushing him down. When that was done, he gave the horse fresh water and put oats in the feeding bin. While Flash ate, Adam ran a curry comb through the horse's mane. Taking care of Flash was relaxing, especially after the way today had turned out.

When Adam finished combing Flash's mane, he noticed that his shoulders actually felt somewhat better. He put the brush and comb away then came back to scratch Flash's ears. "You're good therapy for me, you know that Flash? Who needs reflexology anyways?"

Flash nuzzled his nose into Adam's hand and nickered softly.

Adam brushed off some wet oats from his horse's mouth that had stuck to his hands. Glancing over his shoulder, he saw that the dog was still there, watching from the barn's entrance. Closing the door to the stall, he hung the horse's bridle, along with the blinders, on the hook next to the stall door.

Suddenly, Flash started snorting and blowing air through his nostrils. Because he knew his horse so well, Adam was sure something was wrong. He looked around but didn't see anything unusual. Then he noticed that Flash appeared to be looking toward the back corner of the barn. Adam moved cautiously in that direction. Backed into the corner was a portly groundhog, baring his teeth and snarling. The groundhog ran past Adam's feet, toward the open barn door.

Adam ran outside in time to see the barking Lab disappear as he chased the varmint behind the barn. "Good, let him take care of the groundhog." Adam closed the barn door. "I don't need any more hassles today."

Just as he reached the porch steps, Adam heard a distressed-sounding *yip*! Groundhogs had large front teeth and could probably deliver a nasty bite. Without thinking twice, he ran to the back of the barn, but all was quiet, and neither the dog nor the groundhog was anywhere to be seen. Looking closer, Adam noticed a chewed-out hole that went through the wall of the barn. In the dirt in front of the hole was a spot of blood. Adam scanned the area again but saw no sign of the dog or groundhog. Taking off his hat, he ran his fingers through his hair. *Did that groundhog bite him? Or did the Lab bite the groundhog?* Either way, he'd have to get rid of the pest, because he couldn't have a groundhog getting into the barn again, alarming, or even biting his horse.

He hoped the mutt was okay and would find his family, because that dog would never have a home with Adam.

CHAPTER 10

$\mathcal{E}$ntering the kitchen, Adam paused to yawn and stretch his arms over his head. Then he rolled his head from side to side, hoping to get the kinks out. For some reason, he'd had a hard time sleeping last night, and now he had a stiff neck. *Probably from all that went on yesterday*, he decided. *Well, today is bound to be better.*

Before leaving for work, Adam fixed himself a cup of coffee, ate a banana, and then headed outside to the phone shack to check for messages, which he'd neglected to do last night. Opening the back door and stepping onto the porch, he nearly tripped over something. Looking down, he realized that the determined mutt was lying on his porch.

Disgusted, he stepped around the dog and sprinted down the driveway. *Maybe if I ignore the critter he'll go away. Guess that's wishful thinking, 'cause it hasn't worked yet.*

Inside the phone shack Adam took a seat and checked his messages. The first one was from his neighbor, Clarence Lambright, saying they had some extra eggs and asking if Adam wanted a dozen. Adam dialed Clarence's number and left a message, thanking him for the offer and letting him know that he would pick up the eggs on his way home from work.

The next message was from Adam's sister telling him that she and her family planned to hire a driver next week and come to Arthur to celebrate Adam's birthday. As much as Adam looked forward to their visit, he didn't really care about celebrating his birthday. Turning thirty was no big deal. Adam wouldn't discourage her from coming, though. He hadn't seen Mary, Amos, and their girls since Christmas, and it would be good to see them again.

After returning Mary's call and leaving a message saying he looked forward to their visit, Adam stepped out of the phone shack.

Woof! Woof! The Lab looked up at Adam with sorrowful brown eyes.

Adam gritted his teeth. He couldn't believe the mutt had followed him here. Didn't this dog ever give up?

Adam headed back to the house, and as he opened the door, the dog leaped forward. Adam grabbed the Lab's collar to pull him back, stepped inside, and quickly shut the door. The persistent animal remained on the porch and whined. Adam remembered the dog's encounter with the groundhog and figured he'd better check to see if he had been bitten.

"The critter's probably hungry and thirsty, too," Adam mumbled under his breath. "Guess it wouldn't hurt if I gave him a little something to eat and drink."

Adam found a plastic bowl and filled it with water. Then he went to the refrigerator and grabbed a couple leftover hot dogs. While the dog ate hungrily and lapped up the water, Adam checked for wounds. Seeing none, he figured the Lab must have been the victor or at least chased the groundhog off.

Adam patted the dog's matted coat. "What you need is a good bath and thorough combing." He thumped the side of his head. *I must be getting soft in the noggin. If I do all that, I'll never get rid of the mutt.*

"I'm heading to Elaine's now," Leah called to her mother after she'd finished drying the breakfast dishes.

Mom had been gathering up the living-room throw rugs to shake outside, and she poked her head into the kitchen. "Oh, that's right. I had forgotten you were going over there to help her clean. Will you be back in time for lunch, or will you stay and eat with Elaine?"

"I'll stay there. Priscilla is coming over around noon to eat lunch with us. We three haven't gotten together in a while, and it'll give us a chance to catch up with one another's lives."

"Well, have a good time, and don't work too hard."

"Same goes for you, Mom. I know you said during breakfast that your back feels better, but try not to overdo it."

Mom smiled. "I'm not going to do any heavy cleaning—just touch things up a bit."

"I'd stay and help if I hadn't already promised Elaine."

Mom waved her hand. "That's okay. Go and enjoy your day."

Leah took her black outer bonnet down from the wall peg and put it on over her white head covering. "See you later, Mom."

As Leah headed down the road on her bike, she passed Adam's house and noticed a black Lab sitting at the end of his driveway.

I wonder where that dog came from. As far as Leah knew, Adam didn't have a dog. *Well, it's none of my business,* she told herself. *If it's a stray or one of his neighbor's dogs, it probably wandered onto his property looking for food, or maybe it was chasing a cat or some other critter.*

Thinking about Adam, Leah reflected on how he'd fixed her bicycle chain. She'd definitely seen a kinder side of him yesterday. Maybe they could set their differences aside and be friends. Of course, Adam might not be interested in being Leah's friend. He seemed content to be by himself when he wasn't working in his store, so she wouldn't pursue a friendship with him. If Adam wanted to be Leah's friend, he'd have to do the pursuing.

When Adam arrived at his store a few minutes later than usual, he was glad to see Ben already waiting on a customer, Leah's father. There was no sign of his other employee, so Adam figured Henry's shoulder was still giving him problems. He probably wouldn't be in again today, but hopefully by Monday, Henry would be back to work.

Adam stepped up to the counter. "*Guder mariye*, Ben. Same to you, Alton."

Ben nodded, but Alton barely squeaked out a "good morning" in response. Wrinkling his nose, he turned from the counter. "Guess I'll go look again for that blade I need," he called over his shoulder.

"Whew. . .what's that spicy smell?" Ben asked, leaning away from Adam.

Adam's face flushed. "Well, I did use some new aftershave lotion this morning. Guess that could be what you smell."

"What'd ya do, take a bath in it?" Ben plugged his nose.

"Course not." Adam grunted. "Thanks to the time I took to take care of the mutt that followed me home yesterday, I was in a hurry this morning. Guess I must've put on a little too much balm after I shaved."

"What mutt was that?" Ben asked.

"The black Lab that was hanging around here yesterday. The critter followed me home, and I couldn't get rid of him." Adam turned toward the back room. "I'll fill you in later. Right now I need to go to the washroom and try to get some of this lotion off my face so I don't chase away all our customers today. After that, I'll be in my office, going over some paperwork. If you need me, just give a holler."

"No problem. It doesn't look like Henry will be working again today, but I'm sure I can manage on my own unless it gets really busy."

Adam nodded, thankful once again that he'd hired Ben.

A bit later, as Adam was heading toward his office, a teenage boy wearing a baseball cap stepped up to him. It was the shoplifter.

"Came back to return this stuff to you." The boy handed Adam a pair of gloves and the two small shovels he'd taken. "I know what I did was wrong, and I. . .I just wanted to say that I'm sorry."

Stunned, Adam hardly knew how to respond. He'd never expected to get the stuff back, much less receive an apology from the boy. "Why'd you do it?" Adam asked. "Was it just for the sport of it, or to prove that you could take those things and get away with it?"

The boy shook his head. "My dad's out of work, and my folks are short on money right now. So my mom's been trying to sell some produce from her garden." He frowned. "She's been pulling weeds with no garden gloves, and the handle on the shovel she uses broke yesterday morning."

"So you came into my store and took what wasn't yours." A muscle on the side of Adam's neck quivered. He felt bad about the boy's father being out of work, but stealing was wrong, and the kid ought to learn a lesson.

The boy dropped his gaze to the floor. "The stuff I took hasn't been used. When my folks found out what I did, they said I had to bring everything back this morning." His voice cracked. "Dad's making me do extra chores around the place now, and he said I should do some work for you, too, to make up for what I did."

Adam stood with his arms folded, trying to decide what to do. If he let the kid go without making him do any work, would he really learn a lesson? "I'll tell you what," he said, clasping the boy's shoulder. "You can do some cleaning in the store for me this morning, and when you're done and ready to go home, you can take these with you." He motioned to the gloves and shovel. "Not before you tell me your name, though."

The boy's eyes widened. "You mean it, mister? You won't turn me in?"

Adam gave a hesitant nod, wondering if he was doing the right thing. "But you've got to promise that you'll never steal anything from me or anyone else again."

"No, I won't. I've learned my lesson." The boy grabbed Adam's hand and shook it. "My name's Scott Ramsey. I'm pleased to meet you."

"Likewise, I think," Adam mumbled, handing the boy a broom. "You can start by sweeping the floor."

"No problem. I'll do a good job."

"Oh, before you do that," Adam said, "I was wondering if you own a black Lab."

The boy shook his head. "Nope, just a beagle hound. Why do you ask?"

"One was hanging around the store yesterday, and the mutt followed me home. He also brought a package of gardening gloves into the store. I figured it might be one of the pairs you took."

"I did take two pairs, but I dropped one on my way out." The boy shrugged. "The dog ain't mine, and I don't know anyone who has a Lab."

After Scott moved down the aisle, pushing the broom, Adam went to his office and took a seat at the desk. This had been an interesting morning so far. Not only had he fed a dog he didn't want hanging around, but he'd agreed to give the shoplifting kid the very things he'd stolen from him. He really must be getting soft in the head.

Adam wondered if the dog would be waiting for him when he got home. When he'd checked the animal over this morning, he'd looked at the dog's collar for a name tag or license, but there was nothing to indicate who the Lab belonged to. Adam hated to admit it, but deep down, he almost hoped the dog would still be there. He had to stop at his neighbor's first, to pick up the eggs they had for him, but after that, he would be anxious to get home. Even though it meant extra work, having a pet to care for might relieve some of the lonesomeness and tension he often felt.

CHAPTER 11

*A*dam spent the next week getting ready for his sister's arrival, making sure there was plenty of food in the house, the beds were all made, and the house was cleaned. He'd hired a couple young Amish women to do the cleaning, since he had little free time after work each day.

As he sat on the front porch, watching for his family to arrive, Adam wondered what was taking them so long. They'd hired a driver and were coming in a van, but since it was Friday, the traffic might be heavier than usual, with people heading places for the weekend. Mary had said she and the family would arrive before supper and that she would fix the meal. But when Adam checked his pocket watch and saw that it was five o'clock, he figured they might not get here in time for that. Maybe he would take them out to eat, which would probably be better anyway. Since they'd been traveling all day, Mary was bound to be tired.

Feeling a wet nose nudge his hand, Adam looked down. The Lab was still with him, lying on top of his feet. Adam had resigned himself to the fact that the dog had adopted him. He'd asked around to see if anyone had lost a Lab, but no one knew anything about the dog. Adam had even hung several "Lost Dog" flyers around town but had gotten no response. He didn't have the heart to let the dog roam around, neglected, and since the mutt seemed to have claimed Adam as his new master, he'd finally given in. He had named the dog Coal because of the color of the animal's thick coat of hair. Adam knew that naming the Lab was just as significant as if he'd signed adoption papers.

"Guess you and me are stuck with each other now." Adam smiled, moving his feet while Coal let out a low moan. The dog felt like a sack of potatoes and was cutting off the circulation in Adam's ankles. But it was kind of nice, having the dog around. He'd actually caught himself looking for Coal every day when he got home from work. Faithfully, the dog was there, either on the porch wagging his tail or sitting at the end of the driveway, barking when Adam's horse and buggy came into view.

Even in the little bit of time Coal had been around, he'd proven his worth. On Wednesday, Adam had noticed the disgusting smell of a dead animal permeating the barn. After finding a hole coming up through the floor where he kept bales of straw, Adam realized that the groundhog had actually made a tunnel under the barn and was probably the source of the stench. Adam wasn't sure how to get the critter out but hoped that after a while the odor would fade. The next morning, when he walked out onto the porch, Coal sat with the dead groundhog, smelling even worse than the day before. Adam had no idea how Coal managed to get the carcass out from under the barn, and he wasn't even going to try and figure it out, but he was glad the dog had.

Adam snickered, thinking that if his sister had been visiting and found a smelly old carcass right by the door, she would have probably fainted. At any rate, that evening, Coal had gotten a bath, and his coat still shone like a piece of blue-black coal. No more did the Lab have that mangy mongrel look. Now Coal had the appearance of a sleek purebred black Labrador retriever. Not only would Adam have a dog to introduce to his nieces, but he'd have a clean dog at that.

The groundhog wasn't the only thing the dog had surprised Adam with this week. Last evening, Coal had walked into the barn, where Adam had gone to feed his horse, and dropped a ripe tomato at his feet. Adam recognized it right away, being the first to ripen on the vine. He'd been watching it for the last week, and now the plump tomato was perfect. Adam had intended to pick that tomato this morning, to have with dinner tonight, but Coal had beaten him to it. Amazingly enough, the tomato was intact, with no teeth marks on it—just dog slobber. Luckily, that could be washed off.

"How'd you like to play a game of fetch?" Adam asked, as the dog's tail thumped the ground.

"I'll take that as a yes." Adam headed for the barn, and like a shot, Coal followed. Once inside, Adam pulled the plastic lid off an old coffee can. "This oughtta work fine for what I have in mind."

With Coal at his heels, Adam left the barn and stood in the middle of the lawn. "If you can fetch a tomato, then this makeshift Frisbee should be easy for you." Adam flung the lid high and hard, and it flew across the yard.

The dog watched it go, and just before it hit the ground, he chased after it. Returning the lid to Adam, Coal looked up in anticipation. *Woof! Woof!*

Adam chuckled. "Okay, okay, don't get so impatient." He threw the lid again and smiled, watching the dog race across the yard, leap into the air, and catch the object with his teeth.

They continued playing for a while until Adam called a halt to the game. "Enough is enough, boy. We both need to relax."

Coal flopped onto the grass, and Adam stood staring at the trees lining his property, appreciating the fact that this place was his.

Several minutes went by until Coal grunted, drawing Adam out of his musings. He squatted down and rubbed the dog's ears. "You're a fair enough pooch, but don't get any ideas about sleeping in the house. Even though you are nice and clean, a dog's place is outside, so you can just keep sleeping in the barn till I find the time to build a doghouse with a fence around it."

As if in response, Coal put his head on Adam's knee and closed his eyes.

Adam smiled. When Carrie, Linda, and Amy got here, they'd probably be excited to discover that Adam now owned a dog.

As Leah removed a pair of her father's trousers from the clothesline, she thought, once again, about Elaine and Priscilla and their boyfriends. Elaine had been seeing Ben, and Priscilla had Elam. Leah had no one, and even though her reflexology was meaningful, she secretly longed to be a wife and mother. But Leah had never had a serious suitor. Was there something about her that turned men away? Was it her looks, or didn't they care for her personality? While Leah had never considered herself beautiful, she didn't think she was homely, either.

Her father always said Leah had pretty blue-green eyes, and Mom often commented on Leah's lovely golden brown hair.

There must be something about my personality that repels any would-be suitors. Leah sighed, shaking out another pair of dry trousers. *Well, what does it matter? If I'm meant to be married, then it will happen, in God's time.*

Arf! Arf! Arf! Leah's Jack Russell terrier darted across the lawn and skidded to a stop in front of her laundry basket. Before Leah could say one word, the dog stuck its snout into the basket, grabbed one of Dad's clean shirts, and raced back across the yard.

Leah chased after the dog, shouting, "Come back here right now, Sparky, and give me Dad's shirt!" Of all things, it was one of Dad's good Sunday shirts. If Leah didn't get the shirt from Sparky soon, she'd have to wash it again and hope it would dry before the sun went down.

To her annoyance, the dog kept running without looking back. As Leah bore down on him, he darted around the side of the barn, slipped under the fence, and disappeared into the field of corn.

Leah groaned. "Oh, great! Guess Dad won't be wearing that shirt on Sunday." After she took the clothes inside, she was supposed to set the table, because her brother, Nathan, and his family were coming for supper. Well, she'd have to go after Sparky and get Dad's shirt back before heading up to the house. She hoped by the time she caught the dog that the shirt would still be in one piece.

Adam was about to head out to the phone shack to check for messages, thinking his sister might have called to let him know they were going to be late, when the sheriff's car pulled into his driveway. Adam swatted at the annoying little bugs hovering in a cloud around his head. Humid weather seemed to make them worse, and they appeared as soon as one walked outdoors. Those gnats could be so aggravating, especially when they went right for one's eyes or ears.

The sheriff got out of his vehicle, and from the man's serious expression, Adam had a feeling this wasn't a social call. He glanced over at Coal, who moments ago had been rambunctious but was now sitting quietly by the porch steps.

"What can I do for you?" Adam asked. He knew the man because he'd come into his hardware store a few times.

The sheriff cleared his throat. "Brace yourself. I'm sorry to say that I've come with bad news."

Adam's heart started to pound as he waited to hear what the man had to say. *Dear God, please don't let it be about Mary or anyone else in her family.*

"I'm sorry, Mr. Beachy, but there's been an accident. The van your sister and her family were traveling in was hit by a truck just outside of Arcola."

Adam's mouth went dry. "Are. . .are any of them hurt?"

The sheriff nodded. "But I don't know how badly. Everyone, including their driver, has been taken to the hospital. If you'd like to go there now, I'll give you a ride."

Fear such as Adam hadn't known since he was boy rose in his chest. He had no idea what to expect once he got to the hospital; he just knew he had to get there as quickly as possible. Grabbing his straw hat from the porch, he followed the sheriff to his car, not even stopping to put Coal away. All Adam could think about was his beloved sister and her dear family. *Dear Lord, please let them be okay.*

CHAPTER 12

*L*eah had just captured Sparky when a black Lab wandered into the yard. She thought it was the same dog she'd seen at the end of Adam's driveway. Figuring the dog must be a stray, she waved her hands and shouted, hoping to chase it off. Instead, it sniffed around, as though looking for something. The dog looked a bit different from when Leah had seen it before. Its coat was black as night, and there was an almost bluish tint to its fur. This clean animal was not the shabby, dingy-looking mutt from before.

"Go home!" Leah hollered.

The Lab wagged its tail and let out a loud bark. That brought Sparky from the barn, where he'd gone with his tail between his legs after Leah had finally rescued Dad's shirt.

Arf! Arf! Arf! Sparky chased after the black dog, barking and nipping at its heels.

Woof! Woof! The Lab zipped around the yard twice then turned and chased Sparky.

Panting for breath, Leah ran after Sparky, who was now chasing the Lab. After calling several times, her ornery little dog would not stop. The overwrought animal either didn't hear her or chose to ignore her commands, for he wouldn't give up the chase. Desperate to find a way to bring it to an end, Leah picked up the garden hose. Turning it on full force, she sprayed both dogs with a blast of water.

Yip! Yip! Yip! Arf! Arf! Sparky and the black Lab took off like a shot for the field of corn.

"Go ahead and run, you crazy critters!" Leah called, shaking her head. She sure wasn't going to chase them into the field; she'd already gone there after Sparky, and once was enough. Leah pulled her dad's shirt from around her neck, where she'd draped it before chasing the dogs. She wasn't sure how, but Dad's Sunday shirt was still in one piece. But it would need to be washed again.

Turning toward the house, Leah halted when a horse and buggy pulled in. Behind them, the sky was turning a brilliant orange as the sun began to set. Her brother and his family had arrived, and she was a hot, sticky mess. Not only that, but she hadn't done a thing to help Mom get supper on. Because Nathan worked in the bulk food store and had to close it up for the evening, Leah was glad Mom had planned to serve supper later than usual—especially with this dog episode.

"What happened to you?" Nathan asked when he got off the buggy. "Your dress is dirty, and your face is flushed."

Leah could see little Zeke's arms going up and down on his mother's lap. Holding out her own arms to greet Rebecca and Stephen, who were trying to get to her first, Leah smiled. "It's a long story, and I'll tell you all about it when we go inside."

Adam sat in the hospital waiting room with his eyes closed and head bowed, praying fervently and waiting for news on the condition of Mary and her family. All he'd been told was that Mary and Amos were in serious condition and that the girls and their driver had minor injuries. He clenched his fists until his fingers dug into his palms. Mary and Amos had to make it. Their girls were so young and needed their parents. For that matter, Adam needed Mary, too, for she was his only sibling and his closest living relative. Adam's father was dead, and for all he knew, his mother was, too. Not that he'd ever want to see her again. Even if she was still alive, in every sense of the word, his mother was dead to him. All Adam wanted right now was to see his sister and know that she would be all right.

How could something like this have happened? he asked himself. *And whose fault was it, anyway? Was it the driver of the van they'd hired, or was the person in the other vehicle responsible for the accident? Oh, Lord, I can't lose Mary, too.*

Adam's thoughts came to a halt when a young doctor entered the room and took a seat beside him. "Are you Mr. Beachy?" he asked.

Adam nodded. "Do you have word on my sister and her husband? Are they going to be okay?"

The grave look on the doctor's face told Adam all he needed to know. "I'm sorry, Mr. Beachy, but Amos has died, and Mary is seriously injured. She's lost a lot of blood. I'm afraid she doesn't have long to live."

Barely able to believe the doctor's words, Adam sat in stunned silence. His chin quivered as he closed his eyes. It wasn't possible. He felt as though he was in the middle of a horrible dream—a nightmare.

"Is. . .is she awake? Can I see her?" Adam asked when he finally found his voice.

"Yes. She's been asking for you." The doctor stood. "If you'll follow me, I'll take you to see Mary now."

Numbly, Adam followed the doctor down the hallway, which bustled with normal activity. Adam barely noticed.

"She's in here," the doctor said, leading the way into a dimly lit room, where a nurse stood beside a hospital bed.

The window blinds were tilted, allowing pink light from the sunset to flow between the slats onto Mary's bed. How could something so beautiful be happening outside when inside this room everything was horrible? The silence at Mary's bedside was broken only by the slow, erratic beep of the heart monitor.

Adam swallowed around the lump in his throat as he looked down at his sister's battered body. "Mary," he whispered, touching her hand.

She opened her eyes and blinked, tears trickling down her swollen, bruised cheeks. "Adam?"

"Jah, Mary, it's me."

"Amos is gone, and I. . .I think I'll be joining him soon." Mary's voice was barely above a whisper, but Adam understood every word.

A chill ran through him as he leaned closer to Mary's face. "Don't talk like that, Mary. You're going to be fine."

"No, Adam, listen. I. . .I need you to promise me something."

"Anything, Mary. Anything at all." Adam's throat felt so swollen, he could barely talk.

"Please, take care of my girls." Mary drew in a shuddering breath.

"Promise me, Adam. Please say that you will. I'll not be at peace till I know."

Tears pricked Adam's eyes as he slowly nodded. "I promise, Mary. Don't you worry. I'll take care of your girls."

A faint smile played on Mary's lips while Adam gazed at her, knowing it would be the last time. Then her mouth opened as she shuddered her last breath.

The monitor changed from a sporadic beep to an eerie flat-lined tone, and a sob rose in Adam's throat. When the doctor announced that Mary was gone, Adam closed his eyes in grief. Mary's hand was still warm in his, and even though the nurse had switched off the heart monitor, Adam looked down at his dear sister, barely able to accept the fact that she was truly gone. They would never again share precious moments on this earth.

Several minutes passed. As the truth sank in, Adam felt as though a part of him had died with Mary. How brave and thoughtful his sister had been, thinking only of her girls' well-being, while facing her own death. His stomach clenched as the reality of the situation hit him. Mary and Amos were dead, and he had just agreed to be responsible for their children. Who would tell those sweet little girls that their mom and dad had died? Amy was ten years old, but even at that age, would she understand why her folks had been taken? How could she? Adam sure didn't. The younger ones—Linda, who was seven, and Carrie, who'd recently turned four—how would they grasp this tragic news?

And what about me? Adam swiped at the tears running down his cheeks. He loved his sister and would honor her wishes, but he knew nothing about raising children. Adam bowed his head and closed his eyes. *Lord, how can I keep my promise to Mary? I'm scared. Please, show me what I need to do.*

CHAPTER 13

*A*dam placed four plates, knives, and forks on the table and sighed. Two weeks had passed since Amos and Mary's deaths, and Adam's world had been turned upside down. In addition to seeing that his sister and brother-in-law received proper burials at the Amish cemetery back in Nappanee, he'd brought Mary's three girls and their belongings to his house last night and didn't have a clue how to properly care for them. Carrie, who was small for her age, seemed timid and whined a lot. Linda was full of nervous energy and had a bit of a temper. Then there was stubborn Amy. Because she was the oldest, she liked to take charge and tell her sisters what to do.

When they'd arrived last evening, Amy had made it clear that she didn't want to live with Adam. Even when he'd been with them in Nappanee, it seemed nothing he said or did was good enough. The girl's belligerent attitude didn't help at all. Of course, who could really blame her? She'd not only lost both parents, but she'd also been uprooted from her Amish community and the only home she and her sisters had ever known. He understood how lost they must feel, because he felt bewildered and misplaced, too. Adam was sure the girls would miss their paternal grandparents, who lived in Nappanee, but since Amos's father had become disabled after a fall from his barn roof, there was no way their grandmother could be responsible for the care of three young girls. Amos's brother, Devon, who wasn't married, would see that Mary and Adam's home and other things were sold, but he was in no position financially to take the girls in.

Adam knew from personal experience how difficult moving could be for a child. Even though he had only been five when his mother had left, he could still remember the shock and confusion over her leaving. A few months later, Adam's dad had packed up and moved Adam and Mary from their home in Lancaster, Pennsylvania, to Ohio. After several more moves, they eventually settled in Nappanee, Indiana. Adam had not only struggled with resentment toward his mother, but he'd been angry at Dad for taking him and Mary to places where they didn't know anyone and had to start over at new schools. Mary, being the outgoing one, had made new friends right away, but Adam held back and never allowed himself to get close to any of the other children. Mary was not only his sister but his best friend, so he'd never felt the need to develop any other friendships. Besides, with everything that had happened to him at such a young age, Adam wasn't sure who he could trust. It wasn't hard for him to understand what the girls were going through right now, even though he'd lost only one parent when he was child, not both at the same time.

Putting his thoughts aside, Adam concentrated on getting the girls' breakfast made, knowing they would be waking soon and no doubt be hungry. He'd decided to fix pancakes this morning, so he set out a bottle of maple syrup. Adam was glad the girls wouldn't have to start school for several more weeks. It would give them time to adjust to their new surroundings and hopefully help them get to know him better. Having the children home all day was a problem, since Adam needed to be at the hardware store. He certainly couldn't take them to work with him every day, but he couldn't leave them at home alone, either. After the girls had been released from the hospital and he'd taken them to Nappanee for their parents' funeral, Adam had left Ben and Henry in charge of the store. But now that he was home, he needed to get back to work as soon as possible. At the very least, he planned to drop by the store sometime today to check on things.

Adam hated to admit it, but he didn't want to be cooped up in the house on another rainy day with three nieces he didn't know how to entertain. The girls would have to go with him to the store whether they liked it or not. Adam might not know much about parenting, but he wasn't about to leave them home alone. He would need to ask around and see who might be available to watch the girls while he was at work. Once school started toward the end of August, they would only have to be watched for a few hours in the afternoon, until Adam came home from work. His evenings would certainly be different. The freedom he'd enjoyed to do whatever he pleased would now be replaced with the responsibility of caring for the girls' needs. The only way to get through this was to take one day at a time and trust God to see him through.

Chicago

Cora Finley had never liked the rain, and today was no exception. She'd had trouble sleeping last night, thanks to the incessant raindrops beating on the roof of her house. She had finally succumbed to sleep well after midnight, and now it was six o'clock, and she needed to get ready for work. Glancing out her bedroom window, she grimaced. It was such a gloomy day. They'd had too much rain already this summer, and she was tired of it. Unlike some people, Cora didn't find the continuous pelting sound relaxing at all.

In addition to that irritation, she was concerned about her fourteen-year-old son, Jared. He'd become a rebellious teen ever since the divorce, often trying Cora's patience until she was at her wit's end. He'd become friends with a couple boys from broken homes, and they seemed to find trouble at every turn. With Cora's nursing job, she couldn't be with Jared every minute, and since he was too old to leave with a sitter, he often hung out with his friends.

Cora punched her pillow and moaned. It was bad enough that her husband had left her for another woman. Did he have to abandon his only son, too? At least it felt like abandonment, since Evan spent so little time with their son these days. Didn't he care how much Jared missed him? Didn't it bother him that their son was without his father's guidance much of the time? *I was a fool to believe I'd met my Prince Charming and that my future held nothing but good things. Now I have to try and be both mother and father to Jared, and so far, I'm failing miserably.*

When Cora had first met Evan during his residency at the hospital, she'd been convinced that they were meant to be together because they had many things in common. They both had careers in the medical field and were dedicated to their jobs. They enjoyed traveling and had taken trips to several places around the country whenever they could. Once Evan got established in his own private practice, he'd bought them an upscale condo, with all the benefits of high-class living. When Jared was born, they'd sold the condo and bought a house. Evan was thrilled when he found out Cora was having a boy—said he couldn't wait to build a relationship with his son.

"Yeah, right! Where's Jared's father now, when Jared needs him the most?" Cora grumbled. At this stage in their son's life, he needed his father more than ever—especially when Cora didn't have a clue what a teenage boy really wanted or needed. All she knew was that Jared hadn't been happy since Evan walked out of their life, and she had no idea what to do about it. Apparently, Dr. Evan Finley wasn't the dedicated father she'd thought him to be. Emily, the pretty blond nurse who'd stolen him from Cora, seemed to be all he could focus on these days. What kind of power did a woman like her have over a man? Was it because "Miss Blondie" was younger than Cora? Or did she have a personality that meshed better with Evan's?

Sighing, Cora pushed the covers aside and rose from the bed, stretching her arms over her head. *Maybe I should sell this place and move somewhere else—someplace where there aren't so many temptations for Jared. Perhaps a rural area would be better than living here in the big city. Jared might find a better class of friends if he lived in a more wholesome environment. If we moved, I wouldn't be the focus of the hospital gossip mill, either.*

Cora moved over to the window and stared out at the drizzling rain. She and Jared were still living in the house Evan had bought for them several years ago. It had been their dream home, even though it needed some improvements. Over the years, they'd remodeled it nicely, choosing one project each summer, the last one being a new roof. Not thinking anything of it when they chose the type of roof, it was beyond Cora why she'd ever agreed to the fancy roofing tile. It just added to her annoyance this morning, with every *ping* of raindrops hitting the roof reminding her of what used to be. Looking out the window, Cora felt irked by how agreeable she'd always been with Evan—not just concerning the roof he'd chosen but about practically everything else he'd wanted.

We should have chosen regular shingles like most of the other homes in this area have, she fumed, folding her arms. *But no, Evan had to have the best of everything. Humph! Guess that's why he went for someone younger than me.*

It still amazed Cora that Evan had let her keep the house. He was so selfish, she figured he'd not only want his new wife but the house he'd once shared with Cora, too.

Even though Cora's home was lovely, her anger toward Evan made it difficult to look at his favorite chair or the bed they'd once shared. The death of a spouse, whom one loved so dearly, would be difficult for anyone, but divorce was a bitter path, filled with many regrets. Every time Cora saw Evan and Emily together, her slow-healing wounds reopened. A clean break might be the only way for her and Jared to get through this ordeal.

Think I'll call a Realtor after I get off work today and see how much he thinks I can get for the house. Then I'll put my résumé out to a few of the hospitals and clinics in some of the rural areas here in Illinois and see what happens.

Arthur

"What's on your agenda for the day?" Leah's mother asked as they prepared breakfast that morning.

Leah shrugged while stirring cinnamon-dusted apple slices in a frying pan. "Not much, really. I don't have anyone coming for a reflexology treatment today, so I thought I might stop over at Adam's and see how he's doing since his sister's death. I'm sure it must have been a terrible shock for him to lose his sister and brother-in-law."

Stirring a batch of oatmeal, Mom turned her head toward Leah. "I didn't realize he was back from Indiana. I thought Adam would stay there a few more weeks in order to take care of his sister's estate."

"I heard he was coming back last night, and I don't know why he didn't stay longer. I ran into Elaine yesterday, and she said that Ben told her Adam was bringing his nieces home to live with him."

Mom's mouth formed an O. "A bachelor raising three small girls? I don't see how that's going to work."

"I'm sure he will hire someone to help out." Leah removed the frying pan, took three bowls down from the cupboard, and placed them on the table. "Thought maybe I'd take some cookies for the children, because I doubt that Adam does any baking."

Mom raised her eyebrows, giving Leah a questioning gaze. "Are you sure that's the only reason you're going over there?"

Leah's face heated. "Of course that's the only reason. What other motive would I have for going to Adam's house?"

"Well, he is an attractive man."

Leah held up her hand. "Don't get any ideas about me and Adam, Mom. He may be good looking, but he's definitely not my type."

"Exactly what type of man are you looking for, Leah?"

"One who will love me for the person I am. Someone who respects my opinion. Of course, I'm not looking for a man, so there's no point in discussing this." Leah opened the silverware drawer and took out three spoons. She should have known better than to mention Adam, and maybe she shouldn't go over there today. But she loved children and wanted to meet his nieces and see how they were all doing. They'd been through quite an ordeal and needed some reassurance. She was almost certain that Adam didn't have a clue how to care for his nieces. The children needed nurturing, and with Adam working all day, how could he offer them that?

But if she ever decided to go over to his place again, she'd just go without mentioning it to Mom. No point in giving her false hope. Leah was not interested in Adam. *And he's certainly not interested in me.*

CHAPTER 14

What's that supposed to be?" Ten-year-old Amy squinted her brown eyes and pointed to the plate of pancakes Adam had placed on the table.

"It's *pannekuche*." Adam gestured to the maple syrup beside the plate. "You girls like pancakes, don't you?"

"Jah, but these are burned." Linda, who was seven and also had brown eyes, plugged her nose, backing away from the table. "They smell awful, too."

"Aw, they aren't so bad." Adam absently rubbed his arms. "They're just a little brown around the edges."

Amy thrust out her chin and folded her arms. "Our mamm wouldn't have burned the pannekuche, and we're not gonna eat 'em. Besides, they don't even look like pancakes. They're too *flach*."

Before Adam could respond to Amy's comment about the flat pancakes, four-year-old Carrie looked up at Adam, her blue eyes brimming with tears. "I'm *hungerich*."

Carrie reminded Adam of his sister—shiny brown hair and ice-blue eyes. He had to turn away so the girls wouldn't see his tears.

Feeling more helpless by the moment, Adam was tempted to tell the children that the pancakes were all he had for breakfast, but then he remembered there was a box of cold cereal in the pantry. "If you three will take a seat, I'll get some cereal," he said, moving in that direction. "You like cereal, don't you?"

Adam sighed with relief when they all nodded. "Okay, that's good."

When Adam returned with the cereal and milk, the girls were seated at the table. Three innocent faces guardedly watched him, as if to see what he would do next.

He then poured himself a cup of coffee and sat down across from

Amy. "Let's bow our heads for silent prayer."

"Don't you think we need some bowls and spoons? I mean, how do you expect us to eat cereal without 'em?" Amy questioned.

His face heating up, Adam got up and took three bowls down from the cupboard, then he grabbed some spoons from the silverware drawer. After placing them on the table, he sat back down. "There. How's that?"

"Aren't you gonna eat?" Linda wanted to know.

He shook his head. "I'm not that hungry this morning. A cup of coffee's good enough for me." The truth was, Adam's stomach was so knotted he didn't think he could eat a thing.

Amy grunted and pushed a lock of blond hair out of her eyes. She'd obviously made an attempt to braid her hair, as well as her sisters', when they'd gotten up. But Adam could see that the braids were loose and probably wouldn't hold up all day.

"I'm gonna pray that Mama and Papa come and get us soon," Carrie announced.

"They're not coming to get us 'cause they're in heaven with Jesus." Linda's brown eyes filled with tears. "Don't you remember when we put Papa and Mama in the ground at the cemetery?"

Carrie shook her head vigorously. "No! They'd never go in the ground. It's cold and dirty down there."

Adam's throat constricted. Carrie either hadn't realized it was her parents they'd buried, or else the little girl was in denial. Then again, perhaps she was too young to grasp the concept of what death really meant. He tried to think of the best way to explain, but once again her older sister spoke up.

"There's no point talking about this right now 'cause it won't bring Mama and Papa back." Amy took a drink from her glass of milk.

Carrie's eyes widened, and she started to cry. "They're gone for good?"

Amy nodded then grabbed the cereal box and poured some into their bowls, adding some milk. Pushing two of the bowls in front of her sisters, she said in a bossy tone, "Just eat now, and quit talking."

"We can't eat till we've prayed. God wouldn't like it, and neither would Mama and Papa if they were here." Linda looked over at Adam, as if waiting for him to comment.

"That's right," he agreed. "We always need to pray and thank God for the food."

Amy wrinkled her nose. "It's a good thing we don't have to eat those pannekuche 'cause I'm sure they'd taste baremlich. I could never be thankful for that."

The constant rain outside could be heard hitting the roof, and Adam lifted his gaze toward the ceiling. What was he going to do with his nieces today? They wouldn't be able to go outside and play—not in this nasty weather. He had a few games but no puzzles or anything exciting to keep them entertained other than a coloring book and a box of crayons. If there was one thing he knew with certainty, taking care of three little girls was not going to be easy. Short of a miracle, he didn't see how he could manage the task alone. "As soon as we've finished our prayer, I'll take the pancakes outside for the dog."

Amy rolled her eyes. "I'll bet even Coal won't eat 'em."

Adam was tempted to argue the point because so far the dog had eaten anything set before him. But instead of trying to explain that, he bowed his head and closed his eyes. *Heavenly Father*, he prayed silently, *please give me the wisdom and strength to see that Mary and Amos's girls are raised properly.*

Adam's place was less than a mile from Leah's, and had it not been for the steady rain and the food she was bringing, Leah would have ridden her bike. Instead, she'd gotten out the horse and buggy.

In addition to the peanut butter cookies Leah had baked, Mom had sent along a chicken casserole Adam could heat for supper this evening. She hoped he and the girls would like it.

Leah had only met Adam's nieces briefly when their parents had attended church during one of their visits last year. She couldn't imagine how difficult it must be for the girls, losing both of their parents and then having to leave their home and move in with their uncle in another state.

She thought about Elaine, who had lost her parents when she was a girl and had been raised by her grandparents. But there'd been two adults to nurture and guide Elaine throughout her childhood. Adam wasn't married and lived alone. Surely he had no idea how to care for his nieces.

I guess it's none of my business, Leah told herself. *If Adam needs any help with the girls, I'm sure he'll ask for it.*

When Leah pulled into Adam's yard, she spotted the black Lab sitting on the porch. *Guess I was right about the hund,* she told herself. *That dog must belong to Adam.*

She climbed down from the buggy, secured her horse, and picked up the cardboard box she'd placed on the floor of the passenger's side. Dodging puddles and the relentless raindrops, she hurried toward the house, trying not to lose her balance.

When Leah stepped onto the porch, the Lab ambled up to her, let out a pathetic whine, and then flopped down on the porch again. That's when she noticed a plate sitting near the dog, full of what looked like burned pancakes. She could only assume that was Adam's attempt at making the girls' breakfast, which seemed to have not gone so well. Even the dog wouldn't eat the burnt-looking, flat pancakes. The poor pooch didn't look too happy, either.

Leah knocked on the door. A few seconds later, Adam opened it. "Oh, it's you," he said, mouth open wide. "I. . .I wasn't expecting company right now." Leah couldn't help noticing that his shirt was not tucked into his trousers, his hair looked like he hadn't taken the time to comb it this morning, and his eyes were bloodshot, probably from lack of sleep. The poor man looked so disheveled her heart went out to him.

Leah looked down at the box. "I brought a casserole dish and some kichlin," she said.

Adam rubbed his forehead. "Actually, the girls are just having breakfast."

"I didn't mean to interrupt," she apologized, watching as the dog, nose in the air, sauntered over to her, trying to get a whiff of the food she held. "I brought the cookies for the girls, and my mamm made the chicken casserole. She thought you might like to reheat it for supper this evening."

"Danki, that was thoughtful of you both." He took the box and stepped outside. "Coal, go lay down. You have food in your dish."

"I think he's trying to tell you something." Leah grinned, looking from the dog to Adam. "Perhaps he doesn't like pancakes. They are pancakes, right?"

Adam looked at her, showing no emotion, then shrugged his shoulders.

I shouldn't have said that, Leah scolded herself. "I didn't know you had a dog," she said, trying to lighten the conversation.

"Didn't. Until recently, that is," Adam responded.

"He's a beautiful Lab. How long have you had him?"

"Not long. The mutt came into my store one day and followed me home. I tried to shoo him away several times, but he kept coming back. When I had no luck finding his owner, I took the critter in."

"I've seen the Lab at the end of your driveway, and he wandered over to our place once, but I wasn't sure whose dog he was. If I'd have known he was yours, I would have brought something over for him to eat, too." Leah was relieved when a hint of a smile formed on Adam's lips.

"Truth is, I'm not much of a cook, which even the dog can attest to." His voice lowered as he leaned closer to Leah. "I just never expected it would be this hard to have three little girls in my house. They miss their mamm and daed something awful, and I'm grieving myself. I don't know what to do to help them through this."

"I know it must be difficult, but remember, Adam, those in our church district, as well as others in the community, will help out wherever and whenever it's needed. All you have to do is ask, and I'm sure that many will help without being asked."

"Jah, I know." Adam's eyes brightened a little. "Since you're here, if you're not busy the rest of the morning, I do have a favor to ask."

"What is it?"

"Would you be able to keep an eye on the girls so I can go to the hardware store and check on things? I'll only be gone a few hours."

Leah smiled. "I'd be happy to do that."

Adam blew out his breath. "Danki. I sure do appreciate it." He leaned against the door. "Say, you wouldn't be available to watch the girls while I'm at work every day, would you? I'd pay you, of course."

Leah shook her head. "I might be able to on some days, but not every day, since I often have people scheduled for reflexology treatments."

Adam frowned. "Oh yeah, that."

"I could ask my mamm if she'd be free to watch the girls," Leah was quick to say.

Adam's face relaxed a bit. "That'd be great. If she's agreeable, make sure you tell her that she'll be paid for her services." He opened the door. "Come in. I'll introduce you to the girls and let 'em know that you'll be with them for a few hours while I'm at the store."

I hope I didn't overstep my bounds when I mentioned that Mom might be willing to watch Adam's nieces, Leah thought. *What if she doesn't want to?*

CHAPTER 15

After Adam left, Leah took a seat at the kitchen table to watch the girls eat their breakfast. Even though Adam had introduced her, Leah was at a loss for words. It was obvious from the girls' grim expressions that they were in pain. Leah wished there was something she could say or do to make them feel better.

Maybe if I find something fun for them to do, it'll help break the ice, she decided, looking toward the window. The rain had finally subsided, and partial blue sky was visible among the slowly departing clouds.

"How would you all like to go for a walk after I wash the dishes?" Leah asked. "We'll take Coal along. He could probably use the exercise, and I'm sure he would enjoy spending time with you." Leah paused and waited for the girls' response.

Amy, the oldest, shook her head. "We can't go for a walk."

"Why not?" Leah asked.

"Uncle Adam will be worried if he comes home and we're not here."

"We wouldn't go far," Leah assured her. "Just down the road a ways, where I saw some pretty wildflowers growing in a field."

Amy's nose twitched. "Can't do that; Linda's allergic to some flowers. She might start sneezing or wheezing."

"Does she have asthma?"

Amy shrugged. "Don't know. She just sneezes and can't breathe well when she's near some flowers."

Leah glanced at Linda, wondering why the child didn't speak for herself. Was she always this quiet, letting her older sister speak on her behalf?

Linda's chin trembled. "Mama likes flowers, but she never brings 'em inside 'cause she knows they make me sneeze."

"Mama's gone," Amy stated in a matter-of-fact tone. "So quit talking about her like she's still here."

Linda glared at her sister as a few tears escaped and rolled down her cheeks.

In an effort to smooth things over between the girls, Leah said, "Would anyone like to dry the dishes after they're washed?"

No one responded.

"I know it's a bit early to have a snack, but I brought some peanut butter kichlin with me today. After the dishes are done, I thought maybe we could all have a few cookies with milk."

Carrie, the youngest, who hadn't said a word so far, climbed down from her chair and pushed it toward the sink.

"What do you think you're doing?" Amy called.

"I'm gonna dry dishes," Carrie replied.

"You can't dry the dishes," Amy argued. "You're too little for that."

Carrie shook her head determinedly. "Mama lets me dry the plastic things, so why can't I here?"

"Let's give Carrie a chance," Leah spoke up. "She can dry a few of the dishes, and then you and Linda can dry the rest."

"I don't wanna dry the dishes." Linda pushed her cereal bowl aside.

"Then how about this," Leah said patiently. "After we do the dishes, why don't we all go outside and pick up those branches that have fallen from the trees in your uncle's yard? I'm sure he would appreciate that."

"The grass is wet, and we'll get dirty picking up sticks." Amy lifted her chin, looking right into Leah's eyes.

Leah clenched her teeth. *Oh, boy. Looks like I have my work cut out for me this morning. I sure hope Adam won't be gone too long.*

When Adam entered his store, he noticed Henry behind the counter, waiting on a customer. Then he spotted Ben, standing off to one side, talking to Elaine.

Irritation welled in Adam's soul. He was still frustrated from this morning's happenings, and now this? Well, at least the rain had finally quit.

With no regard for who might hear, or how it could look to anyone who was in the store, he stepped up to Ben and said, "I'm paying you to work, not take time out from your duties to visit with your *aldi*."

Ben jumped back, as though startled, and blinked a couple times. "I wasn't shirking my duties, Adam. Henry only has one customer at the checkout, and Elaine came here to get some fertilizer for her garden. She was just asking me what kind I thought was best for her roses."

Elaine nodded. "That's right; Ben's telling the truth."

Adam's face heated; he felt like a fool. "I–I'm sorry for snapping at you, Ben. I've been under a lot a stress since Mary and Amos died, but I realize that's no excuse."

"It's all right." Ben clasped Adam's shoulder. "I understand. It's not an easy time for you right now."

"That's partly right; having lost Mary, and now having the responsibility of raising her children makes it hard for me to cope. But it's not all right that I barked at you like that." Adam shook his head. "I appreciate you and Henry taking charge of things at the store during my absence. Don't know what I'd do without you both."

Ben smiled. "We're glad to do it."

"Did you bring your nieces home with you?" Elaine asked.

Adam nodded. "I almost brought them to the store this morning, but Leah dropped by and agreed to stay with 'em till I get home."

Elaine smiled. "That was nice of her. Will she be watching the girls every day while you're here at the store?"

"Afraid not. Since she has her 'patients' to treat, she's tied up most days. She did say she would talk to her mamm, and see if she might be willing to watch the girls."

"I hope it works out," Elaine said. "Leah's mamm has such a sweet personality. I'm sure your nieces will take right to her."

"That'd be good if Dianna can help." Adam groaned. "Because they're sure not taking to me very well."

"I know how hard it is to lose both parents at a young age. If there's anything I can do to help, please let me know."

"Danki, I will."

❧

Leah's suggestion of picking up sticks in the yard must have appealed to Carrie and Linda, for without complaint, they walked around the yard with her, gathering the smaller branches that had fallen. For the time being, at least the two younger ones had something to keep them occupied. Amy, however, would have no part of it as she sat on the porch steps, watching. The sun shone through the clouds, and a gentle, warm breeze wafted around them. With each drift of air that stirred, it almost sounded like rain falling again, as water dripped from the still-wet leaves. "I'll pick up the bigger branches." Leah pointed to the pile she'd started.

With all the rain recently, nature had a way of trimming the trees, bringing down dead branches and waterlogged limbs that could no longer hold on. Leah had always found that whenever she felt sad, working outside or even watching the hummingbirds that came into her yard helped to lift her spirits. She hoped it would do the same for Adam's nieces, especially Amy, who seemed to be carrying the weight of the world on her small shoulders. Leah figured that if Amy watched her sisters, she would see how much fun they were having and take part. But so far, she kept to the porch, staring absently at her bare feet.

"Look how many I got." Carrie smiled, taking her small bundle over to the stack of branches. "This is *schpass*."

"You're right," Leah agreed. "It is fun."

"I got a lot, too." Linda joined in, looking pleased with what she'd collected.

"That's wonderful, girls." Leah was glad they were both cooperating. "Keep up the good work. I'm sure your uncle will be pleased when he sees what you have accomplished. He'll probably wonder where that stack of branches came from."

Both girls bobbed their heads in agreement.

Leah looked back at Amy and wished once more that she would join them. But Amy just sat staring off into space. Hopefully in her own good time, the girl would come around.

"Look! Look!" Carrie squealed, pointing at the woodpile as Leah ran over to see what had excited her.

"It's a little chipmunk." Linda smiled, standing next to her sister. "Ain't it cute?"

Carrie nodded and grinned back at her.

Leah was tempted to correct Linda's English but decided not to make a big deal out of it. Glancing back at the woodpile, she figured the chipmunk must have discovered the stack of wood and come out to investigate as more sticks were being added to the top. The cute little critter sat quietly, watching them, then quickly scampered under the pile.

"Okay girls, we don't want to disturb the chipmunk, so we'll have to be gentle when we place the rest of the sticks we gather on the top," Leah said. "When we're done, we'll go inside and see if we can find something to feed to the chipmunk. How's that sound?"

"I can't wait!" Carrie clapped her hands and jumped up and down. "Let's name the critter, 'Chippy.'"

"That's a good name for the chipmunk." Leah breathed a sigh of relief. This little critter might be just what the girls needed to bring a little happiness into their lives. She watched as Carrie and Linda quickly went about to get the rest of the sticks. Leah had to admit Adam's yard looked a lot better. Adam had seemed so preoccupied earlier, she wondered if he really would notice.

Leah glanced back at the porch and spotted Coal sitting beside Amy. She was stroking the dog's back. Coal closed his eyes and leaned against the child's knee. It was amazing how Coal seemed to have honed in on Amy's feelings, as though he were trying to make her feel loved and comforted.

Chicago

"What do you mean you don't have time to talk? This is your day off, isn't it?" Cora's voice rose as she sank to the couch, clenching her cell phone.

"You're right, it's my day off, and Emily and I are about to head out."

There was an edge of impatience to Evan's voice that Cora recognized all too well. If she was going to say what was on her mind, she'd better do it quickly.

"I won't take up much of your precious time." She shifted the phone to her other ear. "I just wanted you to know that I'm thinking of moving, and—"

"Why do you want to move? Is the house too big for you to handle?"

"It's not that." Cora fanned her face. "For that matter, it's much easier to keep clean with just Jared and me," she added dryly. "Not so much clutter lying about."

"Well, what's the problem then?" Evan asked, ignoring her sarcasm. "I think you ought to forget about selling and stay put."

Cora plucked at a piece of white lint that had stuck to her dark skirt. "You don't understand, Evan. My wanting to move has nothing to do with this house." After being married to Evan almost twenty years before he dumped her for another woman, Cora figured he ought to know her well enough to figure things out.

"What does it have to do with then?"

Cora heard him take a deep breath and exhale in irritation. She felt like making this phone call last as long as she could, just to make his precious new wife wait for him.

"As I've mentioned before, our son has become rebellious, and I think he needs a better environment," she continued.

"You're being ridiculous, Cora. Jared's just going through a phase. He'll come out of it sooner or later."

"It's not a phase." Cora clenched her teeth. What did Evan know? He hardly came around anymore. "Jared hasn't handled the divorce very well. Now he's running around with some boys who are leading him astray."

"You worry too much. Just cut our son some slack. Give him a chance, Cora. You shouldn't have to feel pressured to move." Evan paused. "Now, if that's all you have to say, I really do need to go."

"Wait, Evan. I need to ask you something."

"For heaven's sake, Cora, what is it?"

Cora cringed. "If we did move, would you be okay with it?"

"I guess so; just don't move out of the country. I'd like to see my boy once in a while."

"Really, Evan! Of course we won't leave the country," she snapped. "I just want to move to some rural area where Jared won't be faced with so many temptations."

"Yeah, okay. Do whatever you want. Just make sure you let me know where you are so I can keep in touch with Jared." Evan hung up.

Cora's eyes burned as she clicked off her phone. Slapping her forehead, she scolded herself. Why did she need Evan's approval? It was obvious that all he cared about was being with Emily and pleasing her. Cora didn't know why she let Evan's indifference bother her so much. *Was I hoping he'd beg us to stay?* she wondered. *Since Evan obviously doesn't care, I'm going to take that as a sign that it's meant for Jared and me to move. Maybe someday he'll realize what he lost.* She picked up her phone. *I'm definitely calling my Realtor. Then I'll go online to look for a job.*

CHAPTER 16

Arthur

*A*dam sank into his recliner with a groan. The day had been exceptionally busy, and he was exhausted. He'd been relieved when, half an hour ago, the girls had gone willingly to bed themselves, because right now, he didn't have the energy to climb the stairs to their bedroom. It had been a week since Dianna had begun watching the girls during the day, and he was grateful for that.

Yesterday had been an off-Sunday for their church district, which had given both him and the girls a little more time to rest and get better acquainted. Many Amish in the area visited another church district on their in-between Sundays, but Adam rarely did. In addition to the fact that he wasn't much for socializing, he needed that every-other-Sunday as a time to rest and reflect on things.

Hearing voices coming from upstairs, Adam gritted his teeth. His nerves were on edge this evening. "You three need to go to sleep," he called, cupping his hands around his mouth. Adam valued his peace and quiet and hoped this kind of thing would not go on every night, because he didn't have the patience for it.

"I'm not sleepy!" Linda's high-pitched voice floated down the stairs.

"You'll never feel sleepy if you don't quit talking! Just lie down now, and please be quiet."

"Why?" Amy chimed in.

"Because I said so." Adam hoped that would put an end their idle chitchat.

When no one responded, he reached for the glass of milk he'd placed on the coffee table and took a drink. He wished he had some cookies to go with it, but the girls had eaten the last of the ones Dianna had brought over when she'd come to watch the kids last Friday. Adam knew he should limit their sweets, but while trying to make them happy, he didn't always do the right thing.

Adam reminded himself that at least the girls were functioning better in the new life they'd been forced to accept. At night no more muffled crying came from behind closed doors, as it had during the first few weeks they'd been here. Adam had wanted to rush into the girls' room and gather them into his arms, but they had been keeping him at arm's length and he feared their rejection. So when he'd heard his nieces crying themselves to sleep, he just stood there, with his forehead pressed against the side of their door, letting his own tears fall along with theirs. Other times, he'd stand there, barely able to breathe, until the girls' whimpers were replaced with even breathing, letting him know they'd fallen asleep. Then he would quietly enter and tuck them in before heading downstairs to his room in the hopes that he could sleep. Linda and Carrie shared a room and slept in the same bed. Adam had set up a cot in their room for Amy so they could all be together. He figured that later, if Amy wanted her own room, she could sleep in the one across the hall from her sisters.

Last night he'd gone into the girls' room after they'd fallen asleep. When he'd pulled the blanket up to cover Carrie and Linda, Carrie had mumbled sleepily, "Good night, Papa." The poor little thing still didn't seem to understand that her parents weren't coming back.

At the supper table this evening, Adam had felt like his head was going to explode. Linda and Carrie talked nonstop about the chipmunk they'd discovered that lived in the brush pile out back. Dianna had apparently brought some popcorn with her today, and they'd placed the popped kernels on the ground in front of the branches. Linda was excited that Chippy, as she'd named the critter, had peeked out a short time later and filled his pouch with as much popcorn as possible before storing it back underneath the branches. Adam had to admit, it was kind of cute when Carrie puffed out her cheeks, trying to show him how Chippy had looked. After hearing their stories, Adam had joined the conversation long enough to suggest that they save some apple peels for their newfound friend.

It was good to see Linda and Carrie smiling once in a while, but

Amy was another story. While her younger sisters jabbered on and on about Chippy, Amy sat quietly, toying with her food. Adam continued to hope that something would bring Amy around and give her a reason to smile, but he'd begun to think that might never happen.

He rubbed his forehead, making little circles above his brows. *Mary should have picked someone else to raise her children, not me. I don't know how to relate to them, and I'll never be able to take their mamm and daed's place.*

"Uncle Adam, Carrie's hogging the covers." Linda's shrill voice scattered Adam's thoughts. A few seconds later, she padded into the room.

Adam grimaced, wondering if he was ever going to have any peace. There was another empty bedroom upstairs, and he thought about suggesting that Linda move into that room, so she'd have her own bed, but the girls had indicated they didn't want to be separated. "Come on, Linda," he said, rising from his chair. "I'll walk you back up to your room and tuck you into bed."

"Will you tell Carrie she can't have all the covers?"

He nodded. "Jah, sure."

As Adam followed Linda up the stairs, he thought about the challenges that lay ahead for him. The only way to deal with the situation was to take things as they came, because if he looked too far ahead, he'd feel even more overwhelmed. He thought once again how grateful he was that Leah's mother had agreed to watch the children while he was at work. Having a woman's influence to help guide them in areas where Adam couldn't was a huge relief. At least that was one phase of this challenge he didn't have to worry about right now.

"How did things go over at Adam's today?" Leah asked her mother.

Mom's lips compressed as she set the magazine she'd been reading aside. "Adam's nieces are well behaved, and they do whatever I ask, but they're having a hard time adjusting. Losing one's parents at any age is difficult, but when a child loses both parents at the same time, I believe they may feel a sense of abandonment."

"Do you think the girls are angry at their mamm and daed for dying?" Leah questioned, seating herself beside Mom on the couch.

Mom gave a slow nod. "That's possible—especially Amy. And the fact that their uncle is gone so much due to his job isn't helping things any."

"But you're there for them during the day, and Adam's with them in the evenings and on weekends."

"True, but it's not the same as having two parents, and a mother who's at home with them during the day. That little chipmunk is about the only thing that seems to have made those two younger girls happy." Mom smiled. "This morning we put some of that old popcorn I took over in front of the pile of branches. Then we all stood back and watched until Chippy came to investigate. He must have liked it, because back and forth he went, storing the kernels underneath there somewhere, where he'll no doubt eat them later."

"Sounds like a positive distraction that gives the children some joy," Leah said. "At least they have you to share it with them."

"True, and while I like the girls, I'll never have the bond with them that their mother had. And Adam. . .well, he's their uncle, and a bachelor at that, so unless he gets married someday, the girls might never feel as if they're part of a complete family."

"I doubt that Adam will ever find a woman who'd be willing to marry him."

"Why do you think that?"

"He's too set in his ways." Leah popped a piece of gum into her mouth. "No woman I know would want to marry a man who thinks he's right about everything."

Just then Leah's father entered the room with a grim expression.

"What's wrong, Alton?" Mom asked. "Was there a problem in the barn when you were feeding the horses?"

"It's not the horses." He took a seat on the other side of Mom. "I just came from the phone shack. There was a message from your brother-in-law James. Guess your sister is having a hard time with her pregnancy, and the doctor's worried she may lose the boppli, so he put her on bed rest."

"That's going to be difficult." Mom looked at Dad and then touched Leah's arm. "Since James and Grace moved to Wisconsin and have no family close by, I should go there and help out."

Leah nodded. "I understand. And don't worry about things here. Dad and I will get along just fine while you're gone." Grace was Mom's youngest sibling, and this was her fifth child. The other children, all boys, were all less than ten years old and had been born every two years. The boys were quite active, and none would be that much help to their mother, so Leah knew Mom's assistance would be greatly appreciated.

"There's just one thing." Frowning, Mom rubbed the bridge of her nose. "If I go to help Grace, Adam won't have a sitter for his nieces. Would you consider taking over that responsibility, Leah?"

"Oh, I don't know, Mom—"

"The girls will be starting school in a few weeks, and you wouldn't need to be at Adam's house all day."

"Adam doesn't get home until close to suppertime," Leah reminded. "That would mean the girls would be alone after they get out of school until Adam gets home. Besides, Carrie's not in school yet, so she'll need someone with her during the day."

"You're right about that."

"But it won't work for my schedule, Mom, because I need to be available for people who need a reflexology treatment."

"Maybe you could schedule appointments during the evening hours," Dad suggested.

"Or perhaps Adam could bring the girls over here every day," Mom interjected.

Leah shook her head. "They'd be by themselves while I was in the basement working on people's feet. I wouldn't be able to concentrate, knowing they were upstairs, unattended." Leah grabbed the throw pillow and pushed it behind her back. "Besides, I'm sure Adam would never go for that."

"If you're willing to watch them, at least we could ask," Mom said with a hopeful expression.

Leah sucked her bottom lip as she mulled things over. "I suppose I could do that, but Adam may want to ask someone else to watch the girls."

"You won't know that till you talk to him about it." Mom rose from her seat. "I'm going out to the phone shack and leave a message for James, letting him know that I'll be coming to help out."

Leah leaned her head against the back of the sofa and closed her eyes. Adam needed someone to care for his nieces during the day, and for some strange reason, she hoped it would be her. Not to see Adam, of course, but to spend time with those precious girls.

Chicago

Cora sat at her desk in the kitchen, searching for nursing jobs on the Internet. For Jared's sake, she'd been keeping her search to the more rural areas in Illinois, not wanting to move too far from Chicago. She wanted him out of the big city but figured she'd have to deal with Evan if she and Jared moved too far away. Besides, it was only fair to her son to live close enough so that he could spend some time with his father—what precious little time Evan gave.

So far, Cora hadn't found any jobs that met her criteria, but she would keep looking. Yesterday, she'd made contact with a Realtor, who'd be coming by tomorrow morning to take a look at the house. Cora was anxious to find out how much he thought she could get for it. Hopefully, it would sell quickly and bring in enough that she'd be able to put a good share of the money into Jared's college fund. Of course, she had to convince him that he needed more schooling once he graduated from high school. The last time the subject of his education came up, Jared had insisted that he didn't need college and wanted to find a job doing something with his hands. Cora couldn't imagine what that would be. Jared didn't seem to have much interest in anything other than running around with his friends and playing video games on their large-screen TV.

Maybe things will change once we're out of the city and away from his friends, Cora told herself, turning off the computer. Tomorrow was another day, and hopefully things would go well with the Realtor. Her one big concern, however, was what she would do if the house sold before she found a job someplace else. She sure couldn't move without suitable employment.

"*You worry too much,*" Cora's mother had often said during Cora's childhood. *"Just take each day as it comes, and trust God for the rest."*

"That was easy enough for you to say, Mom," Cora muttered under her breath. Cora hadn't trusted God for anything in a long time; not since she was a young girl.

"Who you talking to, Mom?" Jared asked, stepping into the room.

Cora jumped. "Oh, you startled me. I thought you'd gone to bed."

"Nope. I ain't sleepy. Thought I'd fix myself something to eat." Jared marched across the room and flung the refrigerator door open. "Is there any of that pepperoni pizza left from yesterday?"

"There probably is, but do you really want to stuff yourself at this hour of the night?"

He lifted his shoulders in a brief shrug. "Don't really matter to me what time it is. When I'm hungry, I eat. So there!"

Cora cringed. When had her son gotten so mouthy? As far as Cora was concerned, she and Jared really needed to move, and the sooner the better. She might have to take the first job that came along, regardless of how much it paid.

CHAPTER 17

Arthur

The next morning before leaving for work, Adam peeled an apple then wrapped the peelings in a paper towel and wrote a note to the girls. He hoped they'd be happy that he'd left a little something for their chipmunk friend.

As Adam began fixing a sandwich to take to work, he heard Coal barking outside. Glancing out the kitchen window, he was surprised to see Leah riding up on her bicycle. It was a beautiful morning, so he could understand why she'd be on her bike. What he couldn't figure out was why she had come here.

Going to the door, he met her on the porch, with Coal wagging his tail and nudging her hand to pet him.

"Guder mariye," Leah said, looking up at Adam.

"Good morning," he replied. "Out for a morning ride?"

"No, actually, I came to let you know that my mamm can't watch the kinner today," Leah said. "Her sister's expecting a baby and the doctor ordered bed rest for her, so Mom is going there to help out with her four children and will probably stay till the boppli's born."

Adam groaned. This was not the kind of news he needed this morning. "I can understand why she'd want to help her sister, but it kind of puts me in a bind right now. I can't very well take the girls to work with me today. There's nothing for them to do at the store, and they'd either be bored or get into things I don't want them to touch."

Leah held up her hand. "I have the answer to that—at least for today."

"What do you mean?"

"I also came here to say that since my mamm will not be available to watch the girls, I can take over that responsibility today and even until Mom returns home. Unless, of course, you have someone else in mind to be here with the girls."

Adam shook his head. "I don't know of anyone right now, but didn't you say before that you wouldn't be available to watch my nieces?"

"Jah, I did say that, but I've decided that I can give reflexology treatments during the evening hours, which will leave me free to watch the girls until you get home from work each day." She paused. "That is, if you think the arrangement will work for you."

"Sounds good to me, and I'll pay you the same as I was giving your mamm," he said, feeling both grateful and relieved. He figured Leah would do as well with the girls as her mother had and certainly better than he could.

"Are you feeling all right this morning?" Jonah asked, coming up behind Sara and placing his hands against her growing stomach. "I heard you get up several times during the night."

"I'm fine," Sara said. "My back hurts a bit, and I had a hard time finding a comfortable position."

"Sorry to hear that. Would you like me to make you an appointment with our chiropractor?"

Turning to face Jonah, Sara shook her head. "I thought I'd see Leah first and see if she can help me."

"Are you sure about that?"

Sara nodded. "When Leah works on my feet, it always helps me relax. I think stress plays a role in causing my back to flare up."

"Why are you feeling stressed?" Jonah's face was a mask of concern. "Is it your MS? Have you been having more symptoms?"

Sara leaned into him. "Now don't look so concerned. My MS symptoms have actually been better since I got pregnant. I'm feeling stressed because Mark is demanding more of my attention lately. He clings to me a lot when he should be happily playing."

"I think that's partially my fault because I haven't been giving him enough attention."

"You've been busy in the buggy shop, Jonah."

"That's true, but it's no excuse. When I'm done working for the day, I'll try to spend more time with him."

Sara smiled. "I know Mark would like that. He thinks the world of you."

"Maybe I'll close the shop early one day this week, and the three of us can go on a picnic," Jonah said.

"That'd be nice." Sara reached around and massaged her back. "I think I'll go out to the phone shack and call Leah. Hopefully she can see me sometime today."

"What about Mark? Will you need me to come up to the house and watch him while you're gone?"

She shook her head. "I can take him with me. Leah's mamm will probably be there, and I'm sure she'd be glad to keep Mark occupied while I'm getting my feet massaged."

Jonah kissed her cheek. "Okay, but if you need me for anything, just let me know."

"I will." Sara was grateful to be married to such a thoughtful man. Her first husband, Harley, had been that way, too, and she felt doubly blessed to have found such a caring man the second time around. After Harley's death, Sara had struggled trying to raise Mark on her own. Then when she'd been diagnosed with MS, everything had become a challenge. How grateful she was for Jonah's friendship during that time and even more so once they had fallen in love.

Turning from the refrigerator, Leah was holding a chocolate-chip cheeseball when Amy entered the kitchen, rubbing her forehead, followed by the other two girls.

"What's wrong, Amy?" Leah asked, feeling concern.

Amy frowned. "When my sisters and I were playing tag, Carrie kept yelling real loud, and now I have a *koppweh*."

"Carrie didn't give you a headache on purpose," Linda said in her younger sister's defense. "She always hollers when we play that game."

Leah figured it did the children good to run and play. Even Carrie's shouting wasn't a bad thing. It meant they were beginning to relax and have a little fun, despite missing their parents. "The chocolate-chip cheeseball I made this morning is ready to eat," she said, placing it on the table. "Why don't you three go wash up while I get out some graham crackers and milk to go with our snack?" Leah gave Amy's shoulder a gentle squeeze. "Maybe after you've had something to eat you'll feel better."

"Okay." Amy followed her sisters down the hall. When they returned to the kitchen, Leah had everything set on the table.

"*Is gut,*" Carrie announced, after she'd eaten a graham cracker Leah had spread with some of the cheeseball.

Leah smiled. "I'm glad you like it. I've made lots of different cheeseballs, but chocolate-chip's my favorite."

"Bet Uncle Adam would like it," Linda said. "We should save him some."

"Jah, we'll do that." Leah looked over at Amy. The child sat with her head down, rubbing her temples. "Aren't you going to try some, Amy?"

Amy moaned. "My head hurts too bad to eat anything, and I feel sick to my stomach. Sure hope I don't throw up."

Remembering how she'd helped several people with sick headaches, Leah touched Amy's arm gently and said, "Would you like me to rub your feet?"

"My head hurts, not my feet."

"I've helped many people get rid of their headaches by rubbing certain spots on their feet," Leah explained. "What I do is called 'reflexology,' and it can be quite effective. Would you like me to try it on you?"

Linda came alongside her sister. "I think you oughtta let her do it, Amy. I wanna see Leah work on your feet."

"Me, too!" Carrie shouted, then she quickly covered her mouth. "Sorry for yelling in the house."

Amy looked up at Leah and shrugged her slim shoulders. "I. . .I guess so. Suppose it can't hurt to let you rub my feet."

"I wanna watch." Linda bounced on her toes.

"Since it's such a nice day, let's all go outside and sit in the yard," Leah suggested. "The fresh air might help Amy's headache, too. I'll take an old quilt out that we can sit on while I work on her feet."

Leah grabbed the quilt from the back of the couch, and the girls followed her outside. After Leah spread the quilt on the grass, they all plopped down on it. Even Coal ambled over and lay down between Amy and Linda. Then Amy took off her shoes, leaned back on her elbows, and closed her eyes.

"Who taught you how to do that?" Linda asked as Leah began to pressure-point Amy's feet.

"My grandma taught me," Leah replied. "I've been doing it since I was a teenager."

"Don't you mind touching strangers' feet all the time?"

"No, it doesn't bother me at all." Leah smiled. "In fact, it makes me feel good to use the gift God gave me to help others."

Carrie wrinkled her nose. "Eww... *Schtinkich fiess.*"

Leah bit back a chuckle. "Not everyone's feet smell stinky, Carrie."

"But some people's do," Linda put in. "And you must like touching their feet to do them."

Leah nodded, and as Amy's younger sisters looked on, she continued to massage Amy's feet. Several more minutes passed, then Amy opened her eyes. "My head quit hurting," she announced.

Leah smiled. "I'm so glad."

"Will you do my feet next?" Linda took off her shoes and stuck her feet out toward Leah.

"Sure, I'd be happy to." Leah massaged Linda's feet, and when she was done, Carrie scooted in front of her. "Me, too, Leah."

"Okay, little one." Leah began to rub the little girl's feet, while the other girls, and even the dog, moved aside.

Carrie giggled, looking up at Leah with such a sweet expression. *"Ich bin ewe kitzlich."*

Leah smiled. "So you're ticklish, huh?" It gave her such pleasure to see the child laugh.

"What's going on here, Leah? What do you think you're doing?"

Startled, Leah looked up. Adam stood a few feet away, looking down at her with a scowl. She'd been so engrossed in what she was doing that she hadn't heard Adam's rig pull in. Even Coal hadn't budged from the edge of the quilt.

"Amy had a koppweh, and Leah made it better," Linda spoke up. "Then she worked on my feet. After that, Carrie wanted hers done, too."

Adam's eyebrows drew together as he continued to stare at Leah. "So you were poking around on the girls' feet?"

Linda shook her head. "Leah weren't poking. She was doing 'flexology."

"Is that so?" Adam's eyes narrowed, looking sternly at Leah. "You can do whatever you want with the people who come to you for foot treatments, but I'll have none of that hocus-pocus here at my place. Is that clear?"

Carrie started to cry, and Leah's head snapped back, feeling as though she'd been slapped. Didn't Adam care that she'd been able to relieve Amy's headache? Wasn't he willing to at least give reflexology a chance?

"It's okay," Amy said, as though she understood Leah's embarrassment. "My koppweh's gone now, so Leah did a good thing." Before Adam could say anything more, the child jumped up and raced into the house. Carrie and Linda followed, both sniffling as they went. Didn't Adam realize how sensitive these girls were? Hadn't he even heard what Amy said?

Leah scrambled to her feet. "You know something, Adam?" she said through clenched teeth.

He tipped his head. "What's that?"

"You have a lot to learn about children, and unless you've had a reflexology treatment yourself, then you shouldn't be so narrow minded."

"I am not narrow minded. Since this is *my* house, and these girls are *my* nieces, I have every right to say what I will and won't tolerate concerning their welfare."

Leah could see by the determined set of Adam's jaw that he wasn't going to back down. "Since you're here now, I'm sure you can manage things on your own for the rest of the evening, so I'll be on my way home. I have some hummingbird feeders that need to be cleaned, and I need to start supper for my daed." She went into the house and grabbed her purse. When she stepped back outside, she met Adam on the porch. "Please tell the girls I said good-bye and that I'll see them in the morning."

As Leah walked away, she heard Adam mumble something but couldn't make out what he'd said. She wasn't about to go back and find out!

With arms folded and lips pressed tightly together, Adam watched out the kitchen window as Leah hopped on her bicycle and rode off.

Dropping into a seat at the table, he groaned. He hated the fact that he was physically attracted to Leah, yet at the same time, she got under his skin. "I probably should have called her back and apologized," Adam muttered. "But then, why should I? Leah shouldn't be introducing my nieces to reflexology." He tapped his foot in agitation. *Maybe I should look for someone else to watch the girls. Someone less appealing and easier to communicate with. But the girls seem to like her, and I need to focus on their needs and making their transition as smooth as possible. Too many changes will only make it more difficult for my nieces right now.*

Linda stomped into the kitchen, her cheeks still damp with tears. "You know what, Uncle Adam?"

"Say what you have to say," he said, trying to hide his irritation.

"You're mean!" With that, Linda plodded out of the room and tramped noisily up the stairs.

Spotting the cheeseball and graham crackers sitting out, Adam helped himself to some. Maybe it would make him feel better if he ate something. *Linda's right*, he decided. *I was rather harsh. Guess I owe everyone an apology.*

After spreading some of the cheeseball on a cracker, Adam ate it and smacked his lips. *This isn't bad. In fact, it's real tasty. I bet Leah made it.* He fixed another one. *If she promises not to practice her hocus-pocus on Carrie, Linda, or Amy, guess I'll let her keep watching the girls. I hate to admit it, but they seem to like her better than they do me.*

CHAPTER 18

Chicago

Cora sat in the living room, holding her laptop on her knees. For the last hour she'd been looking once again for nursing positions in various areas across Illinois. The few openings she found didn't pay well enough. In addition to her wages, the child support Evan paid for Jared would help with expenses, but it didn't come close to what he used to contribute when they were married. Cora had to hold out for a better-paying job, or she and Jared would be getting by on a lot less than they were used to.

On the plus side, she had met with her Realtor a few days ago, and he'd scheduled an open house, hoping to generate some interest in her home. Cora knew it might take awhile, and once it was sold, she'd have plenty of money, but she wanted to move as soon as possible. In addition to her struggles with Jared, seeing Evan whenever he came to check on patients at the hospital, not to mention bumping into his new bride, was taking a toll. If she only had the support of family right now to help her through this difficult time in her life. But Cora's parents were dead, and she'd lost touch with her four brothers years ago—not that they would have offered much support. They'd never been close to Cora. Of course, that was probably her fault, since they had differing opinions on certain things. Cora had several friends in Chicago, including Ellie and Shannon, both nurses. But they were both too busy for her these days. Perhaps once she and Jared relocated, they'd find a new set of friends.

Cora glanced at her watch. It was almost five. Jared should have been home an hour ago. When she'd arrived home from work this afternoon, she'd found a scribbled note from him on the table, saying he'd gone to a friend's house and would be home by four o'clock. Something, or someone, must have detained him.

Rubbing her eyes, Cora set her laptop aside and began to pace. Last week, Jared had gotten into a fight when some kid made a wisecrack about Jared's father cheating on his mother. While Cora appreciated Jared's anger over what Evan had done, she didn't condone fighting and knew nothing good could come from her son beating someone up. Maybe Jared had run into that same boy today and been involved in another skirmish. But if that were the case, why hadn't Jared come home right away, like he had the last time, when he'd been left with a split lip and bloody nose?

She glanced out the front window. No sign of Jared coming up the walk. Should she start calling some of his friends?

Reaching for the phone, Cora was about to make the first call, when the front door flew open and Jared stepped in.

"Where have you been?" Cora moved quickly toward him, relieved that he showed no signs of having been beaten up. "I've been worried about you."

He sauntered across the room, dropped his backpack on the floor, and flopped onto the couch. "Chill out, Mom. I hung out with my friend Chad all day, like I said in my note."

Jared plunked his feet on the coffee table and clasped his hands behind his head. "What are we having for supper? I only had a candy bar for lunch, so I'm starving!"

"I have a meat loaf in the oven," she replied. "And please take your feet off the table."

He dropped his feet to the floor and wrinkled his nose. "I hate meat loaf."

"If you're hungry, you'll eat it."

"Guess I shoulda stayed over at Chad's. His mom works nights, so Chad's on his own all evening. I coulda ate whatever I wanted to over there."

Cora frowned. "Chad being on his own is exactly why he gets into so much trouble." She took a seat on the end of the couch beside Jared and grasped the throw pillow, hugging it to her chest. "I don't like you hanging around him so much. He's a bad influence."

Jared jumped up. "Since you're gonna give me a lecture now, I'm going to my room." He raced up the stairs before Cora could say another word.

Flinching as her son slammed his bedroom door, Cora's jaw clenched. She felt her relationship with Jared slipping further every day. Things weren't like this when she and Evan were married. Jared had been easier to deal with then.

Maybe I should consider one of those jobs I was looking at earlier, even though they don't pay as much as I make now. I really need to get Jared out of here before school starts.

Arthur

"I'm glad you were able to see me this evening," Sara said as Leah worked on her feet. "I've been having trouble with my back again."

"I'm sorry I wasn't able to see you yesterday," Leah apologized. "I was watching Adam's nieces all day and didn't check phone messages till this morning. Otherwise, I could have seen you last evening."

Sara winced when Leah pressed on a particular spot that Leah knew must be tender.

"It's all right. Jonah worked late in his shop last night, but tonight he's home with Mark, so everything worked out." Sara leaned her head against the back of the recliner and drew in a deep breath, which let Leah know she was beginning to relax.

"I haven't had the chance to get to know Adam's nieces," Sara said. "Losing both of their parents has to be difficult for them."

Leah slowly nodded.

"How are they adjusting?"

"Each of them seems to be dealing with it in her own way, but they all have insecurities and behavioral issues."

"Such as?"

"Carrie, the youngest, clings to me most of the day. When Mom was watching them, she said Carrie did that with her, as well."

"It's understandable. Carrie's still very young and misses her mamm."

Leah probed another spot on Sara's foot. "Linda's the middle child, and she's full of nervous energy. She also has a bit of a temper."

Sara's forehead creased. "That can be difficult to deal with. I get stressed out whenever Mark throws a temper tantrum."

"Then there's the oldest, Amy. She tries to act grown up and tends to boss her sisters around, but she's still a little girl and needs to be loved and nurtured as much as the other two. I know she's still hurting, but she holds it in. I figure she uses her bossiness to cover up her pain. Even though Amy trusted me enough to use reflexology to get rid of her headache, she keeps her distance." Leah saw no point in mentioning Adam's reaction to her working on the girls' feet.

"Maybe Amy just needs a little more attention. Jonah and I have recently come to realize that we need to spend more time with Mark. Once the boppli comes, he will require it even more, so he doesn't feel left out."

"I agree. In fact, I think all three of Adam's nieces need more love and attention. I've actually been thinking of a fun thing I might do that could help them focus on something other than their grief," Leah said.

"What's that?" Sara murmured, now appearing to be even more relaxed.

"As you know, we have a lot of hummingbirds in our yard. Watching them around the feeders each day has made me think that the girls might enjoy having a feeder in Adam's backyard."

"That's a good idea." Sara yawned. "It would certainly give them something to look forward to."

"That's what I was thinking. You'd be surprised to see what a little chipmunk has done to give Linda and Carrie some enjoyment. Adam told me that he heard them talking about it the other day." Leah smiled. "Think I'll take one of my unused feeders over there, and if he has no objections, I'll find a place to hang it where the girls can easily watch the hummers feed."

"Next time I come here I'll be anxious to hear how it worked out."

Leah's excitement mounted. "When my neighbor comes over to band the hummingbirds in my yard, I might see if Adam's okay with me bringing the girls over so they get to see how the procedure is done. It might be one more thing to bring a little joy into their lives."

"That sounds interesting," Sara said. "I'll bet Mark would enjoy watching that, too."

"Feel free to bring him. The girls would probably have fun getting acquainted with your cute little guy."

Sara smiled. "You know, I think we will come over that day. Just let me know when."

"Jah, I will." Leah looked forward to seeing the girls tomorrow and hopefully setting up the feeder. She had so much love to give Adam's nieces and wanted to share the enjoyment she got out of something as simple as watching the tiny birds that had brought her so much pleasure over the years. If she ever had any children of her own, she would try to instill in them a love for all things found in nature. But until that time came, if it did, she would enjoy spending time with Adam's nieces, for they clearly needed her love and attention. She just wished Adam wasn't so against her practicing reflexology on the girls. He ought to at least give her the chance to prove that it wasn't hocus-pocus.

Adam yawned as he stood in front of the stove, trying to make supper. He'd been tempted to ask Leah if she could stay awhile longer and fix the meal for him and the girls but figured she'd be anxious to get home and prepare supper for herself and her dad. Besides, things had been strained between them since Tuesday, when he'd forbidden her to massage the girls' feet, even though he had apologized to everyone for being so harsh.

He reached for a package of macaroni and added the contents to the kettle of boiling water on the stove. *Leah may think I'm being impossible, but she doesn't understand the reason behind my opposition to reflexology.* Adam shook his head. *And what's the point of telling her? What happened in my past doesn't concern her, and it's really none of her business.*

Adam grimaced when he glanced at Amy, whom he'd asked to set the table. She ambled from the silverware drawer to the table, dragging her feet as she carried one item at a time and then placed it haphazardly on the table. It was as though she were moving in slow motion. Was she doing it on purpose, just to irritate him, or did Amy's placid expression and lack of interest mean that her heart wasn't in this chore because of her sadness? She was certainly detached, and Adam wished there was something that would bring her out of it.

He had considered setting the girls down and having a talk with them about their folks—maybe try to get them to open up and express their feelings. *Would it help for them to know I'm hurting, too?* he wondered. But Adam hadn't followed through on that, because he wasn't sure what to say. The simple truth was that the girls didn't relate well to him, and frankly, the feeling was mutual. It wasn't that Adam didn't love his nieces; he just didn't feel comfortable in his new role as their guardian. If he were married and had children of his own, he'd have experience as a father and would understand the girls' needs a little better.

Well, I can learn, he told himself. *It would just be nice if I had a wife to help me through this process.* Adam slapped the side of his head. *What am I thinking? I don't want a wife. And even if I did, who would it be? Certainly not Leah—although I find myself fighting an attraction to her.*

Pushing the conflicting thoughts to the back of his mind, Adam concentrated on getting the macaroni and cheese finished. Maybe he'd toss in some cut-up hot dogs with it. The girls would probably like that. Then after they ate their meal and cleaned up the dishes, he'd suggest they all go outside and look at the bright, full moon. Maybe that would have a calming effect on everyone and let the girls know that he was trying a little harder to take an interest in them.

CHAPTER 19

The following day, as Adam watched the girls eat their cereal and toast, he reflected on how things had gone last night when he'd showed them the beautiful full moon. The two younger ones had seemed quite interested, especially when Adam gave them the binoculars to get a closer look. They'd gasped at how big and orange it was when it first crested the horizon. Then as the moon went higher, it turned its typical white color, with the craters becoming more visible.

But Amy acted bored with it all. She'd said that she didn't see what was so special about the moon. It was just a big round ball of nighttime light.

Later, Amy had asked if she could sleep in her own room, across the hall from her sisters. Adam could tell she wanted to be more independent and keep to herself, so he agreed that she could have her own room. He hoped Amy's indifference wouldn't affect her ability to do well in school, which would be starting in two weeks. Both Amy and Linda would be attending, which meant Carrie might be lonely without her sisters all day.

I hope Leah will continue to watch Carrie. The other girls will need someone here with them when they get home from school, too. Adam supposed he could offer to bring Carrie over to Leah's house each morning, after he'd taken Linda and Amy to school, but having her come here was much more convenient. Besides, his home was more familiar, and right now, Adam thought that was important for the girls.

Guess I'd better talk to Leah about this, he decided. *I'll mention it as soon as she gets here this morning.*

Adam finished his bowl of cereal and was putting his dishes in the sink when Leah showed up. This time she arrived by horse and buggy.

He watched out the kitchen window as she unhitched her horse,

Sugar. He could see she was talking to the mare, while gently rubbing Sugar's neck. She was as gentle with animals as she was with children. He'd noticed this when Coal ran out to greet her every morning. The dog would sit patiently, after running circles around her, accustomed to the special treat she often brought him.

Adam continued to watch Leah as she put Sugar in the corral and took a small box out of the buggy. He waited until she reached the porch, then he opened the back door.

"Guder mariye," they said in unison.

"What have you got in there?" he asked, looking curiously at the box Leah held as she stepped into the utility room.

"It's a hummingbird feeder." Leah smiled. "Unless you have some objection, I thought I'd fill it with nectar and hang it somewhere in your yard. The hummers won't be around too many more weeks, but I think the girls would enjoy watching them drink from the feeder until the hummers head south for the winter. Right now, the little birds are quite active, migrating down from the northern states, so I'm sure it won't be long before they discover this new feeder."

"I don't object at all, and I think the girls might like that. At least Linda and Carrie will." Adam lowered his voice. "I'm not sure about Amy. She doesn't seem to be interested in much of anything other than telling her sisters what to do."

"Well, you never know; watching the hummers might catch Amy's attention. She also might find it fascinating to see how those little birds are just as curious about us as we are about them." Leah paused, pushing the sleeves on her dress up a little. "You know, Adam, I'm surprised you haven't figured it out yet."

He tipped his head. "Figured what out?"

"I think Amy is bossy because she's covering up her true feelings. She's trying to be strong for her sisters and doesn't want to appear weak in front of them. Since Amy is the oldest, she probably feels that she's the only mother her sisters have now, even though she's only ten.

Adam nodded slowly. What Leah had said made sense.

"Oh, and there's one more thing I wanted to talk to you about," Leah said.

"What's that?"

"Next Wednesday morning one of my neighbors will be coming over to our place to band the hummingbirds that flock around my feeders every day. Would it be all right if I take the girls over there so they can watch the procedure?"

Adam shrugged. "Sure. It sounds interesting. Maybe I'll go into work a little later that day so I can watch the banding, too."

Leah blinked, and her mouth opened slightly. "Oh, I didn't realize that would be something you'd be interested in."

He nodded. "I may be tied up with my store a good deal of the time, but I do enjoy all things related to nature. I find watching God's critters to be relaxing."

"Same here; and you're more than welcome to join us that day. I'm sure it'll be a learning experience for all of us."

Adam hadn't been sure how Leah would feel about him inviting himself to the banding session, but he was glad he'd mentioned it. Right now, he couldn't seem to take his eyes away from Leah's as he noticed how easily she blushed.

When Leah broke eye contact and started for the kitchen, he touched her shoulder. "Now there's something I need to ask you."

She halted and turned to face him. "What is it, Adam?"

"As I'm sure you're aware, school will be starting the week after next, and even though Amy and Linda will be in school most of the day, Carrie will still need a sitter. So I was wondering. . ."

"If I would continue watching her?"

"Jah."

"Of course, I will, Adam. I enjoy being with the girls, and since I'm seeing people for foot treatments in the evening hours, that leaves me free during the daytime."

"Are you sure? I could ask around and see if there's someone else willing to watch Carrie and be here after Linda and Amy get home from school."

Leah shook her head. "No, really, I'm fine with the way things are now. The schedule I'm on has been going fairly well for me."

Adam breathed in a sigh of relief. "That's good to hear. Jah, real good."

"So, girls, how would you like to help me with something?" Leah asked after Adam left for work.

"What do you want us to do?" Linda looked up at Leah inquisitively.

Leah went to the box she'd placed on the kitchen counter and removed the feeder. "This is a special kind of feeder for hummingbirds. Do you girls know what a hummingbird is?"

"Course we do," Amy spoke up. "They're little birds with long beaks."

"And they fly real fast, too," Linda added.

"That's right," Leah agreed. "And hummers, as they're sometimes called, don't eat birdseed like most other birds do. They drink sweet nectar instead."

"What's sweet nectar?" Linda asked.

"It's sugar water." Amy poked her sister's arm. "I'll bet even Carrie knows that."

Linda poked her back. "Bet she doesn't."

"Let's go ask her then." Amy tromped across the room to where Carrie sat, stirring the milk around in her cereal bowl. "What's sweet nectar, sister?"

Carrie grinned at Amy and said, "It's *zucker wasser*."

"That's right!" Amy patted Carrie's back.

Linda rolled her eyes. "I'll bet she was listening to what we said. That's how she knew."

"Let's mix some of that sugar water right now," Leah was quick to say. "First, we need to rinse the feeder real good, to make sure it's nice and clean. Then we can all go outside and get the feeder hung."

"Do you know how much to mix?" Amy questioned.

"I sure do. The general rule is four cups of water and one cup of sugar. At home, I prepare the mixture every night and keep it in a container in the refrigerator. So if your uncle has something in his kitchen to store it in, we'll do the same thing here." Leah watched as all three girls listened intently. "So what do you say? Are you ready to find a good spot for the feeder?"

Carrie and Linda bobbed their heads agreeably. Amy merely shrugged her shoulders, but she did get a bag of sugar from the pantry while Linda found a plastic container and got the cup to measure water in. Leah had a feeling that Amy was more interested in feeding the hummers than she let on.

"I wonder how things have been going for Leah since she started watching Adam's nieces," Elaine commented as she and Priscilla headed down the road in Priscilla's horse and buggy. They'd gone out for breakfast and were on their way back to Elaine's.

"I don't know. It's been awhile since I've talked to her," Priscilla said. "Maybe we should stop by Adam's and say hello."

Elaine smiled. "That's a good idea. If you have the time, that is."

Priscilla nodded. "Mom closed our store for the day so Dad can paint it. When I left this morning, she said not to hurry back and to take the rest of the day for myself. I can't think of a better way to spend it than with my two best friends."

"I would have invited Leah to join us for breakfast," Elaine said, "but I knew she'd have to be at Adam's early to watch the girls."

Priscilla pulled back on the reins a little to slow her horse some. "I wonder how much longer Leah will keep watching Adam's nieces."

"I would think at least till her mamm comes home. And who knows, she might even keep on after that."

"I guess that's possible, but being at Adam's all day is probably affecting Leah's ability to practice reflexology."

Elaine shook her head. "From what Leah said when I saw her at church the last time, she's been working on people's feet during the evening hours."

Priscilla drew in a sharp breath and released it slowly. "Wow, that makes for a long day. I wonder how long she'll be able to keep up with that schedule."

"We do what we have to at times when it's needed." Elaine reflected on her own situation when her grandmother was alive. She'd put in long hours caring for Grandma, in addition to doing whatever she could to make a little extra money. But she had no regrets. She had made a commitment to Grandma and kept her promise to Grandpa before he died. As tiring and stressful as those days had been, she would do it all again if it meant having Grandma with her right now.

Life keeps moving on, she thought, *and I've had to learn to live by myself and carry on.* The pain of losing both her grandparents was still with Elaine, but she'd learned to trust God and look to the future. The question was, would Elaine's future be with Ben Otto, or did he only see her as a good friend? An easy friendship was all she wanted from Ben for now, but perhaps someday it could turn into something more.

Elaine closed her eyes, and an image of Jonah Miller popped into her head. She'd never loved anyone the way she had him. But that was in the past, and she'd forced herself to let go. Their relationship had ended the day Elaine had learned that Grandma had dementia. She reminded herself once more that her love for Jonah had prompted her to break things off with him. Setting him free to live a life with Sara and her son had been the best thing for Jonah. He and Sara were happy. Every time Elaine saw the couple together, their love and devotion to each other was more evident.

"We're here. Wake up, sleepyhead."

Elaine's eyes opened. "I wasn't really sleeping—just thinking is all."

Priscilla smiled. "I hope they were good thoughts."

Elaine nodded.

Once Priscilla had the horse secured at the rail near Adam's barn, she and Elaine headed across the yard, where they found Leah and the girls sitting in chairs on the porch.

"It's good to see you," Leah said. "Look what I put up for the girls." She pointed to a hummingbird feeder hanging from a hook under the porch eaves.

"How nice." Elaine looked at Amy and smiled. "Have you seen any hummers yet?"

The child shook her head. "Probably won't, neither."

"What makes you think that?" Priscilla asked.

"Nothing good ever happens for me."

Leah put her arm around Amy. "Good things come to those who

wait. It's going to take a bit of time for the hummingbirds to find our feeder, but when they do, more hummers will come. Who knows? We may even need another feeder or two. Oh, and let's not forget that next Wednesday morning we'll be going over to my place to watch my neighbor put little bands on the hummingbirds." Leah looked at Elaine and Priscilla. "If you two aren't busy that day, you're welcome to come and watch, too."

"I wish I could," Elaine said, "but I have a dental appointment that day."

"I'll try to make it," Priscilla said. "I'm sure it'll be fun. Don't you think so, girls?"

Linda nodded, and Amy said nothing, but Carrie moved closer to Leah and climbed into her lap. "I'm gonna sit right here and wait for the hummers to come."

Elaine looked over at Priscilla and smiled. It was obvious that Leah had won Adam's youngest niece over. Elaine figured it wouldn't be long and her friend would have them all coming to her for the love they surely needed.

That night, Adam read Carrie and Linda a bedtime story in their room. According to Amy, it was Carrie's favorite story. Carrie had closed her eyes after he'd only read halfway through the book. Thinking she had fallen asleep so he wouldn't have to read the whole story, he'd skipped to the last page to finish it quicker. When he was about to close the book, Carrie sat up and announced that he'd skipped the most important part. Linda agreed. Sheepishly, Adam went back and finished reading the rest of the story.

He smiled as he came downstairs and headed to the kitchen to get a drink. At least he was making some progress with Carrie, although she still preferred Leah over him. As he stepped into the kitchen, he realized that the moon was very bright. He could see everything he needed by its glow shining in through the window.

"Let's see now, what do we have in here to drink?" He opened the refrigerator door. There was a carton of milk and some orange juice, but he wasn't in the mood for either. Then Adam spied another container he assumed Leah had made for the girls—probably lemonade, he decided. After pouring himself a glass, he stood by the window and took a big gulp. "Ugh! What is this sweet stuff?" Then he realized he'd forgotten all about the nectar the girls had helped Leah mix for the hummingbirds that day. During supper, Linda hadn't been able to stop talking about the feeder Leah had brought them and how they'd waited patiently for the first hummer to arrive.

Adam had to admit he was happy to see Linda's enthusiasm. If only Amy would come out of her shell and try to find some interests. He was glad that Leah was so good with his nieces. Carrie had especially warmed up to her. This evening, she'd started crying when Leah was getting ready to go home. It was hard watching Carrie cling to Leah's dress, pleading with her not to go. Leah had even teared up, assuring the child that she'd be back bright and early the next day. It seemed to satisfy Carrie when Leah said they would have lunch out on the porch tomorrow so they could watch for any hummingbirds that might come to the new feeder.

Adam missed his sister but hadn't had time to mourn her death since his nieces had come to live with him. Although it hadn't been easy at first, he'd begun to think that the girls were there for a reason, and he couldn't help but wonder if Leah might be, too.

CHAPTER 20

The next Wednesday found Leah scurrying about the kitchen, getting the breakfast dishes washed, dried, and put away. Normally, she would have been over at Adam's by now, but since he'd be bringing the girls over to see the hummingbirds get banded, she wouldn't go there until the banding was done. Last evening, Leah had prepared a few snacks to share with everyone after the process was finished. She'd cleaned and cut fresh vegetables, made some creamy ranch dip, and fixed her favorite chocolate-chip cheeseball. She had also found a cake recipe named, of all things, Hummingbird Ring. It was easy to make and the perfect dessert to serve for this occasion.

Leah looked forward to watching this exciting event and was sure the girls, and maybe even Adam, would enjoy it, too. She hoped Sara and Mark would be able to join them, as well as Priscilla.

It's too bad Elaine can't make it, Leah thought as she put the silverware away. *I'm sure she would find it interesting.*

Leah glanced out the window, and when she saw Adam's horse and buggy coming up the driveway, she hurried to the door. When Leah had first started watching the girls, she'd hoped Adam would find someone else, but now she couldn't think of anything she'd rather do than be with Adam's nieces. She didn't even mind having to schedule her reflexology appointments during the evening. In some ways, it was more convenient for those who came to her, since many of them had day jobs and couldn't take time off from work to get a treatment. So it had worked out best for all.

"Look at all the hummers!" Linda exclaimed when she and her sisters looked around the backyard, where Leah's feeders hung, before stepping onto the porch. "Wish we had that many at Uncle Adam's place instead of just a few."

"It took awhile before so many hummingbirds showed up here," Leah explained, patting the top of the little girl's head. "But since I started feeding them, they've become quite active. In fact, I mark the calendar every year on the day that I first see them, and it's pretty much around the same time when they start arriving each April."

"Maybe that's something we can start doing." Linda's eyes sparkled with enthusiasm.

"That's a good idea." Leah leaned down to give Carrie a hug while Amy's gaze remained fixed on the hummingbirds.

"Are we here too early?" Adam asked when he joined Leah and the girls after taking care of his horse.

"No, it's fine," Leah replied. "My neighbor Alissa, who does the banding, should be here soon, along with the others I invited to watch." She gestured to the chairs on the porch. "Why don't we all take a seat, and we can watch the hummers eat at the feeders until Alissa shows up."

The girls scampered over to the porch swing and sat together while Adam took a seat in the chair beside Leah's.

"Sure is a nice day," Adam commented. "There's not a cloud in sight."

Leah nodded. "I was hoping it wouldn't rain today. That would have put a damper on things."

Adam removed his straw hat, placing it on his knee. "I think getting the girls a hummingbird feeder was a good idea, Leah. Even Amy showed some interest in it this morning. She seemed eager to come over here as well." He paused and grinned at Leah. "Course, it may be less about the hummers and more about spending time with you."

Leah smiled in return. "I enjoy being with all three of the girls. They've become very special to me."

They visited a few more minutes, and then Sara and little Mark showed up. They'd just gotten seated on the porch when Priscilla arrived.

"Where's the woman who'll be doing the banding?" Priscilla asked. "She didn't come and go already, I hope."

Leah shook her head. "Alissa must be running late, but hopefully she'll be here soon." She gestured to the one empty chair. "Why don't you take a seat? We can all visit while we wait for Alissa to get here."

Fifteen minutes later, Leah decided to walk out to the phone shack to see if Alissa may have called and left a message. She'd just opened the door to the small wooden building, when Alissa's car pulled in. Leah waved and followed the vehicle up the driveway.

"Sorry I'm late," Alissa said, her auburn-colored ponytail bouncing as she stepped out of her car and joined Leah on the lawn. "I had a few interruptions this morning and it put me a little behind."

"That's okay. Everyone I invited is here, so we're ready and eager for you to get started."

"Perhaps one of the girls can help me bring some of my things to the banding area," Alissa suggested.

"I'll help," Amy volunteered.

"Alissa, this is Amy. She's the oldest of Adam's nieces." Leah then introduced the other two girls, as well as Adam and her other guests.

"It's nice to meet all of you. Amy, would you mind getting my canvas bag? That has all my instruments in it. Leah, if you'll carry the birdcage, I'll get the tables." Alissa reached into the trunk of her car to get the rest of her things. "I think that's everything I'll need." She put the birdcage on a small table near the hummingbird feeders. That way, while everything else was being set up, the hummers would have some time to get used to the cage and fly in and out of it to get to the feeder she'd hung inside.

Alissa laid out all her instruments and rechecked the bands she'd brought, saying she needed to make sure they were in consecutive order. "Amy, how would you like to be my helper today?" Alissa asked. "That is, if it's okay with your uncle and Leah."

Instantly, Leah nodded her approval. Glancing over at Adam for his reaction, she was glad when he also nodded.

"I'd like to help, but I'm not sure what to do," Amy said hesitantly.

"I'll explain everything as we go along." Alissa smiled as she explained how the hummingbirds would be caught. "The door to the birdcage will be left open, but it's operated by a remote control, which Amy will be using. Once a hummingbird flies into the cage to the feeder, Amy will hit the button on the remote to quickly close the door."

Alissa went on to explain how the doorway was lined with soft material, in case a hummer tried to fly out while the door was going down. "In all the years I've been banding hummingbirds, that's never happened," she added. "But we want to do everything possible to ensure the safety of the birds. My husband usually accompanies me when I do bird banding, but he isn't feeling well this morning. He's the one who actually set up this remote to close the door."

Alissa looked at Amy. "Now, once a hummingbird is caught, you will need to carefully take it out of the cage and put it in one of the soft cloth bags I brought, and then bring it up to me."

Amy's eyes widened. "You. . .you mean I get to hold the little birds?"

"That's right, but your hands are small, and I'm sure you'll be very gentle."

Eyes now bright with anticipation, Amy nodded. "I'll do my best not to hurt any of 'em."

Leah was pleased that Alissa had asked for Amy's help rather than one of the adults. The child seemed eager, and Leah hoped everything would go as it should. If Amy were to injure one of the delicate birds, she would no doubt be extremely upset.

"Try not to worry," Adam whispered, leaning close to Leah, as though he could read her thoughts. "I think this is good for Amy."

Leah, feeling almost breathless from the nearness of him, nodded. "Jah, so do I."

Pulling her gaze from Adam, Leah focused on the little white bag that resembled an onion sack, with tiny holes through it. This was the bag that safely held the hummingbird until Alissa was ready to band it.

"The first thing I will do is band the hummingbird," Alissa told them. "After that, I'll determine if it is a hatch-year or after-hatch-year hummer."

"What does that mean?" Adam asked, looking at Leah's neighbor curiously.

"After-hatch-year means the hummingbird is an adult, and hatch-year means it was hatched out that year, so it's an immature hummingbird," Alissa replied.

"That certainly makes sense." Adam's ears turned pink. "Guess it was a silly question."

Alissa shook her head. "Hey, no question is silly. That's how we learn."

"How do you determine if it's an adult hummingbird?" Sara asked, bouncing Mark on her lap.

"I actually use a jeweler's loupe, which is a small round magnifying glass that I hook onto my glasses. It gives me a close-up look at the hummingbird's beak. The beak is also referred to as the *culmen*." Alissa picked up the eyepiece and showed it to everyone. "Grooving on the culmen tells me it is an immature bird. No grooving and a smooth beak indicate it's an adult."

Leah looked around, noticing how interested everyone seemed to be. The girls, especially, were intently watching and listening to every word Alissa said, leaning forward as though anxious to learn more. Leah was pleased that this day was working out so well. Hopefully all the little hummingbirds would cooperate, too.

Alissa then showed them the other instruments she would be using to gather information on each hummingbird. One was the small tool especially made to put the band on the hummingbird's leg. Each band had a number engraved on it, all in sequence.

"Each band gets put on the bird's right leg," Alissa explained. "All bird banders follow that rule."

"Does it hurt the bird?" Linda questioned.

"I was going to ask that, too," Priscilla put in.

"There is no harm to the bird. These bands are especially made for the hummingbird species, and they won't even know it's on them," Alissa assured everyone.

"I've been watching, and several hummingbirds have flown into the cage to get a drink. Then they flew right back out again," Amy stated.

"That's good." Alissa smiled. "It means they're getting used to the cage. We shouldn't have any trouble at all banding a good number of them this morning."

Alissa explained about the rest of the instruments. The small scales were to weigh the bird, and she also described the instrument that measured its culmen, wings, and tail. She told them that the ruby-throated was the most common species of hummingbirds in the state of Illinois. "But it's not unusual for another type of hummingbird to venture into our state," she added. "When that happens, it causes a bit of excitement among the licensed banders and the bird-watching community, especially if it's a rare hummingbird not common to our area."

Leah was amazed at all the things Alissa told them. She had no idea so much was involved with banding a hummingbird. Amy sat forward, as if grasping every word her neighbor said. It was a far cry from the disinterest she had shown about other things since she and her sisters had come to live with Adam.

"I will also check for the gorget feathers, which are the bright red feathers on the hummingbird's throat. Only the male hummingbirds have those types of feathers, and this is why they are called ruby-throated," Alissa said.

"I see another hummingbird just flew out of the cage." Priscilla pointed in that direction.

"Leah, you certainly weren't kidding when you said you had a lot of hummingbirds at your feeders," Sara commented. "They're like a swarm of bees buzzing around."

"How much sugar do you go through each summer?" Adam asked.

"Believe it or not, last year at this time during migration, I almost went through ten pounds of sugar each week. This extreme activity goes on for about three weeks. Then as more hummers head south of here, it slows up a bit." Leah gestured to her feeders. "As you can see, I have six feeders hanging out to accommodate all the hummingbirds I get. By the end of the day, those feeders will be empty."

Adam's eyebrows lifted. "That must really keep you busy."

"It does, but it's a nice kind of busy. I always refill the feeders in the evening so that in the morning when the hummers really need to juice up, the feeders will be full for them."

"I can see this is a good place to band hummingbirds," Alissa said to Leah. "I only have one other place in this area that I go to each year for banding. Maybe I can talk to you later about having a session here next year as well." She looked at Linda. "How would you like to write the information down on the chart as I do each hummingbird? And Leah, maybe you can help her with that."

Linda nodded enthusiastically.

Both Leah and Linda listened as Alissa explained the chart and where all the information should go. After that, everyone watched and waited for the next hummingbird to enter the cage. They didn't have to wait long before one zipped in and landed on the feeder for a drink. This would be their first one to band.

"Okay, Amy, hit the remote button," Alissa advised.

Amy did as she was told, and the door to the cage quickly closed.

Leah couldn't help smiling as she watched Amy follow Alissa to the cage. She could see that Alissa was explaining to her how to gently take the bird and put it in the small sack.

"We caught our first hummingbird." With a look of sheer joy, Amy held up the bag as they returned to the porch.

The first thing Alissa did was call out the number on the band so Linda could write it on the chart. Then all eyes were on the hummingbird as Alissa gently removed it from the cloth bag and put the bird into the small cut-out end of a nylon sock. "This," she explained, "makes it easier to handle the hummer and also helps keep the bird calm."

Everyone watched closely as she carefully crimped the band around the hummer's right leg and then took the rest of the measurements. This hummingbird was an immature male with only two little gorget feathers on its throat. The feathers resembled two red dots. After that, Alissa called each measurement out so that Linda, with Leah's help, could document the information.

"Carrie, now that I'm all done, how would you like to hold a hummingbird?" Alissa smiled as Carrie grinned shyly and nodded her head. "Just hold out your hand and be very still."

Leah had tears in her eyes when she saw the look of joy on Carrie's face as Alissa put the little bird into the palm of her hand. It seemed as if everyone held their breath, watching to see what the hummingbird would do. It sat there quietly for a bit, looking around; then all of a sudden, it flew into the trees where the little birds liked to perch.

Sara clapped her hands, and little Mark did, too, prompting the rest of them to do the same.

"And that, my friends, is how the process is done," Alissa announced. "I think it went very well. Sometimes," she added, "a hummingbird will get away from me before I can get all the information about it. So that's why I band the hummer first. That way, if it gets away, at least we have it banded and can log the number into our data center."

"Data center?" Amy asked. "What's that?"

Alissa told them that all the information they compiled on the chart would be put into a large data system through an Internet site. "This system is assessable to all licensed bird banders, so if a bird is captured that has already been banded, they can check the computer for its information," she explained. "They can find out where that bird was originally banded and compare all the other information. It's exciting to capture a hummingbird and find out that it had been banded in another state."

Little Mark eventually fell asleep on Sara's lap, but everyone else watched the entire procedure; especially the girls.

After about two hours, more hummingbirds had been caught and banded—thirty-seven of them to be exact. Everyone got the chance to hold a hummingbird before it was released. Alissa further explained that she always tried not to have the hummingbirds in her possession for longer than three minutes, in order not to stress the birds.

Leah couldn't believe how fast the morning had gone. It was good to see Amy smiling as she helped Alissa pack up everything and take it to her car.

"Thank you so much for inviting me." Priscilla gave Leah a hug. "It was amazing. I'll never forget this exciting event."

"You're welcome, but aren't you going to stay long enough to have some refreshments?"

"I'd love to, but I need to run to the grocery store for a few things." Priscilla thanked Alissa for a great experience and headed down the driveway on her bike.

"Unfortunately, I need to leave, too, and get this little guy home," Sara added. "Thank you so much for inviting me and Mark. Like

Priscilla said, it was a great experience."

After that, Leah, the girls, Alissa, and Adam enjoyed talking and discussing the hummingbirds as they ate fresh vegetables with dip, crackers, and the homemade cheeseball Leah had made. They also enjoyed the Hummingbird Ring cake.

"Did you put hummingbirds in this cake?" Carrie asked, pointing to a maraschino cherry.

Leah smiled. "No, dear one. Those are cherries. The cake is just called a hummingbird ring."

"Oh, that's good." Carrie giggled, and so did everyone else. But all too soon, the morning ended.

Leah glanced back at Adam, who was waiting on the porch with his nieces as she walked with Alissa to her car. It had been nice to see him relax and enjoy something so much. He actually seemed like a different person today. "I don't know how I will ever thank you for giving us all such a wonderful experience," Leah told Alissa. "The knowledge you have is incredible, and it was so interesting to learn the banding process. Next year if you'd like to come again, you'd be more than welcome." After giving her neighbor a hug, Leah joined Adam and the girls on the porch, and they all waved until Alissa's car was out of sight.

"I also have to get going, but I thank you for including us today." Adam smiled—a genuine smile that showed in his eyes. "I sure enjoyed it. I know the girls did, too."

"You're welcome. It certainly was a wonderful learning experience, and I had fun, as well."

"You girls help Leah clean up after I go," Adam said before he walked to his buggy then turned to wave. "I'll see you all this evening."

"Wait, Uncle Adam. Wait!" Linda yelled, running to his buggy.

Leah watched as Adam jumped out to see what was wrong. Her heart swelled as Linda hugged her uncle and Adam squeezed her right back.

"Danki, Uncle Adam, for bringing us today. It was fun."

Leah thought she saw Adam wiping his eyes before climbing back into the buggy. That one small gesture from his niece had touched him deeply. Leah couldn't have been happier when all three girls gave her a hug once their uncle had gone. A lump formed in her throat when Amy said how much she appreciated Leah inviting them. Leah's only regret was that her mother couldn't have been here to watch the banding, for she was certain that she would have enjoyed it, too. But Mom was still helping out at her sister's and would remain there a few weeks after the baby came, so Leah didn't expect to see her anytime soon.

Chicago

Cora's skirt swished as she hurried down the hospital corridor. She'd just had an encounter in the elevator with Evan, who'd said he was on his way to see a patient. Cora had made the mistake of telling him that she'd put the house on the market, and it hadn't gone over well. Fortunately, no one else had been in the elevator when Evan glared at her and said, "If you didn't want the house, then you shouldn't have fought so hard to get it, Cora. I would have been happy to keep it and give you the money for a smaller place where you and Jared could be comfortable."

"I fought to get it so you couldn't bring your pretty little wife into what used to be our home," Cora shot back. "You knew I wanted to move and planned to sell the house. If you wanted it so badly, then you should have been satisfied with me and not gone looking for someone you thought was better." It angered her that she let Evan get to her like that, and she'd begun to wonder lately if she'd done something to deserve his unfaithfulness.

Maybe I'm being punished for something I did in the past, Cora fumed. *Or maybe Evan never really loved me at all.*

Continuing down the hall, Cora halted when she nearly bumped into Dr. Rogers going in the opposite direction.

"Oops. Sorry about that," she mumbled. "Guess I wasn't watching where I was going."

He paused and touched her arm. "You look upset. Is something wrong?"

Of course there's something wrong. My husband left me for another woman, and now I feel forced to move. Cora swallowed against the lump in her throat. "I–I'm just in a hurry, that's all," she mumbled.

"Okay. Well, no harm was done." Dr. Rogers started to walk away but turned back around. "I heard from one of the other nurses that you're planning to move."

She nodded. "I haven't found another job yet, though, so I'll continue on here until I do."

"You're well liked here, by the staff and also the patients, so you'll surely be missed." The sincerity in the middle-aged doctor's brown eyes was nearly Cora's undoing. Until this mess with Evan had erupted, she'd always enjoyed her job at this hospital. It wouldn't be easy to leave and start over again, but for her sake, as well as Jared's, that's what she needed to do. From the time Cora was a little girl, her life had been full of changes and complications. Leaving Chicago and the painful memories behind would be just one more hurdle to jump.

CHAPTER 21

*W*e'll be moving in two weeks, so you'd better start packing," Cora told her son the next Monday.

Jared's eyebrows shot up. "Moving? To where, Mom?"

"The town of Arthur." She dished some scrambled eggs onto a plate and handed it to him. "I poured you a glass of orange juice, and there's some toast on the table."

"But we can't move. School starts two weeks from Monday, and. . ." He grabbed his chair with force and sat down abruptly.

"And we'll be moved by then, so you'll be going to a new school," Cora said in a smooth, calm tone. "Also Jared, I'd really like it if you'd go to the barber and get your hair cut. It's getting a bit unruly, and as you start a new school, it'll be nice for you to make a good impression. Your appearance is what people see first."

Jared grunted and slunk down in his seat, pushing back his uncombed hair. "I don't wanna move. I told you that before. And I'm not getting my hair cut. I like it this way, and I don't really care what people think of me. If they don't like what they see, that's their problem."

"I know what you said, and I also know how you feel about your hair, Jared. I was young once, too. If you had it styled a little better, or washed it every day, that would make a difference."

"Yeah. Yeah. Whatever." Jared rolled his shoulders, while tilting his head.

"I also know that this move will be the best thing for both of us." Cora placed her plate on the table and took a seat next to him. "Meeting new people and living in different surroundings could be a good thing for both of us."

"What's in Arthur, anyways? I've never even heard of the place."

"If you want to know more about Arthur, check it out on the

Internet. There's an interesting website all about the town. There's also a nursing position at the clinic there, and I applied for the job yesterday afternoon."

Jared's mouth formed an O. "You went to Arthur?"

"No. I applied online and they interviewed me over the phone."

"You're kidding, right?"

Cora shook her head. "I offered to drive down, but the woman conducting the interview said my résumé and work experience spoke for itself, and so did the information they received from the hospital about me."

Jared folded his arms and frowned. "So you found a job, even though our house hasn't sold?"

"That's right, but I'm confident that it will sell in good time." Cora paused and drank some coffee. "Arthur's only a few hours from here, so it won't be hard for your dad to come visit, or for me to take you there."

"Humph! Dad doesn't see me that much anyway, and I doubt he'd go there. I can't believe you waited till now to let me know about this."

"Jared, it just happened," Cora explained. "Don't worry; it won't be a problem when you want to see your dad."

"Yeah, right. Bet I'll never get to see Dad at all." His voice faltered. "What have I done wrong, Mom, that Dad would just leave me out of his new life since he got remarried?"

"You haven't done anything wrong." Cora placed her hands on his shoulders.

Jared's forehead creased as he shrugged her hands away. "Don't see why you and Dad couldn't have worked things out between you, instead of getting a divorce."

"I wanted to work them out, but some things aren't meant to be."

"Well, you'll never get back with Dad if we move."

Cora blew out her breath in a puff of air that lifted her bangs. "You don't understand, Jared. Your dad has moved on with his life, and we need to do the same." She pointed to Jared's plate. "Now please eat your breakfast so you can start packing while I'm at the hospital. I'll be putting in my two weeks' notice today."

༄

Arthur

"You look *mied* this morning," Sara said as she, Jonah, and Mark sat down to eat breakfast. "You've been working late hours again and aren't getting enough sleep."

Jonah yawned. "You're right, Sara, I am tired, and I apologize for that—especially after promising to spend more time with Mark. But as you know, Dad hasn't been able to work since he cut two fingers last week. Even with Timothy's help, I'm getting behind again, and it could be awhile before Dad's able to work with that hand."

"Have you considered hiring another man?"

Jonah shook his head. "No one else in the area is experienced at making and repairing buggies. Even if someone was, it wouldn't be fair to hire him for just a few weeks and then let him go. Timothy and I will just have to manage till Dad's on the job again."

Sara nodded. "I see what you mean." She turned to Mark and handed him a cup of milk.

Jonah reached over and took her hand. "Let's pray about this—that the Lord will get our business through this rough patch."

They bowed their heads and prayed silently. When Jonah finished, he lifted his head. Seeing that Sara had, too, he smiled and said, "As soon as Dad's able to work in the shop again, and we get caught up, things will be back to normal." He tweaked the end of Mark's nose. "We'll do something fun together soon."

Mark giggled. *"Riggel reide?"*

"Sorry, but I can't play on the see-saw with you today, little buddy." Jonah ruffled the boy's hair. "I'll read you a bedtime story tonight, though. How's that sound?"

Mark bobbed his head, grinning widely.

Sara hoped her husband would be able to keep that promise. Last night when Jonah had finally left his shop and came up to the house, Mark was already sleeping. She dreaded seeing the look of disappointment on her son's face if he had to go to sleep without that bedtime story tonight.

Jonah reached for the bottle of syrup and poured some on his pancakes. "Since I've been so busy these past few days, I forgot to ask how things went at Leah's when you and Mark went to watch the hummingbirds get banded."

"Everything went well. It was fascinating to watch the whole procedure." Without going into too much detail, Sara described the process.

"Sounds like it must have been something special to see," Jonah said. "Wish I could have joined you and Mark that day."

"I think Mark is a little too young to understand what was actually going on, but he got very excited when Alissa placed a hummingbird in his hand for a few seconds. Later, though, he got tired and fell asleep."

"Wish you'd had a camera and had taken a picture of those hummers. That would have been a great memory to capture."

"The memory is up here." Sara touched her forehead. "I even got to hold a few hummingbirds after Alissa had them banded. She explained the proper way to hold them. You can't imagine how fragile those little birds feel, yet they didn't seem alarmed that we were holding them. It was so cute."

"That's incredible, when you think about it." Jonah grinned. "I remember one time when I was a boy. I was carrying a box of ripe tomatoes from Mom's garden, and a hummingbird hovered over the box a few seconds before it flew off. It seemed like it thought I had something there for it to eat."

Sara laughed. "From what Alissa explained, the hummingbirds are attracted to red. She said when her husband wears his red ball cap every year at least one hummingbird flies up and hovers in front of his hat."

"When I first saw a hummer, back when I was a kid, I thought it was a big bumble bee." Jonah chuckled. "Their wings go so fast, they make a buzzing sound."

"I'm hoping that maybe next year we can all go there and watch the banding," Sara said. "I believe that Leah's neighbor will be doing it again."

"That would be fun. When the time comes, I'll try to take that morning off."

"Speaking of hummingbirds, I think maybe next spring I'll get a few feeders to hang up in our yard. It'll be fun for us, as well as Mark, to watch the hummers zip back and forth as they drink the sweet nectar." Sara placed her hands against her growing stomach. "It'll be awhile before our boppli's old enough to enjoy watching the little birds, but by the time he or she is ready, I'm sure those tiny hummers will get lots of attention."

"Who let the mutt in?" Adam grumbled, when he discovered Coal sleeping under the kitchen table.

Carrie, Amy, and Linda looked up at him with guilty expressions, but no one said a word.

Adam frowned. "You know the rules about bringing the dog inside. He's to stay out at all times."

"But Uncle Adam, Coal gets lonely out there by himself," Linda spoke up. "Besides, we like him."

Carrie and Amy nodded in agreement.

"I like the mutt, too, but he's a dog, and he belongs outside." Adam opened the back door, clapped his hands and hollered, "Come on, Coal! Outside you go!"

The dog crawled out from under the table, but instead of heading out the door, he ran past Adam and darted up the stairs.

"Come back here right now, you stubborn animal!" Adam's face heated as he tromped up the steps after the dog. At this rate, he'd never get the girls' breakfast served, and he might be late for work.

All the bedroom doors were open, so Adam figured Coal could have gone into any one of them. Choosing the first room, he stepped inside. "Coal, are you in here, boy?"

No response.

Adam squatted down and peered under the bed. No sign of the dog. The closet door was open, so he looked in there as well, but Coal wasn't inside.

Moving on to the second bedroom, Adam checked all the obvious places, but there was no dog. That meant he either had to be in the third bedroom or the bathroom.

Exasperated with all the time this was taking, Adam entered the last bedroom and spotted a long black tail sticking out from under Amy's bed.

"I know you're under there," Adam muttered. "So you may as well come out."

Coal whined pathetically and moved farther under the bed, turning in the opposite direction so that Adam could only see the dog's head.

Adam groaned. This was not a good way to start the day.

Dropping to his knees, he reached under the bed, hoping he could grab hold of the dog's collar, but the mutt was just out of his reach. "Oh, great."

Adam figured he had two choices: he could either crawl under the bed and try to grab Coal, or go back downstairs and let the dog stay where he was. The second idea really wasn't an option.

Crawling on his belly, Adam inched along until he was nose-to-nose with Coal. The next thing Adam knew, the dog's tongue shot out and slurped Adam's mouth.

"Yuck!" Adam jerked his head, bumping it on the slats holding the box spring. "Ouch!"

Arf! Arf! Coal backed out quickly, and by the time Adam crawled out from under the bed, the dog was gone.

Disgusted, Adam tromped down the stairs. "Where is that mutt?" he bellowed, storming into the kitchen. "Did he come back in here?"

Carrie started to howl, Linda whimpered, and Amy's eyes widened. "You don't have to holler like that, Uncle Adam," Amy said. "You oughtta be nicer to Coal. And you're scaring my sisters, too."

Sweating profusely, Adam drew in a deep breath. "I wouldn't have had to holler or run around upstairs if one of you hadn't let the dog in. We'd have all had our breakfast by now." He looked back at the girls, his frustration mounting. "Have you seen Coal or not?"

Amy pointed to the utility room. "He went in there."

As Adam started in that direction, he heard Amy mutter that their dad never yelled at them like that. Pretending he didn't hear, Adam was almost to the utility room, when a knock sounded on the back door. When he opened it, he discovered Leah on the porch. He was about to invite her in, when Coal darted between his legs and zipped out the door, nearly knocking Leah over.

Instinctively, Adam reached out to grab her, and she fell into his arms.

"Ach, my!" she exclaimed, her face turning red as she pulled slowly away and stepped into the house. "What's going on with your hund?"

"It's a long story, but the shortened version is this: Coal was where he doesn't belong, and I would appreciate it if you'd have a talk with the girls about making sure that he stays outside from now on."

Leah looked at him strangely but then gave a quick nod. "Where are the girls?" she asked.

"They're in the kitchen, waiting for their breakfast, which I was going to make till I ended up chasing after the hund." Adam pulled out his pocket watch and grimaced when he saw the time. "At this rate, I'll never make it to work on time."

"Don't worry about breakfast," Leah said sweetly. "I'll fix the girls whatever they want. If you have time to eat, you're welcome to join us at the breakfast table."

He shook his head. "If I don't leave now, I'll be late, so maybe I'll stop by the bakery on my way to the store and grab a doughnut."

"That's not the healthiest breakfast, Adam. Wouldn't you rather take some fruit or a piece of toast along?"

At first, Adam's defenses rose. Who did Leah think she was, telling him what to do? But after he thought it through, he realized she was concerned for his welfare.

"Maybe I will grab an apple," he mumbled, moving into the kitchen and reaching into the bowl of fruit on the counter. With a quick good-bye to everyone, he picked up his Thermos full of coffee and headed out the door. He shouldn't have lost his temper or made such a big deal about the dog. From the way Coal had responded to Leah in the past, she'd probably have better luck taking control over the mutt than Adam did. It was too bad Leah couldn't be here all the time. But in order for that to happen, he and Leah would have to get married.

Adam thumped the side of his head. *I'd better get that idea out of my head. Even if I did propose to Leah, I'm sure she'd say no.*

CHAPTER 22

*A*my and Linda, are you two ready to go to school today?" Adam asked. Though this was the first day of school for Amish children in the area, most English kids wouldn't start back to their schools until next week.

The girls, who had just entered the kitchen, both shook their heads. "I don't wanna go to *schul*," Linda said in a whiny voice.

"Why not?" Adam asked. "It shouldn't be much different than the school you used to go to." As soon as Adam mentioned their other school, he immediately regretted it. *What was I thinking, bringing that up?*

"I'll miss Leah."

"Me, too," Amy put in. "And we hardly know anybody who'll be going to this school. Carrie's lucky 'cause she gets to stay here all day with Leah. She's our only friend right now."

Adam flinched. They obviously didn't think of him as their friend, but then did he really want them to? He was their guardian—a father figure of sorts—so it probably wouldn't be good if they saw him as a friend. The only time any of the girls had shown him affection was after the hummingbird banding, when Linda rushed up to give him a hug. That simple act had kept him whistling all afternoon. He wasn't quite sure how to respond to Amy's statement just now but was glad the girls hadn't gotten upset at the mention of their other school. He was also pleased that his nieces liked Leah.

Even so, they had to go to school, and he wanted them to enjoy it. Leah had said she would take Linda and Amy to school today, which meant Adam could leave for the store on time. He was having second thoughts about that now, knowing that if he took them it would give him a chance to speak with their teacher, Barbara Yoder. But maybe that wasn't necessary, since he had introduced the girls to her at church a few weeks ago.

Adam moved over to the refrigerator and took out a carton of eggs. *Maybe I shouldn't expect Leah to take Linda and Amy to school. I'm their uncle, and it's really my job, after all.*

Adam didn't know why he was going back and forth like this, but as he cracked open several eggs into a bowl, he made his decision. It would be him taking the girls to school this morning, not Leah.

"I hope I'm not late," Leah said breathlessly when she entered Adam's house. "For some reason, Sugar didn't want to do anything but plod along on the trip over here this morning."

Adam glanced at the clock on the kitchen wall. "You're not late, but I do need to head out pretty soon. I'll be taking Amy and Linda to school on my way to work."

Leah smiled at the girls, who sat beside each other at the table. "I'll come pick you up after school, so you won't have to walk." Truthfully, Leah felt that Linda and Amy were both too young to walk home alone. She felt protective of them—almost as if they were her own daughters.

"That's nice of you," Adam spoke up. "Maybe after the girls make some friends who walk this way, you won't have to pick them up anymore."

She smiled. "I don't mind, really, but if the time comes that they want to walk home, I'll be fine with that, too."

Linda's chin trembled as she looked up at Leah. "I don't wanna go to school; I'd rather stay here with you."

Amy nodded in agreement. "It's not fair that Carrie gets to be with you all day. Me and Linda are gonna miss out on all the fun."

"You'll have fun at school," Adam interjected.

Linda shook her head vigorously. "Uh-uh, we'll have to work."

"It won't all be work," Leah corrected. "Barbara Yoder is a wonderful teacher. You'll get to play games and have fun during recess, and learning about new things can be fun, too."

"Leah is right," Adam agreed. "And I'm sure you'll make some new friends quickly. I can almost guarantee that you will like your teacher, too." Picking up his lunch pail and Thermos, he added, "Now get the lunches I fixed for you, and let's be on our way."

Linda jumped up from the table and gave Leah a hug. Amy did the same. Leah felt sorry for the girls, and she would miss them. She was glad she would have Carrie to watch during the day and looked forward to when Linda and Amy came home after school.

"Remember now," she told the girls, "I'll be there to pick you up when school lets out this afternoon, and then you can tell me all about your first day."

That seemed to satisfy the girls, and with a wave, they followed their uncle out the door. Holding Carrie's hand, Leah stood watching as Adam helped the children into the buggy and backed his horse away from the hitching rack. At that moment, she knew exactly how her mother must have felt when she'd sent Leah and her brother, Nathan, off at the beginning of each new school year.

"Well, little one," she said, smiling at Carrie, "it's just you and me now. Should we find something fun to do?"

Carrie's eyes shone as she nodded. "Let's look for Chippy!"

It had been awhile since they'd seen the chipmunk, but maybe it was because all their attention had been on the hummingbird feeder. Once the hummingbirds had found the feeder, poor Chippy had soon been forgotten.

Leah patted the child's head then glanced at the kitchen sink, full of dirty dishes. Apparently Adam hadn't had time to do them before she'd arrived. "Maybe after a while we can go outside. Right now, though, you can color a picture while I wash and dry the dishes."

Cora looked around the small house she had rented just a mile outside of Arthur. Since it was fully furnished, she'd only brought the basic things they would need, plus their clothes and personal items. Once the house in Chicago sold, she would see about purchasing a home here, and then all of their furniture could be moved.

"I'll be heading to the clinic soon," Cora told Jared, taking a seat across from him at the breakfast table. She didn't realize that moving could be so tiresome, but then when she and Evan had moved into their house they'd hired movers, so everything had been done for them.

Pushing a piece of hair behind her ears, Cora closed her eyes for a minute. She was exhausted, not just from the move but from worrying about Jared.

"You're starting work already?" Jared asked.

She opened her eyes and nodded, noticing how much her son had changed since the divorce. His droopy jeans somehow stayed up without a belt. He wore them for days on end, until Cora insisted that he wear something else so she could launder his clothes. Then there was his hair. Jared was lucky to have a thick head of jet-black hair like his father's. When his hair was cut and styled, he was a handsome young man. But now he didn't seem to care how it looked, and it had become a shaggy mess. Jared's eyes were a vivid deep blue, like Cora's. These days though, Cora hardly recognized her son. Hopefully, once he got used to his new surroundings and made a few friends, that would change and he'd pay attention to his appearance.

"What am I supposed to do all day?" Jared mumbled around his piece of toast.

"For one thing, you can get your things unpacked." Cora reached for her cup of coffee and took a drink. "Since you'll be starting school next week, now's a good chance to get your room organized."

Jared wrinkled his nose, as though some putrid odor had made its way into the kitchen. "We've only been here a couple days, and I hate it already, Mom."

"A few days isn't long enough to judge whether you like it or not. I'm sure that once you start school, you'll make some friends and things will seem better."

"I ain't interested in making any friends—not in this backwater town where there's nothing to do."

"The correct word is *isn't*, and I'm quite sure there are fun things in the area for a boy your age to do. I saw a pizza place when we drove into town the other day, and your school will no doubt have activities after classes and in the evenings. Oh, and I saw a barber shop, too." She tapped his shoulder. "Hint, hint."

Jared grunted. "Whatever they have in this dinky town, I'm sure it's boring."

The *clip-clop* of horse's hooves could be heard on the road out front, and Jared glanced out the window. "Oh, I know, Mom. Maybe I could befriend some Amish kid, and we could ride around in a horse-drawn buggy. Now that would be a lot of fun, wouldn't it?"

Cora's jaw clenched. "You're being sarcastic."

"You never told me we'd be moving to Amish country," he said, ignoring her comment.

Living among the Amish wasn't what Cora had planned, either, but the pace would be much slower than it was back home, and she figured there'd be less chance of Jared getting into trouble out here in the country. And though they didn't know anyone here yet, Cora thought it wouldn't take long for both her and Jared to make new friends.

Leah hummed as she clipped one of Amy's dresses to the clothesline. Today had turned out to be quite nice—a good time to be outside in the fresh air. As part of her duties at Adam's house, she'd agreed to do the laundry for the girls. When she'd asked if he wanted her to wash his clothes, too, Adam's face had colored. "Don't worry about that," he'd said. "I've been washing my clothes for a good many years. Of course, if you'd like to wash the sheets and towels, I'd be okay with that."

Leah smiled, thinking how easily Adam blushed. Just the slightest word or look from her, and his face, and sometimes ears, would turn crimson. She wondered if he reacted like that to things other people said. But then, she was one to talk about blushing. Her face heated quite often these days, especially when she was around Adam.

Hearing Carrie calling for Chippy, Leah turned her head. She figured he was probably hiding under the woodpile or had left the yard and found a new home someplace else.

Woof! Woof! Leah smiled, seeing Coal run out to join Carrie on the lawn. But the child didn't seem interested in playing with the dog right now. She gave Coal a pat on the head then continued to call for Chippy, while poking around in the pile of wood.

Turning back to her job at hand, Leah concentrated on getting the rest of the clothes hung on the line. She was getting ready to clip the last towel in place when Coal started barking frantically. A few seconds later, Leah heard a blood-curdling scream.

Whirling around, she saw Carrie running across the lawn, waving her arms while she hollered, "*Ieme!* Ieme! They stung me bad!"

Instinctively, Leah dropped the towel and raced toward Carrie, knowing that if a person was allergic, even one bee sting could have serious consequences.

CHAPTER 23

*A*s Cora headed for work that morning, she realized the drive would take longer than she'd anticipated. In addition to other cars on the road, there were several horses and buggies. She would have to pass them at the first opportunity, or she'd be late for work. Cora had never understood why anyone would be content with such a slow mode of transportation.

Well, it doesn't concern me, and I can't think about that, she told herself. *I just need to make sure I'm not late for work.*

Moving her minivan toward the center lane and seeing that it was clear, Cora pulled out and passed two Amish buggies. Pulling back into the right lane, she sped up a little and was relieved when the clinic came into view. She'd actually made it with a few moments to spare.

Turning into the parking lot, she couldn't help but compare the small size of the building to the enormous hospital she'd left behind in Chicago. *Of course,* she rationalized, *this is a clinic, not a hospital.* It was adequate for this rural area and serviced the needs of the people who required medical assistance but weren't in need of a hospital.

Continuing to observe the building, while applying some lip balm, Cora had a feeling she'd made the right decision. Something about this small clinic appealed to her simple side.

Outside the clinic stood a few mature trees, and a rustic-looking picnic table had been placed under one of them. It would be a peaceful place to eat lunch every day—at least before the weather turned cold. Brightly colored mums in various shades were beginning to bloom among the shrubbery near the building, and two planters were positioned on either side of the entrance door. The building seemed unusually quiet, with no hustle and bustle of nurses, doctors, and visitors coming and going. If it weren't for the four cars in the parking lot,

Cora would have thought the place was closed.

Pulling down the visor for one last look in the mirror, she tucked her short brunette hair behind her ears. *Oh my, look at those eyes. I hope no one thinks I've been crying.* Cora's eyes were a bit bloodshot from not getting enough rest, so she quickly applied some drops from the bottle she kept in her purse. Stepping out of the car and taking a deep breath, Cora headed toward the doors that would open to a new beginning for her.

Once inside, Cora introduced herself to the office manager and was taken to the back of the clinic, where she met two doctors, as well as another nurse. Everyone seemed friendly and said they looked forward to working with her. Dr. Franklin, the older of the two doctors said that if she had questions or needed anything, to let him know. Already she felt at ease with everyone's relaxed attitude. It was a far cry from the constant buzz of activity Cora had become used to at the hospital in Chicago.

A short time later, a young Amish woman with a small child entered the clinic. Cora knew her day was about to begin.

Leah was relieved when she and Carrie were taken to an examining room right away. Even though Carrie hadn't exhibited any life-threatening symptoms from her bee stings, her little arms and legs were covered with raised welts, which she said itched and burned something awful. She'd also received a few stings on her neck and face.

"My name is Cora." The middle-aged nurse with short brown hair who had brought them into the room looked at Leah and said, "Do you know what kind of bees stung your daughter?"

Leah decided now wasn't the time to explain she wasn't Carrie's mother. All that mattered was getting Carrie the treatment she needed.

"They were yellow jackets," Leah replied. "Apparently they had built a nest under a woodpile, and when Carrie was poking around in there, she must have disturbed them."

"Has she been short of breath or had trouble swallowing?" Nurse Cora questioned as she took Carrie's vitals.

Leah shook her head. "Just itching and burning where she was stung. I gave her half a dose of an antihistamine while we were waiting for our driver to pick us up. I also applied ice packs that I'd wrapped in a towel to help with the swelling. If she'd had any trouble breathing or swallowing, I would have called 911 instead of bringing her here in a neighbor's car."

"Bringing her by car was better than horse and buggy," the nurse said before asking Carrie to open her mouth. "I don't see any sign of stings in there, so that's a good thing. Even a single sting in the mouth or throat could cause swelling and obstruction of the airway." She patted Carrie's shoulder. "Children are at increased risk for these types of breathing problems from a sting."

Leah nodded. "Yes, I know. That's why I brought her here to be checked out."

Leah was impressed at how well the nurse handled Carrie. The child seemed to relax because of the nurse's calming manner. Leah couldn't help but notice that Nurse Cora's complexion was flawless. But behind those blue eyes was a sadness similar to the sorrow Leah had seen in Amy all these weeks. *I wonder what might be going on in this woman's life.*

The doctor came in then, so the nurse stepped aside as he began to examine Carrie. When he told Leah that Carrie wasn't in serious danger, she felt relieved. But she was worried about what Adam would say when he came home from work and saw Carrie's arms and legs. She hoped he wouldn't think she'd been neglectful in watching the child.

Leah glanced at the clock on the far wall. Her other concern was that she might be late picking Amy and Linda up from school.

As Adam worked at the back of his store, putting new inventory on the shelves, he thought about Leah and how the girls had reacted to her this morning. They were clearly becoming attached to her, and he couldn't blame them. With no mother to nurture them and with him making a weak attempt at filling their father's role, the children were starved for attention and in need of a parent's guidance and love.

Taking the girls to school this morning had been difficult. Riding in silence, he hadn't been able to find the right words to ease their apprehension about going to a new school. Bravely, though, they had walked beside him while he took them inside to meet the teacher. Linda had even reached up to take his hand. At that moment, he'd felt more like a father than the uncle he truly was. Being a father figure was harder than Adam had ever imagined. He never quite knew if he was saying or doing the right things. *If Mary could see how things are going with me and the girls, would she regret having asked me to take care of them?*

Adam pushed a box of hammers closer to the shelf where he was working. *I wonder what Leah would say if I asked her to marry me. It would be a marriage of convenience of course, because I'm sure she doesn't love me.* Weighing the idea further, he pursed his lips. *Would she think I've lost my mind if I brought up the subject? It would be in the girls' best interest if they had a substitute mother. Having Leah there full-time to cook, clean, do laundry, and take care of the girls would take a lot of pressure off me.*

As Adam continued to stock the shelves, he let the idea of marriage roll around in his head. He'd been opposed to finding a wife all these years because of his mother's abandonment, but Leah seemed grounded in her faith. He was fairly certain that if she had any plans of leaving their Amish community, she would have done so by now.

Maybe I should talk to someone about this—see if they think Leah might be willing to marry me. But who? Adam's mind raced, searching for answers. He could speak to Ben about this, since they'd gotten to know each other fairly well, but then Ben wasn't that well acquainted with Leah. *I might talk to Ben about my mother, though. It would feel good to share the feelings I've kept bottled up all these years with someone I can trust.*

Finished with his task, Adam rose to his feet and took the empty boxes to the storage room. When he stepped out again, he nearly bumped into Elaine Schrock, one of Leah's closest friends. If he could talk to anyone about Leah, it would be Elaine.

"I'm glad you're here, Elaine," Adam said. "If you have a few minutes, could I talk to you?"

She smiled up at him. "Sure, Adam. I came in to get some birdseed, but I'm not in a hurry."

Adam gestured to his office. "Could we talk in there? I don't want anyone to hear our conversation."

"I guess that would be okay." Elaine glanced around before taking a few hesitant steps in that direction.

Adam entered his office and motioned for her to take a seat at his desk.

"Don't you want to sit there?" she asked, barely meeting his gaze.

"No, that's okay; I'll just stand." While Elaine took a seat, Adam positioned himself in front of the desk, where he could look directly at her. He wanted to see the expression on her face when he asked his question.

Moistening his lips, Adam spoke quickly, before he lost his nerve. "I need to ask you something. It's about Leah."

"If it's about Leah, then shouldn't you be talking to her?"

He shook his head. "I'd rather not talk to her until I know how she might respond."

Elaine leaned forward, resting her arms on Adam's desk. "I can't really speak for Leah, but what is it you want to know?"

"Do you think she would agree to marry me?"

Elaine touched her fingers against her parted lips. "I knew Leah had been watching your nieces, but I didn't realize you two had been courting."

A tingling sensation crept up the back of Adam's neck. How was he going to explain this to Elaine? It was so embarrassing.

"Well, uh. . .we're not exactly courting." He paused and swallowed a couple times. "Actually, we're not courting at all."

"Then why would you be thinking of marriage?"

Adam shifted nervously, giving his shirt collar a tug. "Well, umm. . .the thing is. . ."

"Oh, wait! I think I get it." Elaine pushed her chair aside and stood. "You want Leah to marry you so she can take care of the girls all the time; not just when you're here working. Am I right?"

Adam nodded. "I know it may seem selfish, but I'm really thinking of Carrie, Linda, and Amy. In the short time Leah's been caring for them, they've grown attached to her."

Elaine's eyes blinked rapidly. "So if Leah agreed to marry you, your marriage would be based on need, rather than love?"

"Jah, but I do have a high regard for Leah. She's been good with the girls, and I believe she cares for them as much as they do her."

"Do you want my opinion, Adam?"

He nodded once more.

"You ought to talk to Leah about this, because I have no idea whether she'd be willing to marry you or not. I just know that if it were me, I wouldn't marry a man I didn't love."

When Elaine left Adam's office, he sat down at his desk and wiped his forehead with a hankie. This evening, when he got home from work, he would do as Elaine suggested.

CHAPTER 24

*W*hen Cora arrived home from work that afternoon, she went straight to the kitchen to fix herself a glass of iced tea. As she'd pulled into the driveway, she'd noticed that Jared's bike wasn't on the porch, and she figured he might have gone out for a ride. Looking out the kitchen window, Cora gazed into the backyard. She was lucky to have found this house to rent, even though it was rather small. Across the road was a cornfield that belonged to the farm sitting farther back. The rental agent had told Cora that the land this house was built on was once a part of that farm, but a good many years ago the owner sold off a section of the property and kept only what was on the other side of the road. It was peaceful, and even with the road out front, the meager traffic was made up mostly of horses and buggies.

I hope Jared gets home soon, because I'm hungry and would like to start supper, Cora thought, moving to the living room and plopping down on the couch. She took a sip of iced tea then set her glass on the coffee table. Yawning, she removed her shoes and stretched out on the couch. Even though there were no long corridors to walk at the clinic, she'd been on her feet most of the day, and they'd begun to ache. With one last peek at the cozy living room, Cora closed her eyes, letting her mind wander.

Things had gone fairly well with her first day on the job. The doctors seemed nice and weren't demanding, like a few of the physicians at the hospital in Chicago had been. The other nurse, Sandy, had been helpful, too. Compared to the hospital routine, the amount of patients that came to the clinic today had been few.

She thought of the little Amish girl she'd seen first thing this morning. For some reason, Cora couldn't seem to get that child off her mind. She hoped Carrie would be able to sleep tonight. Just one bee sting could be miserable, but Carrie had so many of them. It was good that she hadn't had a severe reaction. While the child's mother had shown concern, she'd seemed quite calm about it. Cora figured that was probably why Carrie hadn't overreacted, as she'd seen some children do when they were frightened or in pain.

Several other Amish people had come to the clinic today, in addition to a few people who weren't Amish. Living and working in this rural area would take some getting used to, but Cora felt that she'd made the right decision by moving here. Evan and his pretty new wife weren't about to leave Chicago and the private practice he'd worked so hard to establish. Cora couldn't live with the painful reminder that she'd been jilted by the man she still loved.

When the front door opened and slammed shut, Cora opened her eyes. "Jared, I'm glad you're finally home. Where have you been anyway?" she asked, stretching as she sat up.

He sauntered across the room and flopped into the recliner. "I rode around on my bike for a while, checking things out in town. Then I went to the pizza place for lunch."

"Do they have good pizza there?"

"It was okay."

"I'll have to try it sometime. Did you do anything else today?"

"Met this kid named Scott Ramsey. He's my age, and guess I'll be going to the same school as him."

Cora smiled. "That's good. I'm glad you've made a friend already. I'm anxious to meet him."

Jared shrugged. "Didn't say he was my friend. Just said I met the guy."

"Do you like him?"

"He's okay, I guess." Jared rose from his chair.

"Where are you going?" she asked in irritation. "I'm going to be starting supper soon."

"I'm going outside for some fresh air." As Jared shuffled toward the door, the hem of his jeans dragged on the floor. "It's hot and stuffy in here."

"That's fine. I'll call you when supper's ready. Oh, and you need to throw those jeans you're wearing in the laundry basket tonight. After they've been washed, I can hem them up a bit."

"No way, Mom! I like these jeans just the way they are," Jared called as he went out the door.

Cora rose from the couch with an exasperated sigh. *Whatever happened to the darling little boy Jared used to be?*

Walking back to the kitchen to start supper, she had to admit her son was right. It was a bit warm in here. Fanning her face, she opened the kitchen window then went back to the living room to open the front door. Thankfully, there was a screen door to keep the bugs out. Cora hoped this good country air would cool things off soon.

This little two-bedroom house was a far cry from the spacious home they'd left in Chicago. It didn't even have an air conditioner. Cora thought about buying a portable one and putting it in one of the windows, but fall was just around the corner and the weather should be turning cooler soon. For now, they'd get by with what they had.

Leah scurried about the kitchen, getting a snack for the girls. She'd been late picking Linda and Amy up from school and wanted to make sure their treat wouldn't be eaten too close to suppertime.

"Are you doing okay?" Amy asked, gently patting Carrie's arm.

Tears welled in Carrie's eyes. "Jah, but Chippy's gone."

"I'll bet he's hiding out in that pile of wood," Linda spoke up.

Carrie sniffed deeply, as more tears fell. "*Die ieme* will get him."

"I'm sure that Chippy won't be bothered by the bees," Leah said, placing a platter of cheese and crackers on the table for the girls. "He may even have left the woodpile and found another home by now."

"I don't think so," Linda said with a shake of her head. "Chippy liked our woodpile."

"If he is in there, he'll come out when he's ready." Leah poured each of the girls a glass of milk and joined them at the table. "How was school today? Did you make some new friends?"

"I did," Linda said around a mouthful of cracker. "Her name is Carolyn. She's the same age as me."

"I'm glad you made a friend." Leah looked over at Amy. So far, the child hadn't eaten a thing. "How was your day, Amy? Did you make a new friend?"

Amy slowly shook her head, as she fingered her napkin. "I miss my friend Mandy back in Nappanee."

"I understand," Leah said. "Good friends are special, and some friends we keep for the rest of our lives."

Amy heaved a sigh, dropping her gaze to the table. "Don't think Mandy and I will be friends for life, 'cause we live too far away now. I'll probably never see her again."

"Maybe Mandy and her family will come here to visit sometime. Or maybe you'll get to go visit her there," Leah gave Amy's arm a light tap. "In the meantime, it would be good if you made some new friends here."

Amy frowned. "Don't want any new friends. Never wanted to move here, neither. I wish things could be like they were when Mama and Papa were alive."

Leah's heart went out to Amy. The girl still grieved the loss of her parents. Amy's sisters did, too. Leah was sure that being here in a strange place with no special friends probably made it seem even worse.

"Who would like to help me make a tossed green salad for supper?" Leah asked, hoping a new topic might help.

"I will!" Carrie's hand shot up.

"Are you staying for supper?" The question came from Linda.

"No, but I thought a tossed salad might go well with whatever your uncle decides to prepare."

"He usually just fixes sandwiches or soup," Amy mumbled.

"Oh. Well a tossed salad would go with soup, don't you think?"

The two younger ones nodded their heads, but Amy sat staring at her glass of milk.

Leah left the table and was about to get the lettuce from the refrigerator, when Coal started barking from the porch. Leah liked it when the dog alerted her that someone was coming. She presumed it was Adam. She watched from the window as the girls' uncle stooped down to pet the black Lab. Although she'd never heard him say so,

Leah knew Adam liked the dog.

Soon after, Adam entered the kitchen. His cheeks were pink, and perspiration gathered on his upper lip. "Hello everyone." Deep wrinkles formed across Adam's forehead as he stared at Carrie. "What happened to you?"

"She got stung by bees," Linda spoke up before Leah or Carrie could offer an explanation.

Adam stiffened. "How did that happen?"

Leah explained how Carrie had gone looking for Chippy in the woodpile and disturbed a yellow jackets' nest. "Even though she didn't appear to have a serious reaction, since she had so many stings, I took her to the clinic to be checked out."

Concerned for his niece's welfare, Adam bent to take a closer look at the welts on Carrie's arms and legs. Then he looked back at Leah. "What did they say at the clinic?"

"Carrie was seen by a new nurse there first, and then the doctor came in," Leah replied. "He gave us some medicine for Carrie to take that will help with the swelling and said I should continue to put ice on the places where she'd been stung."

"You said the hive is under the woodpile, right?" Adam asked.

Leah nodded.

"I'll take care of this problem, once and for all!" Adam opened one of the kitchen drawers and took out a package of matches. Then he grabbed a can of kerosene and headed out the back door.

"Where're you going, Uncle Adam?" Linda called.

Adam glanced over his shoulder and saw that the girls and Leah were following in quick pursuit.

"I'm doing what needs to be done. Something I should probably have done long before now." Adam dashed into the yard, doused the woodpile with kerosene, and threw in a match. In an instant, the wood went up in flames.

"No! No!" Carrie shouted, running toward Adam before Leah could pull her back. "You're gonna kill Chippy!"

Adam's brows pulled together. "Chippy?"

"The little chipmunk that's been living in the woodpile. Remember when the girls told you about it?" Leah stepped up to Adam. "We haven't seen him for a while, so I think he may have found another home."

Adam gave a nod. "Guess I'd forgotten about him."

"Chippy! Oh, poor Chippy!" Carrie sobbed. Then Linda started crying, and soon Amy joined them.

Adam was flustered and didn't know how to make things right. In his state of confusion, he turned to Leah and said, "I. . .I really need your help with the girls. Will you marry me, Leah?"

CHAPTER 25

*L*eah stood in stunned silence, staring at Adam and wondering if he'd lost his mind. Surely he couldn't have meant what he had just said. Until now, he'd given no indication that he wanted to marry her. They weren't even courting, for goodness' sake.

She glanced at the children and noticed their wide-eyed expressions, as their tears were brushed quickly away. They were obviously as surprised by Adam's proposal as she was. Except for Carrie's hiccups after she'd stopped crying, not a sound could be heard. At this moment, the chipmunk was obviously far from their minds, but what were Adam's nieces thinking right now?

"Uncle Adam, are you and Leah getting married?" Linda finally asked, looking at him with astonishment.

Adam shuffled his feet a few times. "Well...umm....We are, if Leah agrees to it."

Rubbing the back of her neck, Leah looked at Adam and said, "I...I think we need to talk about this in private, don't you?" She couldn't imagine why Adam had suddenly asked her to marry him—especially in front of the girls. He certainly wasn't in love with her.

Adam's face turned a brighter shade of red as he nodded. "But I want to stay here with this fire a little longer to make sure it goes out. Why don't you go into the house with the girls? I'll come in when I'm finished out here."

"I have a better idea," Leah responded. "The girls can go inside and finish their snack, while you and I talk out here in the yard."

"Guess that would be okay."

Leah opened the back door and gestured for the girls to go in. They hesitated a minute before stepping inside. Then Leah joined Adam on the lawn and stood watching the fire. When the branches burned to glowing embers, Adam stirred through them with a garden rake.

"Let's sit in my buggy so we can talk without our conversation being heard," he suggested. "I can still watch the embers from there."

Leah nodded but turned her attention to the small pond at the far end of Adam's property. He'd told her once that the water was always cold, no matter what time of year it was. The pond was spring fed, and at the lower end, the water emptied into a small stream. Adam had said that even during the drought they'd had last year, the pond stayed full of water.

Right now, Leah wished she were a little girl again, because as warm as she felt, she'd like nothing better than to kick off her shoes, run down to the pond, and jump in. Suddenly, the air seemed so heavy, she could hardly breathe. *Those lucky ducks*, Leah thought when she noticed a pair of mallards swimming in the center of the pond.

"Leah, are you coming?"

Startled, Leah looked back at Adam. "I'll be right there." Her palms grew sweaty as she followed Adam across the yard. When they reached his buggy, she took a seat in the passenger's side, and he went around to the driver's side.

"Leah, I. . ." Adam paused and cleared his throat. "I'm sorry for blurting that out in front of the girls. It was stupid."

Leah tipped her head. "Which part was stupid—asking me to marry you or saying it when the girls were present?"

"The second one. . .or maybe both." Adam gave his earlobe a tug. "I mean, you might think I'm dumb for proposing marriage when we haven't even courted." Adam paused again, as though waiting for her response.

"I'll admit, you took me by surprise," Leah said. "I assume the reason you suggested we get married is because you're concerned about the girls and want them to have a full-time caregiver."

"It's true, but it's more than that."

Leah held her breath, waiting for Adam to continue. Part of her hoped, even wished Adam had asked her to marry him because he felt something for her. The truth was, she'd begun to have feelings for him. While she might not be in love with Adam, a friendship was forming, and if given the chance, she was sure it could turn into love.

"What else were you going to say, Adam?" Leah prompted, trying to control her uneven breathing.

"It's just that. . . Well, the girls have developed a fondness for you, and I've seen the way you are with them. I believe you must care a lot for my nieces."

"You're right. I've come to love Carrie, Linda, and Amy very much."

"As do I," he said. "That's why I want what's best for those girls. I believe having you as their substitute mother would be a good thing for all of them."

"What about you, Adam? What's best for you?"

He glanced at Leah, looked quickly away, and turned to face her again. "Clearly, you can see that I need help with the girls."

Leah released an exasperated sigh. "I know that already, which is why I've been coming over to help every day while you're at the store."

Adam undid the top button of his shirt then pulled the collar away from his throat. "You're making this hard for me, Leah."

"I'm not trying to be difficult. I'm just trying to understand how us getting married would be the best thing for me."

"Does the idea of marrying me repulse you?" His unreadable expression made Leah even more confused.

She shook her head slowly, unable to look away. "Of course not. But since we're not marrying for love, I have to wonder what kind of life we would have."

He paused, tapping his chin. "It would be a marriage of convenience, Leah. You can sleep in the guest room, because I wouldn't expect you to share my room."

"I see. And you would be fine with that?"

"Jah. Unless there comes a time that we both felt differently."

Holding her hands tightly in her lap, Leah forced a smile that she didn't really feel. This truly wasn't the type of proposal she'd romanticized about. Glancing over at the embers that had nearly gone out, she murmured, "For the sake of the girls, I will marry you, Adam."

"R–really?" he stammered. "How soon?"

"I think the soonest I could plan and get ready for a wedding would be the second week of November. That's less than three months from now, and I don't think our church leaders would approve of us getting married any sooner than that."

Adam drew in a deep breath, pressing his palms against his chest. "Danki, Leah. I promise to be a good provider for you and the girls."

Provider? Leah swallowed hard, as the reality of the situation hit her like a bale of hay falling from the loft in the barn. She had just agreed to become Mrs. Adam Beachy, but they would be married in name only. *What in the world have I agreed to? I've thought many times that I would never marry a man unless we had been seriously courting and were deeply in love. Oh my. I wonder what Mom and Dad are going to say about this—especially when I haven't even taken the time to pray about my decision.*

"Can we go tell the girls our news?" Adam asked, feeling like a sudden weight had been lifted from his shoulders. He could hardly believe that Leah had said yes to his proposal.

"I think that's a good idea," she responded. "Since they heard you ask if I would marry you, I'm sure they're anxious to learn whether I agreed to become your wife."

My wife. Adam let the words play over and over in his head. All these years he'd sworn that he would never marry, yet in a split second, here he was an engaged man. Could a marriage of convenience such as theirs really work, or was it wishful thinking on his part? For Carrie, Linda, and Amy's sake, he needed it to work, and he would do his best to make everyone happy and see that Leah had everything she needed.

She'd have to give up doing reflexology, of course, because she would be too busy for that once they were married. Adam wouldn't mention anything about that to Leah yet—not until after they were married. She may not be willing to give up something she thought was helping people. If he said anything now, it could be a bone of contention, and it might keep Leah from marrying him.

Adam stepped down from his buggy and went around to help Leah get out, but by the time he got there, she was already on the ground. "If you'll wait a minute, I want to pour a bucket of water on the ashes. I think the fire's almost out, but I want to make sure before we go inside."

"Sure, that's fine."

As Adam put water into the pail, he glanced at Leah. She was looking toward the pond again. *What is she thinking about? Is she watching those ducks, or wondering what she's agreed to? What was I thinking with a proposal like that? Shouldn't I have prayed about this first? Well, I can't take back my proposal now.*

Adam poured water where the branch pile had been. White smoke wafted through the air as the last of the embers sizzled out. "I think that about does it." He motioned to Leah, and they headed for the house. "Would you like to tell the girls, or would you prefer that I make the announcement?"

Leah stepped onto the porch and turned to face him. "Since it was your idea, I think you ought to be the one who tells them."

"You're right." Adam opened the door for Leah and then followed her into the house. Thinking the girls might be in their rooms by now, he cupped his hands around his mouth and shouted up the stairs, "Amy! Linda! Carrie! Would you please come down here? I have something I need to tell you."

"Adam, look at me a minute," Leah said, brushing his arm with her hand.

When he turned his head, she wiped her thumb over a spot on his cheek. "You had something smeared on your face. I think it was a piece of ash from the fire."

Adam ran a finger over the spot where Leah had made contact. Was the sudden flush he felt from her gentle touch?

"It's gone now." Leah lowered her gaze.

A few minutes later, the girls appeared. "We were watching out the living-room window," Linda said. "Saw you and Leah sitting in your buggy."

Carrie bobbed her head in agreement, rubbing one of the spots where she'd been stung.

Adam bit back a chuckle. When he glanced Leah's way, he noticed a smile tugging at her lips. Did she think it was funny that the girls had been spying on them?

"Why don't we all go into the living room so we can talk?" Leah suggested, ushering the girls into the other room.

"Good idea," Adam agreed, wondering why he hadn't thought of it.

After everyone had taken a seat, Adam got right to the point. "Well, girls, as you know from what I said earlier, I've asked Leah to marry me." He paused and waited, hoping at least one of them would say something, but they just looked at him with curious expressions.

Adam rubbed his sweaty palms along the sides of his trousers. "Leah said jah, so unless you object, we're going to be married in November."

"Do you have to wait that long?" Linda asked.

Adam glanced at Leah and noticed her look of relief. He was glad, too, that none of the girls had objected.

"It's not really that far off," Leah said, slipping her arm around Linda, as she sat beside her on the couch. "I'll need time to make my dress and complete some preparations for the wedding."

"Can I help?" Amy asked.

Leah nodded. "I'm sure there will be plenty that all three of you can do to help me get ready for the wedding."

Carrie climbed into Leah's lap. "Are you gonna be our new mamm?"

Tears welled in Leah's eyes. "I could never take the place of your mother, but I won't have to go home every evening once your uncle and I are married, and I'll love you like you were my very own kinner."

The girls seemed satisfied with that as they clustered around Leah, expressing their happiness at this news. Even Amy, although looking guarded, seemed okay with the idea.

Adam leaned back in his chair, suddenly exhausted. Maybe he'd made the right decision, asking Leah to marry him. Of course, he might feel differently in the morning.

CHAPTER 26

*L*eah could hardly believe Adam had suggested they invite their friends over for a bonfire on Saturday night. But here they were gathered around the fire by the pond, roasting hot dogs. The girls sat between them, and on the other side of the fire sat Priscilla with her boyfriend, Elam, and Elaine with Ben.

It was a cool evening, perfect for sitting around the fire pit. The end of August had a way of giving little hints of the fast-approaching autumn weather. One day it could be sweltering and uncomfortably humid, and the next, it could be the exact opposite.

The girls seemed to be having a good time, and after getting stung by all those bees, Carrie seemed to be healing well. Leah didn't think she'd ever forget the sound of little Carrie's screams that day. Thankfully, as with most children, Adam's youngest niece had recovered rather quickly.

Earlier, while Adam was gathering wood for the bonfire, Leah had stood watching the girls trying to catch frogs near the pond's edge. Their laughter, as well as the excitement they still exuded after learning about the upcoming marriage, put a smile on Leah's face. Already she felt as if they were a family. *How could this be wrong? Surely God would not object to me helping raise Adam's nieces, whom I already love so much.*

Leah had always enjoyed cookouts, especially roasting hot dogs over an open fire. But as the evening wore on, she found that with each bite she took, it was getting harder to swallow. Even with the hot dog on the verge of being burned and smeared with lots of mustard and relish, just the way she liked it, Leah couldn't seem to enjoy it. Somehow she managed to take the last bite. That little bit of happiness she'd felt earlier had been replaced with apprehension. Was it too soon to be announcing their news? How would her friends react when Adam told them that he and Leah were planning to be married?

Elaine sputtered as smoke wafted from the fire in her direction then lifted into the air. "Oh my!" She coughed. "I thought I might have to move my seat, but it seems to be better now."

Ben grabbed hold of her hand. "You know what I've always heard? 'Smoke follows beauty.'"

"Behave yourself." Elaine blushed while the others laughed.

Spending time with her two best friends had always been fun, and when times got tough, they'd been there for one another. But this evening, knowing the reason she and Adam were having this gathering, Leah felt tense and ill at ease. She couldn't stop wondering what Elaine and Priscilla would think of her sudden plans to marry Adam. She swallowed hard, getting the last mouthful of her hot dog down as she watched Adam stand up to make his announcement.

"I'm glad you could all be here this evening," he said, shifting his weight, as though unsure of himself. "Leah and I have an important announcement to make, and except for the girls and Leah's parents, you are the first ones to know."

With the glow of the fire, Leah could see that all eyes were focused on Adam as everyone got quiet. The only thing that could be heard was the croaking of a frog and the crackling wood in the flames of the fire. She held her breath, waiting for him to continue.

"Leah and I have decided to get married," Adam proclaimed. "The wedding will take place the second Thursday in November, and we would like the four of you to be our witnesses."

No one said anything at first, making Leah wonder if they all disapproved. Maybe the frogs approved, though, because now there was a chorus of them singing.

Finally, Ben left his seat and came around to shake first Adam's and then Leah's hand. "Congratulations."

Elaine joined him, and after shaking Adam's hand, she gave Leah a hug. But Leah suspected from the look on her friend's face that she had some misgivings.

Priscilla and Elam came next, offering handshakes and hugs as well. Priscilla's smile appeared to be forced, and Leah figured Priscilla wasn't happy to hear this news, either. Since she couldn't come right out and ask in front of the others, Leah decided to wait until she had a chance to speak with Elaine and Priscilla alone.

"Sure wish Leah could move in with us right now," Linda said after Adam handed her another hot dog to roast. "November's a long way off."

Leah reached over and touched the child's arm. "It'll be here before we know it."

"The girls are pleased that Leah and I getting married," Adam spoke up.

"I imagine they would be, especially since Leah's such a good cook." Elam bumped Priscilla's arm with his elbow. "Don't you think Leah's a good cook?"

Priscilla responded with a brief nod. Something was wrong, and Leah planned to find out what it was before the evening was out. Watching the tips of the flames as sparks disappeared into the air, Leah prayed that her friends would understand and be happy for her.

After everyone had eaten and the girls began roasting marshmallows, Leah gathered up the rest of the food and took it into the house. She was glad when Elaine and Priscilla came along, carrying some of the items.

"Are you in love with Adam?" Elaine asked the minute they entered the kitchen.

Placing the tray of food on the counter, Leah smiled and said, "Adam has many good qualities. I think he'll be a good husband."

"But do you love him?" Elaine repeated, setting her items on the table.

"Well, I..." Leah's face heated. "Adam and I are not in love, if that's what you mean, but we do respect each other."

Priscilla's gaze flicked upward. "Then you shouldn't have agreed to marry him."

"I agree with Priscilla," Elaine interjected. "I've always felt that a person should marry for love."

"I love Adam's nieces. That ought to count for something."

"Is that the reason you've agreed to marry Adam—because of the girls?" Priscilla crossed her arms in front of her chest.

"That's mostly the reason," Leah admitted. "He needs someone to be with the girls full-time. Even when Adam's at home, he has a hard time managing things."

"Have you prayed about this?" Elaine questioned.

"Well, not exactly, but I feel confident that—"

"So you're going to make the ultimate sacrifice and marry Adam in order to make his life easier because he can't take proper care of his nieces?" Priscilla uncrossed her arms and tapped her foot. "Look what happened when Elaine sacrificed her needs to take care of her grandma. She ended up losing the man she loved to another woman, who was more than happy to marry him, I might add." Priscilla's hands shook as she held them close to her sides.

Elaine's chin quivered and her eyes filled with tears. "I thought you understood why I broke up with Jonah. I thought you supported my decision to put Grandma's needs ahead of my own."

"I did, but. . ." Priscilla turned and fled the room.

Leah watched as her friend dashed down the hallway and into the bathroom, slamming the door shut behind her. Stunned by Priscilla's outburst and feeling sorry about what had been said, Leah slipped her arm around Elaine's waist. "I'm sure Priscilla didn't mean to hurt you. She's just concerned about me marrying Adam and doesn't want me to sacrifice my own needs."

Elaine sniffed. "I don't regret caring for Grandma. Jonah is happy being married to Sara, and I'm glad for them. Someday, Lord willing, I'll find the right man and know the kind of joy Sara feels when she's with Jonah."

"What about Ben? He's been courting you for a while now. He seems quite attentive tonight, so I assumed you two might be getting serious."

Elaine twisted her finger around her head covering ties. "I enjoy being with Ben, but right now we're just friends."

"Friendship should always come first," Leah said. "Perhaps it will blossom into love." She cringed, thinking about her own situation. *Are Adam and I really friends?*

Priscilla leaned against the bathroom door, sobbing and berating herself for the hurtful things she'd said to Elaine and Leah. She didn't know what had come over her to spout off like that. Elaine and Leah were both good friends, and she'd never intentionally hurt either of them before. Yet that's just what she'd done.

Pressing her hands against her forehead, Priscilla tried to figure out what had just happened. *When Elaine broke up with Jonah, I tried to be understanding and supportive. So what made me say what I did just now? I should have just congratulated Leah on her engagement to Adam and shown support, even if I'm concerned about her reason for marrying him. And I never should have brought up the topic of Jonah to Elaine. She didn't deserve that.*

More tears fell as Priscilla came to grips with her feelings. As much as she hated to admit it, she was jealous because Leah would soon be getting married. All these months Elam had been courting her and he'd never said a word about marriage. Yet Adam hadn't courted Leah at all, and he'd asked her to marry him.

Of course, she reasoned, *he only asked her because he needs a wife— someone to take care of his nieces and cook and clean.* If Adam and Leah were deeply in love, she'd be even more envious. And it hadn't helped to hear Ben make that remark to Elaine about her beauty and then tenderly hold her hand. Priscilla felt even sorrier for herself. Elam had never said such sweet things to her, although he did sometimes hold her hand.

It wasn't right to envy her friends, and she should never have taken her disappointment and frustration out on them. Grabbing a tissue from the vanity, she wiped her eyes and blew her nose. She owed Leah and Elaine a heartfelt apology.

When Priscilla stepped into the kitchen, she found Leah and Elaine sitting at the table. "I'm sorry for the way I acted and the horrible things I said." She placed her hands on Elaine's shoulders. "I do understand why you broke up with Jonah, and I shouldn't have brought that up. I hope you will forgive me."

Elaine reached back and patted Priscilla's hand. "You're forgiven."

Priscilla touched Leah's shoulder. "If you feel that marrying Adam is the right thing to do, then I'm happy for you."

Leah smiled. "Danki. I appreciate that."

"It's hard for me to admit this," Priscilla said, taking a seat across from them, "but the truth is, I'm jealous."

Elaine's forehead wrinkled. "About what?"

"I've known Elam since we were kinner, and we've been courting for several months, yet he hasn't said a word about marriage. Makes me wonder if he's stringing me along until someone better catches his eye. Or maybe Elam only sees me as a friend."

"I've seen the dreamy way he looks at you," Leah said. "No man looks at a woman like that unless he cares deeply for her."

"Then why hasn't he asked me to marry him?"

"Perhaps he's afraid you'll say no," Elaine suggested.

Priscilla shook her head, gripping the tissue she held tightly in her fingers. "I wouldn't say no."

"Does Elam know that you love him?" Leah questioned.

"Well, he ought to. I think my actions have proved that. Surely he must realize that I would have broken things off with him by now if I didn't love him."

Elaine nodded. "But have you actually said the words?"

"Course not. That would be embarrassing. Besides, I think he should be the one to say it first, don't you?"

Leah shrugged. "I suppose so, but then I'm no expert on love."

"If my grandma were still alive, I'll bet she'd say, 'If you love someone, you ought to let them know; if not in word, then by your actions,'" Elaine put in.

"Is there something you could do to let Elam know you love him?" Leah asked.

"I'm not sure."

"Maybe you could cook a tasty meal and invite him over for supper," Elaine suggested. "You know what they say about the way to a man's heart being through his stomach."

Priscilla snickered. "I don't think that would get a marriage proposal from Elam. He's sampled my cooking several times, and even though he said what I fixed was good, he didn't mention marriage."

"You could let him know that you think he's handsome and strong," Elaine said. "His love language might be words of affirmation."

Priscilla's eyebrows lifted. "Love language?"

Elaine nodded. "There's a book about it. According to the author, certain things cause a person to feel loved. One is words of affirmation, and then there's—"

Linda tromped into the kitchen with her hands on her hips. Turning to Leah, she said, "Uncle Adam wants to know if you three are coming outside to roast marshmallows with us. He said if you're not, then he's gonna eat the whole bag himself."

Laughing, Leah pushed back her chair and stood. Elaine and Priscilla did the same.

"Guess we'd better get out there," Leah said, still chuckling, "because we sure wouldn't want Adam to eat all the marshmallows and end up with a *bauchweh*."

Linda shook her head. "No one likes to have a stomachache."

Feeling a little better about things, Priscilla followed the rest of them out the door and headed toward the fire burning brightly in the yard. She wasn't planning to tell Elam that he was handsome, but maybe there was something she could say that would let him know she thought highly of him. If words of affirmation really was his love language, maybe they would give him what he needed to finally pop the big question.

CHAPTER 27

*C*ora stood in front of the living-room window, staring out at the darkened sky. It was the last Friday of September, and Jared was spending the night with his friend Scott again. She had met the boy, as well as his parents, but wasn't sure if he would make a good friend for Jared. While Scott seemed nice enough, he wore his hair too long, dressed sloppily, and had so much dirt under his fingernails she wondered if he ever washed his hands. Of course, Cora realized that she shouldn't judge the boy by his looks. As long as Jared didn't get into any trouble when he was hanging out with Scott, she had no objections to their friendship.

Shivering, Cora pulled the collar of her pink velvet bathrobe tightly around her neck. It was a bit chilly this evening. She wished she'd thought to ask Jared to bring in some wood before he'd left so she could build a cozy fire in the fireplace. A small house had its advantages, for it didn't take long to warm things up with a roaring fire. But that wouldn't happen tonight, because Cora wasn't about to go outside and haul in wood. That would risk ruining the beautiful robe Evan had given her for Christmas last year. She fingered the silky ribbon decorating the sleeves. Evan had chosen pink because it was Cora's favorite color.

Tears trickled down Cora's cheeks as she reflected on that beautiful morning. If she'd only known then that it would be the last Christmas she, Evan, and Jared would spend as a family, she might have said or done things differently. Of course, looking back on it now, she wasn't sure what she could have done differently. If Evan wanted to cheat on her, she probably couldn't have done anything to prevent it.

Pulling her thoughts back to the present, Cora left the window and turned on several of her decorative battery-operated candles. She preferred them not only because they created the ambience of real candles, but they also were handy in case the lights went out and were safer than regular candles. A few of the battery-operated ones were also scented, which released a nice aroma into the room.

Taking a seat in the rocking chair, Cora leaned back and set the chair in motion. She and Jared had been here almost a month now, but she hadn't made any real friends. She couldn't count on Jared for companionship, either. After school when she got home from work, he was either in his room doing homework or making some excuse to be outside by himself. While he hadn't actually said the words, Cora knew he was still angry at her for moving to Arthur.

Thankfully, Cora's job at the clinic kept her busy during weekdays, but the weekends were the worst. She hadn't even made any close connections with the people she worked with at the clinic. During the day, as expected, most of the conversations were on a professional level; then after work, everyone went home to their own lives. Cora hoped that as she got to know everyone better, maybe some close friendships would form. In the meantime, she had suggested several things she and Jared could do together, including a trip to one of the nearby lakes, but he'd said he wasn't interested. Cora was convinced that her son didn't want to spend any more time with her than he had to.

Cora had tried to set things up with Evan so he could have Jared over the weekend, but Evan had said he had something else going on and he'd have Jared some other time.

"I'll bet you will," Cora muttered, clenching her teeth until her jaw ached. "When you walked out on me, you apparently deserted our son, as well." She stared into the flame of the flickering candle she had placed on a doily in the center of the coffee table. She loved the feel of velvet, and while rubbing her hand over the sleeve of her robe, she continued to think about Evan. They'd been so happy during the first several years of their marriage. At least, she'd thought they were. Evidently, she'd been too blind to see that he'd lost interest in her and had started seeing the other woman. *Maybe I'm just too naive*, Cora thought, remembering how her mother used to call her that. *I should have seen the warning signs when Evan lost interest in me.*

Because it signified happier times, Cora had almost gotten rid of the robe she wore this evening. But as she looked around at the few things she'd unpacked, just about everything Cora owned reminded her of the marriage she thought had been made in heaven.

Leaning her head against the back of the rocker and enjoying its soothing motion, Cora closed her eyes and allowed her mind to take her on a trip down memory lane. Back to when she and Evan were newlyweds. . . .

"Have I told you lately how much I love you?" Evan asked, caressing Cora's cheek with his thumb.

Her eyelids fluttered as her lips curved into a smile. "I think you told me an hour ago, but I never get tired of hearing it." She leaned into his embrace. "I love you, too, Evan."

"I can't imagine us being any happier than we are right now, but I think as the years go by, our love will grow even stronger." He kissed Cora's cheeks and her nose, and then his lips settled on hers, in a kiss so tender and sweet, Cora felt that it would stay with her forever. Nothing and no one could ever come between her and Evan. He was her soul mate—the man she was destined to marry. And this was the life she was meant to live.

Cora's cell phone rang, jolting her eyes open and bringing her memories to a halt. The phone lay on the small table beside her, and she quickly reached for it. Looking at the caller ID, she realized that it was her Realtor, so Cora answered the call. "Hello, Mr. Sherman. I hope you're calling with good news."

"No, not really," he said. "No offers have come in on your house yet."

"Then why are you calling me?" she asked a bit too sharply. This was not what she wanted to hear.

"The house has been on the market for a month now without even a nibble, so I think it might be time to lower the price."

"Lower the price?" Cora nearly jumped out of her chair. "Are you kidding me? That house is in top-notch condition, and it's worth every penny I'm asking for it."

"It may be worth that much to you, Mrs. Finley, but during the last open house I conducted, several people said they thought it was overpriced." There was a pause. "If you really want to sell your home, then I think we ought to drop the price by ten thousand dollars."

Cora's face felt like it was on fire. She needed every penny she could get. "Ten thousand dollars is a lot of money, Mr. Sherman!"

"Do you want to sell it or not?"

Cora could hear the impatience in his voice and knew she'd better give him an answer quickly. Drawing in a deep breath, she said, "Okay, you can lower the price by eight thousand, but I won't go down any more than that." Even as she spouted the words, Cora knew if the house didn't sell at the lower price, she might have to relent and let it go for even less. If it meant getting out of this dinky rental, it might be worth the sacrifice.

"Sounds good, Mrs. Finley. I'll keep you posted."

Feeling defeated, Cora clicked off the phone, turned the candle switches off, and headed down the hall toward her bedroom. Maybe things would look better tomorrow.

The next morning, as Cora sat at the kitchen table drinking a second cup of coffee, she stared at the tablet and pen in front of her. She needed to make out a grocery list, as well as record a few things she needed at the health food store. She glanced at the clock. It was a few minutes past ten. If she waited to leave the house until closer to noon, she could stop somewhere for lunch before doing her shopping.

Maybe I'll try out that pizza place where Jared met Scott awhile back. Since he found a new friend there, maybe luck will be on my side and I'll meet someone, too.

Cora knew that probably wouldn't happen, but the thought of a Canadian bacon with pineapple pizza sounded pretty good to her. If she bought a large size, she could bring the leftovers home for her and Jared's supper this evening. She'd told him to be home by three, so that meant he planned to be here for the evening meal.

Cora hurried to finish her lists and then gulped down the last of her coffee. She would take a shower, get dressed, and head out the door by eleven.

A chilly wind blew under the eaves of the porch as Leah stepped out to shake some throw rugs. Since Adam let his employees run the store most Saturdays, it gave her a chance to get some cleaning done at home. She'd been at it since early this morning and was almost done.

Arf! Arf! Arf!

"What's the matter, Sparky?" Leah looked toward the screen door, where the dog stood, peering out.

Sparky turned and ran through the house, barking. Then he came back to the door again.

"I know, boy, I miss her, too." Leah felt sorry for Sparky. Ever since Mom had gone to Wisconsin to help Aunt Grace, the little terrier had been watching for her return. He whined like a child crying on their first day of school, not wanting to be separated from their parents. If a dog could mope, Sparky had certainly been doing a lot of that lately. The other night Dad had laughed and said, "That dog's gonna wear a path to the door, watching for your mamm."

Leah glanced at the single feeder she had left hanging near the porch. It had been almost two weeks since they'd seen the last hummingbird. She smiled, remembering how just yesterday she'd mistaken a dragonfly for a hummingbird. She was surprised to have seen even that.

Alissa had suggested leaving at least one feeder out until closer to December. That way, she'd explained, any late-migrating hummers would have a place to stop and juice up before heading southward to warmer climates.

I'm sure going to miss those flying jewels, Leah thought as she scanned the yard, just in case. *Think maybe I'll treat myself to lunch in town. Then I need to make a visit to the Stitch & Sew to choose the material I want for my wedding dress.*

Leah knew she should have done that already, since the wedding was only two months away, but she'd been so busy taking care of Adam's nieces and trying to keep up with everything that needed to be done at home. With Mom still gone, Leah had taken on more responsibilities, although Dad helped out as much as he could when he wasn't working. Hopefully Mom would be home by the first week of November, so she would not only be able to attend Leah and Adam's wedding but could take over her household chores again, too.

Leah smiled, thinking about her folks' reaction to Leah's acceptance of Adam's proposal. Dad had simply said he thought Adam was a good man and that he hoped they would be happy. When Leah had called Mom and told her the news, she'd chuckled and said, "I'm not a bit surprised, Leah. Remember when I told you that I thought Adam was a handsome man? I figured it was just a matter of time before you saw that about him, too."

Leah shook the last rug and stepped back inside. *Surely Mom has to know I'm not marrying Adam just because he's good looking.*

Leah had actually been surprised when neither Mom nor Dad had questioned the reason behind Leah's hasty decision. *Maybe they're so relieved that I won't be living at home the rest of my life as an old maid that they don't care what made me decide to marry Adam.*

Leah placed the rugs on the living-room floor and headed to the bathroom to wash up. "I wonder if Adam thinks I'm pretty," she mused, glancing in the mirror. "I guess it doesn't really matter, but I'd kind of like to know."

After washing her face and hands and changing into a clean dress, Leah slipped her black outer bonnet on her head, grabbed her purse and shawl, and headed out the door. She would stop at the pizza place in Arthur for a quick lunch and afterward go straight to the fabric store.

CHAPTER 28

*C*ora tapped her fingers impatiently on the table as she waited for the pizza she'd ordered. It seemed like it was taking a long time. Maybe that was because she was so hungry. Her stomach growled noisily, and taking a quick scan of those sitting closest to her, Cora was glad that no one seemed to notice. The pizza shop was busy this afternoon, typical of the ones back in Chicago. Some folks came and went, picking up takeout orders, while others like her were eating in the restaurant.

A few teenagers sat at a booth in the corner. Cora noticed Jared wasn't among them. *I wonder what he and Scott are doing today.* Jared rarely talked about the things he and Scott did. As a matter of fact, Cora's son didn't share much of anything with her these days. But at least she knew who he was with, and having spoken to Scott's mother on the phone the other evening, Cora felt once again that Scott was a nice enough kid. His mother had mentioned that her husband had been out of work for a while but had found another job recently. It was one more reminder of how grateful Cora felt for her position at the clinic.

Turning her attention to a young Amish couple with two small children, Cora watched as they bowed their heads before eating. *How long has it been since I said a prayer?*

Cora smiled when one of the little boys, who couldn't have been much older than three or four, closed his eyes like his parents. Taking a closer look, Cora realized the boys were twins with the blondest hair she'd ever seen. When their prayer was over, one of the boys looked at her and grinned. She returned his smile and gave a discreet wave. *I wish Jared was still that young and innocent. Things were much easier when he was a small child.*

Looking toward the counter where the pizzas were made, Cora's nose twitched. The aroma of pepperoni, onions, peppers, and sauces made her stomach rumble again. *What in the world could be taking so long to make my pizza?*

Cora glanced toward the door and saw a young Amish woman with golden brown hair enter the restaurant. Even though it had been several weeks, Cora remembered meeting her when she'd brought her little girl into the clinic.

Cora waved, and the young woman waved in response before placing her order. When she took a seat at a table near Cora's, Cora looked over at her and smiled. "Do you remember me? I'm Cora Finley—the new nurse at the clinic. We met when you brought your daughter in after she'd been stung by yellow jackets."

The woman nodded. "My name is Leah Mast, and Carrie's not my daughter. I take care of Carrie and her two older sisters while their uncle's at work."

"Oh, I see." Cora thought it was odd that Leah had said the girls' uncle, and not their parents, but she didn't think it would be proper to ask about it.

"If you're not waiting for someone, would you like to join me at my table?" Leah asked.

Cora didn't have to be asked twice. "It's no fun eating by yourself, and since I'm all alone, it would be nice to have the company." She scooped up her glass of iced tea and took a seat across from Leah. "How is Carrie doing now?"

"She's fine. We were relieved that she didn't have a serious reaction to the stings."

"Allergic reactions can be quite serious," Cora agreed.

"You're right about that. I practice reflexology, and one of the women I treat had a reaction to some walnuts awhile back, so I know how frightening things like that can be."

Cora's eyebrows lifted. "Are you a licensed reflexologist?"

Leah shook her head. "I'm not licensed, but I've been doing reflexology for several years. In fact, my grandmother taught me when I was a teenager. Since I don't charge a set fee, I'm not required to get professional training or be licensed."

"Don't you think you'd make more money if you could charge a set fee?" Cora questioned.

"I don't know. I've never really thought about it." Leah shrugged. "Besides, I don't practice reflexology just to get paid."

Cora leaned her elbows on the table and looked closely at Leah. She wanted to know what made this young woman tick. "Why do you do it, if not for the money?"

"I want to help others. I see my ability to help them feel better as a gift."

Cora reflected on that before responding. *Do I see my nursing abilities as a gift or just a way to make money?*

When Cora had finished her nurses' training, her focus had been on helping others, but she'd also needed the money she made—especially since she'd had to go into debt to pay her way through nursing school. There'd been no financial help from any of her family. Cora had been given no choice but to make it on her own—until she'd met Evan. Dr. Evan Finley had been to Cora everything that her family had never been. He'd understood her reason for wanting to be a nurse and had even paid for her to get more schooling.

Unfortunately, things were quite different these days. *Evan wouldn't lift a finger to help me now*, she thought bitterly. *All he thinks about is satisfying his own needs and catering to the whims of his pretty new wife.*

"Are you okay?"

Cora's thoughts scattered at the sound of Leah's voice. "Oh, um. . . Yes, I'm fine. Just thinking about the past—that's all. Sorry for spacing off like that."

"It's all right. I've done the same thing myself." Leah chuckled. "One little thing can get my mind wandering, and then my thoughts will start drifting."

Both of their pizzas came, and although Cora was starving, she waited patiently as Leah bowed her head for silent prayer.

How long has it been since I uttered a prayer of any kind, much less one of thanksgiving? she asked herself once more. *Well, God's never answered any of my prayers before, so why would He now?*

When Leah opened her eyes, she smiled at Cora and motioned to the personal-sized pizza she had ordered. "Feel free to have some of mine if you like."

"It's nice of you to offer, but I have plenty of my own to eat. In fact, I'll be taking the leftovers home, so if you want some of mine, please help yourself."

"This will probably be enough for me." Leah picked up a piece of her sausage and black olive pizza. "I ordered a small one because I'm not going directly home from here. As soon as I'm done eating, I'll be heading to the fabric shop to buy some material for my wedding dress."

"Oh, you're about to get married?"

Leah nodded. "In a couple months. The second week of November, to be exact. In fact, I'll be marrying Carrie's uncle."

Cora reached for her glass of iced tea and took a sip. "I'm sure Carrie will be happy about that. From what I witnessed between the two of you at the clinic, she seemed quite dependent on you."

"Yes, and since I started watching Carrie and her sisters, I've grown attached to them."

Cora heaved a sigh. "I wish my son, Jared, and I related to each other better. Seems like he's always looking for some excuse not to be around me these days. It all started when his father left me for another woman." Cora didn't know why she was telling a near stranger all of this, but it felt good to get it off her chest. "I think Jared blames me for the breakup."

Leah reached over and touched Cora's arm. "I'm sorry you had to go through that. I'll remember to say a prayer for you."

"Thank you." It was nice to know someone would be praying for her, because she sure wouldn't be praying for herself.

As Cora and Leah continued to eat, they talked more about Leah's reflexology.

"Would you mind giving me your phone number?" Cora asked. "My feet get sore sometimes from being on them all day. I'd probably benefit from a foot massage."

Leah hesitated at first, but then she reached into her purse for paper and pen. "I'll write my number down for you, but when you call, you'll have to leave a message, because our telephone is outside in a small wooden building that we call our phone shack."

"That's not a problem. I'll leave you a message, and you can return my call to let me know when you'd be available for an appointment. I'm so looking forward to having you work on my feet."

"Since I watch the girls during the day, I've been scheduling people's foot treatments during the evening hours," Leah explained.

"That's perfect for me since I'm working at the clinic on the weekdays." Cora didn't know if it was her imagination or not, but she felt as though she and Leah had made a connection today. Perhaps this young woman would turn out to be the friend she so badly needed. At the very least, Cora had found someone to massage her feet.

When Leah entered the fabric store a short time later, she spotted Sara Miller looking at some bolts of material. "Wie geht's?" Leah asked.

"I'm doing pretty well." Sara placed one hand against her protruding stomach and smiled. "In a few months the boppli should be here. Jonah and I are both getting anxious."

"I can imagine." Seeing Sara's excitement over having another baby caused Leah to feel a bit envious. She'd be getting married soon, but to a man who didn't love her. It wasn't likely that she'd ever have any children of her own. But at least she'd have Carrie, Linda, and Amy to help raise, and she looked forward to that. "Are you hoping for a *bu* or a *maedel?*" Leah asked.

"It really doesn't matter to Jonah or me whether we have a boy or a girl," Sara replied. "As long as the boppli is healthy."

Leah nodded. It did her heart good to see the joyful smile on Sara's face. She'd been through a lot and deserved every bit of happiness she could get.

"I'll bet you're excited," Sara said. "It won't be long until you and Adam will be getting married."

"That's why I'm here," Leah said. "I need to buy some material and get my wedding dress made."

"I'm pretty good with a needle and thread, so if you need any help, just let me know," Sara offered, rubbing her stomach.

Leah slipped her arm around Sara's waist. "Danki for the offer. I just might take you up on that if I can't get it done by myself."

Sara gave Leah a hug. "I hope you and Adam will be as happy as Jonah and I are."

All Leah could manage was a brief nod. *I wonder what Sara and other people in our church district would say if they knew Adam and I aren't marrying for love.*

As Leah moved on to choose her material, she thought about Cora and how sad she'd looked when she talked about her husband walking out on their marriage. It was distressing to think that anyone could get married and not keep their vows. Even if she and Adam never fell in love, divorce would never be an option for them.

CHAPTER 29

*A*dam rolled out of bed and glanced at the clock on his bedside table. He couldn't believe it was almost noon. He'd been awakened in the wee hours of the morning when Coal decided to go into barking mode. At one point, he'd been on the verge of getting up to check on things, but the dog had finally settled down. After Adam finally got back to sleep, he slept harder and longer than he normally did. It was one of those deep slumbers that put him in a fog once he finally woke up. Moaning, he stretched his arms above his head, trying to get the kinks out of his back from sleeping so long. "I'll most likely be paying for this all day," Adam mumbled, bending down to touch his toes. "Wonder why those girls didn't wake me up?" This was not the way he'd planned to start his Saturday.

Hurrying to get dressed, Adam noticed that the house was quiet as he ambled down the hall. Hearing nothing from the girls, he wondered if they, too, had slept in.

When Adam entered the kitchen, he halted. All three of his nieces sat at the table, eating peanut butter and jelly sandwiches.

"Uncle Adam, you missed breakfast, but you're just in time for lunch," Linda announced. She grabbed a napkin and wiped the end of Carrie's nose, where a blob of grape jelly had stuck.

Adam glanced at the clock and grunted. "Someone should've woken me up."

"I was gonna," Carrie spoke up, "but Amy said no."

Adam looked at Amy, but she barely gave him a second glance. She was too busy chewing her sandwich.

"She said you must be tired," Linda intervened, "so we just let you sleep."

"I would have gotten a good night's sleep if it hadn't been for Coal barking in the middle of the night," Adam explained. "Did any of you hear him carrying on?"

"I didn't hear anything. Did either of you?" Linda asked her sisters.

Carrie shook her head.

"Me, neither," Amy said.

"Guess it could have been something down by the pond that had him alerted." Adam figured the girls must have really been tired to be able to sleep through all that barking. He grabbed his straw hat and plunked it on his head. "I'd better get outside and tend to the animals. They probably think I'm not coming to the barn at all."

"Want me to help?" Linda asked. "I'm almost done with my lunch."

"That's okay. I can manage." Adam figured he could get the chores done quicker if he didn't have her trudging after him, asking a bunch of silly questions or stopping to play with the dog or one of the barn cats.

He watched as Amy took a napkin and wiped Carrie's hands and jelly-stained mouth. Then she cleared off the table and put water in the sink to do the dishes. Adam couldn't help thinking that someday the girl would be a good mother.

When Adam stepped out the door he nearly tripped over Coal, who lay stretched out on the porch. "Thanks for keepin' me awake last night," he mumbled, nudging the dog with the toe of his boot.

Coal lifted his head lazily and grunted. Then he stood, shook himself, and ambled into the yard with Adam.

Adam snickered when the dog yawned in a whinnylike manner. "Serves you right. Now you know how I feel when I'm tired and have to get up."

As Adam walked across the lawn, he noticed several bruised and battered apples. They were too far from the apple tree that was on the other side of the yard, so he figured the girls must have found the apples lying on the ground and tossed them onto the lawn. As soon as he finished his chores he'd go back inside and tell the girls that they needed to clean up the mess.

Nearing the barn, Adam halted, causing Coal to plow right into his leg. Adam couldn't believe it. The window closest to the door was shattered, with a good-sized hole in it.

"That's just great!" Adam jerked the barn door open and stepped inside. Going over to the broken window, he spotted a mangled looking apple on the floor. It didn't take a genius to realize what had happened. "Those girls are really in trouble now," Adam grumbled, rubbing the back of his neck. He stood, moving his head in a slow circular motion, which relieved some of his tension. "The least they could have done was told me what happened. But no, they just sat there at the table, looking wide-eyed and innocent."

Adam bent to pick up the apple, placed it on a shelf near the door, and fed the livestock. When that was done, he grabbed the apple and headed back to the house.

"Carrie! Amy! Linda!" Adam shouted when he entered the kitchen and found it empty. "I need to speak to you right now!"

A few minutes passed, then Carrie and Linda showed up. "Where's Amy?" Adam asked, struggling to keep his temper.

"In the bathroom. Want me to get her?" Linda responded.

Adam shook his head. "You and Carrie can go to the living room and take a seat. When Amy comes out, the four of us need to have a little talk."

The two girls looked at him strangely but did as they were told.

Adam followed them into the other room and seated himself in his recliner, while they sat on the sofa.

"Is something wrong, Uncle Adam?" Linda asked. "You look like you've been sucking on sour candy."

Adam folded his arms. "We'll discuss it when Amy joins us."

They all sat quietly, until Adam heard the bathroom door open. "Amy, would you please come into the living room?" he hollered. "There's something we need to talk about."

Amy shuffled into the room with a disinterested expression and flopped onto the couch next to Linda.

"I discovered a broken window in the barn, and this on the floor below it." Adam held up the apple. "There were also several apples on the lawn." He leaned slightly forward, squinting his eyes. "What I want to know is, which one of you did it?"

"Not me," said Carrie.

"Me, neither," Linda added.

Adam looked at Amy. If the younger girls didn't do it, then she had to be the guilty one.

Amy pursed her lips and shook her head determinedly. "I never threw any apples, and since Carrie and Linda said they didn't do it, you'd better ask someone else."

"There's no one else here to ask, unless you think the dog did it." Adam gripped the arms of his chair. "And none of you had better leave this room until the guilty party fesses up."

Carrie and Linda started to cry. Amy just sat, staring defiantly at Adam. "I'm not gonna say I did something when I didn't, even if you make me sit here all day. I won't say I threw those apples just to make you happy. Somebody else must've come into the yard and tossed the apples."

Adam groaned. He wished Leah were here today watching the girls. She had a better way of dealing with them than he did. Maybe he'd been too harsh accusing his nieces, but if they hadn't thrown the apples, then who?

Leah had been looking at bolts of fabric for a while when Priscilla and Elaine showed up. They'd promised to meet her and help choose the fabric for her wedding dress, as well as for the dresses they would wear as her witnesses. If Leah had planned the day better, she would have asked them to meet her at the pizza place for lunch, but that had been a last-minute decision.

"Have you found anything you like?" Priscilla asked.

"I'm thinking maybe this." Leah gestured to a bolt of olive-green material. "Green seems to go well with my hair color." She pointed to another shade of green. "I thought this might work for your two dresses."

"Whatever you think's best." Elaine smiled. "After we leave here, I'm going right home to get started on my dress."

"Same here," Priscilla said. "With the wedding less than two months away, there's no time to waste."

"You're right," Leah agreed. "Since I'm at Adam's on weekdays and have foot treatments scheduled on many evenings, I asked Adam if I can move my sewing machine to his house so I can sew during the day."

"What'd he say?" Elaine questioned.

"Said it was fine with him. After all, once we're married, I'll be moving all of my things to his place."

Priscilla bumped Leah's arm. "It's going to seem strange having one of us married and the other two still hoping."

"Don't worry. I'm sure it's just a matter of time before you and Elaine will have your wedding dates published during one of our church services."

Priscilla shook her head. "That might be true for Elaine, but I've about given up on Elam. I may look for someone else—someone who might actually be interested in marriage."

"Really?" Leah could hard believe Priscilla was giving up on Elam. "I thought you were going to give him more words of affirmation and see if that made him feel loved."

"I did, but it didn't work," Priscilla said with a huff. "Now let's pay for our material and be on our way."

Cora's head jerked when the front door opened. She'd been reclining on the couch since she got back from town and had nodded off while waiting for Jared.

"Do you know what time it is?" she asked sharply when Jared sauntered into the room, looking disheveled. His wrinkled shirt made her wonder if he'd slept in it last night.

"Sure, Mom. It's five o'clock."

Cora's jaw tightened. "What time did I ask you to be here?"

He shrugged and tossed his backpack on the floor near the door. "I can't remember."

"I said three o'clock."

He shrugged again. "So what's a measly two hours?"

Cora sat up. "It's not about the difference in time. It's about you learning to do as I say."

Jared sank into a chair. "Well, I'm home now, so that oughtta make you happy."

"It does, but I wish you had listened to what I said and come home on time." Cora studied her son, noticing that in addition to his shirt being wrinkled, it appeared to have several splotches on it. "What's that all over your shirt?"

He looked down and brushed at the smudges. "Nothing much. Scott and I had a fight with some apples. Guess I ended up with most of 'em on my shirt."

Cora frowned. "I'm sure Scott's mother didn't appreciate that."

Jared made no reply.

"Are you hungry?" she asked.

"Maybe a little."

"If you'll change out of those dirty clothes and take a shower, by the time you're done I'll have some pizza heated for our supper."

"Where'd you get pizza?"

"I ate lunch at the pizza place in Arthur today. There was a lot left over, so I brought it home."

"What kind is it?"

"Canadian bacon and pineapple."

Jared wrinkled his nose. "Not my favorite, but I guess it'll fill the hole." Scooping up his backpack, he meandered down the hall.

Cora sighed and rose from her seat. *If that boy moved any slower, he'd stop.* She was glad Jared had made a new friend since they'd moved here, but his attitude sure hadn't improved. Even his posture had an "I don't care" stance. He still hadn't gotten his hair cut, and even worse, he now wore it in a ponytail. *Think I'll give Evan a call and see if he'll have a talk with our son.*

CHAPTER 30

*T*hanks for seeing me on such short notice," Cora said as she settled into the recliner in Leah's basement.

"It's not a problem." Leah smiled. "You're the only person I have scheduled for this evening, so it worked out just fine. Often Monday evenings are pretty busy. I guess that's because things happen over the weekend to cause people pain."

Cora nodded. "That's exactly what happened to me. I was unpacking some boxes from our recent move and ended up straining my back. In hindsight, I think I picked up one too many boxes, and knowing that reflexology can help with something like that, I decided to come see you before I resort to muscle relaxers or pain meds."

"Do you ever see a chiropractor?" Leah asked as Cora removed her shoes and socks.

"I had a good chiropractor when we lived in Chicago, but I haven't found one here yet."

"I can give you the name of the one I go to," Leah offered. "Before you leave, remind me."

"Thanks, I will."

Cora reclined her chair, and Leah put some massage lotion on Cora's right foot and began massaging and probing, searching for sensitive areas. "You said you knew that reflexology can help with some back issues. Does that mean you've had foot treatments before?"

Cora nodded.

Leah was pleased to hear that. It meant Cora was a believer in the advantages of reflexology. *Unlike some people*, Leah thought as a vision of Adam came to mind. *Maybe after we're married I can make a believer out of him. He needs to stop being so narrow minded.*

"Is that spot sore?" Leah asked when Cora flinched after she'd touched a certain area just below her big toe.

"Jah, just a bit."

"Jah? Did you just say yes in Pennsylvania Dutch?"

Cora snickered. "Over half the patients we see at the clinic are Amish, so I've been trying to learn a few Pennsylvania Dutch words. *Jah* is one of the easier ones, right?"

Leah nodded. "Jah, it sure is."

Leah continued to work on Cora's right foot. When she finished, she moved on to the left one. "How are things with your son? Did he enjoy the leftover pizza you took home last Saturday?"

"The kind I bought isn't Jared's favorite, and it didn't do anything to help his attitude. Yesterday I gave his father a call and asked if he would have a talk with Jared." Cora sighed. "Of course, my request fell on deaf ears. Evan's only response was that he was too busy to talk right then. Oh, and then he said I needed to take a firmer hand with our son. Evan never seems to have time for Jared anymore. I guess other things are more important to him."

"It sounds like you have a lot of responsibility on your shoulders right now. Trying to be both mother and father to your boy must be difficult."

"You've got that right, and I feel like I'm failing miserably."

"I'm sure you're doing the best you can."

"I try, but it never seems to be enough." Cora closed her eyes.

As Leah continued to work on Cora's feet, she lifted a silent prayer on her behalf. Just the stress of what Cora was going through right now was reason enough for her back to have tightened.

"If this foot treatment helps, which I'm hoping it will, don't hesitate to call me again," Leah said.

"I certainly will, and danki for letting me blow off a little steam."

"Is that another word you learned from your patients at the clinic?"

Cora smiled. "Jah."

As Priscilla sat across the table from Elam at the pizza shop, a lump formed in her throat. When he'd suggested they come here tonight, she'd decided this might be a good time to break things off. Of course, if he brought up the subject of marriage, she would reconsider. The question was, what excuse should she give Elam for breaking up? She couldn't simply blurt out that she didn't want to see him anymore because he hadn't asked her to marry him.

Priscilla took a drink of root beer and stared at the pizza on her plate as she continued to mull things over.

"Aren't you hungerich? You've hardly touched your pizza." Elam gestured to her plate. "And you haven't said more than a few words since we sat down."

Priscilla set her glass down, watching the bubbles of the root beer rise. "I've been thinking." Not only was she holding back tears, but her stomach felt like it was tied up in knots. Pizza was one of her favorite foods, but tonight Priscilla could hardly eat. Since she'd known Elam so long, would she be comfortable with another suitor if one came along? After all, Elam was kind, and he'd been good to her. But Priscilla wanted more. She wanted marriage, children, and the chance to grow old with the man she loved. What if she broke up with Elam but never fell in love with anyone else?

"What are thinking about?"

Startled, Priscilla jumped. "Umm. . . I've been thinking about us."

"What about us?" Elam grabbed a slice of pizza and took a bite as melted cheese stuck to his lip. "Ouch, that's hot!"

"Are you okay?"

"I'll be fine. Just need to be more careful is all."

Satisfied that Elam hadn't been seriously burned, Priscilla continued. "We've been courting for some time now, right?"

He gave a quick nod.

"Well. . ." She moistened her lips. "Maybe it's time that we go our separate ways." There, it was out. Only trouble was, Priscilla didn't feel one bit better.

Elam's eyebrows lifted high on his forehead. "You're kidding, right?"

She shook her head, holding firm and hoping he wouldn't try to dissuade her.

"Why now, after all this time, do you wanna break up with me? I thought things were going along good between us."

"So did I, for a while, at least." Priscilla paused and cleared her throat. "But things are different now."

He plunked his elbows on the table and leaned closer to her. "How are they different, Priscilla?"

She turned her head, unable to look into his hazel eyes. This wasn't going well. She felt like she was backed into a corner.

"You care about me, don't you, Priscilla?" Elam reached across the table and took hold of her hand.

The feel of his warm skin and the sight of his tender gaze were almost her undoing. She did care about Elam, so how could she break up with him? Maybe if she stuck it out awhile longer, he would finally pop the question.

"Forget I said anything." Priscilla took a small piece of pizza. "I wasn't thinking right when I said we should break up."

A slow smile spread across Elam's face. "That's gut, Priscilla. Jah, real good."

Priscilla drew in a deep breath. *What have I done? Elam will probably never ask me to marry him, and I'll end up becoming an old maid. Maybe I should have broken up with him, but then, maybe I need to give him another chance.*

Before Adam went upstairs to say good night to his nieces, he decided to relax on the porch and watch the stars for a while. The sky was crystal clear, and the stars looked more vivid than ever. He felt like he could reach out and touch them. The Big Dipper hung low in the eastern sky and looked as if it were standing on its handle. The Milky Way stretched out overhead, with its twinkling pathway to the starry heavens.

Coal lay at Adam's feet, with his head tilted to one side and ears perked as a neighbor's dog started howling in the distance. "Don't get any ideas of running off," Adam warned. After a few seconds Coal laid his head down between his front paws and went back to sleep.

Reflecting on how his day had gone and how busy they'd been at the store, Adam was glad to be off his feet and relaxing at home. He was thankful that Scott Ramsey had come in after school to work a few hours before closing time. He'd ended up hiring the kid part-time, and Scott had turned out to be a good worker, except for the times his new friend showed up.

Adam wasn't sure who this kid was; he hadn't seen him around Arthur before. It could be that a new family had moved into the area and Adam just hadn't met them yet. Anyone new to these parts usually ended up coming into the store at some point.

Adam hadn't said anything when Scott's friend showed up the first couple times. And he really wouldn't have minded if the boy had been there to purchase something, but it soon became apparent that he only wanted to hang out. Adam didn't take kindly to the way this teenager kept Scott from doing his work. This afternoon, when the kid showed up again, it had been the last straw. Adam hated to do it, but he'd ended up saying something to Scott and his friend. The two boys had gone outside together. After twenty minutes passed, Adam went out to find them. If Scott wanted to get paid, then he had to work. Scott and the other boy, whom Scott had introduced as Jared, were pitching a football back and forth. When Adam told Scott that it wasn't the time to be fooling around and that he needed to get back to work, Scott said he was sorry and returned to the store. Jared, however, stood with a smirk on his face. A few seconds later, he finally stalked off, mumbling something under his breath.

Adam wondered if he should have said something more to the boy before he took off. He was obviously a bad influence on Scott.

Pushing his thoughts aside, Adam resumed his appraisal of the star-studded night. Looking up at the twinkling, sprawling sky, Adam thought of his sister. *Is heaven up there, somewhere?* he pondered. *Is that where Mary and Amos are? Can they see what we're doing down here? Do they approve of how I'm caring for their girls?*

Adam missed his sister and her husband so much. He hated to think that every year he would associate his birthday with their deaths. After all, they'd been coming to help celebrate his thirtieth birthday when the accident happened. Adam was never much on celebrating his birthday, and usually the day would pass like any other. Most people, except his sister and her family, didn't even know when it was.

If I had never been born, two precious lives would not have been lost, and three little girls wouldn't be without their mother and father, Adam thought with regret.

Coal got up and sat directly in front of Adam. Whimpering, the dog laid his head in Adam's lap.

"Somehow, boy, I think you can read my mind." Adam scratched behind the dog's silky ears. Wiping away a tear, he looked up at the sky. *Good night, sweet Mary. Pleasant dreams.*

Knowing he needed to make sure the girls had gotten ready for bed, Adam rose from his seat and went into the house.

He was about to head upstairs, when he remembered the letter he'd found in the mailbox this afternoon. Busy getting supper and doing evening chores, he'd forgotten about it. He hoped the letter would perk Amy up a bit.

Adam went upstairs, and seeing that Carrie and Linda were asleep already, he went across the hall to Amy's room. He knocked on her door, which was slightly ajar, and found her still awake, sitting up in bed.

"I have a letter that came today, and I thought you'd like to hear what it says." Adam sat on the edge of her bed.

"Who's it from?"

"Your friend Mandy's mother." Adam pulled the letter from his pocket. "Should I read it to you?"

Amy nodded.

" 'Dear Adam: We got your wedding invitation, and if all goes well, we should be able to attend. Mandy is excited to see Amy again, and we look forward to meeting your bride. Sincerely, the Burkholder Family.' "

Adam didn't know Mandy's family that well—he'd only met them a few times when he'd gone to Nappanee. But thinking it would be good for Amy to spend some time with her friend, he'd invited Mandy and her folks to attend the wedding.

A huge grin spread over Amy's face. It was the first time since his sister's death that Adam had seen her look so happy. He saw it as a sign that she might be on the road to healing.

At least he hoped she was.

CHAPTER 31

*O*ver the next few weeks, Cora saw Leah regularly for foot treatments. Her back felt much better, and her feet weren't nearly as sore, even though she wasn't getting reflexology specifically for that. The real reason Cora kept returning to Leah's was because she felt so comfortable with her. Leah had become the friend Cora needed so badly.

The young Amish woman was real, not phony, like some of Cora's so-called friends in Chicago. Leah was someone she could count on and even confide in. A few of the nurses she'd worked with at the hospital had been genuine, but none of them had as caring an attitude as Leah's. Whenever Cora talked about her problems with Jared, Leah offered a listening ear and promised to pray for Cora. Despite the fact that Cora didn't put much stock in prayer these days, it was comforting to know that someone cared enough to petition God on her behalf.

Cora had grown up with Bible knowledge, but she'd never really taken it to heart. As far as Cora knew, none of her siblings had ever strayed from their faith. Not like Cora, who had always been a bit of a rebel. Cora's father used to accuse her of being selfish and self-centered, which wasn't pleasing to God.

"Maybe Dad was right," Cora murmured as she pulled her car up to Leah's house. "Maybe that's why God doesn't answer my prayers—because my selfish ambitions displease Him so much."

Tears welled in Cora's eyes, and she looked in the rearview mirror to make sure none had fallen onto her cheeks. She would rather not go in to see Leah in a tearful state; she'd already shed more tears than she should have while telling Leah her woes.

Cora remained in her car a few more minutes, watching the sun's gradual descent in the west. The sunset's glow cast a beautiful radiance on the few leaves still clinging to the trees in the Masts' front yard. Some of the maples still had their autumn color, glowing with the brilliance of a blazing fire. The reflection it cast on all that it touched was breathtaking. Cora rolled down the car window for a better look, enjoying the sight. Inhaling, she could actually smell autumn in the air—that damp, earthy scent. Breathing deeply, she inhaled its fragrance.

A slight breeze picked up, creating a whirlwind of leaves, lifting them into the air, and just that quickly, floating them slowly back down to the grass. Some ended up wedged into the corners by the house, joining others that had already accumulated there. As Cora continued to watch, she couldn't help comparing the leaves to herself. Like the leaves clinging to the tree branches, Cora sometimes felt as if she was just barely hanging on. Her life had been a whirlwind, with so many highs and lows. Just when everything seemed normal and calm, something happened to ruin it all.

Recently, though, Cora had begun to feel as if she was drifting toward some kind of normalcy in her life, something she yearned for in the worst way. Cora felt more confident every day that she'd made the right decision to move to Arthur. She had a good job and was making a few friends. Even if Jared hadn't wanted this move, something about this area made her feel that she belonged here—in a place she could call home.

Cora dabbed her eyes with a tissue and opened the car door. Walking toward the house, she enjoyed the sound she made from shuffling her feet through dried leaves. Another gust of wind brought down more leaves, falling like big golden snowflakes. The chrysanthemums planted on the side of Leah's house and those still in planters on the porch added to the beauty of this wonderful season. Their purple, yellow, rust, pink, and white created a rainbow of color so pleasing to the eyes that Cora found it hard to look away. The breeze coming in her direction brought the flowers' musky smell to her nostrils. The odor wasn't as pleasant as some other flowers, but there was something about their fragrance that Cora enjoyed. It was a smell that described autumn.

Maybe someday when I'm able to buy my own place here, I can plant pretty flowers like this, too.

⌒∕⌒

"It's a bit breezy out there," Cora mentioned as she went down the stairs with Leah. She quickly ran a hand over her hair to put some wind-blown strands back in place.

"You are so right," Leah agreed. "We usually have all the leaves raked by now, but with the wedding coming up, we haven't had time."

Cora thought about offering her son's help with the leaves. It would give him something constructive to do and hopefully make him realize how good it felt to help someone out. But she didn't suggest it to Leah, knowing Jared would probably refuse. She could barely get him to do a few simple chores at home.

"How are your wedding plans coming along?" Cora asked as she settled herself into Leah's recliner.

"Fairly well. My dress is finished, the guests have been invited, and everything we'll need for the wedding meal has either been bought or rented."

"Will it be a large wedding?"

"Just a couple hundred or so."

"Will you continue doing reflexology after you're married?" Cora questioned.

"I hope so, but it will depend on what my husband has to say." Leah put more lotion on Cora's right foot and massaged the pressure points on her toes.

"I don't know why men think they have to decide everything for us." Cora frowned. "If a woman has a career or wants to do something special, he ought to respect her wishes."

"Did your husband respect your wishes?" Leah asked.

"Which husband? I've been married twice."

Leah's eyes widened. "Oh, I didn't realize that."

"I left my first husband because he tried to control me. Now I'm the one who's been left in the lurch, since my second husband left me for another woman." Cora flinched but not from anything Leah was doing to her foot. It was from the pain she always felt when she thought about the past.

"Your tone makes me think you have many regrets," Leah said, moving on to Cora's left foot.

Cora sighed so deeply, it came out as a groan. "My whole life has been full of regrets." She closed her eyes as a wave of painful memories washed over her. "I've never told anyone else this before, not even Evan, but my parents were Amish, which is truthfully why I'm able to say some words in Pennsylvania Dutch."

Leah's jaw dropped, and she sucked in her breath. "You were born Amish?"

Cora nodded, wondering what she had been thinking, blurting that out. Well, since she'd said that much, she may as well tell Leah the rest of her story. She had been holding in the things concerning her past life so long that she couldn't seem to stop talking now. It would feel good to get it all out. "I was born and raised in Lancaster County, Pennsylvania. I joined the church when I was eighteen and married an Amish man a year later. We had two children—a girl and a boy."

"In addition to Jared, you have a daughter as well?"

Cora shook her head. "I had Jared after I married Evan."

"So you have two sons and a daughter?"

Cora nodded and swallowed hard, hoping she wouldn't fall apart. "I haven't seen my Amish children in over twenty-five years, and I'm sure they've forgotten all about me by now."

Deep wrinkles formed across Leah's forehead. She stopped working on Cora's foot and just stared at her with a strange expression. "You left your Amish husband and your children?"

"Jah," Cora murmured, unable to meet Leah's accusing gaze. *I should have known better than to blurt that out. Now Leah thinks I'm a terrible person and our friendship will be over.*

Leah sat on the stool in front of Cora as though frozen.

Tears welled in Cora's eyes as she lifted her gaze to meet Leah's. "Please don't judge me until you've heard the rest of my story."

Slowly, Leah shook her head. "I'm not judging you, Cora. God is our one true Judge, and the Bible says we are not to judge others. If you'd rather not tell me anything more, that's fine, too."

Cora pulled the lever on the recliner and sat up. "No, I really need to get this off my chest. I've kept it bottled up inside for far too long."

Leah sat silently as Cora began telling her incredible story.

"I was barely eighteen when I got married, and, like you, I practiced reflexology."

"You. . .you worked on people's feet?" Leah asked, almost disbelieving. If Cora had been a reflexologist, then why hadn't she said something until now?

Cora's eyes blinked rapidly. "I can only imagine what you're thinking. You're probably wondering why I've kept this a secret."

Leah could only nod in response.

"At first, the fact that I used to practice reflexology didn't seem important enough to mention. Then later, as we got better acquainted, I was afraid if you knew I used to work on people's feet, you might think I was critiquing as you worked on mine." Cora paused to take a breath. "As far as me having once been Amish, that's a part of my life that I've tried to forget."

"But how could you forget that you had two children, whom I assume stayed with their father when you left?"

Cora nodded. "I never forgot Mary and Adam, though. Not for one little minute."

Leah's hands went straight to her mouth, stifling a gasp. *Is it possible that. . . Oh, no, surely not. It just can't be!*

"I want you to understand why I left my husband and children," Cora continued. "I wasn't satisfied just doing reflexology. What I really wanted was to be a nurse. Of course, Andrew, my husband, thought that notion was ridiculous. He reminded me often that in order to become a nurse, I'd have to leave the Amish faith. My desire to be a nurse was something I just couldn't let go. I pleaded with Andrew to leave with me, but he said no, that the English world was not for him."

It wouldn't be for me, either, Leah thought. *Especially not without my husband and children.*

"Andrew said that if I left, it would have to be alone. He would not allow me to take our children." Cora's eyes pooled with tears, and when Leah handed her a tissue, she wiped her eyes and blew her nose.

"I thought I could stick it out, for my children's sake, but I guess my selfish desires got in the way of sensible thinking. So one day when Andrew took the children for ice cream, I packed my bags, left a note, and called our driver for a ride to the nearest bus station."

"Where did you go?" Leah asked, still reeling with shock.

"Chicago. I found a job as a waitress in a small café and saved up my money until I had enough to begin my nurse's training. Soon after that, I met Evan. When we fell in love, I divorced Andrew and married Evan." Cora grimaced. "Of course, when I left the Amish faith, I was shunned, and I knew the stand the Amish take against divorce."

"It's biblical," Leah reminded.

"I know."

"How old were the children when you left?"

"Mary was eight and Adam was five."

"Did you ever go back to see them?"

Cora's head jerked as though she'd been slapped. "I tried to, but when I returned to our home in Pennsylvania, Andrew and the children were gone. They'd packed up and moved, and no one would tell me where." Cora sniffed deeply. "I'll probably never see Mary or Adam again. I can only imagine how Andrew has poisoned them against me, and I can't really blame him. Looking back, I realize I was a terrible mother." She paused to wipe away more tears. "I've lived a life full of bitter regrets and tried to hide it by focusing on my life in the English world. But, of course, I've messed that up, too."

Leah hardly knew what to say. She'd liked Cora from their first meeting and thought she was a nice person. Now having learned all this about her past, Leah's heart was torn. She felt sorry for Cora, knowing it must have been hard not seeing her son and daughter all these years, but at the same time, wasn't that punishment well deserved for abandoning her family? Leah knew from something Elaine had shared with her that Adam had told Ben that his mother had abandoned him and his sister when they were small children. It had to be more than a coincidence that Cora's children had the same names as Adam and his sister. Surely, this woman must be Adam's mother.

Should I say something to Cora? No, I need to wait until I've talked with Adam. Tomorrow was Saturday, so she wouldn't be watching the girls. Adam planned to take them all out to supper that evening, including Leah, so she would speak to him about this then. Perhaps Adam would want to meet Cora right away, to confirm that she really was his mother.

CHAPTER 32

*A*ll day Saturday Leah had trouble concentrating, and by five o'clock that evening she was a ball of nerves. Adam and the girls would be coming by any minute to pick her up for supper. Tonight, when the opportunity arose, she would ask Adam about his mother.

Leah wished her own mother were home already so she could ask her opinion, but Mom wouldn't be coming home until early next week. *The one thing I do know,* Leah told herself, *is that I shouldn't say anything about Cora in front of the children. A topic as sensitive as this must be raised to Adam alone.*

At the sound of a horse and buggy approaching, Leah peered out the kitchen window. *Maybe when Adam brings me home this evening I will get the chance. I'll let Adam know that I want to talk to him about something and suggest that the girls go inside and visit with Dad for a few minutes so we can talk privately.*

Watching as Adam's horse pulled his rig up the driveway, Leah's heart began to pound. She'd been looking forward to this evening until Cora had shared her story about abandoning her children. Now Leah looked on the evening with dread. How would everyone be affected by what she'd just learned? If Cora was Adam's mother, would a reunion be sweet, or could it go the wrong way? Would Adam accept his mother into his life again, or would he reject her? If Cora really was his mother, Adam had a stepbrother he knew nothing about. And poor Cora wasn't even aware that her daughter had been killed in a tragic accident. She also didn't know she had three precious granddaughters. And how would Jared feel, knowing he had an older brother who was Amish?

So many things hung by a thread, depending on what Adam said once she told him about Cora. Of course, it wasn't certain that Cora was his mother, but there were too many things that fit for it to be coincidental.

For the girls' sake, Leah would try to relax during supper and show them a good time. Since she and Adam would be getting married in two weeks, tonight was an opportunity for them to do something fun together as the family they would soon become.

"Leah, you're awfully quiet tonight, and you haven't eaten much of your pizza." Adam motioned to Leah's plate.

"Maybe she don't like plain sauce and cheese pizza," Linda said before Leah could respond.

Leah shook her head. "No, it's not that. Guess I'm just not real hungry."

"How come?" This question came from Amy, who'd been more talkative than usual this evening.

Leah reached over and patted Amy's hand. "I have a lot on my mind."

"I have a lot on my mind, too," Adam put in, "but it won't stop me from eating." He grabbed another piece of pizza and took a big bite, wiggling his eyebrows as he did so.

Carrie snickered and jiggled her eyebrows back at him.

"What's on your mind, Leah?" Amy prompted. "Are you thinking about the wedding?"

Leah shifted in her chair, searching for words that wouldn't be a lie. "That is one thing I've been thinking about." She picked up a slice of pizza and took a bite. "Guess maybe I should quit thinking so much and finish what's on my plate."

Carrie looked over at Leah and smiled. "I'm glad you're here."

Leah leaned over and gave Carrie a hug. "So am I." She felt so much love for Adam's nieces. That, in itself, made her look forward to becoming his wife. She just hoped things went well when Adam took her back to the house this evening and they had their little talk. If he didn't like what she said, would he call off the wedding?

"How are you feeling, Sara?" Jonah asked, his face a mask of concern. "I saw you wince. Are you in pain?"

"I'm having some cramping and lower back pains." She forced a smile. "This is how it went before Mark was born, so I'm pretty sure my labor has started."

"But you still have a few weeks to go. Do you think something is wrong?"

"Everything is all right, Jonah." Sara almost felt sorry for her husband as she watched him begin to pace. "It's quite normal if a baby is born a little early, or even a few weeks late, especially if the calculations are a little bit off."

Jonah's eyes widened. "Then we'd better take Mark to my parents' house and get you to the hospital right away."

She shook her head. "Not yet, Jonah, and don't look so worried. My pains aren't close enough yet. I'll let you know when, so just try and relax." Sara had to remind herself that this was a first for Jonah. She remembered how nervous Harley had been when she was in labor with Mark.

"I think I should at least take Mark over to my mamm and daed's place so when it's time to head to the hospital, we can just go there directly."

"Okay, whatever you think is best. I'll pack the things Mark will need to spend the night, and then you can deliver him right to their door."

"Maybe I should pack his things so you can rest," Jonah was quick to say.

She waved her hand. "There's no need for me to rest, Jonah. In fact, I'm going to walk around for a bit and see if I can get things moving along a little quicker."

He slipped his arm around her waist. "Now, don't get too carried away. I don't want you having the boppli while I'm gone."

"Your folks don't live that far away, and I don't think you'll be gone that long."

His cheeks and the back of his neck colored as he grinned

sheepishly at her. "You're right. I'm feeling kind of *naerfich* right now. Guess I'm not thinking straight."

She squeezed his arm. "There's nothing to be nervous about. Women have been having babies since Eve gave birth to Cain and Abel."

Jonah bent to kiss her cheek. "Jah, I know. But you're having *our* baby."

Smiling, Sara started down the hall for Mark's room, where he'd gone to play after supper. She was sure he'd be excited to know that he would be spending the night with Jonah's folks. Since they'd moved here from Pennsylvania and been able to see them quite often, Mark had become very fond of them.

As Sara neared the door of her son's room, she paused to pray. *Dear Lord, please help me have a safe delivery, and may this little one who's about to be born be healthy and a blessing to You throughout his or her life.*

"I hope you don't mind, but I'd like to speak to you alone for a few minutes before you go home," Leah whispered to Adam when he pulled his horse up to the hitching rack near her father's barn. "The girls can go inside and visit with my daed while we sit on the porch and talk."

Adam's eyebrows squished together. "You want to sit outside and talk? Don't you think it's a little chilly for that?"

"No, not really, but if you'd rather, we can sit here in the buggy."

Adam couldn't imagine what Leah had to say that couldn't be said in front of the girls, but whatever it was he figured he ought to hear it. He hoped she hadn't changed her mind about marrying him. Besides the embarrassment of having to call off their wedding, if Leah backed out, he'd be left with the full responsibility of raising Mary's girls. He'd already tried that and hadn't done so well.

"Adam, did you hear what I said?" Leah touched his arm.

He nodded. "Jah. If you want to take the girls inside, I'll wait here in the buggy so we can talk."

Leah climbed down, helped the children out, and then led them to the house. As Adam waited for her to return, he became even more apprehensive. *The girls will be so disappointed if Leah and I don't get married. They're all excited about having her move into our house, and I'll have to admit, I'm looking forward to it, as well.*

With regret, Adam realized that with the exception of his three nieces, he wouldn't have any family members at the wedding—assuming it took place.

Adam wished his father had lived long enough to really get to know his granddaughters. He was sure they would have loved him as much as Adam had. For a man to be both father and mother to his children had been no small feat, but somehow his dad had accomplished it. Adam wondered if Dad had ever wished he could have gotten married again after Adam's mother left and filed for a divorce. But that was not to be, because unless Adam's mother had died, Adam's father would not have been free to remarry.

I wonder if my mother is still alive. If so, has she ever thought of me and Mary? Adam's jaw clenched. *If she was selfish enough to walk out on her family, she probably never gave us a second thought.*

Startled out of his musings, Adam's head jerked when Leah stepped into the buggy and took a seat beside him. "Oh, you're back."

"Jah, and the girls seemed happy to visit with my daed. He's been working on a puzzle and asked them to help."

"That's good. Now what did you want to talk to me about?"

Leah cleared her throat. "Well, I've been wondering about something."

"What's that?"

"You have talked about your daed and how much you miss him, but you've never really mentioned your mamm."

A muscle on the back of Adam's neck knotted. "I don't talk about her because there is nothing to say. She walked out on me and Mary when we were kids, and we never saw or heard from her again."

"Jah, I know about that."

He quirked an eyebrow. "You knew before I said anything?"

Leah nodded. "Elaine told me."

"Elaine? How'd she find out about it?"

"Well, I think—"

Adam held up his hand. "No, don't tell me. It had to be Ben. He's the only one I've ever told about my past." He frowned. "Guess I should have known better than to trust him to keep my secret."

"If Ben told Elaine after you'd asked him not to say anything, then that was wrong," Leah said. "But when Elaine told me, she thought I already knew."

Feeling a headache coming on, Adam rubbed his temples. He couldn't help wondering how many other people Ben had told. If he didn't nip this in the bud, it wouldn't be long before everyone in their community knew about his past.

"Do you know your mother's first name?" Leah asked.

"She was always Mom to me, but when I asked Dad what her first name was, he said it was Cora." Adam looked over at Leah and blinked. With only the light of the moon shining into the buggy, he couldn't see her expression, but he heard her gasp. "Where's this conversation leading, anyway, and why'd you inhale so sharply?"

"What is your daed's name?"

"His name was Andrew. Why do you ask?"

"I think I might know your mother."

A cold chill swept over Adam. "What do you mean? And where and when did you meet this woman you think is my mother?"

"She lives here in Arthur."

Adam shook his head vigorously. "No she doesn't. If she did, I would know."

"She moved here recently." Leah placed her hand on his trembling arm. "After all these years, I don't think you would recognize her, Adam. I'm sure she wouldn't know you, either, since you were just a boy when she left. Besides, in your memory she wore Amish clothes. Now, she's every bit English."

"How do you know her? Did she talk to you? Where did you meet?" Adam's sentences were running together, as his mind whirled.

"Her name is Cora, and she's a nurse at the clinic. We met the day I took Carrie in after she'd been stung by those yellow jackets. I found out later that it was her first day working at the clinic."

"You met this woman you think is my mother that long ago and have never said anything to me about it till now?" Adam flexed his fingers until they bit into his palms.

"I didn't know who she was then, Adam. And you have never told me anything about your mother. It wasn't until she started coming to me for foot treatments that she started to open up about her recent divorce from her husband who's a doctor and lives in Chicago." Leah paused and drew in a quick breath. "When Cora saw me last evening for a foot treatment, she blurted things out about her past. It really took me by surprise when she said she used to be Amish but had left her husband and two small children to pursue a career in nursing."

Adam moaned as he leaned forward, letting his head fall into his outstretched hands. He remembered Dad telling him that his mother used to say working on people's feet wasn't gratifying enough—that she wanted to be a nurse. But he hadn't thought about that until now. What he also remembered was his mother massaging and pressing on his and Mary's feet, which she'd done the night before she left. That memory had left Adam with a sense of bitterness toward reflexology. He'd always associated it with something bad—something that had left him and Mary motherless.

Adam lifted his head. "Does the woman know about me—that I live here in Arthur?" he asked, wanting to know the answer, yet hoping Leah would say no.

"I did not mention your name. I wanted to talk to you about this first."

He sighed with relief. "That's good to hear."

"Adam, there's more." Leah placed her hand on his tense shoulder.

He turned to face her, wanting to hear what she had to say but at the same time dreading it.

"Cora said she had two children—a girl named Mary and a boy named Adam—and that she had tried to—"

"I don't want to hear any more!" White-hot anger rolled through every part of Adam's body, nearly scorching his soul. "If you talk to this woman again, please tell her to leave, because I never want to see her. Is that clear?"

Leah remained quiet.

"Leah, is that clear?" he repeated.

"Jah," she murmured. "But, Adam, I think maybe—"

"And you are not to mention anything to that woman about Carrie, Linda, or Amy. I don't want her anywhere near my nieces!"

CHAPTER 33

*L*eah sat on the edge of her bed that night, looking in the Bible for answers to her dilemma. It would be difficult not to tell Cora about Adam when she saw her again. But she couldn't do that without going against Adam's wishes. And if she told Cora about Adam and he found out, he'd be furious. This was not a good way to start a marriage.

Of course, Leah reasoned, *we're not starting it out the way most Amish couples do. The people I know who've gotten married were deeply in love.*

Leah swallowed hard. She never thought she would admit this, not even to herself, but until last night when she'd heard the anger and bitterness in his voice, she'd thought she might be falling in love with Adam. But since he didn't feel that way toward her and seemed unable to get past his resentment of Cora, Leah would hold her feelings inside. Adam would never know that she'd begun to have strong feelings for him. She must learn to be content as his wife in name only. For now it was enough to be a mother figure to his precious nieces.

Turning to a verse she'd marked in her Bible some time ago, Leah read James 1:5 aloud: "If any of you lack wisdom, let him ask of God, that giveth to all men liberally, and upbraideth not; and it shall be given him."

Knowing that it wasn't her place to tell Cora about Adam, she closed her eyes and prayed. *I need Your wisdom right now, Lord. Please help me keep my promise to Adam.* Leah paused, as another thought entered her mind. *And please soften Adam's heart so that he will willingly speak to his mamm.*

Basking in the glow of motherhood, Sara gazed at the precious baby in her arms. "What shall we name her, Jonah?"

With a look of pure joy, Jonah stared at their infant daughter, born just an hour after they'd arrived at the hospital. "I don't know, Sara. What would you like to name her?"

"I was thinking we could call her Martha Jean. Her first name would be after my mamm, and her middle name in honor of my good friend Jean Mast."

Jonah grinned. "That's a good idea. I'm glad you thought of it, and I'm sure those two ladies will be pleased."

"I had thought about using your mamm's name, but it might be a bit confusing with two *Sara*s in the family already, even if your mamm's name is spelled a bit different than mine."

"You're right, and I'm sure Mom won't have a problem with you choosing your mother's name." Jonah stroked the baby's cheek with his thumb. "I can't wait to see the look on my folks' faces when they see their new granddaughter for the first time."

Sara nodded. "I'm excited for my parents to meet Martha Jean, too. But since they live in Indiana and Dad might be busy with his business right now, it could be a few weeks before they can come here."

Jonah laughed. "From what I've come to know of your mamm, I'm guessing the minute she hears the news, she'll be packing her bags. I bet she'll want to be here to help out for a while, too."

"You're probably right." Sara sighed, rubbing her cheek against their daughter's downy head. "I can't believe the way God has blessed us, Jonah. It almost seems too good to be true."

Jonah clasped Sara's hand and gave her fingers a gentle squeeze. "It is true. We are blessed beyond measure, and I am so thankful."

Sara gently kissed the baby's forehead, amazed at the infant's dark wavy hair, a trait she'd inherited from her father. Sara could hardly wait to take Martha Jean home to meet her big brother. They were now a family of four.

Adam punched his pillow, rolling this way and that, unable to find a comfortable position. He'd gone to bed over an hour ago, but sleep would not come. He couldn't stop thinking about the things Leah had told him. It didn't seem possible that his mother was living right here in Arthur or that she'd been seeing Leah for foot treatments.

Maybe it really isn't her. But Leah said the woman's husband was named Andrew, and her kids were Mary and Adam, so it must be her. Sure don't know what I'd do if I came face-to-face with that woman, Adam fumed. *Of course, like Leah said, I probably wouldn't recognize her, nor would she know me. She could have come into the hardware store already, and I'd never have known it. This lady doesn't even know her own daughter has died. Wonder how she would feel about that.*

It was hard to refer to Cora as Mom, because she surely hadn't been a mother to him and his sister. Adam was almost glad Mary was safe in heaven and didn't have to deal with this unsettling news. *If Mary were still alive, what would she do?* he wondered. *Would she want to see this woman?*

When they were growing up, that was one subject Adam and his sister never really discussed. Oh, they'd talked about their mother leaving when it first happened, but as time went on, her name was hardly ever mentioned. And Adam had never asked Mary what she would do if their mom came back.

Why'd Cora come here, anyway, and why now? He continued to stew. *I should've thought to ask Leah that question. If I get the chance, I'll talk more to Leah about this after church tomorrow morning.*

Adam sat up, throwing his legs over the side of the bed. It was no use. He wasn't going to fall asleep anytime soon. Just that quick, he flopped back down on the mattress, covering his face with his hands. Why did this have to happen now, when everything with his nieces and with Leah had been falling into place? *Would this alter their wedding plans?*

Spreading his fingers and then clutching the sheets, he stared at the ceiling. *This is going to change everything. I'll be looking over my shoulder everywhere I go, wondering if Cora is near.*

Adam's thoughts took him back to his childhood. He remembered how hard it was going to school programs and seeing the other kids who had both parents in attendance. Adam had felt left out because he didn't have a mother like the other scholars. Some mothers would bring a hot lunch to school for everyone, while others brought cookies or some special dessert at certain times. One of their neighbors who sometimes watched Mary and him while Dad was working came to school a couple times with treats, but she wasn't their mother, so that didn't count.

Knowing he wouldn't be able to sleep and sick of reliving the past, Adam pushed himself back up. After slipping into his trousers, and pulling on a shirt, he quietly left the room, using a flashlight as his guide.

When Adam entered the kitchen, he turned on the gas lamp hanging above the table. If he were here by himself, he might have gone to the store, even though it was the middle of the night. There were certainly enough things to do to keep him busy. A new shipment of winter items had arrived, including snow shovels, salt pellets for driveways, more birdseed, suet cakes, and feeders, and they needed to be set out. Working might help take his mind off Cora, but with the girls sleeping upstairs, he couldn't leave them alone.

Maybe if I eat something I'll feel better and quit thinking so much. Adam opened the refrigerator and looked around. Nothing in there really appealed, until he spotted a chocolate-chip cheeseball Leah had made the other day and left for him and the kids to enjoy. He took it out, as well as a container of milk, grabbed a box of graham crackers, and took a seat at the table.

As Adam ate his snack, he thought of Leah. She was a good cook, kept the house clean, and was great with the girls. She was also kind and had a pretty face. He'd begun to have strong feelings for her, although he'd kept them to himself. But could she be trusted to keep her word and not tell Cora about him?

"The practice of reflexology is a complete waste of time," Andrew hollered as Cora stood at the sink peeling potatoes for supper. "And your idea of becoming a nurse is just plain lecherich!"

"It's not ridiculous," she countered. "It's what I've always wanted—even when I was a girl. I need to help others, and I want to be a nurse. What's wrong with that?"

*"Then you should not have joined the church or married me."
Andrew's face grew redder with each word he spoke, and Cora flinched
when he shook his finger at her. "You can help within our community if
you have this need."*

*"It's not the same, Andrew," she argued. "I could do things as a nurse that
I can't do here."*

*"I won't allow you to talk like this in my house where the kinner could
hear. What kind of example are you setting for them?"*

*Tears flooded Cora's eyes and dribbled down her cheeks. She hated it
when she and Andrew had words, and when he shouted at her like this, it
made her feel like packing her bags and running away to someplace where she
could never be found. She didn't understand why Andrew wouldn't give up
his life here and go English so she could follow her dream. But they'd had this
conversation before, and Andrew always remained firm. He was not going
to back down on his vow to God and the church, and he did not want Cora
to, either. She'd have to stay here and forget about nursing or leave without
him. Perhaps if she left, he'd change his mind and follow. It would be a test
of Andrew's love for her.*

*At that moment, Cora decided. Tomorrow when Andrew took the kids
to town for ice cream, she would make some excuse not to go along. While
they were away, she'd pack her bags, and by the time they returned home, she
would be gone.*

Drenched in sweat, Cora cried out as her eyes snapped open. She bolted
upright in bed. She'd been trapped in a recurring dream about events
that had actually happened to her. She felt as though she couldn't
breathe.

Pushing the covers aside, Cora climbed out of bed and quickly
opened the window. As a cool November breeze wafted in, she gulped
in several deep breaths. *I should never have told Leah about having once
been Amish and abandoning my husband and children. She must think I'm
an awful person, and probably talking about my past has brought on this
nightmare.*

Tap. Tap. Tap. "You okay over there, Mom?" Jared's muffled voice could be heard between the walls that separated their bedrooms. "I heard you scream."

"I'm fine, son," Cora muttered. "Just had a bad dream."

Holding her arms tightly against her chest, Cora gave in to the threatening tears. She'd done a terrible thing by abandoning her children, but she couldn't undo the past. Unless some twist of fate should occur, it wasn't likely that she'd ever see Adam or Mary again. But if somehow she did, she would apologize and beg their forgiveness.

CHAPTER 34

ow come you're not dressed for church?" Leah's father asked when she placed a cup of coffee in his hand the following morning.

She blinked against the harsh sunlight streaming into the kitchen. "I have a pounding koppweh, so as soon as I fix your breakfast, I'm going back to bed."

Dad's forehead wrinkled as he looked at Leah with obvious concern. "Are you grank? Maybe you've come down with the flu."

She shook her head slowly, so as not to aggravate the pain. "I'm not sick. It's just a bad headache. I don't think I got enough sleep last night, either."

"Maybe you're stressed out about the wedding next week." Dad set his coffee cup down and motioned for Leah to take a seat. "Are you sure you want to go through with this, Daughter? I mean, your decision to marry Adam was awfully sudden."

"It's not about the wedding." Leah poured herself a cup of coffee and sat in the chair across from Dad. She wished she felt free to tell him about Adam's mother. If she broke her promise to Adam and told Dad, he'd probably tell Mom when she got home tomorrow evening. And if Mom knew about it, she would no doubt tell someone else, because Mom had never been one to keep a secret.

"If it's not about the wedding, then why'd you have trouble sleeping?" Dad asked.

"Some nights are like that, I guess." Leah massaged her forehead, thinking if she gave herself a foot treatment it might help. "I'm afraid if I go to church today, my koppweh will turn into a sick headache, and I may throw up. Now wouldn't that be an embarrassing thing to do in the middle of church?"

Dad gave Leah an understanding nod. "Then you'd better go back to bed and take care of yourself. And don't worry about fixing breakfast. I'm perfectly able to make something for myself."

Leah felt relieved. As much as she'd looked forward to seeing Adam and the girls this morning, she needed to return to her darkened room and try to sleep off this headache.

Adam had a hard time concentrating on the church service, knowing Leah wasn't there. Had she been so upset by what he'd said to her last night that she'd stayed home from church in order to avoid him? Or could Leah have come down with something and be sick in bed? He could hardly wait until church was over so he could talk to Leah's father and find out.

Adam glanced over at Amy, Linda, and Carrie. Usually they sat with Leah, but since she wasn't here today, Adam had asked Elaine to sit with them. They seemed to be doing fine, for which he was glad. When snacks were given out to the younger ones, Carrie appeared to be quite content. Adam was thankful that Leah had good friends like Elaine and Priscilla. She'd told him once that they would be there for her if she had any need. They'd both been willing to be Leah's witnesses at their wedding, just as Ben and Elam had agreed to be Adam's. It should work out well, since Ben had been seeing Elaine, and Elam was courting Priscilla. He figured it wouldn't be long before both couples would be getting married.

Maybe we can all be friends and do some fun things together, Adam thought, letting his mind wander even further from the sermon that was being preached. Since he and Leah would be getting married, Adam figured it would be good for him to establish a few friendships.

Thinking more about the conversation he'd had with Leah about his mother, Adam wondered just how much Leah knew about Cora. He'd been so upset by the news that she was in the area that he hadn't let Leah finish telling him everything.

Sure wish I hadn't told Ben anything about my childhood. I'll need to speak with him about that after church.

Sometime later, Adam was roused from his musings when all the men around him stood. Church was obviously over, and he'd missed nearly all of it.

Not a very upright, Christian thing to do, Adam thought as he made his way out of Marcus Gingerich's barn. *I should have been paying attention, and I probably missed out on a timely sermon.*

"I'll keep the girls with me until you're ready to go home," Elaine told Adam as the men began to set up tables for their noon meal.

"Danki. I'll probably leave as soon as we're done eating. I want to drop by Leah's and find out why she didn't make it to church today."

"I've been wondering that myself." Elaine's voice tensed. "I hope she's okay. With your wedding coming up next week, she's been working too hard to get things ready. She may have worn herself out."

"You could be right. Leah's a hard worker and sometimes doesn't know when to stop and rest," Adam agreed. "She's taken on quite a bit in these last couple months."

"Hopefully after the two of you are married, she won't have quite so much to do. It's been difficult for her to watch the girls, keep up with everything at your place as well as her folks' house, and squeeze in time for her reflexology patients."

She won't be doing people's feet once we are married, Adam thought, but he didn't say anything to Elaine, because he didn't want her to tell Leah. Surely after they were married, Leah would understand his reasons for wanting her to quit practicing reflexology.

Seeing Leah's father on the other side of the barn, Adam excused himself. "I noticed that Leah's not with you today," he said, catching up with Alton. "Is she grank?"

Alton shook his head. "Said she wasn't sick—just woke up with a koppweh and didn't get enough sleep last night."

Adam frowned. "Sorry to hear that. If it's all right with you, I think I'll stop by after we're done eating and check up on her."

"I have no problem with that." Alton smiled. "If she's awake and feeling better, I'm sure Leah would appreciate seeing you."

Adam wondered if Leah's headache had anything to do with their discussion last night. Could Leah be as upset about Cora coming to town as he was?

"Hey, Adam, how's it going?" Ben asked, stepping up to Adam and thumping his shoulder.

"I was just going to come looking for you. Could we talk privately for a minute?"

"Sure, what's on your mind?"

"Let's go outside." Adam led the way and found a place on the other side of the yard where no one was at the moment. "Remember when I told you about my mamm running out on my daed when my sister and I were kinner?"

"Jah."

"I heard that you told Elaine about it, even after I asked you not to tell anyone."

Ben averted his gaze. "I'm sorry about that, Adam. Elaine and I were discussing you and Leah getting married, and it just sort of came out. I don't think Elaine will blab it to anyone though."

Adam's muscles tensed. "She already has. I found out last night that she told Leah."

Ben sighed and rubbed his chin. "Isn't Leah supposed to know? I mean, she'll be your *fraa* soon, and—"

"I never saw the need to tell her until last night. Then I found out she already knew." Adam wasn't about to tell Ben that Leah had said his mother was in the area. If he knew that, too, he'd probably tell Elaine and maybe some others. From this point on, Adam would be careful what he told Ben, and it sure wouldn't be anything about his personal life.

"It's about time you got up," Cora snapped when Jared made an appearance at noon. "What were you planning to do—sleep all day?"

Jared yawned and stretched his arms over his head. "Cut me some slack, Mom. You're getting yourself all worked up for nothing."

Cora's jaw clenched. "Don't talk to me like that, young man. I'm your mother, not one of your friends."

"Sorry," he muttered, while sauntering over to the refrigerator. Pulling out a carton of milk, he drank right out of the container and then flopped into a seat at the table.

Cora rolled her eyes. What had happened to the manners she'd taught her son? "Jared! Don't drink from the carton. How many times have I told you that?"

"You don't have to get so bent outta shape, Mom." Jared smirked. "There was hardly any milk left. See." He turned the carton upside down, and only a few drops dripped onto the table.

"It's still an unsanitary habit, and I wish you wouldn't do that."

"Thought I was saving you a glass to wash." Jared sauntered across the room and threw the empty milk carton away.

"Would you like me to fix you a piece of toast?" she asked, lowering her voice in the hope that she and Jared could have a sensible conversation for a change.

He shook his head. "Naw, I'm not that hungry. I'll just get some more milk and head back to my room."

"Please drink it from a glass this time."

"Yeah, okay. . .whatever."

Cora bit the inside of her cheek. If Jared hid out in his room all day, she'd be sitting here alone with nothing to do but feel sorry for herself. "I thought the two of us could go for a ride. Then maybe we can stop somewhere for a bite to eat."

Jared looked at Cora as if she'd lost her mind. "What's the big deal in going for a ride? That sounds really boring."

"Well, I just thought—"

"Scott and I planned on doing something today."

"Like what?"

Jared shrugged. "We're just gonna hang out."

Cora shook her head. "I don't think so, Jared. You saw Scott yesterday, and today is going to be our family day."

"Family day?" Jared jammed his hands into his jeans pockets. "We ain't no family anymore, Mom. Not since you made Dad leave."

Anger bubbled in Cora's chest. "I did not *make* your father leave! He's the one who wanted a divorce so he could marry someone else."

Jared finished the rest of his milk and set his glass in the sink. "I don't blame Dad for leaving. Listening to you yammering away all the time would make any man leave."

Cora's hand shook as she pointed at Jared. "Now, you listen to me young man, your dad left because—"

"I don't wanna hear it, and I'm getting sick of you bad-mouthing Dad all the time!" Jared tromped across the room, opened the back door, and stepped outside, slamming the door behind him.

Tears streaming down her cheeks, Cora sank into a chair and sobbed. She was almost at the end of her rope. Would things ever be right between her and Jared again? The other night, she had felt good about the decisions she'd made. But now, Cora wasn't so sure. Had she made a huge mistake leaving Chicago? Should she give up and move back or keep trying to make a go of things here?

CHAPTER 35

*L*eah, are you up?" Dad called from the hall outside Leah's bedroom.

"Jah, Dad, I'm out of bed," she responded. "Just putting my head covering in place."

"That's good, because Adam is here with the girls, and if you're feeling up to it, they'd like to visit with you awhile."

"My koppweh is better. Tell them I'll be down in a few minutes."

"Okay."

It pleased Leah that Adam cared enough to come by. Perhaps he had missed seeing her at church and stopped on his way home to check on her. She took one last look at herself in the mirror to be sure her covering was on straight and that no stray hairs stuck out. After smoothing the wrinkles from her dress, she hurried from the room.

Downstairs, she found Adam and the girls in the living room, visiting with Dad.

"We missed you at church," Adam said, rising from his seat on the couch. "Your daed said you stayed home because of a koppweh, so we decided to drop by and see how you're feeling."

As Adam moved closer to Leah, she could see such a look of concern in his eyes that it made her wonder if he might feel something more for her than friendship. *Don't be ridiculous*, she chided herself. *If Adam cared for me in a romantic sort of way, I'm sure he'd have said so by now.*

"I'm doing better," she said, smiling up at him. "A couple aspirin and a few hours' rest in a darkened room cured the headache."

"Glad to hear it." Adam motioned to the door. "Do you feel up to going for a walk? There's something I'd like to talk to you about."

Leah glanced at the girls, and seeing that they were occupied with some of her childhood books Dad had given them to look at, she said,

"That would be fine, Adam."

Leah slipped her shawl over her shoulders and followed Adam out the door. Then, taking a seat in one of the wicker chairs, she turned to him and said, "What did you wish to talk about?"

Looking more than a little nervous, Adam lowered himself into the chair beside Leah's. "Umm. . .guess here is fine for us to talk."

"Oh, I'm sorry. You wanted to take a walk, didn't you?" Leah couldn't believe she'd forgotten that. *I must be as nervous as Adam appears to be.*

"That's okay. We can talk here just as easy. It concerns my mother."

Leah waited quietly for him to continue, sensing that he was having a difficult time talking about this sensitive subject.

Adam clasped his fingers together and flexed them as he stretched his arms out. "I've been wondering why Cora came here to Arthur."

"She's recently gone through a divorce and was looking for a new start."

Adam snorted, as he tapped his foot against the floor of the porch. "Another divorce, huh? Why am I not surprised by that? If I could just find some way to get that woman to leave town, I'd feel a whole lot better."

Leah gulped. She wasn't sure how that could happen. With Cora working at the clinic, it wasn't likely that she'd quit her job and move. If she really was Adam's mother, then Leah wished Cora and Adam could meet and find healing from the past.

After Elaine finished eating at the Gingeriches', following their church service, she'd come right home and decided to rest, since she had no plans until the evening, when Ben would be coming over for a visit. Before lying down, however, she took out the rock she'd painted for Leah to see how it looked now that the paint had dried.

Painting rocks had always been a relaxing diversion for her, especially when she needed a break from her everyday routine. It was fun to see the transformation of an ordinary stone as it turned into something unique and pretty.

Elaine had found this particular stone among her collection of rocks she hoped to paint someday. It was one she hadn't really noticed before, but after looking at it closely, she realized the stone would be perfect for Leah. Along with the quilted pot holders and table runner she planned to give Leah and Adam for their wedding, the rock would be something special just for Leah—a gift from one good friend to another. It was because of her friend's interest in hummingbirds that Elaine had painted this unusually shaped rock. It was similar to the shape of a hummingbird. Even the piece that had been broken off left enough of the stone to resemble a beak. The rest of the rock was in the shape of outstretched wings, looking like most hummingbirds taking flight.

Thumbing through some magazines, Elaine had found a picture of a ruby-throated hummingbird, which she used as a guide for painting. It was nearly done, except for the hummingbird's red throat, which she would work on tomorrow.

Reclining on the living-room couch, Elaine let her thoughts drift. She thought about how busy she kept hosting dinners since Grandma died and how little time she had to herself these days. Although Elaine enjoyed having the tourists come to her home for a meal, it was nice having some time off to relax.

Elaine's thoughts continued as she reflected on all the memories she'd accumulated in this stately old house. Even the backyard, where her favorite swing still hung, held pleasant memories. Elaine had enjoyed that swing during her childhood, as well as during her teenage and young-adult years. Many times she'd dreamed there of a future with a wonderful man and children.

Her mind drifted back to a special night when she'd been sitting on the porch with Jonah, gazing at a beautiful sunset that had taken her breath away. Even after all this time, Elaine couldn't help thinking how different her life would be now if she had said yes to Jonah's proposal.

Today in church, she had overheard someone say that on Friday night Sara had given birth to a baby girl. If Elaine had said yes to Jonah that evening, perhaps she might have had Jonah's baby by now.

This isn't right, Elaine scolded herself. *I should not be thinking such thoughts. Jonah is happily married, and he's the father of a brand-new baby.*

He will never know how badly I'd wanted to say yes to his proposal that night. The timing just wasn't right.

Shaking her head to clear her thoughts, Elaine got up from the couch. *Things happen for a reason, and maybe it wasn't meant to be. Besides, now that Ben is in my life, I should be happy about that and enjoy his friendship.*

"Take it slow and easy now, Sara," Jonah cautioned when they entered the house. Sara clutched his arm as he carried their baby girl.

"I'm fine. Just feeling the need to sit while we introduce Mark and your folks to the newest addition in our family."

As soon as they stepped into the house, they were greeted by Jonah's mother. "Oh, let me have a look at that baby." Tears welled in Mom's eyes as she touched the baby's downy head. "How are you feeling, Sara?" she asked.

"I'm a little weak and shaky, but I guess that's to be expected," Sara replied.

"Go on into the living room and take a seat," Mom instructed. "Mark's in there with his grandpa, and I know they'll be excited to see you."

After Jonah saw that Sara was situated on the couch, he placed the baby in her arms and invited his dad and little Mark to come take a look.

"She's a nice-looking girl." Dad smiled down at the baby.

Sara motioned to Mark. "Come over here and meet your little sister."

With a dubious expression, he inched his way over to the couch. "Boppli?"

Sara nodded. "Her name is Martha Jean."

Mark reached out and touched the baby's small hand.

"I think he likes her." Jonah grinned.

"Of course he does. What's not to like?" Mom extended her hands. "May I hold her?"

"You sure can." After Mom took a seat in the rocker, Jonah picked up the baby and placed her in his mother's arms.

"When are your parents coming, Sara?" Mom asked as she began rocking the baby. "I'm sure they're as anxious to see this little girl as we've all been."

"I believe they'll be here by the end of the week." Sara yawned. "Excuse me. Guess I'm more tired than I thought."

"Why don't you go lie down in bed and rest awhile?" Jonah suggested. "You didn't get much sleep last night at the hospital, so a nap might be just what you need right now."

"You're right. Think I'll go rest for a bit. Bring the boppli to me if she gets fussy and needs to be fed." Sara rose from the couch and started across the room. She was almost to the door leading to the hallway when she let out a little gasp and fell to the floor.

"Sara!" Jonah shouted, dashing across the room, fear clutching his heart. Had she just gotten up too quickly, or was something else wrong?

CHAPTER 36

Sara's body was damp with perspiration, and her eyelids felt heavy, but she forced them open. "Wh–what happened?" she asked as Jonah's anxious expression came into view.

"When you were heading to our room to lie down, you fainted."

Feeling the familiar comfort of the pillow beneath her head and realizing that she was lying on her bed, Sara asked, "How did I get here?"

"I carried you." Using a damp washcloth, Jonah wiped the perspiration from her forehead. "You really gave us a scare."

"Where's the boppli?" Sara asked, rubbing her temples before trying to sit up.

Jonah put his hands on her shoulders and held her gently in place. "She's fine. My mamm's rocking her in the living room, and my daed's waiting to hear whether he should call 911 or not."

Sara shook her head. "There's no need for that. The doctor said I might feel a bit light-headed for a few days from a loss of blood, but I'm sure it's nothing to be concerned about. I probably got up too quickly and should have asked for some assistance instead of trying to walk to the bedroom by myself. I'm so thankful I wasn't holding the baby when I fell."

Jonah's mother stepped into the room just then. "How is she, Jonah? Do we need to call for help?"

"I'm fine," Sara replied before Jonah could respond. "But I'm kind of hungerich."

"Of course." Jonah's mother gave her forehead a thump. "Don't know what I was thinking. I should have offered to fix you something to eat or drink as soon as you got home. Little Martha's sleeping in Raymond's arms right now, so I'll just run into the kitchen and fix you and Jonah some lunch." She hurried from the room.

"I'd really like the *boppli* here with me," Sara said, looking up at Jonah. "She might wake up and need to be fed or have her *windel* changed."

"I'll get her." Jonah leaned over and kissed Sara's cheek. "Now please stay put and just rest."

When Jonah left the room, Sara closed her eyes and lifted a silent prayer. *Heavenly Father, please help me get my strength back soon so I can take good care of my family.*

An hour after Adam and the girls left, Leah heard Sparky barking. She had just let the dog out. "What in the world has that pooch so worked up?" She glanced out the living-room window and saw a car pull in. Normally, her dog was pretty docile and rarely barked when someone pulled into the driveway. Suddenly, Leah knew why Sparky was carrying on. She grinned, surprised to see her mother get out of the passenger side of the vehicle.

"Wake up, Dad! Mom's home!" Leah called.

Roused from his nap on the couch, Dad bolted upright. "Really?"

Leah nodded. "She just got out of her driver's car."

Dad clambered to his feet and hurried out the door. Leah was right behind him, struggling not to laugh at the way his hair stood up. Any other time, she was sure he would have taken the time to comb it, but he was obviously so excited to see his wife that he hadn't given a thought to the way his hair looked.

Though Mom and Dad rarely hugged in front of Leah, not to mention with Mom's driver in plain view, Leah was pleasantly surprised to see her parents embrace. She giggled, watching Sparky trying to get Mom's attention as he jumped up and down, pawing at her dress. It was as if he had springs on his feet.

"It's been too long, and it's so good to be home," Mom said, while Dad patted her back.

Leah held back until Mom pulled away and Dad went around to retrieve her luggage. She gave Mom a hug. "This is such a surprise. We didn't expect you until sometime tomorrow."

Mom smiled, giving Leah's arm a tender squeeze. "I decided to leave a day sooner than planned because I wanted to be here to help with all those last-minute things that will need to be done before your wedding."

"I appreciate that. How's Aunt Grace doing?" Leah asked.

"She and the boppli are fine. You'd hardly know she's recently had a baby. Grace was up the next day, acting like everything was normal. I'm so glad I was there for the birth and was able to stay awhile to help out," Mom said. "You should have seen the look on James's face when the midwife announced that it was a boy."

"Now they have five sons." Dad grinned, while wiggling his brows. "What'd they name the baby?"

"They chose Paul." Mom smiled. "I know James had mentioned that he'd like a little girl this time, but that was all forgotten when they put baby Paul in his arms. No father looked more pleased."

"I don't know about that." Dad chuckled. "I was pleased as fruit punch when I held Nathan and Leah for the first time."

As if in protest of Mom's lack of attention, Sparky sat down and started barking. "Come here, you sweet pooch." Mom leaned down with outstretched arms. "I missed you, too."

Dad and Leah both laughed as Sparky bounded into Mom's arms, almost knocking her down. Mom chuckled when Sparky slurped her cheek. "I'm guessing that even our hund must have missed me."

Tears sprang to Leah's eyes. "Oh, Mom, I'm really glad you're home. Dad and I have both missed you so much. And you're right, so did Sparky. We never heard so much whining going on. From the minute you left, and then every day after, he'd go to the window or sit by the door, waiting and watching for you."

Mom put Sparky down, and after sniffing her luggage for a bit, the dog sat right down on Mom's feet. "You know what they say: 'Absence makes the heart grow—'"

"My heart couldn't be any fonder of you—even if you never went anywhere without me." Leah gave Mom another hug. She couldn't help thinking about Adam's mother and how she'd abandoned her children.

What an awful thing to do. "I really appreciate having you as my mamm. You've always been so good to me and Nathan, and I want you to know that I'm grateful for everything you and Dad have ever done for us."

Sparky barked, as if agreeing with what Leah had just said.

Mom smiled. "I appreciate you saying that, Leah, but it's our responsibility, as well as privilege, to love and nurture our kinner. Your daed and I have always been thankful that God blessed us with two special children. We love you and Nathan so much and want only the best for you."

"I know, Mom," Leah said with feeling.

Mom clasped Leah's hand. "Well let's get inside so I can hear all about what's been going on around here since I've been gone."

Leah wished she felt free to tell Mom and Dad about Adam's mother, but she was sure Adam wouldn't appreciate that.

Elaine was about to doze off when she heard a horse and buggy outside. Getting up and going to the window, she was surprised to see Ben's rig coming up the lane. *He's here early. Did I misunderstand when he said he'd be coming by this evening?*

Elaine hurried to the door.

"I know I'm here a few hours earlier than planned," Ben said when she greeted him, "but I didn't want to wait till this evening to talk to you."

Ben's somber expression caused Elaine to feel concern. "Is something wrong? You look anxious."

"Nothing's wrong, really. I just need to talk to you about something."

"Let's go into the kitchen. I'll fix us some tea or a cup of coffee."

"Coffee sounds good to me."

Elaine led the way, and after Ben removed his jacket and hat and took a seat at the table, she poured them both some coffee.

"Hey, that's nice." Ben pointed to the hummingbird rock she'd placed on the counter. "Did you make it?"

"As a matter of fact, I did, and it's nearly finished. What do you think?"

"I've never seen anything like it before. That rock looks like a picture of a hummingbird I saw in a magazine once."

Elaine smiled. "Funny you should say that. I actually used a picture in a magazine as a guide to paint it. I think the colors match pretty closely to what that kind of hummingbird looks like."

"Very nice, Elaine. You've done a good job on it."

"Danki. The rock is going to be something special for Leah. She gets such enjoyment watching the hummingbirds that come into their yard every year. I thought she'd like something like this."

"I'm sure she will. That was thoughtful of you."

"So, what did you want to talk to me about?" Elaine asked, handing Ben his cup and taking a seat across from him.

Ben blew on his coffee and took a sip. "Remember when I told you what Adam had shared with me about his mother running away from home when he was a boy?"

Elaine nodded soberly. "That must have been hard on Adam, as well as his sister and their daed."

"Jah." Ben drank some more coffee. "I can't imagine living through something like that."

"Me, neither. As difficult as it was to lose both of my parents when I was a girl, at least they were taken in death and didn't leave the way Adam's mamm did."

Ben fingered the quilted placemat in front of him. "Adam and I had a conversation after church today. He found out from Leah that I'd told you what he'd shared with me about his mamm. Honestly, Elaine, I didn't think you would say anything to Leah about that."

Elaine nearly choked on the coffee she'd just started to drink. "Ach! You didn't tell me I wasn't supposed to say anything. I thought Leah already knew. I assumed Adam had told her. Is he *umgerennt* with me?"

Ben shook his head. "I think he was more upset with me."

"How are we going to fix this?" Elaine asked. "Would it help if I talked to Adam?"

Ben shook his head. "I don't think so. Just, please, don't tell anyone else what you know about Adam's past." He leaned slightly forward. "You haven't, I hope."

"No," Elaine was quick to say, "and I surely won't." She leaned back in her chair with a groan. "This isn't going to affect Adam and Leah's marriage, I hope."

"I don't think so. Before Adam headed out to check on Leah, he said he'd see me at the wedding."

Elaine sighed with relief. Now all she had to be concerned about was whether Leah had made the right decision in agreeing to marry Adam for the sake of his nieces. Above all else, she wanted her friend to be happy and blessed.

"There's one more thing I wanted to say." Ben clasped Elaine's hand. "I've fallen in love with you, and I know we haven't been courting even a year yet, but I was wondering if you would do me the honor of becoming my wife."

Feeling a bit dazed, Elaine sat there, unable to answer his question. She cared for Ben, and he'd become a good friend, but she wasn't certain that what she felt for him was love. Without a deep, abiding love, she didn't see how she could say yes to his proposal. "You've taken me by surprise," she said breathlessly. "Could I have a few weeks to think about it?"

"Jah, of course." He stroked her hand tenderly. "Take all the time you need."

CHAPTER 37

*W*hen Cora got off work Monday afternoon, she felt more tired than usual. On top of that, her lower back hurt again. It made no sense, because working at the clinic was a lot easier than trekking up and down the long corridors at the hospital in Chicago. While she'd had some trouble with her back then, it was nothing like what she'd encountered since she and Jared had moved to Arthur. She wondered if these back spasms had more to do with her stress levels than with being on her feet so much. Even though Jared had made a friend since they'd moved here, he wasn't doing well in school, and his belligerent attitude toward Cora was more than she could take.

I wonder if Leah would be free this evening to give me another reflexology treatment, Cora thought as she approached her car. She slid into the driver's seat, pulled out her cell phone, and punched in Leah's number. *Hopefully Leah will check her answering machine and return my call before the evening is out. But just in case, I think I'll stop by there after supper and see if she's free to work on my feet.*

Cora started her car and pulled out of the parking lot. Before she headed for home, she needed to stop by the hardware store she passed on her way to work and pick up some lightbulbs and an extension cord. Besides the outlets for the stove and refrigerator, the home she'd been renting had only one other outlet in the kitchen. She was getting tired of unplugging the toaster or coffeepot in order to plug in the electric can opener and blender. Maybe she should look for a power strip, too. That might work well, especially in the kitchen. Cora remembered how, in Chicago, Evan had used a power strip in his garage, and he'd said that it even protected against power surges.

"Chicago? Why am I even thinking about that place?" Cora berated herself. For some reason, that city had been on her mind lately. She had thought moving to Arthur would be the right change for her, but was she, once again, only thinking of herself?

Maybe I should have discussed it more with Jared and opened up to him about how I was feeling. But if I had, would he have even cared or understood?

Cora knew the reason she hadn't. She was sure that Jared's response would have been negative. And what good could have come from her expressing how she felt about the divorce? At the time, Cora thought she was sparing Jared the ugly details and an explanation of why she felt the need to start over at a place where she could use her nursing skills the way she'd always felt called to do. She couldn't really tell Jared that she'd wanted to move in hopes that it would solve his behavioral issues. That would have made him angry and perhaps even more belligerent. Cora had hoped that by now Jared would have adjusted to their new surroundings. She certainly felt comfortable and at home here. It was much more laid back than living in Chicago, but then, what kid would find that important? It didn't seem to matter to Jared. He complained that there was nothing exciting to do. Having too much time on his hands could get Jared into trouble. She was pleased that he'd made a new friend but wondered what the boys did and where they went when they spent time together.

In any event, Cora wondered if going back to the city would be the best thing for Jared. At least then his father wouldn't have any excuse for not spending time with him.

Although not keen on the idea, Cora figured she could probably get her old job back at the hospital or perhaps find something else in her field in the city. She could take the house off the market, and things would go back to the way they were before she'd come up with the idea of starting over in a new place. The more she thought about it, the more sense it made. She hadn't received even one offer on the house, and since Jared had become increasingly rebellious since the move, what was the point in staying here? She just wished that God, if He cared about her at all, would give her some direction as to what she should do.

When Cora entered the hardware store, she wandered up and down the aisles for a bit, curious as to what was for sale. Since there were just gas lamps overhead, it didn't take long for her to realize this was an Amish-run store. She'd just begun to browse, when a tall Amish man came up to her and asked if she needed any help.

"I'm looking for an extension cord and some lightbulbs, and also wondered if you have any power strips. But since this an Amish store, you probably don't have any of those, right?"

The young man raked his fingers through the sides of his thick blond hair, while giving Cora a quick shake of his head. "We never carried the power strips, but we did have some lightbulbs and extension cords for our English customers. Unfortunately we're out of those right now. You should be able to get all of the things at the hardware store in downtown Arthur, or even at the grocery store."

"Thanks. I'll head over to one of those places right now." Cora hesitated a moment. There was something familiar about this Amish man, making Cora wonder if she'd met him before. But that wasn't likely, since this was her first visit to this store. Of course, he could have been a patient at the clinic, she supposed.

"Is there something else I can help you with?" he asked.

"Umm. . .no. Guess I'll be on my way."

As the man walked away, Cora felt even stronger that she'd met him before. His dark eyes and striking blond hair, reminded her of someone she used to know, but who? Well, she couldn't waste time thinking about it now. She needed to finish running her errand and get home to make sure Jared was there. Then as soon as they'd had supper, she would head over to Leah's and see if she had time to give her a reflexology treatment.

"Have you ever seen that woman who was just here?" Adam asked Ben, after he'd finished waiting on one of their regular customers.

"What woman was that?" Ben asked.

"The middle-aged English woman with short brown hair. She came in looking for lightbulbs and an extension cord and mentioned something about a power strip."

"Did you tell her we were out of those things and to go to the hardware store in downtown Arthur?"

"Jah, I did. Said she could probably find what she's looking for at the grocery store, too." Adam tapped his chin thoughtfully. "It was kind of odd, though. She looked at me so strangely. Made me feel uncomfortable."

"Maybe she's new around here and has never seen an Amish man before." Ben chuckled. "Some of the tourists who stop by the store can't seem to keep from staring at us."

Adam nodded. "I've often wondered how they would like it if we stared right back at them."

"Or started asking a bunch of questions about their lifestyle," Ben added.

Adam shrugged. "Guess they can't help being curious, since we dress differently than they do, not to mention our slower-paced mode of transportation." He thought about the English woman again and wondered if she could be his mother. Adam quickly pushed that thought aside. *If she is my mother, wouldn't she have said something? Of course, how would she have recognized me? I'm not the frightened little boy she left behind twenty-five years ago.*

"Get a hold of yourself," Adam murmured after walking away from Ben. "You can't go thinking every English woman you see is Cora."

Leah had just ridden her bike up her parents' driveway, when a car pulled in behind her. Turning, she saw that it was Cora. *I wonder what she wants.* Leah parked her bike and waited for Cora to get out of the car.

"I'm sorry for just showing up like this, but I wasn't sure whether you'd check for messages this evening," Cora said, joining Leah near the barn. "My back hurts again, and I was wondering if you'd be able to give me a foot treatment."

Since she was hungry and wasn't anxious to speak with Cora again,

Leah hesitated. But she could see from Cora's pinched expression that she was truly in pain. Leah hoped during the treatment that there would be no mention of Adam. "Okay. Let's go inside. You can head on downstairs, and I'll join you there shortly."

Sparky rushed over to greet Cora, like he did whenever they had visitors. Leah watched as Cora bent down to pet the terrier. "You're sure a cute little fellow," Cora said when Sparky licked her hand. "I wouldn't mind having a dog like you." Cora gave Sparky's head a pat, and he seemed content with that, for he went back to his spot on the porch and lay down.

As Cora descended the basement stairs, Leah stopped briefly to say a few words to Mom and explain that Cora had come for a treatment. She then went over to the stove to see what was simmering, because something sure smelled delicious. Mom had made a pot of chicken-corn soup and had just taken a loaf of bread from the oven. The kitchen had such a wonderful aroma that it almost made Leah light-headed.

She smiled, glancing at Sparky, now lying by the stove. He certainly wasn't going to let Mom out of his sight for very long. Leah could understand that, for she was equally glad to have Mom back home.

"What about supper?" Mom asked, placing the bread on a cooling rack. "Surely you must be hungry, Leah."

"It's okay. I can wait awhile to eat. Cora's hurting, and I'm hoping a treatment will help. You and Dad go ahead and eat supper without me."

"All right," Mom said. "I'll keep some soup warming on the stove, and you can eat when you come up from the basement. Oh, and I made a blueberry pie this afternoon. We can have that for dessert." She chuckled. "Your daed was hinting last night about blueberry pie."

"Dad's always liked your blueberry pies." Leah smiled as she headed to the basement.

Seeing that Cora was settled in the recliner, Leah poured some massage lotion on her hands and began to pressure-point Cora's right foot. "Does this seem to be helping at all?" she asked.

"I can't tell yet if my back pain has lessened, but my feet feel better than they have all day."

"I can imagine being on your feet for so many hours would cause them to ache an awful lot." Upstairs, Leah could hear Mom talking to Sparky, and every now and then, Sparky would bark.

"That dog of yours is sure sweet." Cora smiled. "Sometimes I wonder if I should get Jared a puppy. But what if he didn't want it? I'd end up being the one taking care of the dog. And with my schedule, I just don't have the time for that. Although, on a positive note, a dog would make a good companion for me, since Jared doesn't seem to want much to do with me anymore."

"I'm sorry," Leah murmured. "Perhaps in time he will come around."

"I'm still hoping for that." Cora closed her eyes and seemed to relax a little. Leah was glad. It would be better for both of them if they didn't make idle conversation. She could concentrate more fully on finding the right pressure points, and Cora could just let everything go.

Leah had just started on Cora's left foot, when Cora surprised her with a question. "How are your wedding plans coming along?"

"We still have some last-minute things to do, but we should be ready on time for the wedding this Thursday."

"After you're married, will you continue to see people for foot treatments here, or will you have a place to do that at your new home?"

"I'm not sure," Leah replied. "I'll need to speak to Adam about that."

"Adam?"

"Yes, Adam Beachy, my soon-to-be husband."

Cora bolted upright in her chair, nearly knocking the bottle of massage lotion out of Leah's hand. "Adam Beachy? I don't know if it's a coincidence or not, but my first husband's last name was Beachy, and as I had mentioned before, my Amish son's name was Adam. Oh, Leah, if there's even a chance that it's him, I need to know where he lives, so I can go talk to him."

While Cora babbled on, Leah gulped. A wave of heat spread across her cheeks. She couldn't believe she'd been dumb enough to blurt out Adam's name like that. *Oh my, what have I done? If Adam finds out, he'll probably never speak to me again. And he might even call off the wedding. What do I say to Cora? I don't dare tell her where Adam lives, because she's bound to go there, and that wouldn't sit well with Adam at all.*

Cora touched Leah's arm. "Oh, Leah, do you think your Adam Beachy might be my son?"

Leah nodded. "Jah, I believe he is."

CHAPTER 38

Cora trembled, and her mouth felt so dry she could barely talk. "How long have you known that the man you're engaged to is my son, and when were you planning to tell me about it?"

Leah lowered her gaze as she squirmed on her footstool. Cora figured she was uncomfortable talking about this. After several awkward moments, Leah looked up at Cora and said, "I haven't known very long. After the things you told me, plus the few things I already knew, the pieces started coming together. Then, the other day, I spoke to Adam about you, and he—"

"Adam knows I'm here?" Cora was suddenly filled with hope.

Leah nodded slowly. "But he's bitter about the things that occurred in the past, and I'm sorry, but he wants nothing to do with you. In fact, he said if I saw you again, I was to tell you to move back to Chicago."

Cora shook her head determinedly. "I can't do that, Leah. I need to see my son and make things right between us. Please tell me where he lives, or maybe you could set something up so we can meet."

"I cannot go against Adam's wishes," Leah said. "It would cause dissension between us."

Cora sat, mulling things over. "What about my daughter? Does Mary live in this area, too?"

Leah clasped Cora's hand. "I'm sorry to tell you this, but Mary and her husband were killed in an accident several months ago."

Cora covered her mouth to hold back the sob rising in her throat. "Oh, no! That just can't be. It wasn't supposed to happen this way. I wanted to make things right with my children." As reality sunk in, Cora let her tears spill, while Leah sat quietly, gently patting her back.

"Oh, Leah, it's too late to make amends with my daughter. I'd hoped that someday I would see both of my children again so I could apologize to them."

Heartfelt sympathy showed on Leah's face, and Cora thought she saw tears in Leah's eyes. "It was hard for Adam to accept Mary's death, but I think having her girls to raise has been a comfort to him in many ways," Leah said.

Cora gripped the armrests on the chair as this new information penetrated her brain. "Are Adam's nieces the girls you've been caring for?"

Leah bobbed her head. "And I'll be more involved in their care after Adam and I are married."

Cora drew in a sharp breath. "Those little girls are my grandchildren." Pausing, she let out a whispered sigh. "I have granddaughters." Looking up at Leah through blurry vision, she said tearfully, "I'd like the chance to get to know them."

"Leah, Elaine's here to see you!" Leah's mother hollered from the top of the basement stairs.

"I'll be up soon. Tell her to wait for me in the living room," Leah called in response. She looked at Cora. "I'm sorry, but I need to go now. My friend probably came by to talk about last-minute details for the wedding."

"I understand, and I surely won't keep you." Cora rose to her feet. "Before I go home, can I ask a favor?"

"What is it?"

"Would you at least put in a good word for me with Adam? Ask if he'd be willing to meet with me—or, at the very least, allow me to visit my granddaughters?"

"I'll try," Leah said, "but you'll need to accept whatever Adam decides."

I'm not sure I can do that, Cora thought. If Leah couldn't get through to Adam, then Cora would decide what to do next. One thing was for sure: she wouldn't be moving back to Chicago now. Her place was here—with her son and granddaughters. Now Jared would get to know his stepbrother.

Elaine had been waiting in the living room for twenty minutes before Leah showed up, and when she did, she appeared to be quite upset.

"What's wrong, Leah?" Elaine asked. "Have you received some bad news?"

Groaning, Leah flopped onto the couch next to Elaine. "I have, in fact."

"What is it?" Elaine clasped Leah's arm. "Has someone you know been injured or taken sick?"

Leah shook her head. "Remember the talk we had about Adam's mother leaving when he was a boy?"

"Jah."

"Well, that woman who was here getting a foot treatment is Adam's mother, and she wants me to set something up so she and Adam can meet."

Elaine's eyes widened. "What did you tell her?"

"Said I'd see what I could do but made no promises." Leah folded her arms in front of her chest, rocking slowly back and forth. "I'm the reason Cora made the request. I stupidly blurted out that the man I will be marrying is Adam Beachy." She sniffed. "Worse than that, I broke my promise to Adam by telling his mother about him and the girls."

"Are you going to tell him what happened?"

Leah nodded. "And I'd better do it before this day is over, because if I don't talk to him about it now, Cora may decide to seek Adam out on her own. That could make things even worse."

"I'll pray for you, and for Adam, too."

"We surely do need some extra prayers."

Elaine picked up the cardboard box she'd placed on the coffee table when she'd first arrived. "I doubt this will make you feel any better, but I made you a pre-wedding gift."

"What is it?" Leah asked, taking the box from Elaine.

"Open it and see."

Elaine held her breath as Leah opened the lid and removed the rock.

"Oh, how beautiful! It looks like a ruby-throated hummingbird."

Elaine smiled. "When I found that rock the other day among my collection and realized it resembled a hummer, I knew I had to paint it for you."

Leah set the rock down and gave Elaine a hug. "Danki. Your timing was perfect. I miss the hummingbirds when they leave for the south. Now I'll have this cute little rock to look at all year long. This special gift has brightened my day."

Elaine was on the verge of telling Leah about Ben's marriage proposal but thought better of it. *Leah has enough on her mind right now, and it wouldn't be fair to ask her to help me decide whether I should marry Ben. Besides, that's something I need to decide for myself, after I've prayed about it. If I agree to marry Ben, then I'll tell Leah.*

As Cora drove down the road, her hands shook so badly she could hardly steer. It was completely dark, and the tears she tried holding back blurred her vision. Adam, her son, lived right here in Arthur. Oh, how she had missed him all these years, but thinking there was no chance of her ever seeing him again, she'd kept it all bottled up inside. And to have found out about Mary. . .

"Oh my sweet daughter, how can you be gone?" Cora cried out as more tears spilled down her cheeks. "I wanted so badly to make things right with you. Please forgive me, Mary. I'm so sorry I put you and your brother through all that." Cora continued to sob, hoping against hope that somehow Mary could hear her pleas.

Even though she wasn't far from home, Cora was so upset she had to pull over, unable to go on any farther. Sobs came over and over from deep within. It was hard to breathe. She turned the car off and screamed out more pain. Sounding like a wounded animal, her throat constricted and started to hurt, but she didn't care as she howled even louder. Leaning her head against the window, she cried, "Oh, what have I done?" Her punishment had come, and she deserved it. "I was wrong to think of only myself. How could I have thought being a nurse was so important that I heartlessly left my husband and two small children like that?"

Cora let her forehead fall against the steering wheel and grieved over the fact that she would never see Mary again. She'd never get to meet the man her daughter had married or have the chance to make things right with her. Life could be so cruel, and she had no one to blame but herself.

Slowly, her sobs subsided, but the hiccups that followed remained. Fishing into her purse for a tissue, Cora wiped her eyes and blew her nose. She jumped when she heard someone knocking on her car window. When Cora saw the sheriff standing outside with a flashlight, she rolled the window down.

"You all right, ma'am?" he asked, leaning in to look at her.

"Yes, yes. . .*hic*. . .I'm fine," she stammered. "I'm on my way home and needed to pull over for a bit. *Hic! Hic!*"

"Well, if you have to pull over again, remember to put your blinkers on. It's dark out, and you don't want someone to accidentally hit you."

"Thank you, Officer. I'll remember that."

Relieved that her hiccups had finally subsided, Cora watched in the rearview mirror as the sheriff got back in his vehicle and pulled away. Sighing, she turned on the ignition and headed for home.

When she walked into her home sometime later, she was greeted by Jared, who stood with his hands on his hips. "Where you been all this time?" he demanded. "I'm hungry!"

"Then you'd better fix yourself a sandwich," Cora mumbled on the way to her room. "I have a headache, and I'm going to bed." She fled past Jared straight to her room, not wanting him to see her puffy eyes. There was no way Cora could discuss with Jared all that she'd just learned. Not tonight anyway. She had too much information to digest. Somehow, Cora had to come to grips with the knowledge that her daughter had died, her son lived here in Arthur, and she had three granddaughters. To top that off, Leah would soon be married to Cora's son and, technically, would be her daughter-in-law.

Cora undressed, slipped a nightgown over her head, and climbed into bed, pulling the blankets up to her chin, as if to wrap herself in a safe cocoon. "Sleep is what I need," she whimpered. "Maybe things will make more sense in the morning and I can figure out what I need to do."

⟡

Adam had just finished tucking the girls into bed, when he heard a knock on the back door. He made sure the girls' doors were shut then went quickly down the stairs.

When he opened the door, he was surprised to see Leah on the porch, her black outer bonnet slightly askew.

"Leah, what are you doing here at this time of night? Is everything all right?"

"I need to talk to you," she said breathlessly.

Concerned for her welfare, he opened the door wider and invited her in. "Let's go into the kitchen."

Once they were seated at the kitchen table, Adam said, "You look umgerennt."

"You're right. I'm very upset."

"What's wrong?"

"Cora came to see me for another foot treatment earlier this evening, and I. . .I accidentally mentioned your name."

Adam's head fell back. He felt like he'd been kicked by a mule. "You told her about me?" He could hardly believe Leah would betray him like that.

Tears gathered in Leah's eyes. "I'm sorry, Adam. I didn't mean to blurt it out. We were having a casual conversation, and she asked me about the wedding. It was just a slip of the tongue."

Adam sucked in air between his teeth. *Why did this woman have to come here now? She'll ruin everything.*

"Adam." Leah touched his arm. "She asked about Mary, too. I had to tell her. I had no choice."

"I bet that was a jolt to hear. Serves her right!" He thumped his knuckles on the edge of the table. "I suppose she wants to see me now?"

Leah gave a quick nod. "And the girls, too. She's anxious to meet her granddaughters."

His back muscles tightened. "You told her about them? Leah, how could you?"

"I didn't mean to, Adam. It just slipped out. Besides, she sort of figured that out for herself."

Adam's hand came down hard on the table. "It'll be a snowy day in sunny Florida before I allow her to see those girls!" His lips compressed. "You'd better talk her into leaving Arthur, Leah, because if she comes anywhere near me or the girls, I'll do just like my daed after that woman left us. I'll pack up our things and move so far from here that she'll never find us!"

CHAPTER 39

$\mathcal{I}$'m tired. It's too early to get up," Jared complained when Cora prompted him to get out of bed Thursday morning.

"You've got school today. Did you forget?" She gestured to his clothes piled up on the floor. "And when you get home, I expect you to get this messy room cleaned. You weren't born in a barn, Jared, and I'm getting tired of reminding you to pick up after yourself."

Jared moaned, rolling to the edge of his bed. "Okay, I'll do it later today. Maybe after I get back from Scott's."

Cora frowned. "I don't recall giving you permission to go over there after school."

"Yeah, Mom, you did. Said it last night, remember?"

Truth was, Cora had been so tired and stressed out last night, that she barely remembered fixing supper or going to bed. She was sure she hadn't given Jared permission to go anywhere after school. Ever since her visit with Leah Monday evening, when she had learned that Leah was going to marry Cora's own son, she'd been in a fog, trying to decide what to do. She didn't know how she'd made it through work the past couple of days after learning all that, but somehow she had managed to act in a professional manner. That's exactly what it had been: an act. All she'd been able to think about was Adam and poor Mary. Every time Cora had gone into the waiting room to get the next patient, she half expected one of the Amish men waiting there would be Adam. But if Leah had said anything to him, wouldn't Adam have made an attempt to see her by now?

Yesterday, when Cora got home from work, she'd made a decision. She was going to Leah and Adam's wedding, even though she hadn't received an invitation. Cora knew it wasn't the right thing to do, but as soon as she'd gotten out of bed this morning, she'd called her boss at the clinic and said she was sick. She'd thought about taking Jared to the wedding but didn't want him missing any time from school. Besides, Cora still hadn't told him about Adam. She figured that could wait until she'd spoken to Adam and made things right. It would be a shock for Jared to find out he had a half brother.

"Mom, did you hear what I said?" Jared asked, scattering Cora's thoughts.

She jerked her head. "Uh, yes, son, I heard you."

"So can I go over to Scott's after school?"

"I guess it would be okay. But stay out of trouble. Do you understand?" He nodded.

"Good. Now get dressed, and pick up some of your clothes before you eat breakfast." Cora hurried from the room. She'd wait until Jared left for school before she drove over to Leah's. She felt sure that was where the wedding would take place.

Leah's stomach tightened as she took a seat across from her groom, inside her brother's oversized shop. She'd seen Adam on Tuesday, and again yesterday, when she'd gone to his house to care for the girls, but not a word had been said about Cora. Perhaps Adam had calmed down now that he'd had a few days to think things over. And maybe, if the Lord answered Leah's prayers, at some point Adam would agree to see Cora. She felt sure that his comment about moving if Cora tried to see him had been spoken out of anger and frustration. Surely he wouldn't give up his home and business and uproot the girls now that they were getting settled and used to living here in Arthur.

And what about me? Leah wondered. *Would Adam expect me to leave my folks and the only home I've ever known and move someplace else so that he could run from his past?* Adam's relationship with his mother—or the lack of it—was eating him up, and Leah felt powerless to do anything about it.

She closed her eyes and offered a brief prayer. *Heavenly Father, please soften Adam's heart and heal the pain that's been there for so many years. Help me to be the helpmate he needs, and, if possible, let healing occur between Adam and his mother.*

Opening her eyes and glancing at her soon-to-be husband, Leah couldn't help but notice the perspiration that had gathered on his forehead. Was he as nervous as she was? Could he be having second thoughts about making her his wife? What would she do if he ran out of Nathan's shop?

Get a hold of yourself, and stop thinking such negative thoughts. Leah licked her dry lips and fought the urge to pick at a hangnail on her thumb. If she had noticed it before she'd left home this morning, she would have trimmed it off with nail clippers. But if she started pulling on it now, she'd draw attention to herself, and that would be embarrassing.

Pulling her gaze from Adam, she glanced at her two witnesses sitting beside her. Elaine seemed focused on the sermon being preached by one of their ministers, but Priscilla kept her focus on Elam, sitting directly across from her.

I wonder if she's wishing they were getting married today. The couple had been courting for quite a while, and Leah was still surprised Elam hadn't asked Priscilla to marry him by now.

Maybe he's waiting till he has enough money saved up, Leah thought. *Or perhaps, for some reason, he's afraid of marriage.*

Leah looked at Ben and noticed that he couldn't take his eyes off Elaine. *Now there's someone who's obviously in love. I wonder if Elaine realizes the way Ben feels about her. If it's this apparent to me, I would think it would be to her, as well.*

She looked at Adam again. If anyone had a reason to fear marriage, it was him. She couldn't imagine how it must have been for Adam's father when Cora walked out on her family. It must have been heart-wrenching, not to mention humiliating. She wondered what other people in Adam's Pennsylvania community must have thought. Would there have been some who believed Adam's dad was to blame—that he may have done something to drive Cora away? Or had most folks blamed Cora, thinking she was a terrible person for what she'd done, especially leaving her two small children? Adam certainly believed that. But unless he could forgive his mother, he would never truly be at peace.

As the service progressed, Adam felt himself beginning to relax. He'd come here feeling exceptionally nervous, fearful that something might happen to ruin the wedding. His eyes kept darting toward the door, hoping a particular person didn't unexpectedly show up, although he was certain that he wouldn't recognize her. It had been three days since Leah had admitted telling his mother who he was. Much to his relief, Cora had not gone to see Leah again or tried to contact him. Maybe she'd given up and decided to leave Arthur. That would be the sensible thing to do, because there was no hope of her having a relationship with him or the girls. All Adam wanted was the chance to begin a new life and, with Leah's help, raise Mary and Amos's girls the best way he could.

When Cora arrived at Leah's home, she knew immediately that the wedding was not taking place there because no buggies were parked in the field and there was no sign of a bench wagon or anything else to indicate that a wedding was being held.

Cora tapped the steering wheel. *Let me think. Where might the wedding be held?*

Unsure of where to go or what to do, Cora turned her car around and headed back down the driveway. The only thing she could think to do was drive around the area and see if she could locate the home where the wedding was being held. Surely it couldn't be that hard to spot. She just had to find the right road.

Turning onto the main road, Cora looked at the sky. "At least my son has a beautiful day for his wedding." It was a cold, crisp November day without a cloud to be seen. The air was sharp and so nippy it felt as though she could almost touch it. A sheet of ice glazed over the top of a pond she passed. Most of the trees were nearly bare, with only a few leaves hanging on the branches.

The other morning, driving to work, Cora had seen a few snow flurries. It reminded her of living in Chicago, where she had become used to the wind and snow. At least Cora didn't have snowy roads to contend with today. She was good at driving in the snow, but everyone else worried her. Over the years, she'd witnessed people making terrible mistakes when they drove on icy and snowy roads. But being a nurse and having to drive herself to work every day, Cora had learned to get over her fear and pay attention to what other vehicles were doing.

Cora glanced at her reflection in the rearview mirror. She had chosen to wear a simple outfit because she would be attending an Amish wedding. Her closet was full of fancy dresses she'd brought with her from Chicago, but none of them would have been appropriate. She had attended many hospital functions, weddings, and parties with her now ex-husband, but those dresses were too flashy to wear to a simple gathering such as this. Cora certainly didn't want to bring attention to herself, so she had chosen a dark blue skirt with matching jacket, and a light blue blouse. Since Amish women wore no jewelry, she avoided wearing earrings or a necklace.

Cora took a deep breath and concentrated on the matter at hand, slowing down at each farm she came to, hoping to see a crowd of horses and buggies. So far she'd had no luck. To make matters worse, a few minutes ago, her vehicle had started making sputtering noises.

Oh, please, not now, Cora silently prayed. *I don't need this on top of everything else.* She checked the gauge, but that was okay. She still had a half tank of gas. No other lights on the dash were lit up, and the steering seemed to be okay. Inspection was due sometime soon, but Cora hadn't had a chance to seek out a garage where she could take her vehicle. That was the first thing she planned to do when she went back to work the next day. Perhaps her coworkers could let her know of a reputable place to get her car inspected.

A few more miles down the road, Cora's car sounded normal again.

Sure wish I'd thought to ask Leah where the wedding was going to be. But then, she might not have told me.

Cora clutched the steering wheel tightly and berated herself. "What am I doing?" She was slowly beginning to lose her nerve. "What will I say to Adam if I come face-to-face with him?"

She'd planned out what she would say, but now she was so nervous she couldn't remember the words. She didn't want to talk herself out of it, but her nerves were on edge. What if she located the place where the wedding was being held and found out that she wasn't welcome? Cora didn't think she could handle the rejection.

After driving another mile up the road, she spotted a line of buggies parked in a field. *This must be the place.* Biting her lip, she slowed to let another vehicle pass before pulling in.

She turned up the driveway and parked her car near the edge so that if anyone needed to get out she wouldn't be in the way. Besides, she didn't want to alarm any of the horses, even though most of them were probably used to vehicles. Cora had to admit, she wanted to park in a space where she could get out easily, in case she had to leave quickly.

Opening the car door, Cora froze when the car started drifting forward. She realized then that she'd forgotten to put the gear in PARK. After doing so, she sat for a few minutes, taking deep breaths. "Pull yourself together," she whispered. "You came here to see Adam, so you can't chicken out now."

Gathering her courage, Cora grabbed the door handle and stepped out of the car. Despite the butterflies in the pit of her stomach, there was no stopping her now.

CHAPTER 40

Cora heard singing coming from inside the oversized shop on the right side of the property, so she headed in that direction. When she got to the door, she stopped, running her damp hands down the side of her skirt. Earlier she had been concerned that she hadn't dressed warmly enough, given the cool weather. But now, Cora's nerves were keeping her plenty warm enough.

Looking back at her car to make sure it was still parked where she'd left it, Cora wiped her hands one more time then grasped the shop door handle. Taking a deep breath, she stepped inside and slipped quietly onto one of the backless wooden benches on the women's side of the room, near the rear. She couldn't see the bride and groom because other heads blocked her view. Cora sat silently, willing her heart to quit beating so wildly and uncrossing her legs to keep her feet from bobbing.

Leaning slightly forward, she looked past the women in front of her and saw several children. Some sat with their mothers, grandmothers, or some other person, and a few sat with their fathers. Cora wondered which of these children might be Adam's nieces. Then she spotted little Carrie, whom she'd met at the clinic the day Leah had brought her in. The child looked so cute, wearing an olive-green dress with a white apron. Her small hands were folded as she looked straight ahead. On either side of Carrie sat two other young girls. Beside them was an older woman, who Cora recognized as Leah's mother. She'd only seen her briefly the last time she'd gone to Leah's for a foot treatment, but she was sure it was her.

I wish I were the one sitting on the bench with those girls, Cora thought. *I gave up the privilege of knowing my children when they were young, but, oh, I would cherish each moment if I could spend that lost time with my grandchildren now.*

Cora's attention was drawn to the front of the room when one of the men, whom she assumed was a minister, stood and gave a message on the topic of marriage, speaking in German. The language came back to her as if she'd never stopped using it, and Cora was able to understand every word he said.

The focus of the message was on the serious step of marriage, for in the Amish church, the people were taught that divorce was not an option. The sermon and Bible passages emphasized the relationship between husband and wife, as God intended.

Cora had heard something similar the day she'd married Andrew but hadn't really taken it to heart. Today, however, the man's words penetrated her soul. Even though she'd spoken her vows before God and man and promised to be true only unto her husband, Cora had broken that vow the day she'd left Andrew and filed for divorce. Then by some twist of fate, Evan had done the same thing to her. If only she could go back in time and reverse her decision. *What goes around, comes around.* And what she had done so many years ago to her family had certainly come back around to her. *I didn't leave my husband for another man, though,* Cora justified, comparing what she'd done to Evan's reason for divorcing her. Wanting to be a nurse was a burning desire she'd had years ago, but had it been worth it in the end? Cora knew she had done wrong by leaving Andrew and had cheated herself out of the joy of knowing their children and being the kind of mother to Mary and Adam that they deserved. She had also robbed herself of the privilege of knowing her granddaughters. But maybe it wasn't too late for that.

As the minister continued, Cora's face burned with shame. Tears dripped onto her blouse. It felt like he was directing his words at her; yet he was speaking to the bride and groom. *Father, forgive me,* she silently prayed. *I was a selfish woman who knew better but wanted my own way. I know it's a lot to ask, Lord, but I'd like the chance to make amends.*

When the sermon ended, the wedding couple was called to stand before the bishop. Cora craned her head to get a look, and her heart nearly stopped beating when she caught sight of Leah standing beside a young Amish man with blond hair. It was the same man she'd spoken to at the hardware store the other day. Cora knew now why he'd looked so familiar. He resembled his father.

Swallowing against the lump in her throat, Cora couldn't take her eyes off the couple as they said their vows. Her son wasn't the little boy she remembered from long ago. Adam had been such a cute kid, and now he'd grown to be a handsome young man who had taken on the responsibility of raising Mary's daughters. No wonder Leah had fallen in love with him.

Cora continued watching as Leah glanced shyly at Adam. It took Cora back to the day she and Andrew had shared their wedding vows and looked bashfully at each other.

Adam and Leah were asked by the minister if they would remain together until death and if they would be loyal and care for each other during adversity, affliction, sickness, and weakness. They both answered affirmatively, and then the minister took their hands in his, and after wishing them the blessing and mercy of God, he said, "Go forth in the Lord's name. You are now man and wife."

Tears clouding her vision, Cora sat very still as the couple returned to their seats. Then she stood and quietly left the building, hoping neither Leah nor Adam had seen her. She had come here, planning to speak with her son and reveal who she was, but now she realized that this was not the time to make an appearance. She didn't want to spoil Leah and Adam's wedding day, so she would wait for a better time to speak with Adam.

When Leah took a seat after saying her vows, she glanced over at Adam's nieces and smiled. Those precious little girls would be in her care full-time from now on, and she looked forward to that. Unless things changed between her and Adam, she would probably never have any children of her own. That was one more reason for Leah to find satisfaction in being able to nurture and care for Carrie, Linda, and Amy. If the look of happiness on the girls' faces was any indication of how they felt, then they were equally glad that she'd become Adam's wife.

Adam's wife, Leah mused. It was hard to believe, especially given the fact that at one time she hadn't cared for Adam that much. Things were different now. Since Adam had become the caregiver of his nieces, Leah had seen him in a different light. He didn't annoy her like he had before, although he could still be pretty stubborn. If it weren't for the bitterness he carried toward his mother, Leah could give Adam her whole heart.

Turning her attention to the final sermon, Leah listened as the minister praised the institution of marriage and quoted more scriptures. She thought about the vows she'd just spoken and wondered what the rest of her life would be like. Would Adam ever give his heart to her in love? Was there any chance that he would agree to speak with Cora? So many questions and doubts floated through Leah's mind. The best response was to simply take one day at a time and trust God to work things out for everyone.

Adam's throat felt dry as he alternated between listening to their bishop speak about marriage and looking at Leah's rosy cheeks. She'd looked at him so sincerely when she'd answered the bishop's question only moments ago: "Can you confess, sister, that you accept our brother as your husband, and that you will not leave him until death separates you?"

"Yes," Leah had said with a decisive nod.

Why didn't my mother stay true to those vows when she married my daed? Adam wondered. *Did Dad, Mary, and I mean so little to her that she could forget about the promise she'd made before God and the church?*

That old familiar bitterness welled in Adam's soul. It was wrong to harbor such feelings of anger and resentment toward his mother, but he couldn't seem to help himself.

I won't let it consume me, Adam told himself. *My concentration needs to be on raising my nieces and trying to be a good husband to Leah, even though we won't be married in a physical sense.*

He glanced at Leah once more and relaxed a bit when she smiled at him. Adam was convinced that God had brought them together—if not to be husband and wife in every sense of the word, then to make sure that Mary and Amos's girls received the love and care they truly deserved. Although Mary had never met Leah, Adam was sure she would have approved of the young woman he'd chosen to marry.

That evening when Leah and Adam arrived at his house with the girls, Leah told Adam that she would help the girls get ready for bed.

"That's fine," Adam responded. "While you're doing that, I'll put your suitcase upstairs in the room next to Amy's."

Leah nodded. She'd known she would not be sharing a room with Adam downstairs, but the reminder that she'd be sleeping in the guest room was most troubling.

What have I done? she asked herself as she and the girls went into the house. *Marriage is for life, and I've just committed to a man who does not love me and who will never truly be my husband.*

Resolving to make the best of her situation, Leah followed Carrie and Linda up the stairs and into the room they shared, while Amy went to her room next door. After the younger ones changed into their nightclothes and said their prayers, Leah tucked them into bed. After kissing Carrie and Linda good night, she entered Amy's bedroom.

"How come Uncle Adam said he was gonna put your things in the room next to mine?" Amy asked when Leah took a seat on the end of her bed.

Unsure of how best to respond, Leah smiled and said, "I want to be close to you and your sisters right now."

Amy gave Leah a hug, apparently satisfied with that answer. "I'm glad you'll be living here with us now. I don't miss my mamm so much when you're around."

Tears pooled in Leah's eyes. "I'll never be able to take her place, but I want you to know that I'll be here for you in every way." After kissing Amy's forehead and telling her good night, Leah turned off the gas lamp and slipped quietly from the room. When she entered her own bedroom, where her luggage now sat, she went to the window and looked out. A full moon illuminated the yard, and Leah could see Adam's barn clearly. A light shone through the windows, letting her know that Adam was probably tending the horse. She wondered what he was thinking. Did he have any regrets about marrying her? Was he still upset because she'd told Cora about him? He hadn't said anything more about his mother or what he planned to do, and Leah was afraid to bring up the subject. She hoped Adam wouldn't make good on his threat to move. As far as she was concerned, that would be the worst thing to do.

After opening her suitcase, Leah took out her Bible. Taking a seat on the bed, she looked up Isaiah 30:15. *"In quietness and in confidence shall be your strength,"* she read to herself.

Closing her eyes, Leah prayed, *Lord, please help me remember to put my trust in You to work everything out according to Your will.*

CHAPTER 41

*L*eah scurried around the kitchen, getting breakfast on before Adam and the girls came in. It just didn't seem possible that a whole week had gone by since her and Adam's wedding. Even though Leah had been coming over for the past few months to care for the girls, it felt strange to actually be living in Adam's house, knowing she was his wife.

But I'm his wife in name only, she reminded herself. *Adam doesn't see me as anything more than a housekeeper, cook, and someone to take care of his nieces.*

As Leah stirred a kettle of oatmeal on the stove, her thoughts took her back to their wedding night, when she and Adam came home with the girls. After a whole week had gone by, Adam still hadn't mentioned Cora. Was he ever going to say anything? Should Leah bring up the topic? She was confused and didn't know what to do.

"God is not the author of confusion, but of peace, as in all churches of the saints." Leah silently quoted 1 Corinthians 14:33.

"What's for breakfast?" Amy asked, stepping into the kitchen and scattering Leah's thoughts.

Leah smiled as she turned from the stove. "Since this is such a chilly fall morning, I decided to fix *hawwermehl.*"

Amy's nose crinkled. "I don't like oatmeal that much."

"I like it, and so does Carrie," Linda said, holding her little sister's hand as they skipped into the room.

"Amy, would you please set the table?" Leah asked. "I'm making toast, so you can have a piece of that."

"What can I do?" Linda wanted to know.

"Why don't you get out the brown sugar and butter?" Leah suggested. "Oh, and Carrie, you can put some napkins by each of our plates."

While the girls did their jobs, Leah turned the stove down and toasted several slices of bread. By the time they came out of the oven, Adam had come inside from doing his chores in the barn.

"Brr. . ." Adam rubbed his hands briskly over his arms. "It feels more like winter than fall this morning. You can really smell the wood smoke in the air. Guess a lot of folks did what we did and fired up their woodstoves and fireplaces this past week." He glanced at Leah and smiled. "Is breakfast about ready?"

Smiling in return, she nodded.

"Great. I'll get washed up, and then we can eat." Adam headed down the hall toward the bathroom. When he returned, everyone took a seat at the table. "I'll bring more firewood in before I leave for work," he said. "That way you can keep the fireplace going."

"Danki, Adam. The warmth from the fire makes the living room cozy." Leah lowered her eyes, feeling the heat of a blush on her cheeks. She appreciated his thoughtfulness, and the gentle way he'd looked at her just now made her feel kind of giddy.

After their silent prayer, Leah dished everyone a bowl of oatmeal and passed Amy the plate of toast. As they ate, Amy and Linda talked about school and how their teacher would soon be giving out parts for the Christmas program. Leah looked forward to attending along with the parents and other family members of the scholars who went to the one-room schoolhouse. For her, Christmas would be different than it had been in the past, since she was no longer living at home with her parents. Now, she was a parent, of sorts.

"Will you be washing clothes today, Leah?" Adam asked. "I spilled some glue on my trousers yesterday, and they need to be cleaned."

"I'll do my best," Leah responded, "but I can't promise that the glue will come out."

"It's okay if it doesn't. They're an old pair of trousers."

"I'll start washing as soon as I get Linda and Amy off to school," Leah said. "I need to get it done before Priscilla comes for a foot treatment."

Adam's eyebrows squished together. "I've been meaning to talk to you about that, Leah. Now that we're married, I'd prefer that you stop practicing reflexology."

Leah stiffened. "But Adam, there are people in this community who count on me to help them with various ailments."

"If they're sick, they can see a doctor." Adam reached for his cup of coffee and took a drink.

"Some folks who see me aren't sick; they may have back problems or—"

"That's what chiropractors are for," he interrupted.

"But, Adam—"

He gestured to the girls. "I rather not discuss this right now. Since you've already scheduled Priscilla to come over, you can go ahead and work on her feet, but you'll need to let her know that this will be the last time you will see her for that." As if the matter were settled, Adam got up from the table and put his dishes in the sink. After he'd said good-bye to the girls and Leah, he grabbed his hat, jacket, and lunch pail, and headed out the door.

It's not fair of Adam to ask me to quit doing reflexology. Leah teared up. *It's my gift.*

As Cora drove to work that morning, she spotted a group of Amish children walking along a path on the side of the road. No doubt they were headed to school. She recognized two of the young girls, as she'd seen them sitting with Carrie at Leah and Adam's wedding. One of the girls looked so much like Mary when she was a little girl that Cora was tempted to stop and talk to them. But she didn't want to frighten the girls. Once more, she thought about how she had cheated herself out of knowing these children. Was it too late for that? If the girls knew she was their grandmother, would they welcome her into their lives?

Cora had to find out, and the only way she could do that was to speak with Adam. She didn't know where Adam lived, but she would go by his hardware store before the week was out. She just hoped and prayed he would be receptive to what she had to say.

That afternoon, Leah scurried around finishing up the housework. She hadn't done the laundry yet, because she'd gone over to her folks' house to get her massage lotion for Priscilla's foot treatment. The old recliner she had always used was still in Mom and Dad's basement, so she would have Priscilla sit on one of the chairs in Adam's living room. Oh, how she dreaded telling her friend that she could no longer practice reflexology. If Leah had known Adam was going to take that away from her, she'd have thought twice about marrying him.

Before Leah and Carrie had gone to her folks', she'd taken Adam's pants to the laundry area and rubbed some spot remover on the area he'd told her about. Now the house was all clean, including the floors, and she had just gotten Carrie up from her afternoon nap. "Do you want to go for a walk with me out to the phone shack, Carrie? I need to check for messages."

Carrie eagerly agreed and got her coat, which hung on a low-hanging hook in the utility room. Hand in hand, they walked to the phone shack, with Coal following close behind. The Lab was so good with the girls, and he'd taken a liking to Leah, as well. She missed seeing Sparky every day, but he was better off staying at home with Mom. No doubt Sparky and Coal would have vied for her attention, and two dogs were just too many for Leah to deal with right now.

"Now just stand here and wait until I check for messages." Leah smiled when Carrie reached for Coal and hung on to the thick fur on the back of his neck, while the dog sat close to her feet.

There was only one message, and it was from Priscilla. Her plans had changed. She wasn't going to be able to make it for a foot treatment after all.

Going back into the house, Leah decided to start the laundry. Hopefully the spot remover had worked and the glue would come out once Adam's pants were washed. Carrie seemed content to sit by the living-room window and watch the birds at the feeder outside.

"Carrie, I'll be right back as soon as I wash your uncle's clothes. Do you want to come with me to the laundry room while I do that, or would you like to stay here and keep watching the birds?"

"I wanna watch the birdies eat," Carrie responded.

Leah reminded Carrie that she wouldn't be long and to come to her if she got tired of watching the birds. There were some children's puzzles Carrie could play with that were kept on a shelf in the laundry area, but Adam's youngest niece seemed quite content to sit quietly looking out the window.

Leah was happy when she saw no evidence of the glue in Adam's trousers after she'd washed them with a few other things. "He should be pleased with that," she murmured, putting the clothes in the basket to take outside to hang on the line.

Setting the laundry basket by the back door, Leah went to check on Carrie, but the little girl was no longer at the window. "Carrie, where are you?" Leah called, going from room to room. "Now where could that child have gotten in so little time?"

Leah looked toward the hook where she'd hung Carrie's coat when they'd come inside earlier. When she saw that it, too, was missing, Leah grabbed her own coat and immediately went outside.

Leah stood on the porch, yelling Carrie's name. Silence. She realized that Coal, who always greeted her when she went outside, hadn't appeared, either. Leah hurried to the barn and checked there, but Carrie was nowhere to be found. Leah continued searching, walking all around the outside of the house. Her heart beat wildly as she raced toward the pond, but luckily she saw no evidence of Carrie or the dog. She'd hoped at first that the girl might be playing hide-and-seek, but now Leah was afraid. "What am I going to do?" She nearly choked on the words.

Just then, she spotted Amy and Linda walking with a few other children, coming home from school. When the girls entered the yard, Leah told them that their little sister was missing.

"Oh, no!" Linda gasped. "What if we never find her?"

"I'll bet she saw something she liked and wandered off someplace," Amy put in.

"Well, we need to find Carrie before your uncle gets home from work," Leah said. "Will you two help me look for her?"

Both girls nodded soberly.

While the three of them searched for Carrie, Leah tried to remain calm. Where was Carrie? Why did she leave the house? How would she explain to Adam what had happened, and what would he think? They'd only been married a week and already something had gone wrong. Leah told the girls to go back in the house while she went to the phone shack to call the sheriff. It was the last thing she wanted to do, but, at this point, she saw no other choice, especially since it would be getting dark in a few hours. After giving a description of Carrie to someone at the sheriff's office, Leah mentioned that there might be a black Lab with her. She was beside herself, but she'd done all she could.

When Leah entered the house, Amy and Linda were sitting in the livingroom crying. Gathering them into her arms, Leah tried to offer the girls hope that their little sister would soon be found. She had to hold things together until they heard something from the sheriff.

Leah looked at the clock above the fireplace and couldn't believe it had been an hour already since she'd first realized Carrie was missing. In that amount of time the child could have gone almost anywhere. *Please, Lord, let her be okay.*

Suddenly, all three of them heard a slight barking sound from outside. Trying to get through the door at the same time, Leah, Amy, and Linda rushed outside. Leah was so relieved when she saw Coal walking next to Carrie, coming toward them from the edge of the backyard. Carrie clutched the Lab's thick fur on the back of his neck. The dog, Leah realized, was Carrie's protector, walking slowly beside the child so her two little legs could keep up with his four. Carrie was smiling, big as you please, while Coal's tail wagged rapidly back and forth.

Leah couldn't get to the child quickly enough. Running down the porch steps, she scooped Carrie into her arms, holding on for dear life.

"You're squeezing so tight." Carrie giggled, while Leah eased up but continued to hug her. Coal was barking loudly now, his tail going in circles.

Linda and Amy bent down and hugged the dog. "Good boy, Coal. Good dog," they said in unison.

After Leah put Carrie down, Linda and Amy hugged their little sister.

"Where have you been, Carrie?" Leah asked. "We were so worried."

"I saw Chippy and went after him, but he ran away."

"I'm glad you saw the chipmunk, but you should not have left the yard," Leah scolded.

Carrie's chin trembled. "Sorry."

Leah gave one of Carrie's braids a gentle tug. "Please, don't ever do that again."

"I won't," Carrie promised. "I'll stay in the yard."

After Leah sent the children inside, she went to the phone shack and called the sheriff's office again, letting them know that Carrie had been found. When she returned to the house, she put another log in the fireplace to warm the house up a little more for Carrie. In the meantime, Linda took some fresh water out on the porch for Coal. When they were all back together in the house, Carrie continued to tell them her story. While she'd been watching out the window, she'd seen Chippy in the backyard under the bird feeder.

"We thought he died," Linda spoke up. "I'm so glad he's okay."

Carrie's lower lip jutted out. "When I went outside, Chippy ran, so I followed him."

"But where did you go?" Leah asked. "We looked everywhere for you."

"I went far away—in a field, where Chippy ran." Carrie paused, tears pooling in her eyes. "Then I didn't know how to get home."

"Didn't you hear us calling for you?" Leah asked calmly, so as not to further upset the little girl.

"Uh-uh. I'm sorry." Carrie hid her face with her arm.

"Come here, sweetie." Leah lifted Carrie onto her lap.

"How did you get home?" Amy questioned.

"Coal kept tuggin' on my coat, so I gave up looking for Chippy." Carrie looked up at Leah and sniffed. "Are ya mad at me?"

"Of course not." Reaching for the child's small hands, Leah squeezed them gently. "We're just glad you're home, safe and sound."

Leah was so happy she was about to burst. As a reward for bringing Carrie home, Leah had thought about letting Coal come inside. That way he, too, could enjoy the warmth of the house. She decided to wait until Adam got home, however, since Adam had made it clear that he didn't want the dog inside. Leah hoped that after he heard the details of Carrie's safe return, Adam would change his mind and let Coal come in.

✏

When Adam got home, Leah explained what had happened with Carrie. His heart hammered in his chest, thinking about what could have happened, but he'd quickly calmed down, seeing that Carrie was okay. Leah had apologized for not watching Carrie closer, but Adam knew she couldn't be with the child every moment of the day.

Like he normally did each evening after supper, Adam had gotten a bowl ready and fixed Coal's food, but this time he'd opened the door and called the dog inside. As Coal came running in, Adam stole a glance at Leah and the girls and grinned back at them as Coal hungrily slurped his chow.

Adam turned off all but one of the gas lamps and stood by the wall where the glow of light reflected. Even Coal, who'd been lying near Leah's feet, looked up and watched.

"Can any of you guess what this is?" Adam asked, making a shadow figure on the wall.

"It looks like a dog!" Linda shrieked with delight, while Carrie clapped her hands. Even Amy wore a grin.

Next, Adam made a bird and flapped his hands, making the shadow look as if it were flying. After that, he made a rabbit and several other animals. Linda was so intrigued that she jumped up and joined Adam, asking if he would teach her how to do it.

"Okay, now you put your hands like this." He positioned her hands and showed her how to make an easy hand shadow. "This one you can do with one hand, raising your index finger a little."

"It looks like a dog," Linda squealed.

"Now make him bark by moving your thumb up and down a little." Adam watched as Linda succeeded in making the motion.

Carrie came forward, and Linda showed her how it was done, while Adam stood off to one side. He glanced at Leah, who smiled as she, too, sat watching the girls. Being here with his nieces and Leah made Adam feel like he was complete, like he had a family. How could he have ever been content to keep to himself for all those years?

Only one thing was missing, and that involved Leah. Did he dare express the way he felt about her? He'd be taking a risk if she didn't share his feelings of love. Adam knew from the way Leah responded to the things he said that she respected him as the head of the house. But he wanted more.

As Adam sat down on the couch next to Leah, he made a decision. When the time was right and he felt a little more confident, he would open his heart to Leah. But he couldn't do that until Leah showed some sign that she loved him, too.

"That's really good, girls," Adam said, focusing once more on Carrie and Linda. "The hand shadow you made looks just like a bird. Now see if you can make him fly."

Unexpectedly, a vague memory worked its way into Adam's consciousness. He remembered someone else making shadow figures on the wall when he was a child. Until now, he'd kept this memory buried all these years. *My mother taught Mary and me how to do this.*

"Are you okay, Adam?" Leah asked. "You've become very quiet."

"I'm fine. Just watching the girls." Adam broke out in a sweat. There was no way he was going to let this one little memory make him forget what his mother had done to him and Mary, not to mention Dad. *We suffered all those years without a mom, and I won't let one good memory erase all of that.*

CHAPTER 42

When Jonah entered his buggy shop on Friday morning, he found his father hard at work. "Am I late?" Jonah asked. "Thought I was getting here right on time."

"You are." Dad grinned. "I woke up early this morning and decided to come on into the shop and get started. We've still got two buggies we need to complete before Christmas, you know."

Jonah nodded. "And I'm ever so thankful to have you working with me, Dad."

"How are Sara and the boppli doing?" Dad asked, reaching for one of his tools.

"The baby is doing well, but I'm worried about Sara." Jonah moved across the room to his desk.

Dad's forehead creased. "What's wrong? Has she been doing too much?"

"Not really," Jonah replied with a shake of his head. "Between Mom and Sara's mamm, now that she's arrived, they're taking over the household chores and cooking." He grimaced. "I think Sara's MS is flaring up. She's had a few dizzy spells, and her legs have been kind of weak. She's been using a cane to get around the house, and I can't help but worry."

Dad set his work aside and joined Jonah at his desk. "Try not to worry, son. Remember what God's Word says in Philippians 4:6: 'Be careful for nothing; but in every thing by prayer and supplication with thanksgiving let your requests be made known unto God.'"

Jonah clasped Dad's shoulder and squeezed it. "That's good advice. Danki for the reminder."

✑

Dianna parked her bicycle and joined Leah by the clothesline, where she was removing her clean laundry.

"It's good to see you. What brings you by here today?" Leah asked.

Dianna smiled and gave Leah a hug. "Can't a mother drop by to see her daughter without there being a reason?"

"Of course." Leah placed one of the little girls' dresses in the basket. "I just thought maybe you came by for a special reason."

"I did. Came to see you." Dianna playfully tweaked the end of Leah's nose, like she'd done many times when Leah was a child. "So, how are you doing?"

Leah dropped her gaze to the ground. "Just trying to get these clothes off the line. I left them hanging outside all night."

"I can see that. But I didn't ask what you were doing; I asked how are you doing?"

"Okay, I guess."

"Just okay? You're a new bride, for goodness' sake. You ought to be smiling from ear to ear."

When Leah made no comment, Dianna felt concerned. "Is something wrong, Leah? You look unhappy this morning."

"I am unhappy, Mom." Leah glanced at Carrie playing with Coal on the porch, and lowered her voice. "When I told Adam yesterday morning that Priscilla would be coming by for a foot treatment, he said he didn't want me doing that anymore."

"Really? Why not?" Dianna could hardly believe Adam would object.

"He didn't explain. Just said he didn't want me doing it anymore, and then he left for work."

"Don't you think you ought to find out the reason for his request?"

"Jah, but I don't want to do it in front of the kinner. They don't need to hear Adam and me involved in a disagreement—especially now that we're married."

Dianna shook her head. "I should say not." She was tempted to say more on the subject but decided it would be best to let Leah and Adam work out their differences. It might be that after Adam had time to think about it, he would change his mind.

"I'll help you get the clothes off the line," Dianna said, reaching up to remove another dress."

"Danki."

Dianna remained quiet as she and Leah finished the job. When they stepped onto the porch, Carrie announced that she was hungry.

"Guess it is about time for lunch," Leah said. "Would you like to stay and join us, Mom? Thought I'd reheat some chicken noodle soup I made for supper last night. Does that sound good to you?"

"That'd be nice." Dianna smiled. "While you're doing that, I'll fold the clothes and put them away."

"Come on, Coal. You can come inside, too." Leah held the door open until Coal walked through.

Dianna followed Leah and Carrie into the house, and when they went to the kitchen, she took the clothes to the dining room, where she placed them on the table to fold. Once that was done, she carried Adam's trousers down the hall, remembering that when she'd been watching the girls, Linda had mentioned that her uncle's room was downstairs.

Dianna stepped into the bedroom and opened the closet door to hang up the trousers. *Now that's sure strange. Where are all of Leah's dresses?* she wondered, looking around.

Going to the dresser, she opened each of the drawers, but there was nothing in any of them to indicate that Leah shared this room with her husband. *What in the world is going on here? Could Leah have moved her things to one of the rooms upstairs because she was upset with Adam after he'd said she couldn't practice reflexology? Should I say something to Leah about this or just let it go? If Leah and Adam are having marital problems, she may need someone to talk to about this. Maybe I'd better discuss it with Alton first and see what he thinks I should do.*

During lunch, Leah chatted with Mom about the usual things going on with her friends and how some of the stores in Arthur were having preholiday sales.

When Carrie finished eating, she went to the living room to be with Coal, who had bedded down by the fireplace. "Since Carrie's in the other room, now's a good time for me to tell you what happened yesterday."

"What was that?" Mom asked.

Leah explained how Carrie had run off and how frantic she'd been when she couldn't find her. "Even when I realized that Coal was with her, I was still scared." Leah continued to explain the details of how Carrie and the dog came back and how Adam had allowed the dog to come in the house last night.

"I would have done the same thing myself," Mom said. "And I'm pleased to hear that everything worked out okay."

Leah was about to say more, when Carrie yelled for them to come quick. Thinking something must be seriously wrong, Leah jumped up and hurried into the living room. There stood Carrie by the fireplace, giving the dog her own performance of making shadow figures on the wall.

When Cora got off work that afternoon, she headed straight for Adam's store. She'd gone there yesterday, but because she worked later than usual, by the time she'd arrived, the hardware store was closed.

As she drove along, she noticed a horse and buggy pulled off to the side of the road. An Amish man with his back to the road was squatted down by the buggy wheel, as though there might be a problem.

Cora pulled in behind the buggy and got out of the car. "Is there anything I can do to help?" she asked.

When the man turned around, Cora felt as if her heart had stopped beating. She'd seen him at the hardware store the day she'd gone looking for lightbulbs and an extension cord. She had seen him again a week ago, when he'd stood before the bishop with Leah, saying his wedding vows.

"I appreciate you stopping, but I don't think there's much you can do," he said.

He doesn't recognize me. He has no idea I'm his mother. Cora moved closer to Adam. "You don't know who I am, do you?"

He stared at her several seconds. "Oh, now I remember. Aren't you the lady who came into my store a week or so ago, looking for lightbulbs?"

"Yes, Adam, that was me."

He blinked rapidly. "How do you know my name? Don't think I introduced myself when you came into the store."

Barely able to get the words out, Cora murmured, "My name is Cora. I'm your mother."

CHAPTER 43

*A*dam's throat tightened as he stared at the person claiming to be his mother. She was the same woman who'd come to his store, but he hadn't recognized her then, nor did he now. "You're not my mother," he mumbled, forcing himself to look into her eyes. "A real mother would not have abandoned her own flesh-and-blood children."

Cora reached out her hand but pulled it back when Adam moved aside. "I know what I did was wrong, and I—"

Adam held up his hand. "I don't want to hear your excuses, because that's all they would be, excuses. A real mother loves her children and wants to be with them. A real wife doesn't run off and get a divorce for no reason." Adam's hands shook as he dropped his arms to his sides. "Didn't the vows you took when you married Dad mean anything?"

"I thought they did at the time, but then things changed."

"You mean, *you* changed! One day you were my mother who wiped my nose when I had a cold and created hand shadows on the wall when I was afraid of the dark. The next day you were gone." Adam gulped in a breath of air. "You never returned or kept in touch with me or my sister."

"I know how it must seem, but if you'd just let me explain—"

"I'm not interested in your explanation. Nothing you could say or do would ever make up for all those years that you were not a part of our lives."

Tears welled in Cora's eyes, but Adam felt no pity. Why should he? Had she felt pity for him or Mary when they'd called out for their mother and cried themselves to sleep so many nights? Did she care that she'd not only broken her husband's heart but had also left him to raise their children alone?

"You're not welcome here." Adam motioned to her car. "You left me and my sister by your own choice. Now I'm asking you to leave again, but this time it's my choice."

Cora shook her head determinedly. "I can't do that, Adam. I lost you once. I won't let that happen again."

"You lost me?" His jaw clenched so tightly it was a miracle he didn't break a tooth. "You didn't lose me. You threw me away! If you don't leave Douglas County, I'll have no choice but to take my family and move."

Cora gasped. "Oh no, Adam. Please, don't do that. I have a new job here, and it's given me a new start. I promise I won't bother you or try to force myself on you at all. If the day ever comes that you reconsider and allow me to be a part of your life, then—"

"That will never happen!" Adam turned away abruptly. "Now please go."

As he moved back to his buggy, Adam heard her car door open. When the engine started, he let out his breath in relief. Even if Cora didn't come around or try to see him and the girls, she'd still be in the area, and Adam would no doubt see her from time to time. He wasn't sure he could deal with that painful reminder of the past and be constantly looking over his shoulder for fear of running into her again. It might be better for him and the girls if he did leave Arthur, and it would serve Cora right!

"Alton, I need to speak to you about something," Dianna announced when she arrived home from Leah's that afternoon.

Alton set his newspaper aside. "What is it, Dianna? You look umgerennt."

She took a seat on the couch beside him. "I am upset. I was at Adam and Leah's today, and when I went to put some clothes in their bedroom, I discovered that none of Leah's things were there—only Adam's."

Alton gave his beard a quick tug. "Are you sure about that?"

She nodded.

"Did you talk to Leah about it?"

"No, I wanted to discuss it with you first." Dianna sighed. "Leah said something while I was there that troubled me, too."

"What was that?"

"She said that Adam asked her to stop doing reflexology."

Alton's expression turned grim. "Did she say why?"

"No, but it got me to thinking that if Leah is upset with Adam about this, maybe she moved her things out of their room and is sleeping upstairs in the guest room or with one of the girls."

Alton crossed his arms. "I'm thinking maybe I should have a little talk with our new son-in-law. Find out why he doesn't want Leah doing foot treatments anymore. I'm also going to ask how come they are sleeping in separate rooms."

"Oh, dear." Dianna clutched the folds in her dress. "I hope Adam won't think you're interfering in things that are none of your business."

Alton's knuckles whitened as he clasped his hands tightly together. "Anything that concerns our daughter is very much my business."

Cora was beside herself and barely remembered driving home. Her talk with Adam had gone all wrong, and now because of her, he and his family might move. What would she do then, after just finding him? Adam had made it clear that he wanted nothing to do with her. She didn't even get the chance to tell him about Jared. Maybe he wouldn't have cared to know that he had a half brother. Would it be easier for her to move so that Adam and his family could remain here in Arthur? Cora didn't feel right about him feeling forced to leave. At the same time, if she moved back to Chicago, she might never repair the damage she'd done to her son—if that was even possible.

Cora got out of the car and was fishing for her house key that had somehow disappeared to the bottom of her purse, when Jared flung open the front door and stepped outside.

"Jared, you startled me. I didn't expect you'd be home yet. I thought you'd made plans with Scott after school."

"I did, but Scott had a dental appointment. Said he forgot till his mom reminded him this morning."

"Oh, I see." Cora followed him into the house. *Should I tell him about Adam? Would it help anything if he knew he has a big brother?*

Exhausted, she shuffled into the living room and flopped down on the couch. With all that had happened today, plus the decisions she needed to make, Cora couldn't decide anything right now. If she moved back to Chicago, she'd never resolve things with Adam. If she stayed, it would most likely drive him away. She needed to take a few days to think about things and, yes, even pray.

⁓

Leah had started making supper and was getting ready to set the table, when Adam entered the house, red-faced and nostrils flaring.

"Adam, what's wrong?" she asked, feeling concern.

He glanced around the room. "Where are the girls?"

"In the bathroom, washing up."

"That's good. I don't want them to hear this."

"Hear what, Adam?" Leah set the dishes down and moved toward him.

"On my way home from the hardware store, I stopped along the side of the road to check a wobbly wheel." Adam paused and glanced toward the doorway leading to the hall where the bathroom was located. Leah figured he was worried that the girls might come into the kitchen. "While I was stopped, a car pulled up behind my buggy and a woman got out, asking if I needed any help."

Leah waited as Adam paused again. He sank into a chair at the table. "She introduced herself and said she was my mother."

Leah gulped. "Cora?"

"Jah."

"Did anything get resolved between you?" Leah asked hopefully.

His lips curled slightly as he shook his head.

"I'm sorry to hear that. I was hoping once you two had—"

"I asked her to leave Douglas County, but she flatly refused."

"That's understandable, don't you think? I mean, she wants to make things right between you, and I'm sure she'd like to get to know her granddaughters."

Adam slammed his fist on the table. "That will never happen!"

"But don't you think—"

"If Cora won't move, then I'm going to put the store up for sale, and we'll move to another part of the country." The determined set of Adam's jaw and the cold, flinty look in his eyes told Leah that he was serious. Thanksgiving was next week, and her parents, along with her brother Nathan and his family, would be coming for dinner. Then there was Christmas. Surely Adam wouldn't think of uprooting everyone before the holidays. Leah knew it was imperative that either she get a hold of Cora and convince her to move, or figure out some way to get through to Adam. But that seemed impossible.

"I'm going out to the barn to feed the *katze*," Sara told her mother.

Mom's dark eyebrows furrowed. "Can't that wait till Jonah comes up to the house? I'm sure he'd be willing to do it. Or your daed can feed the cats when he comes out of the bathroom."

"Jonah will have enough to do feeding the horses, along with his other chores this evening." Sara slipped into her sweater. "Besides, the fresh air will do me some good. I've been cooped up in this house since we brought the boppli home from the hospital."

Mom turned from the stove, where she'd been stirring a kettle of stew, and nodded. "All right then, but don't be too long. Supper will be ready soon, and when Jonah gets home, we can eat."

Sara smiled and stepped out the back door. The air was a bit nippy this evening, but it felt refreshing. She walked halfway to the barn and paused, breathing in the odor of decaying leaves, mingled with wood smoke from the fire Dad had built in the fireplace before he'd gone to take a shower.

After several minutes, Sara moved on. When she entered the barn, she identified another aroma: horseflesh coupled with the scent of baled straw stacked against a wall. It felt good to be out here with the animals, even if she did feel a bit weak and shaky. But that was to be expected since she'd recently given birth.

Not seeing any of the cats, Sara picked up their metal dish and banged it a couple times with a small shovel. Then she poured some food into the dish and waited. A few seconds later, Fluffy, the mama cat, along with three of her six-week-old babies, darted across the barn and poked their heads into the dish.

That's strange, Sara thought. *Where is Fluffy's other kitten?*

No sooner had Sara thought the words, when she heard a faint, *meow*!

Sara looked up. There sat a little gray-and-white kitten in the loft overhead, looking down at her so pathetically. *Meow! Meow!*

"What's the matter, little guy?" Sara tipped her head back for a better look. "You found your way up there, so why can't you find your way down?"

Meow! Meow! The kitten continued to cry.

"Oh, all right, I'll come up and get you." There was no way Sara would chase a kitten all over the loft. If it wasn't where she could easily reach it, then it would have to find its own way down.

Grasping the sides of the ladder, Sara made her way slowly up, while the kitten sat patiently waiting for her. "Now don't you move. I'm almost there."

She was nearly at the top, when her right leg gave out and she missed the next rung. It threw her off balance, and letting go with one hand, she tried to regain her balance. Just then, the kitten screeched, leaped onto Sara's right shoulder, and dug its needlelike claws into her skin.

The room started to spin, and as an inky blackness moved in, Sara lost her grip on the ladder. Her last thought as she tumbled toward the floor was, *Dear Lord, take care of my family.*

CHAPTER 44

*J*onah whistled as he made his way from the buggy shop to the house. It had been a long day, and he was anxious to see how Sara and the baby were doing. He looked forward to spending some time with Mark, too, and enjoying a pleasant evening visiting with his in-laws during supper. It was a comfort having Sara's folks there to look after things while Jonah was working; although he knew his own parents would have continued that task if Rueben and Martha hadn't come to see their new granddaughter.

Jonah looked forward to being with both sets of parents on Thanksgiving. His twin sister, Jean, and her family would be there as well. Jonah had always longed for a wife and children, and now that he had them, his life seemed complete. He loved Sara and their children with all his heart and would do anything for them.

When Jonah entered the house, he found Sara's mother standing at the sink, washing a head of lettuce. "Guder *owed*, Jonah." She turned and smiled at him.

"Good evening," he responded. "How's my fraa doing? Is she resting like the doctor told her to do?"

Martha motioned to the kitchen window. "Said she wanted some fresh air and insisted on going out to the barn to feed the katze."

"How long ago was that?"

"Now that I think about it, it's been quite a while." Martha glanced at the clock on the wall near the stove. "She really should have been back by now unless she found something else to do out there in the barn."

Jonah frowned. "Sara shouldn't be doing anything in the barn. I'll go out and see what she's up to." He turned and headed back outside.

When Jonah entered the barn, it was dark, so he called Sara's name.

No response.

Could she have left the barn and gone into the house without Martha seeing her?

Jonah lit one of their gas lamps. Holding it up so he could see better, he moved across the barn. The mama cat was sitting on a bale of straw, and her kittens were grabbing at her tail. Below them sat the cat dish, but it was empty. Looking back at the cats, Jonah noticed that one of Fluffy's kittens was missing. He walked over to the mama cat and stroked her head. "Where's your other little one?" He smiled as the cat leaned in, purring, while rubbing her whiskers on the back of his hand.

When Jonah went farther into the barn, he heard a faint *meow*. "Where are you, kitty? Here, kitty kitty."

As he looked around, he froze. Sara's twisted body lay on the floor beneath the ladder leading to the loft. Wedged under her arm was the missing kitten. "Sara!" Jonah dropped to his knees in front of his wife, setting the lamp on the floor. "Sara! Sara, what happened? Can you hear me?"

When Jonah picked up Sara's arm to hold her hand, the kitten took advantage and ran out. Her hand was like ice. He felt for a pulse, but his hands shook so badly he couldn't find it. She was so still. He detected no movement or response from her whatsoever. She looked like a sleeping angel.

Jonah checked for any sign of breathing. Then he put his ear against her chest and held his breath, praying to hear the beating rhythm. Silence. He realized then that sweet Sara, his beloved wife, was gone.

Adam was getting ready to check on the horses when he heard a noise. Turning, he came face-to-face with Leah's dad. "Alton! You startled me. Have you been here long?"

Alton shook his head. "Just got here. I was heading to the house till I saw light coming from the barn."

"Jah, we just finished eating supper, and I'm checking on the horses." Adam didn't like the furrow of Alton's brows. "Is something troubling you? Sure hope you didn't come with bad news."

Alton moved closer. "I came to ask you a question, and I'd appreciate it if you were up front with me."

"Sure, Alton." Adam nodded. "What did you want to know?"

"It's about you and Leah." Alton cleared his throat. "Are you two having marital problems? Is that why her things are not in your room?"

Adam winced. "Did she tell you that?"

"No, her mamm did."

Adam was on the verge of asking how Dianna would know anything about his and Leah's sleeping arrangements, when Alton spoke again.

"My wife was here earlier, helping Leah with the laundry. When she took some things into your room, she was surprised not to see any of Leah's clothes there."

Adam shifted his weight and leaned on the stall door, feeling the need for support. "Well, you see—"

"Dianna also said that you asked Leah to stop doing reflexology. Is that true?"

Adam nodded slowly.

"Is that the reason she moved her things out of your room?"

"Well, no, but—"

"Leah's ability to help people through the use of reflexology is her gift. How could you take that from her, Adam?"

Adam pulled nervously on his shirt collar, feeling like he'd been backed into a corner. Should he tell Alton the truth? Well, what did he have to lose? Sooner or later, Leah's folks, and maybe others, would figure out that his and Leah's marriage wasn't based on love, but on a very special need.

"Okay, there's something you need to know," Adam began cautiously. "Leah and I got married so she could give my nieces full-time care."

Alton's eyebrows shot up. "I knew Leah was fond of the girls, but I didn't think she'd marry you just to be their substitute mother."

"She's more than that," Adam interjected. "She's also my friend."

"Humph!" Alton screwed up his face. "If she were your friend, you wouldn't have asked her to give up something she feels is so important."

Adam felt like a heel, but in order to explain his reasons for asking Leah to stop foot treatments, he'd have to tell Alton about his past.

I may as well tell him, 'cause if I don't, Leah probably will. Maybe she already has. I just won't mention that Cora is living here in Arthur.

Adam took a step closer to Alton. "I think you should know the reason I asked Leah to give up reflexology."

"I'm all ears."

Adam quickly told the story about his mother leaving when he was a boy and how she used to do reflexology, even though his dad disapproved. He heard them arguing about it and had always wondered why she wouldn't give it up when Dad had asked her to. When she finally did give it up, it was to become a nurse—something she couldn't do and remain Amish. She obviously cared more about helping other people than taking care of her own family.

Alton stood silently for several minutes, as though trying to let everything Adam had said sink in. Slowly, he reached out his hand and touched Adam's shoulder, giving it a squeeze. "Sounds like you went through a lot as a child, and I'm real sorry about that. But the past is in the past, and just because your mamm practiced foot doctoring and left to become a nurse doesn't mean Leah would do that, too. She's a good woman, devoted to God, your nieces, and I believe to you. Don't you think you oughtta give her the chance to prove that, Adam?"

Adam swallowed hard, trying to dislodge the lump in his throat. "Maybe you're right. I'll tell Leah that I've changed my mind. As long as it doesn't take time away from the girls, she's free to see people here in our home for reflexology treatments."

Alton gave Adam's shoulder another squeeze. "That's good to hear. Jah, real good."

Adam was tempted to tell Leah's dad about the sudden appearance of his mother, and how he was thinking of moving, but then he thought better of it. He needed to do something he should have done sooner. He needed to commit everything to prayer.

Cora turned off the kitchen light and was about to head for the living room to watch TV and spend a little time with Jared, when her cell phone rang. She paused. Seeing that it was her ex-husband, she answered the call. "Hello, Evan."

"Hey, Cora. How's it going?"

How do you think it's going? she silently screamed. *I'm here trying to raise our rebellious son by myself, and I've just met my other son, whom you know nothing about, but unfortunately, he would barely speak to me.* "Fine, Evan. Everything's just fine and dandy," she said dryly.

"Okay, good. Well, the reason I'm calling is I thought I'd drive down to Arthur on Tuesday and pick up Jared so he can spend Thanksgiving with me and Emily."

Oh, great. Now you want to spend time with our son. Cora was tempted to say that she'd made plans for her and Jared's Thanksgiving, but the truth was, she had no real plans. Besides, it might do Jared some good to spend a little time with his dad. After all, they hadn't seen each other since Cora and Jared left the city.

"Sure, Evan, that would be fine. I'll let Jared know right away. I'm sure he'll be glad."

"Okay, great. I'll be there late Tuesday afternoon to pick him up, and I'll bring him back on Sunday."

"That sounds fine."

When Cora hung up, she headed to the living room to give Jared the news. She knew he'd be glad, and she was happy for him, too, but oh, how she dreaded spending Thanksgiving alone.

CHAPTER 45

Saturday morning, Adam awoke at the crack of dawn. He'd spent several hours last night praying and mulling over the things Leah's father had said to him. He'd come to the conclusion that asking Leah to give up reflexology just because his mother used to practice it probably wasn't fair. Perhaps Alton had been right when he'd said Leah had a gift for helping others. He remembered how Amy had said Leah's foot treatment had relieved her headache, so maybe foot doctoring wasn't hocus-pocus. Maybe he'd just associated it with that because of negative things his dad had said.

Could my mother have had that gift as well? Adam threw the covers aside and crawled out of bed. He wouldn't think about his mother right now. Even if she'd had the gift, she quit doing it and ran off to become part of the English world. No God-fearing Christian woman would have done something like that. Not if they had been in their right mind.

Adam shook his head and muttered, "It would be a lot easier to forget about the past if she hadn't shown up." He still had to make a decision about whether to sell out and move to another state. If Cora would just leave, he wouldn't even consider moving. But how could he get her to do that?

I need to clear my head. Maybe I'll take a walk before breakfast and have another talk with God.

After getting dressed, Adam left the house, being careful to close the door quietly so he didn't disturb Leah or the girls while they slept upstairs. He'd just reached the end of his driveway, when Jonah's father, Raymond, pulled in with his horse and buggy.

"Guder mariye," Adam said, stepping up to the buggy. "You're sure out and about early this morning."

Raymond's grim expression gave Adam cause for alarm. "Is something wrong?"

The older man nodded. "I came with bad news."

"What's wrong?"

"Sara passed away last night. Since she and your wife were friends, I thought she'd want to know."

Adam drew in a sharp breath. "What happened?"

"Jonah found her in the barn, lying on the floor beneath the ladder leading to the loft. He thinks she may have climbed up to get one of their kittens and fallen." Raymond's voice faltered, and his eyes glassed over. "It appeared that her neck was broken."

Stunned by this news, Adam touched his pounding chest. "That's baremlich! I'm so sorry for your family's loss. Please let us know when the funeral arrangements have been made and also if there's anything we can do to help out."

Raymond nodded. "Guess I'd better move on. I still have others in the community that I need to notify this morning."

Adam turned and shuffled back to the house. He dreaded telling Leah this news.

Leah yawned as she entered the kitchen to start breakfast. She hadn't slept well last night, tossing and turning as she thought about the situation with Adam. Seeing his tender way with the girls had made her fall in love with him, but Adam's bitterness toward his own mother troubled Leah. It was a wedge that would always stand between them unless Adam's heart softened and he became willing to forgive Cora for what she'd done.

I need to keep praying about the situation, she told herself as she opened the refrigerator and removed a carton of eggs. There was no time to dwell on this now; the girls and Adam would be up soon and they'd expect to have breakfast ready.

Leah took out a bowl and cracked open several eggs. She'd just begun mixing them, when the back door opened and Adam entered the room.

"Ach, you startled me, Adam." Leah gestured to the bowl. "I was just getting breakfast started and figured you were still in bed."

"I went outside to clear my head, but then. . ." Adam paused and moved closer to Leah. "Raymond Miller stopped by to deliver some very distressing news."

"What is it, Adam? You look umgerennt."

"I am upset, and you will be, too, when you hear what I have to say."

Leah held her elbows tightly against her sides. "Adam, what is it? Tell me what's wrong."

"It's Sara Miller. She. . .she's dead."

Leah clasped her hands over her mouth to cover a gasp. "Oh, no! Oh, no! That just can't be. What happened, Adam?"

She stood in stunned silence as Adam told her everything that Raymond had said. Her legs felt so weak she could barely stand. Had it not been for the fact that Adam had taken hold of her arm, she might have collapsed.

As the reality of the situation sank in, Leah began to sob. Sara had visited her regularly for foot treatments, and they'd gotten to know each other quite well. In addition to Elaine and Priscilla, Sara was Leah's good friend. She had confided in Leah many times during her treatments, and Leah's heart had gone out to Sara when she'd learned that she had MS. Then when Sara married Jonah and had his baby, Leah had shared in their joy. Poor Jonah was alone now with the responsibility of raising Mark and baby Martha on his own. It wasn't fair. Life wasn't fair. Where was God in all this?

Adam pulled Leah into his arms, gently patting her back. "It's all right, Leah. Let the tears flow and grieve all you want."

Despite her pain, Leah found comfort in Adam's embrace. It was the first time they had been this close, emotionally or physically.

When Leah's sobs subsided, Adam leaned down and gently kissed her forehead. "This may not be the best time to say this, but there's something I need to get off my chest."

She tipped her head back and looked up at his face. "What is it?"

"Your daed came by last night while I was in the barn."

"Really? I didn't know Dad was here." Leah paused to use her apron to wipe at the tears wetting her cheeks. "Go on, Adam. Tell me the rest."

"You were probably preoccupied doing something with the girls and didn't hear his horse and buggy come in."

"What did Dad want?"

"He wanted to talk to me about something."

Leah waited for Adam to continue, finding comfort in his embrace.

"He thinks we're having marital problems."

Leah blinked. "What made him think that?"

"Apparently your mamm was in my room putting some laundry away, and when she saw that none of your things were there, she figured out that you don't sleep there. So she just assumed—"

Leah groaned. "Oh no."

"Your daed also said that your mamm had told him that I'd asked you to stop doing reflexology."

Leah pulled away from Adam and sank into a chair at the table. Not only did she need to deal with her grief over Sara's death, but now she also faced having to explain her relationship with Adam to her folks.

Adam pulled out the chair beside her and sat down. "I admitted to your daed that the reason we got married was so you could live here full-time and help me care for my nieces." He paused. "I could tell that Alton was none too happy about that. He accused me of marrying you just so you could be a substitute mother for the girls."

"Didn't you?"

"Well, yes, but that wasn't the only reason." Adam's cheeks colored. "The truth is, Leah, I care about you, and you've become a good friend."

Just a friend? Is that all I am to you, Adam?

"That's not the only thing I told your daed, Leah." Adam rushed on. "I told him about the situation with my mother—how she used to practice reflexology and then ran out on me, Mary, and our daed."

"Does he know that your mother is here in Arthur and that she wants to make amends with you?" Leah questioned.

Adam shook his head. "I figured, at that point, enough had been said."

"Sooner or later, it's bound to come out, Adam."

"Not from me, it won't. And I hope you won't say anything, either."

"I won't say anything without your approval, but we can't know about Cora. She could tell someone she works with or anyone else she may know."

"I'll deal with that when the time comes. Right now, we have issues of our own to deal with." Adam touched Leah's flushed cheeks, lightly brushing away her tears. "I thought hard and prayed about things last night, Leah, and I've decided that it was wrong of me to ask you to give up reflexology. Since my mother practiced it when I was a boy, I saw it as something evil, like her."

Leah shook her head. "No, Adam, I don't think Cora is evil. What she did was wrong, but I believe she's truly sorry and regrets her decision to leave like that. I think she deserves another chance."

Adam lowered his gaze. "You might be right, but I don't think I'm ready for that. I do want you to know, however, that if you'd like to continue doing foot treatments, you have my blessing. I may even ask you to work on my feet once in a while."

"Really, Adam? You don't mind if I do reflexology here in this house?"

He shook his head. "As long as it doesn't interfere with the care of the girls, you can foot doctor whenever you like."

Leah smiled, despite her tears. "Danki, Adam. Danki for that."

CHAPTER 46

*C*ora stared out the living-room window at the falling rain. It was such a dismal day, which only added to her depression over having to spend Thanksgiving alone. She'd thought about going out to dinner at one of the restaurants that were open on the holiday, but the idea of eating by herself held no appeal. So she'd stayed home and fixed a small turkey, just so she would have the leftovers for making sandwiches and soup.

Cora moved away from the window and took a seat in the rocking chair to be closer to the warmth of the fireplace. *I wonder what Adam and his family are doing today?* She squeezed her eyes tightly shut, willing herself not to cry. She'd done enough of that already, and where had it gotten her? Tears wouldn't change the fact that she'd been dumped by Evan, nor would they bring Adam back into her life. Crying and feeling sorry for herself wouldn't give her a good relationship with Jared, either. He'd been angry with her ever since the divorce and hated living here in Arthur.

Maybe it would be best for everyone if Jared and I did move back to Chicago. Since my house hasn't sold, we could take it off the market and move into it. And I don't think it would be that difficult to find a nursing job. It just won't be at the hospital where I'd have to see Evan and Emily.

A horn tooted from outside, and Cora's eyes snapped open. Obviously a car had pulled into the yard. Moments later, the front door opened and Jared stepped in.

"Jared! What are you doing here?" Cora asked in surprise. "I didn't expect you to come back until Sunday."

Jared frowned and tossed his coat on a chair. "As soon as we finished eating dinner today, I asked Dad to bring me home."

Cora's eyebrows rose. "How come?" *Did Jared just call this place home?*

"Dad didn't really want me there, Mom." Jared grunted as he flopped onto the couch. "The first night I was at their house, he and Emily went to a party and left me home alone. Then on Wednesday, they both went about their business as though I wasn't even there." He folded his arms. "Guess they thought I could entertain myself by watching TV or playing some computer games."

Cora frowned. "I thought he wanted to spend some quality time with you. That's what he said when he called." She glanced at the door. "What'd he do—just pull into the driveway and drop you off?"

Jared gave a nod. "He's bent out of shape because I asked him to bring me home. Guess he didn't like being pulled away from his fancy friends."

"What friends?"

Jared shrugged. "Beats me. I can't remember any of their names, but I think they were all doctors from the hospital. A few of them brought their wives and kids along."

"Did Emily host the meal?"

"Nope. The dinner was held at one of the other people's homes, but Dad pretty much ignored me the whole time. Made me feel like a stranger—even to him. To tell you the truth, Dad seems like someone I don't know anymore."

"I'm sorry, Jared." Cora got up and sat on the couch beside him. "I was hoping you would have a good time."

"Yeah, me, too."

"Do you still want to move back to Chicago?" she asked.

He shook his head. "No way! Being around Dad, Emily, and their snooty friends made me anxious to get back here to be with you."

Cora's heart melted, and she gave Jared a hug. "I'm glad you're back, because I missed you. It wasn't Thanksgiving without you."

"Same here."

"If you're hungry, I have some leftover turkey. Would you like some of that?"

Jared shook his head. "Not now, Mom. Maybe later, though."

"Okay." Cora smiled. Today had turned out better than she'd imagined, at least where she and Jared were concerned. She didn't know when or if she would ever mend fences with Adam, but at least she had Jared, and for that she was thankful.

The day after Thanksgiving as Elaine stood beside Ben, along with several others who had come to the cemetery to say their final good-byes to Sara, her heart went out to Jonah. He stood beside Sara's parents, holding little Mark, while his mother-in-law held the baby. On the other side of Jonah were his parents and his sister and her family. Obviously they were all in pain. Sara and Jean had been good friends, so Sara's death had been a huge blow to everyone in the family.

Jonah's drooping shoulders and dull-looking eyes let Elaine know that in addition to his grief, he hadn't had much sleep. Losing a loved one was difficult in any situation, and an unexpected tragedy such as this had to be devastating. Elaine wished there was something she could do to ease his burden. It would be difficult for him to go on without Sara. But Jonah was strong, and Elaine felt sure he would make it through with the help of his folks and Sara's. Others within their Amish community would be there for Jonah and his children, too.

As Jonah stood on shaky legs, staring at Sara's simple wooden coffin being lowered into the ground, he struggled to keep his emotions under control. For little Mark's sake, he did not want to break down.

It still didn't seem possible that such a tragedy had happened. Things had been going along so well, and he and Sara had been so excited about the safe arrival of their new baby girl. It grieved him to know that their precious daughter would never get to know her mother—at least not on this earth. He loved Sara and wondered how he could make it without her. For the sake of his children, though, he had to find the courage and strength to go on.

He remembered the words to Isaiah 30:15, a verse of scripture their bishop had quoted during Sara's funeral service: *"In quietness and in confidence shall be your strength."*

Jonah would need to memorize that verse and quote it many times in the days ahead, for he had never been more fully aware that he could do nothing in his own strength. He needed every bit of help he could get—from his family and friends, but most of all from God.

Leah's heart was saddened as she stood beside Adam and recited the Lord's Prayer along with the others in attendance. She was confident that Sara was in a better place, but she would be sorely missed by her family and friends—especially Jonah. Mark was still young, and even though he would miss his mother, in time his memory of her would fade. And the precious baby girl would have no memory of Sara at all. *What will Jonah do now?* Leah wondered. *Will he eventually remarry or simply rely on his family to help him raise Martha and Mark?*

Leah knew how important the children were to Jonah. She'd been convinced that he'd married Sara mostly to be a father to Mark. That wasn't to say that he didn't love Sara. No, it had been quite evident from Jonah's tender, caring ways that he was committed to Sara and their marriage and would have done most anything for her.

She glanced over at her brother, Nathan, and his wife, Jean, who stood near Jonah and his parents. *Poor Jean, seeing her brother go through something like this. It seems so unfair to all of them.*

"Leah, are you ready to go?" Adam asked, placing his hand on her arm while leaning close to her.

She blinked a couple of times and slowly nodded. She'd been so immersed in her thoughts that she hadn't even realized the service was over.

Leah followed Adam over to offer their condolences to Jonah once more. "If there's anything you need, please let us know," Leah said, swallowing against the sob rising in her throat.

"Jah," Adam agreed. "We'll do whatever we can to help."

"Danki for your kindness." Jonah tousled Mark's hair. "It's going to be tough, but with the support of family, friends, and most of all God, we'll make it through."

Several others came up then, so Leah moved aside and followed Adam to their horse and buggy at the hitching rack just outside the fence surrounding the cemetery. They'd left the girls with Leah's mother today, thinking the funeral might be a harsh reminder of their own parents' death.

Adam helped Leah into the buggy, untied his horse, and took his place in the driver's seat. Turning to Leah, he said, "There's something I think you should know."

"What's that?"

"I've been thinking about our marriage and how it's only a marriage of convenience." He clasped her hand. "What I'm trying to say is that I've been dead inside, but you've brought me back to life. I'm in love with you, Leah, and I'd like us to be married in every sense of the word."

"I love you, too, Adam, and I love Carrie, Linda, and Amy. I've come to realize that you and the girls are God's gift to me. But we need to work out some things."

"You mean about my mother?"

Leah nodded, while squeezing his hand. "We are Christians, Adam, and God's Word says we need to forgive others."

"I know, and I've been praying about that. I'm not ready yet to establish a relationship with Cora, but God's helping me to be able to forgive her." Gently, he caressed Leah's face. "You don't have to worry about me selling out and moving, either, because we'll be staying put."

Tears welled in Leah's eyes, clouding her vision. "I'm so glad."

"I've been meaning to ask you something. That night when you told me about Cora, it seemed that you were going to say something else, but I cut you off. Was it important, Leah?"

"Jah, I think it was, but I didn't say anything because it seemed as if you'd made up your mind, and I was waiting for just the right time."

"What is it, Leah? I'm willing to listen."

"Cora told me that awhile after she'd left you, Mary, and your daed, she'd come back to see you, but you'd moved, and no one would tell her where you had gone."

"She really came back?"

Leah nodded. "That's what she said."

"Do you think she planned to stay, or was it just for a visit?"

"I'm not sure. That's something you'd have to ask her yourself."

"Maybe someday, I will." Adam leaned closer and gently kissed Leah's lips.

His words gave Leah hope. Maybe after a little more time, Adam would be willing to talk to his mother and would learn that he had a half brother. Perhaps someday soon, he'd allow Cora and Jared to be a part of their family. Now that would be the best gift of all.

DISCUSSION QUESTIONS

1. Leah felt that her ability to help people with reflexology was a gift from God. But some people, like Adam, didn't see it that way. Have you ever had an ability that you felt was God's gift but others did not? How did you deal with their negative comments?

2. Since Adam's mother had abandoned him when he was a child, he was afraid of establishing a relationship with any other woman because she might reject him. Have you or someone you know ever been in a similar situation? How did you deal with those feelings?

3. What can we do to help someone whose parents have abandoned them? What are some verses of scripture that might help someone like Adam cope with their past?

4. Cora made several unwise decisions during her adult life, including her decision to leave the faith of her people. How did walking away from the faith that she'd been taught during her childhood change the course of her life?

5. Should Cora have included her son Jared in the decision to leave their home in Chicago and move to Arthur where they had no friends or family? Do you think Jared may have been more receptive to change if he'd been included in the plans?

6. After Cora's divorce, her son became rebellious. How can a single parent deal with a defiant teen?

7. Jonah suffered yet another loss when an unexpected accident shattered his world. What are some things we can do to help someone get through a tragic loss?

8. Despite his decision to remain single, Adam felt the need for a wife. His marriage was one of convenience, rather than love, since he needed someone to help him raise his nieces. Was that the best course of action for Adam, or should he have looked for a full-time babysitter?

9. Leah agreed to marry Adam even though he didn't love her. Leah's

love for Adam's nieces was a driving factor. Is there ever a time when a couple should marry without love? What obstacles would they have to overcome in order to make the marriage work?

10. Leah's friend Priscilla became tired of waiting for her boyfriend to propose and was thinking about breaking up with him, but she didn't tell him why. Do you think Priscilla should have been up front with Elam, or should she have been more patient and waited awhile longer to see if he would bring up the subject of marriage? How long do you feel a couple should date before marriage?

11. Was it fair for Leah's friend Elaine to allow Ben to court her when she still had feelings for Jonah?

12. When Leah knew she had feelings for Adam, she kept them to herself. Should she have opened up and admitted how she felt instead of fearing rejection?

13. Forgiveness, acceptance, and tolerance of others are some of the themes in this book. What verses of scripture were mentioned in the story? Can you think of some other helpful Bible verses that deal with these topics?

14. What life lessons did you learn from reading this book? Were there any particular verses of scripture that spoke to your heart?

15. Did you learn anything new about the Amish by reading this story? What are your thoughts about their way of life?

LEAH'S CHOCOLATE-CHIP CHEESE BALL

1 (8 ounce) package cream cheese, softened
½ cup butter, softened
¼ teaspoon vanilla
¾ cup powdered sugar
2 tablespoons brown sugar
1 (10½ ounce) package mini chocolate chips
¾ cup nuts, finely chopped

In mixing bowl, beat cream cheese, butter, and vanilla until fluffy. Gradually add powdered sugar and brown sugar until combined. Stir in mini chocolate chips. Cover and refrigerate for 30 minutes. Place on large piece of plastic wrap and shape into a ball. Refrigerate at least 1 hour before serving. Roll ball in nuts. Serve with graham crackers or any other cracker you like.

LEAH'S HUMMINGBIRD CAKE

1 package yellow cake mix
⅓ cup vegetable oil
1 (8 ounce) can crushed pineapple, well drained with juice reserved
3 eggs
1 teaspoon cinnamon
1 ripe banana, cut up
¾ cup walnuts, chopped and divided
1 (12 ounce) jar maraschino cherries, well drained, chopped, and divided

Glaze
4 ounces cream cheese, softened
¼ cup powdered sugar
2 to 3 tablespoons milk

Preheat oven to 350 degrees. Coat 10-inch Bundt pan with cooking spray. In large bowl, combine cake mix, oil, pineapple, eggs, and cinnamon. Add enough water to reserved pineapple juice to make ½ cup. Add to bowl and beat thoroughly until mixture is combined. Stir in banana, ½ cup walnuts, and ¼ cup cherries. Mix well. Sprinkle remaining nuts and cherries in prepared pan then pour in batter. Bake 40 to 45 minutes, or until toothpick inserted in center comes out clean. Let cool 15 minutes then invert onto serving platter and cool completely. In medium bowl, combine cream cheese, powdered sugar, and milk. Beat until smooth. Drizzle glaze over cooled cake.

ABOUT THE AUTHOR

New York Times, award-winning author, Wanda E. Brunstetter is one of the founders of the Amish fiction genre. Wanda's ancestors were part of the Anabaptist faith, and her novels are based on personal research intended to accurately portray the Amish way of life. Her books are well-read and trusted by many Amish, who credit her for giving readers a deeper understanding of the people and their customs. When Wanda visits her Amish friends, she finds herself drawn to their peaceful lifestyle, sincerity, and close family ties. Wanda enjoys photography, ventriloquism, gardening, bird-watching, beachcombing, and spending time with her family. She and her husband, Richard, have been blessed with two grown children, six grandchildren, and two great-grandchildren.

To learn more about Wanda,
visit her website at www.wandabrunstetter.com.

Let's Keep In Touch!

Want to know what Wanda's up to and be the first to hear about new releases, specials, the latest news, and more? Like Wanda on Facebook!

 Visit facebook.com/WandaBrunstetterFans